Praise for
JANE LINDSKOLD

"Jane Lindskold is one of the best new writers to emerge in the fantasy field in the '90s. In *CHANGER*, she imbues the modern world with rich mythic resonance. If you love the urban fantasy novels of Charles de Lint or Emma Bull, here's an unusual, magical, and thoroughly entertaining new book to add to your shelves."

Five-time World Fantasy Award-winning editor and author
Terri Windling

"One of the brightest new writers
to come along in years."
Roger Zelazny

"A worthy new heir to Mary Shelley."
Locus

"Worth a reread, let alone a read."
Philadelphia Weekly Press on *When the Gods Are Silent*

"*Donnerjack* read[s] like a Zelazny novel, and one of the best. Kudos to Lindskold for a remarkable job."
Starlog

"An intricate, dense novel woven with myriad threads . . . *Donnerjack* will enthrall anyone willing to ponder the future."
Albuquerque Journal

Other Books by
Jane Lindskold

BROTHER TO DRAGONS, COMPANION TO OWLS
MARKS OF OUR BROTHERS
THE PIPES OF ORPHEUS
SMOKE AND MIRRORS
WHEN THE GODS ARE SILENT

With Roger Zelazny

DONNERJACK

Changer

JANE LINDSKOLD

AVON • EOS

This is a work of fiction. Names, characters, places, and incidents either are the product of the author's imagination or are used fictitiously. Any resemblance to actual events, locales, organizations, or persons, living or dead, is entirely coincidental and beyond the intent of either the author or the publisher.

AVON BOOKS, INC.
1350 Avenue of the Americas
New York, New York 10019

Copyright © 1998 by Jane Lindskold
Published by arrangement with the author
Visit our website at http://www.AvonBooks.com/Eos
Library of Congress Catalog Card Number: 98-92629
ISBN: 0-380-78849-7

First Avon Eos Printing: December 1998

AVON EOS TRADEMARK REG. U.S. PAT. OFF. AND IN OTHER COUNTRIES, MARCA REGISTRADA, HECHO EN U.S.A.

Printed in the U.S.A.

WCD   10 9 8 7 6 5 4 3 2 1

This one is for Jim Moore, with love.

Dream tonight of a compass rose
Points smashed finny flat
The scent of my blood on the wind

There are people whose watch stops at a certain hour and who remain permanently at that age.

—SAINTE-BEUVE

DEATH COMES IN MANY FORMS, BUT IT HAS ONE SMELL, a smell of blood stagnating, of flesh stiffening, of breath grown stale. Later there is decay, and that can have many smells: sweet and sick and sour. But death has one smell. Returning from hunting, a limp rabbit in his jaws, the dog coyote smells another death carried in the wind from his den.

Dropping the rabbit, the dog coyote crouches and sniffs the breeze. Death is there, death in quantity, and with it other smells. The smell of human sweat, of gunpowder, of horses, and of blood—coyote blood. He does not need to see more to know who has died, but he creeps forward nonetheless, a very uncanine dread blending with his coyote terror.

From the shelter of a low-hanging bush he sees two humans, both dressed for riding. Their horses are picketed to a tree a few paces away, shifting nervously, either at the smell of fresh blood or at the scent of carnivores; the dog coyote cannot tell. Nor does he care: His attention is all for the humans.

One is skinning a dead coyote. The overwhelming smell of blood should mask identification, but the dog coyote knows the scent, knows the reddish pelt of his older daughter;

1

her black-tipped tail is blown by a faint breeze in a parody of life. He does not need to see the thin scar running from shoulder to flank to know that the pelt already hanging from the saddle of one of the horses is that of his mate.

He bites back a wail of grief and rage. Still crouched in concealment, he looks to where the second human kneels by the mouth of the den, twisting something with his gloved right hand, his head tilted to listen.

The dog coyote's hearing is much more acute than the human's, and he hears the frightened whimpers of the pups beneath the earth. Perhaps those infant cries would have softened the human's heart, but he does not hear the cries, only the sharp, short scream as the wire gig rips into the puppy's belly.

"Got it!" the man grunts, satisfied. Pulling on the wire, he hauls out the pup. One thump from his hand breaks the puppy's neck, and the crying stops.

The dog coyote, who is more than a coyote, can do nothing but watch as his baby's body is tossed into a sack already lumpy and bloodstained by the corpses of its littermates. Bitter lessons from centuries past have taught him to hold still at such times, to preserve himself even when he cannot preserve those he loves.

Watching while the two ranchers depart, he weeps within, chides himself for not relocating the den, for not keeping a tighter watch on where the young female roamed. With little reason, ranchers hate and fear coyotes; there are few places coyotes can live that do not infringe on human territories. Once again, the coyotes have lost, and with them so has the Changer.

Then he hears a faint sound, a whimper and a scrabbling. In two bounds he is at the entry to the den. The smell of blood and urine almost covers another scent.

Aware of his danger should the two humans return, he forces head and shoulders into the den. The entryway is tight, dug for his mate's slimmer build, but he can make his way. In the dim light from the second entry, he sees a chubby form blindly trying to dig its way into the dirt at the back of the burrow.

It is his daughter, the runt, the smallest and weakest of the litter. Small to begin with, unable to compete fairly with the others, she had not grown as quickly; now her littleness has been the saving of her life.

With his teeth he drags her from the hollow in which she had taken refuge from the searching gig. Mother and siblings dead, she would have died of starvation or fallen prey to owl, fox, or hawk if he had not found her.

Quickly now, the dog coyote hauls his daughter into the sunlight. Her whimpering increases when she sees the skinned bodies of the others. First he must get away and wait for darkness. Then he will consider what to do next.

As he is ascending the hill into safer ground, he freezes at a flicker of motion down where the pasture meets the highway. Thinking it might be more humans, perhaps the same two returning, he sets down his daughter and watches.

The two ranchers have ridden to meet someone in a car, someone who hands them money in exchange for the raw pelts and the bloody, dripping sack. Their bulky forms keep him from seeing who is in the car, but here the smell of death does not so dominate.

Through the clear air, the dog coyote catches a new scent, one that registers with the dormant portion of his mind, a smell that recalls flowers and musk, seductive and artificial.

A growl rumbles in his throat, a growl so furious that his daughter rolls on her back, pissing in submission and fear. He ignores her, his entire attention focused in a very uncoyote-like fashion on gathering information. When the car pulls away, he memorizes the license number. Then he watches until the two horsemen stop at a ranch where they clearly reside.

Now is not the time, but soon he will have some calls to make, some questions to ask, and, quite possibly, some deaths of his own to arrange.

¤◻¤

Elsewhere, in a cheap but clean motel room, a whippet-thin, sharp-featured, red-haired man punches an unlisted number into a telephone. That the number is not only unlisted but the connection impossible delights him. He has a fondness for amulets and charms, for tools of all sorts that permit him to expand his own eclectic but not terribly powerful talents.

After a series of chimes, soft and high, like a crystal goblet tapped with a silver filament, a voice speaks, deep and resonant, in cadences pedantic: "Greetings to you, fire-born, fire's self, flickering fastness, impossible imp."

The red-haired man sighs. "Can't you just say 'Hi, Sven'?"

"Without body, with naught but mind, I make shape, shapeless one, from words, from fancy."

"We're working on fixing that, buddy," Sven says. "I've pinpointed where the Changer is hiding. He's definitely in New Mexico, out in the Salinas District. All the portents indicate that he's living as a coyote."

"Salinas? So salt calls sea-born master of shapes, such said I when searching started."

"You said you thought he was near an *ocean*," Sven retorts sarcastically. "New Mexico is about as different from an ocean as you can get: hot and dry, cold and dry, mountainous and dry. I don't think anyone could mistake it for an ocean."

Sven's auditor maintains a dignified—or perhaps offended—silence, and, after a moment, Sven continues, "When I get him—and that's not going to be easy, let me remind you—I'll try to get you your pound of flesh."

An indignant hrumph precedes the inevitable alliteration: "Embodied blood, not flaccid flesh is what sorcery seeks to build bodies. Ocular oracles so ordain."

"I know," Sven says. "I'll try not to harm the Changer. I have plans to use him against another of my targets. When they've worn each other out, then I'll catch him for you."

"Seize swiftly, this one, oldest of us all."

"I've promised, haven't I?" Sven retorts. "In any case, I have a lot going on right now. Revolution isn't easy to manage."

"Easier," his cohort reminds him, "when alongside I stand."

Sven nods as if the creature on the other end of the phone could see him—as perhaps he can.

"I haven't forgotten. I'll check back in a few days."

"Farewell, fire's friend."

"Bye."

Hanging up, Sven considers what to do next. He needs to make a bunch more calls tonight, uplink to his website, then continue scouting for the Changer. Quickly he punches the extension for the motel restaurant and orders a snack. No rest for the wicked, his mother might have said—if he'd ever had a mother. To be perfectly honest, he doesn't remember.

The gap in his memory doesn't bother him a great deal.

✡◻✡

The night following the deaths of his mate and pups, the dog coyote sits on a rough, rocky hilltop about five miles from where his former den had been. Superficially, the area is exposed, but given his current situation, it is far preferable to where he had denned before.

Humans and their creatures do not care for these places. The bristly foliage of piñon, juniper, and four-wing saltbush do not offer grazing, only shade. The mica-flecked sand slips under boots or all but the cleverest hooves. Nor do the creatures who often reside in such copses invite visitors: biting ants, rattlesnakes, millipedes, scorpions. Not that a coyote is particularly fond of such crawlers and biters, but he knows how to scent them, to avoid them.

Here he takes his motherless daughter for protection. An old ground-squirrel burrow can be enlarged enough to hide a scrawny whelp such as she, and, regardless of what other ways in which she may be a poor excuse of a coyote, she is a survivor. She is the last of his family, the last except for the scattered litters of other years, most of whom are most probably dead already. There are reasons that coyotes litter six pups a year.

Scratching behind his right ear with a rear leg, the dog coyote contemplates the moon, considers what he must do. That teasing scent on the wind has led him to believe that the deaths of his family were not merely vermin extermination, but were murder. The humans who did the kills might or might not have known what they did. This is something he must resolve.

But before he can do this, he must do other things, things that are tangled in with yet other things. His mind is not a coyote's mind, for all that it resides in a coyote's brain, but even his other-than-coyote mind rebels from the complexities he must resolve before he can do the simple thing of asking the two ranchers why they slew his family.

First there is his daughter. At least she is no longer so dependent on nursing. He can take many shapes, but they are all male. Mother's milk is the one thing he cannot give her. Although she is just reaching the age where she would be learning to hunt, she cannot be expected to provide for herself.

Scrawny as she is, she is still vulnerable to numerous predators. Accident could also claim her: a fall, a chance encounter with a rattler, poison, or bad water. No, whatever he does, he must make provisions for her.

Abandoning her does not even occur to him. She may have been the runt of this litter, but she is his daughter and has claim on his protection for at least her first year. And, in all honesty, he no longer thinks of her as the poorest example of this year's pups. Her attempt to avoid the wire gig rather than giving in to terror has won his admiration.

So he must provide for her. For several days, she should be safe enough on this scrubby hilltop. He will regurgitate food for her and warn her to stay near the ground squirrel's burrow. Having learned the practical uses of caution, she should obey.

Next, he must consider how to confront the humans. Unlike other of the Earth's inhabitants, humans only know how to converse as equals with other humans. He tries to remember how long it has been since he lived as a human for any extended period of time and decides that it has been about fifty years. During that time there have been many changes, changes he has observed but not taken part in. Still, if he does not claim too much, he should be able to pass himself off as a human.

Now things become difficult. He can take human form, but human society demands things that he cannot shape from his own body: clothing, money, transportation, personal history. His exasperated growl sends his daughter, who had been battling a twig, scuttling into the ground squirrel's burrow.

A moment later, her little black nose peeks up over the edge, sniffing vigorously for sign of whatever had annoyed her father. Turning his mind back to his problems, he lets her decide for herself when it is safe to come forth. It is a lesson she will need to learn.

Bright and laughing, the moon stares down at him, offering him a partial solution. Her face shines over more than this hilltop; her gaze encompasses the ranch house and the pastures. Although the Changer has no form that can fly as high as the moon, he can take other forms, something he has been resisting until he knows better what he needs.

Now he admits that what he needs will not be found on this hilltop. Nor will he find what he desires in coyote form. Reluctantly, for he has loved being coyote as he has loved only a handful of other forms, he reaches for a new shape.

¤◙¤

"WHAT HAS THE KING EVER DONE FOR YOU?" ask words printed in red on a sheet of canary yellow paper.

The envelope containing this flyer had been delivered to a rural mailbox at the edge of a large tract of forested land in Oregon, bordering on Umatilla National Forest. No one ever saw the person or persons to whom this mailbox belonged. Much of the mail was simply addressed to "Box Holder" but some was sent to "Mr. and Mrs. Trapper" or to "J.Q. Fuzzy."

The letter carrier knew that a week or more could pass before the box was emptied. Then the junk mail would be sorted into a bag neatly labeled "Please Recycle." Sometimes a stack of boxes waited for pickup. Often a small envelope containing five or ten dollars "For Your Troubles" would be attached.

Today the sheet of canary yellow paper is almost dropped into the recycling bag without a careful reading, but a hairy hand reaches out and intercepts it before it can fall.

"Wait," says a voice, distinctly female for all its guttural inflection. "I want to read that."

The creature that takes the letter cannot be called a woman. She is too hairy—furry might be a better word—and as muscular as a professional football player. She is also at least six feet tall. Next to her husband, who towers over seven feet in height and is covered with thick, coarse reddish brown fur, she is a dainty thing. With her silky black coat and delicately pointed head, she knows herself a young and beautiful representative of her kind.

"Listen to this," Rebecca Trapper says. She begins reading aloud to her husband, who politely looks up from a report on fashion models protesting against fur coats:

WHAT HAS THE KING EVER DONE FOR YOU?

THE HUMANOCENTRIC POLICIES OF THE CURRENT ADMINISTRATION NEED TO BE CHALLENGED AND NOW! SINCE THE DAWNING OF THE INDUSTRIAL REVOLUTION, THOSE INCAPABLE OF HUMAN FORM HAVE BEEN TOLD THAT THEIR ONLY REFUGE IS IN SECRECY. WHY?

BECAUSE IT SUITS THE NEEDS OF THE HUMAN-FORMED!

OUR COALITION BELIEVES THAT THERE ARE OTHER OPTIONS AVAILABLE TO THOSE AMONG US WHO HAVE BEEN RELEGATED TO THE STATUS OF MONSTERS AND MYTHS. LET'S BAND TOGETHER AND TAKE ADVANTAGE OF MODERN SOCIETY'S NEED FOR MYSTERIES TO BALANCE MATERIALISM!

ASK THE DRAGONS!

BEFORE YOU DISMISS OUR APPEAL WITH THE TRIED-AND-TRUE RESPONSE "THE KING IS ALWAYS RIGHT" WHY NOT ASK THE DRAGONS ABOUT THEIR FEELINGS ON CURRENT POLICY?

"Ask the dragons!" grunts Bronson Trapper. "What kind of nonsense is that? Everyone knows that dragons are extinct!"

"I think that's the point, my dear," Rebecca Trapper says calmly. "There's an address and a website here for further information. I think I'll look into it."

"Politics has never done us any good," Mr. Trapper protests, turning into the forest. "The King helped us purchase this land and secure the equipment we need to run a business without exposing ourselves to ridicule and rude inquiry."

"Still," Rebecca Trapper muses, thinking of the places and things she has seen on television via satellite dish, of the friends she has made via computer chatrooms whom she would love to meet in person, "this flyer does have a point. There's no harm in looking up their website, is there?"

"No dear," says Bronson Trapper, his mind already back on what this latest antifur crusade could do to business. "No harm at all."

¤▣¤

After considering his needs, the Changer decides an owl will suit, a large spotted owl, capable of covering vast distances, of seeing with little light, and of carrying away prey. The idea pleases him, and his blood thrills in anticipation of flight. Too long has passed since he took wing.

Warning his daughter that strange things are coming (news that she acknowledges by diving into her burrow and peering out over the edge), the Changer begins the shift from coyote to owl.

With some amusement he has perused human legends regarding those who can alter their shape—legends that have remained legends because, even when confronted with the truth, most humans are unwilling to relinquish their myth that they are the dominant creature upon the Earth. As the human race has spread, those cultures which believe in humanity's dominance have tended to overwhelm or absorb those that do not. Thus the truth is further obscured beneath legend.

One of the dominant "truths" that humans use to deny the presence of shapeshifters among them is the question of matter and mass. Logically, they argue, something the size of a coyote could not become something larger (like a human) or something smaller (like an owl) because there would either not be enough matter or there would be too much matter.

Only with the advent of modern subatomic physics have humans begun to come close to the truth. Matter is mostly space. Moreover, the building blocks of matter are, at a most basic level, interchangeable. One such as the Changer knows how to make such exchanges. The only difficulty is in the individual template. Thus, he can become anything living, but its gender must be male. Others of his kind have fewer shapes (indeed, all do, for he is the supreme shapeshifter), but are not restricted by gender.

What templates are available to a shapeshifter vary from type to type. This issue interests him only slightly, since he is little restricted in his choices. Even as he considers such abstractions, he is beginning to alter his form.

Feathers dark and brown over wings, tail, and round, puffy, head. The eyes, set frontally in that round head, are dark as well, but this brown-on-brown scheme is relieved by bars and spots artistically scattered along the owl's underside.

Yes.

The details he needs are stored in the slowly awakening portion of his mind. Anything he has studied he can shape. Long ago he committed a vast number of creatures and their variations to memory. Some of the animals he can shape are extinct, but he has made no effort to restore them. To do so would be to court stagnation, and he is the Changer.

When he has designed this particular owl form (and sent the black nose of his daughter deep into her burrow), he strokes a quick brush of memory over the shape. If he has need, he can reassume this shape with minimal effort, go in moments from coyote to owl. There are other such stored shapes in his repertoire, even other stored owls, but he enjoys the act of design. Making new shapes is part of his delight in being the Changer.

Without further ceremony, he beats his wings, and, faster than magic, he is aloft. Shapeshifting has made him hungry. He sweeps down, a rodent's silent nightmare, and takes a shivering mouse. This is eaten not only still warm, but so close to living that he can feel the beating of its heart. The kill has been easy, so easy that it reminds him why he does not frequently take the shapes of the smaller members of the order *rodentia*.

Then he is over the ranch to which he saw the two men ride earlier that day. It is an attractive place, although built to serve practical needs. There is a large house, a single-story structure that has been added on to over the years. Parts of it are thick, solid adobe brick, others more modern frame-stucco. The building materials have dictated its rectangular form and its brownish color, but color touches doorframes and window frames.

The livestock barns are more modern, constructed largely of sheet metal and concrete. Most reek of cattle, but there is one for horses and another with a few pygmy goats. Off to one side, there is a large vegetable patch, planted with tomatoes, onions, chilies, and squash. This early in the season, the plants are small and seem set too far apart. Near the vegetable patch is a little white wooden chicken coop. Doubtless the chickens are encouraged to forage in the vegetable patch during the day.

Tonight they are locked safely behind wire and metal, safe from the predations of the local red or grey foxes and ambitious owls like himself. Several large dogs sleep in the shelter of the barns. One sprawls across the back door to the house. No doubt any more usual prowler would find himself receiving an unpleasant welcome.

Finishing his circuit, the Changer notices another, smaller, house set in a copse of cottonwood and tamarisk along an irrigation-ditch bank. While not precisely hidden, the house is effectively shielded from casual observation from either road or field. Curious, he swoops down to take a closer look.

Perched in a tree branch outside of a window lit by the bluish glow of a television set, he observes.

Four men sit within, watching a program on a screen whose sharpness of resolution and clearness of color surprises the Changer—especially since its battered case suggests that it is not a particularly new model. His brief ventures into the human world have not included taking time to watch television. Apparently the technology has advanced quite a bit since he last bothered to look at it.

Judging by what is playing on the screen, the programming does not seem to have advanced very far. His interest in the television is passing, however; he studies the four men.

Neither of the two who killed his family is among their number, nor does he catch the disturbing scent of flowers and musk that had made his hackles rise earlier that day.

All four of the men are brown-skinned and dark-haired. Although the television program they are engrossed in is in English, the few comments they exchange among themselves are in Spanish. During a commercial, a debate over the virtues of the two *gringa* actresses breaks out. Listening to the cadences of their speech, the Changer becomes certain that they are Mexicans.

A small mystery is solved then. These men are most probably wetbacks, illegal aliens hired by the rancher to augment his workforce at minimal cost to himself. If the rancher is Hispanic, they might even be relatives.

Had the owl's face been constructed to smile, the Changer would have smiled. Now he has a means of bringing pressure on the rancher. The Changer takes wing then and continues his survey.

Changes in farming practices make absolute judgment difficult, but he guesses that the rancher is doing well enough but is certainly not prosperous. A severe drought or an unfavorable fluctuation in cattle prices could put him deep in debt. If a stranger came and offered him a couple hundred dollars for a bunch of freshly killed coyotes, no questions asked, doubtless he would welcome the opportunity to earn some easy money and rid himself of vermin at the same time.

The Changer's last sweep takes him by the black-metal mailbox at the edge of the road. The name "Martinez" is stenciled neatly in white on the side.

Very good. He knows precisely how he is going to acquire the human goods that he needs before he can call on Mr. Martinez.

Ravens, another of the Changer's favorite shapes, share with their cousins the jays a fondness for shiny objects. Over the years, the Changer has collected a variety of useful objects which he has cached throughout his territory.

Because he is the Changer, and not merely a raven or coyote, the caches contain cash as well as coins and jewelry. They also contain some fairly useless items, for a bit of broken glass or bent metal can catch his fancy and hold it.

The Changer spends the remainder of the dark hours winging from cache to cache, collecting his finds and carrying them to the hilltop where his daughter is hiding. It is onerous work, for while only a winged creature could reach his caches, transferring their contents efficiently is difficult without hands. He remedies part of his problem by scooping up a plastic grocery bag from the side of the road and using it as a carryall. Still, he must stop frequently to forage, and by dawn he is quite exhausted.

With the last of his energy, he brings his daughter a ground squirrel (possibly kin to the one who so kindly provided the burrow) and stretches out beneath the thick growth of juniper. Sleep claims him almost immediately.

¤◎¤

On an isolated website, unlinked to any others, unlisted by web-browsing programs, its address distributed only to those who have found a certain canary yellow flyer in their mail, the chatroom is untenanted except by two.

Rebecca>> Have you seen the latest posting?

Demetrios>> The one on the proposed referendum? Yeah. What do you think?

Rebecca>> I like it. Bronson isn't so sure. He says the King has always been good to us. Why rock the boat?

Demetrios>> To get your feet wet? :) Sure the King has been good to us, but what does it cost him? We've become his serfs.

Rebecca>> :(Is it that bad? We live lots better than most Americans.

Demetrios>> Are we really Americans? I know: you live in Oregon; I live in California, but we aren't permitted to take part in governing the states or counties in which we live.

Rebecca>> We don't pay very high taxes either!!! We can handle what we pay and if we're to own property we must be in human databases.

Demetrios>> True. But what about our dues to the King? What are those if not taxes?? An extra tax.

Rebecca>> Bronson says that the King's help in securing our land is worth years of dues.

Demetrios>> Still . . . There's more to life than having good hideouts. What about being able to experience the joys of life? I miss beaches and moonlit glades.

Rebecca>> Don't you have a glade at your place?

Demetrios>> Sure, but one patch of greenery gets old after a while. I long for the freedom of the world. Anyhow, fauns are cute, not monstrous like dragons.

Rebecca>> Or sasquatches??? Don't fool yourself. Fauns look like medieval depictions of the devil, at least some people think so.

Demetrios>> You've got a point. Sorry.

Rebecca>> Do you really think the Moderator can give us that freedom?

Demetrios>> He says the human world is ready to accept us— more than that—it yearns for us. I agree.

Rebecca>> I wish I was so certain. . . .

When evening comes, the Changer uses the waning light to survey his haul. Pawing through, sorting and counting, he is impressed with the value of what he has collected.

In cash, there is something in the neighborhood of a thousand dollars—mostly in one- and five-dollar bills, although there are bills of larger denominations. There are several fifties with sequential serial numbers. These, he remembers, came from a wallet he found dragged by the current in a narrow mountain stream. He had flown the wallet to a postal drop and left it, but had kept the money for his troubles.

In addition to the cash there is almost a hundred dollars in American coins and a smattering of foreign currency (mostly Mexican, although there is some German and British). He also possesses fifteen rings, numerous single earrings, five necklaces, and about a dozen bracelets. Since he has a good deal of cash, he decides to leave the jewelry. Some of it is merely costume jewelry, but he has lived long enough to see the trash of one age become the valued antiques of another.

Finally, there is the pure junk, including large quantities of broken glass and countless twists of scrap metal. Much of the latter is chrome from automobiles, but there is also copper, aluminum, steel, and brass. He turns an automobile antenna over with his paw, recalling the day his raven self had proudly ripped it from an elderly auto.

Some of the broken glass is far lovelier than the jewelry. Teal green, ruby red, various shades of blue, delicate lavender, it recalls to him his mate of several seasons, a she-raven who enjoyed foraging for treasures in the ruins of a burned house that was at the heart of their nesting grounds. He had kept much of the glass out of memory of her, and he does not discard it now for the same reason.

The money makes his current task easier, but it does not

solve all his problems. Even with something like a thousand dollars in his possession, he cannot stroll stark naked onto the Martinez ranch and expect to be spoken to man to man. No, first he will need clothing, but without clothing he cannot enter an establishment to purchase clothing. Without much regret, he decides that first order of the night (after he has fed his daughter) is to steal something to wear.

Stealing does not bother the Changer overmuch. As he sees it, humans take property too seriously and life too lightly. Therefore, after he has introduced the girl pup to some of the joys of mousing, he shifts into owl form and goes seeking human attire.

He has never paid a great deal of attention to human fashions, but memories from his coyote years reassure him that blue jeans and a button-down shirt are still considered reasonable menswear. Underclothing would be nice but can wait until he can carry it.

Choosing a course that will carry him away from the Martinez ranch, he comes across a trailer court. Most of the folks who reside in this place apparently economize by hanging their laundry out to dry. In the darkness, the owl examines each of the clotheslines. From a particularly overloaded line, he takes a long-sleeved Western shirt and a pair of jeans.

Immediately, he realizes that he has chosen poorly. The shirt is light, but he will not be able to carry the jeans any distance. Dropping these on the ground with a silent apology to their owner, he takes a pair of khaki shorts and a tee shirt. These he can lift, although he will need to rest frequently.

As he wings away, the Changer considers what any who glimpses him might think. Had he possessed shoulders at that moment, he would have shrugged. Everyone in the Southwest knows that witches can turn themselves into owls. A sighting of an owl carrying off a shirt and a pair of shorts would add to local legend, nothing more. Certainly there would be nothing to indicate that once again the Changer walks among humankind.

Stowing the stolen clothing in an isolated copse at the edge of sprawling pasture many miles from the Martinez ranch, he hunts mice and makes his plans for the morrow. Then he returns to his daughter and sleeps as a coyote beneath the juniper bush.

In the morning, daughter fed and cautioned not to stray too far afield, the Changer assumes the form of a particularly magnificent raven. His beak is large, horny, and slightly curved. His plumage is black, but the light reveals highlights of green, blue, and even purple. With a wingspan in the area of four feet, an elegant wedge-shaped tail, and a bright eye, the raven knows himself the king of birds, bowing not even to the eagle or the hawk.

Pleased, the Changer grasps his stash of bills in one clawed foot and launches into the sky, croaking farewell to his coyote daughter. A few flaps of his great, dark wings, and he is en route to his hidden clothing and closer to the vengeance his inhuman heart craves.

¤◙¤

The e-mail message is anonymous: "You're missing a story both sensational and true! Does the name Arthur Pendragon mean anything to you? He's living right here in Albuquerque, reigning in secret for all to see."

Chris Kristofer, junior reporter for the *Albuquerque Journal*, runs a hand through his brown hair. He is about to delete the message when he glimpses another line farther down the screen: "If you don't believe me, it's your great mistake. Look up Pendragon Productions! That's all it'll take."

Chris sets a search program running and is rewarded when a webpage takes shape on his screen. Even in a commercial art form dominated by amateurs, this page is badly designed. Blurry photos are captioned in glaring turquoise. The text is presented in solid blocks of tiny print almost impossible to read. Hot links to other pages proliferate.

The business of Pendragon Productions is listed as "outreach and support." Arthur Pendragon is president, Edward Zagano vice president, Vera Tso secretary and treasurer. Each hot link connects to information about various government projects, some local, some statewide.

Despite his initial reluctance, learning that there really is someone calling himself Arthur Pendragon who is trying, however ineffectually, to influence public opinion, awakens

Chris's journalistic fervor. He composes an e-mail message of his own.

"Bill: Check out a business called Pendragon Productions . . ."

Go where he will, the wise man is at home,
His hearth the earth—his hall the azure dome.
——RALPH WALDO EMERSON

THE CHANGER DOES NOT PUT PARTICULAR CARE INTO crafting his human form, since he does not plan to use it more than this once. Instead, after studying the stolen clothing, he draws a basic human male design from his repertoire, alters it by adding a few inches of height and a bit of breadth to the chest, and dresses himself in his pilfered attire.

No longer a wild creature, the Changer stands as a young man with medium-length sandy blond hair and light blue eyes. His complexion is fair, touched with freckles. About his eyes are faint lines as if from squinting at the sun. Since he could not steal shoes, the Changer compromises by toughening his feet. Placing his money in his pocket, he walks to the highway.

As he trudges roughly north, he tries to thumb a ride from the passing vehicles. Either the thumb-out gesture has gone out of style since last he tried this, or humans have grown more cautious, but he walks three miles before a truck slows.

After his ride drops him off in Mountainair, the Changer locates a general store. There he purchases a pair of sneakers, socks, a comb, jeans, a shirt, underclothing, a roll of tape, and an inexpensive wallet. The clerk is quite willing to throw in a medium-sized cardboard carton and a stack of old newspapers. Mountainair is not a large town, but it does include a garage alongside of which is a used-car lot.

Dickering is not his favorite sport, but he has millennia of practice, so without exhausting quite all of his money, he purchases an elderly sedan.

Now he has clothing, money, and transportation. He will speak with Martinez, gather up his daughter, and head into Albuquerque. He wonders what the orphan coyote will think of the city, wishes that he could explain more clearly what is happening. He shrugs. One problem at a time.

He only stalls the car three times before he feels confident driving his purchase. After filling the gas tank, he heads back south toward the Martinez ranch. As the little sedan carries him effortlessly across lands he has traversed more laboriously on wings or pads, he reflects that, whatever else they have done, humans have mastered the art of transportation. The cost, needless to say, is isolation from their world.

From the first time a human slung his leg up over some cooperative equine, thus freeing himself from the need to slog along on his own two feet, the faster and farther a human has traveled, the further he has traveled from knowing the land he traverses.

The Changer doesn't feel particularly judgmental about this. The car will make it possible for his daughter to exceed the limits of her four legs. That she may be unable to find her way home again is a minor concern since that home is inhospitable to an orphaned coyote pup.

He debates visiting her first, then discards the notion. She will do well enough, and he will endanger her more if anyone sees him crossing the fields in human-form. Instead he revs the engine and heads for the Martinez ranch.

✪◧✪

Red hair, Sven decides, is a bit of a liability if one wishes to go unnoticed, especially if one wishes to go unnoticed in Santa Fe, where dark hair and tanned skin are the rule. Still, he has established this persona, and creating another would take more effort than he wants to invest. Besides . . . he'd hate to give up his snappy new wardrobe.

Humming softly, he glances in the window of the *Prima!* gallery. He sees Lil inside, talking intently with a chunky woman with permed black hair. A customer. Good. With the bitch busy here, his meeting with Tommy should go quite well.

And soon, hopefully soon, Lil will be gone for good.

Leaving downtown, he redeems his rented Lumina from a parking garage and heads toward an exclusive gated community at the northern end of the city. He has no difficulty getting in, though the name he signs to the register is false. The license number the guard neatly jots down will do nothing more than cause confusion if anyone tries to check his trail.

Sven likes that. Chuckling to himself, he parks the car a short walk from his destination. Then, eschewing the labeled trails, he crosses a decadently green lawn to a pair of attached town houses. Both of these, along with those to either side, belong to Lil and Tommy—privacy that appears to be public living. The rich can do such things with ease.

Straightening his cream-colored raw-silk jacket, Sven presses the buzzer on the door of the left-hand town house.

"Yeah?" The voice that answers is sleepy, but for all that sensually masculine.

"Hello, Tommy. I'm the person who left a certain . . . present for you at the club last night."

There is a long pause, long enough that Sven wonders if Tommy has fallen asleep again.

"Yeah?" The tones on the other side of the connection are more alert now. Sven can almost taste the tang of the cocaine that fuels them. "Well, hey! Come in, man."

The man who opens the door for Sven is belting a silk tapestry-print lounging robe about his waist, but that is as far as he goes in the direction of social graces. Sven doesn't mind. His earliest memories of this man recall him draped in a leopard skin, dappled with fresh blood and red wine, his hair tousled, a wreath of vine leaves askew on his brow.

Tommy's last identity had possessed jet-black hair, pouting lips, and seductive blue eyes. With the aid of mass media, it had been his most successful persona since the earliest— and those had tended to end up both deified and violently dead.

This time around the pouting lips and seductive eyes remain, but the build is lean, almost angular, height accented by a leonine mane of golden brown hair cut in a stylish shag. Although his official bio claims he is half–Native American, half-French, Tommy Thunderburst looks like nothing so much as the incarnation of rock 'n' roll—and that he is.

"Hi, Tommy," Sven says, stepping past the man in the doorway, a bantam strutting beneath the leopard's jaw. "Thanks for seeing me."

"Yeah, right, man." Befuddled still, Tommy closes the door and follows Sven into the living room.

Remnants of a fire fill the kiva fireplace in one corner, cigarette ashes overflow several Indian pots around the room. Glasses half-filled with flat soda or stale fruit juice randomly decorate any available tabletop where the drinker had distractedly put them aside and forgotten their existence.

The source of that distraction is even more evident than the mess. Sheet music is scattered on stands and the floor. Two acoustic guitars lean against a grand piano. A flute and a lyre rest atop the piano. Electronic gear is heaped in another corner. Through an open door, Sven spots enough recording equipment to make a major studio envious.

Eyes sleepy no more, Tommy views the chaos, clearly aware of it for the first time.

"Sorry about the mess, man. I didn't expect company."

"No, don't worry about it," Sven says jovially. "I did drop by unannounced. Tell me. Did you like my gift?"

Tommy's eyes narrow. "Maybe."

"Hey!" Sven warms his tones. "I'm not a narc, and I'm not from *her* either."

Neither of them need to clarify who the female in question is. Tommy's lovers have been countless, but only one woman is a constant in his life.

"She don't care," Tommy says bluntly.

Without volition, he has strayed over to one of the guitars. He picks it up, sits on the edge of one of the chairs, and starts strumming something atonal yet melodious. Sven feels himself being captivated by the music, shakes himself.

"Tommy, I'm a big fan of your music."

"Ain't had any out yet, bud."

"I've heard you in the clubs. You're good. I think you're

going to be as big as Elvis . . .'' He pauses, watches for some flicker of acknowledgment in the downturned gaze. ''As big as Angus . . . as Orpheus.''

The gaze that lifts from the guitar is no longer sleepy.

''Who are you?''

''A friend. One who knows what you can do, who is glad to know that you are walking among us once more and who wants to . . .''

''Use me?''

Sven arches his brow. ''Hardly.''

He lies easily. Deception is easier for him than truth. With truth he always feels he is giving something away. However, since no one gets something for nothing, he has made himself comfortable with the necessity for truthfulness from time to time. With Tommy, this time, there is no need for awkward truth.

''No, Tommy, I'm just a fan. After your last 'fall,' I researched how you might avoid your . . . tendency toward excess?''

He makes the last a question, as if he himself is less than certain what he means, although he knows precisely. Many athanor have patterns they live over and over again. For Tommy Thunderburst the pattern involves music, tragic love, drugs, and self-destruction.

''Excess,'' Tommy laughs bitterly. ''Call it that, if you want.''

''I have,'' Sven continues cheerily, ''taken advantage of modern chemistry. There are designer drugs that give highs unlike anything in wine or dope, but safe—nonaddicting.''

''That's what they said about cocaine,'' Tommy says, fingers working through a syncopated scale. ''And about lots of other shit. And there are drug tests, now. Get you arrested. The days of wine and roses are gone, my red-haired kinsman.''

''What,'' Sven says, leaning forward, ''if I gave you a charm that would protect you from all of that?''

He quickly pulls out a dark purple stone carved into the shape of a thunderbird, lightning gripped in its claws. With anyone else, he would have teased longer, but, for anything except music, Tommy's attention span is tragically short.

"Cool," Tommy says, taking the pendant from Sven's hand.

"It's amethyst," Sven explains, "long believed to be sovereign against the ills of intoxication. It's also the birthstone for February and associated with the eighth hour of the day."

"Yeah?"

"Yeah. And it's also an emblem of deep, pure love."

"Cool."

"I've had it ensorcelled to protect against detrimental intoxication—whether from alcohol or drugs. It will also neutralize your bodily fluids so that you will pass drug checks."

"Wild!"

"Do you want it?"

Tommy doesn't let go of the satin cord holding the pendant, but he looks suspicious.

"What's the price?"

"Nothing. Just be my friend."

Tommy ties the cord around his neck. "Okay, friend."

He picks up the guitar again and begins playing. At first, he glances at Sven from time to time, as if seeking audience response. Then he clearly forgets all about him.

Rising, Sven tiptoes from the room. With luck, Tommy will forget all about Sven's visit until next time they meet. Well, with luck . . .

And a little help from his friends.

¤■¤

Almost as soon as the Changer turns his car into the Martinez's dirt-and-gravel driveway, his arrival is heralded by the barking of several dogs. He does not need to be a coyote to know that they are saying: "Stranger, Boss! Stranger!"

Prudently he rolls down the window so that the dogs can get a whiff of his scent. He has been told that no matter what shape he takes, there is a hint of wildness about him, a strange scent that identifies him as more than he seems. Although he cannot smell this himself, he has concluded that it may be an ancient defense mechanism, something that warns potential predators that he is dangerous.

Two great dogs, one a shepherd mix, the other a mutt that

looks like an unfortunate cross between a blue heeler and a coon hound, come baying up to the car. The shepherd looks as if he is about to plant his paws on the side of the car and learn what the interior acoustics will do to the sound of his bark, when suddenly he drops back onto his haunches.

"Easy fellows," the Changer says, opening the car's door and getting out. "We don't want any trouble."

The shepherd rolls over and shows his belly. The other dog is less submissive, but he sits and begins scratching vigorously behind one ear. Knowing that his apparent ease with their animals will help ingratiate him with the Martinezes, the Changer rubs the shepherd's belly with the toe of his shoe, then bends to stroke the other mutt's ear.

Hearing the house's back door open, he straightens. A woman in her late forties, her black hair untouched with grey, but her carriage slightly stooped, has stepped out onto the back step. She studies him with a confidence that tells him someone is close enough for her to call if he proves to be trouble.

He takes a few steps in her direction, trailed by the now-obedient dogs.

"Mrs. Martinez?"

"Yes."

There is a lilt to that single word that makes him suspect that her first language is Spanish.

"I'd like to speak with your husband."

"My husband?"

He is close enough to see the lines around her mouth and eyes and reestimates her age as perhaps twenty years older than he had first believed. So many women of Spanish or Indian descent do not grey at all until they are quite old.

"Or perhaps your son," he continues, "a tall man with dark hair cut short. He rides a bald-faced brown horse with a white stocking on its off hind leg. There was another man, younger, but enough like him to be his son. He rode a chestnut with four white stockings and a scar across its near shoulder."

She smiles, perhaps because he can better identify the horses than the men. Then she nods.

"My son and his son. Why do you wish to see them?"

"I want to discuss some business with them."

The Changer knows that on the surface he is an unlikely one to be coming to discuss business. His car and clothing do not telegraph money. He is too young, too fair to be a farmer. Idly, he wishes that he had taken more time crafting this human form. Had he looked like a cattleman or a horseman, they might have believed him a potential buyer.

Mrs. Martinez studies him a moment longer, glances at the shepherd dog leaning against his leg, then nods.

"My son is out in the cattle barn. Come into the kitchen, and I will send someone for him."

"I can go myself and spare you the trouble."

"No, come in. There is hot coffee and some *sopaipillas*."

He accepts her hospitality, knowing that she does not want him out in the barns where he might see the wetbacks at work. Doubtless they are ready to hide if anyone official-seeming arrives, but his unprepossessing car might not have given warning.

Admiring her prudence, he takes a seat at the kitchen table. This room is part of the oldest portion of the house. The walls are adobe, painted white and bordered with flowered tiles. The floor is dark brown tile, threaded with fine cracks from years of use, but as clean as if it had just been mopped.

Another woman, this one also dark-haired and Hispanic, but plump with rosy cheeks, grants him a brilliant smile as she half turns from where she hovers over a kettle of hot oil.

"Fresh *sopas* in a moment," she says. "I am also Mrs. Martinez. You spoke with my husband's mother just now."

The Changer notices that the older Mrs. Martinez has vanished. Through the lace-curtained window, he sees her marching across the yard to the barn. Mrs. Martinez the Younger nods toward the coffeepot.

"Help yourself. There's creamer and sugar next to it."

"Thanks," he says, pouring a cup. "I don't mean to impose."

"No imposition," she says, dropping batter into the oil. "There's always coffee, all day. We're getting the *sopas* ready to stuff for dinner. I think we can spare you one."

Again she turns that brilliant smile on him. The Changer finds himself liking her for her easy hospitality. She must be an asset to her husband in more ways than just her domestic skills. Whatever else they are, the Martinez family does not seem to be made up of unpleasant people.

He regrets this, for it will make his task more difficult, but the memory of his mate's pelt hanging from the back of a saddle and his pups' blood leaking from a sack makes him hard.

He is finishing his *sopa* with honey when the outer door opens admitting first Mrs. Martinez the Elder, then the man he had seen methodically skinning his yearling daughter.

Swallowing a surge of rage along with the remnants of his coffee, the Changer attempts to see the man for who he is, rather than for what he represents.

What he sees is a tall, lean man with skin browned as much by exposure to the elements as by genetics. Like his mother and his wife, he is dark-haired and dark-eyed, but unlike them he is thin as a rail. A drooping mustache conceals his upper lip, a marked contrast to his hair, which bristles short enough to suggest military influence. He is clad as the Changer had seen him before, in heavy, worn jeans and a blue work shirt.

Having turned the man back into a person, the Changer is able to smile politely, rise, and offer his hand.

"Mr. Martinez, my name is John Anderson."

"Pleased to meet you, Mr. Anderson," Martinez says, gesturing for him to sit and motioning for his wife to refill the coffee and *sopaipilla* plate. "My mother says that you have business with me."

The flavor of Spanish is less noticeable in his voice, but present nonetheless. His body language is of a man who is accustomed to being obeyed. The Changer knows that nothing but directness will answer.

Nodding thanks at the younger Mrs. Martinez for his newly filled coffee cup, he forgoes another *sopaipilla*.

"Two days ago, you and your son killed a bunch of coyotes."

Mr. Martinez starts. Coyotes are not on the bounty list in New Mexico, but neither are they protected. Still, technically, he should have a proper hunting license before taking one.

"So you say," he replies guardedly.

"So I know," the Changer counters. "Two females, one

older than the other. There were also five pups gigged from a den."

"They are vermin," Martinez says. "They were troubling my calves."

"They were not. You were paid to kill them and to sell their pelts to someone. I'll leave you alone if you tell me what you know about the buyer."

"Leave me alone?" Martinez says angrily. "What can you do?"

"Report you for suspected violations—a hunting license, perhaps." The Changer pauses, lets the predator look out of his blue Anglo eyes. "Perhaps for some hiring irregularities."

Martinez meets the challenge in the Changer's eyes like a sheepdog facing off against a prowling wolf. Again, the Changer accepts that he likes these people. No matter what they have done, they were only tools in others' hands.

The men glower at each other for a long moment, the tension broken when the elder Mrs. Martinez pulls out a chair and takes a seat at the table. She speaks in rapid idiomatic Spanish:

"*He knows, Diego. Give him his answer. You know little enough, and I did not like that blond witch.*"

The word she uses for "witch" is "*bruja*," a term far more derogatory than "*curandera*," which also can mean witch. The distinction is not as clean-cut as black or white magic, but there is something similar.

Allowing mild puzzlement to color his features, the Changer reaches for one of the cooling *sopaipillas*. Squeezing honey onto it from a bottle shaped like a bear, he looks at it.

"Must be tough making a living on honey and a few head of beef cattle," he muses. "Nice to get paid well for a few hours' easy work."

Martinez stiffens, but a mercenary glint enters his dark eyes. Knowing now that the man can be bribed, the Changer reaches for his wallet. The navy-and-white nylon isn't very impressive, but its bulge is promising. Resolving not to let Martinez learn that most of the bills are ones, the Changer sets the wallet down and covers it with his hand.

"I've taken you from your work. Certainly, I can pay you

for your time. What is a rancher's hourly wage these days?''

He knows from his brief ventures into the general store and the used-car lot that money is not worth what it once was, but those same ventures have given him an idea of current values.

"Perhaps twenty dollars?" he says, pulling out a crisp bill.

Martinez snorts and drizzles honey on a *sopa*.

"Thirty?"

Martinez doesn't pause in his chewing.

"Forty?"

Martinez seems prepared to continue stonewalling, but his mother leans forward.

"*Diego, the* gringo *is being fair with you. Don't forget that he can cause trouble for Juanito's cousins. Your greed makes a fool of you.*"

Diego Martinez continues to chew, but the Changer does not add another bill to the pile. Instead, he scoots his chair back a few inches as if preparing to rise.

"*Diego!*" the elder Mrs. Martinez snaps, "*Tell the* gringo *about the* gringa bruja *or I will tell him myself. Then I will take the money and visit my sister in Chimayo and beg her to pray with me for your soul.*"

"Very well," Martinez says in English, although it is unclear whether the words are intended for the Changer or for his mother. "I will tell what I know.

"Three days ago, a blond woman came here to the ranch looking to buy coyote pelts. I told her I had none. She was disappointed and told me she had seen several coyotes in my fields. She thought I would have hunted them.

"When I told her no, she asked if I would get those coyotes for her. I asked her why she didn't go to a furrier. She said that she had a particular fancy for these coyotes. When she offered me two thousand dollars in cash for the skins—and said that she would take care of the tanning—I agreed."

His shrug is eloquent. It seems to say, "Who would not take advantage of such insanity?"

The Changer feels bile surge in his throat. He swallows, maintaining his calm with effort.

"She wanted the pups as well?" he asks.

Martinez nods. "She said if there were pups, she wanted them, too. They are easy enough to kill, so we did."

"Did she give you a name or phone number?"

"Both." Martinez glances at the pile of money on the table, but a soft hiss from his mother warns him to keep speaking. "They may be by the telephone."

At his unspoken command, his wife exits, returning a moment later with a piece of paper torn from an envelope. Written on it in a neat, feminine hand is "Lil Prima" followed by a number.

"She said to call her when we went out for the coyotes," Martinez continued, "and when we were coming down to the road, she was waiting there in her car. We gave her the skins then."

The Changer nods and hands a fifty to the elder Mrs. Martinez.

"Gracias," he says, and continues in Spanish, "*You may wish indeed to pray for your son. That woman is very wicked. The holy shrine at Chimayo may be needed to counteract her power.*"

The older woman gasps and crumples the money tightly in her hand. "*What should we do if she comes here again?*"

"I don't think that she will," the Changer says, reverting to English and rising from his chair. He nods politely to his hosts. "If she does, you may tell her that I came asking after her. That will divert her attention from you."

He leaves then, bowing slightly to the ladies and shaking Martinez's hand. Tonight, he knows, they will call in a priest to bless the house. The elder Mrs. Martinez will go to Chimayo and pray fervently for protection. None of this will make a difference; nothing, really, will matter.

Just as Lil Prima has what she had come for—the deaths of his family and, she may hope, of him—so he has what he came for. The unnatural element he and his kind represent will have touched the Martinezes' lives briefly, and now it will depart, leaving them richer by $2,090, and a story for around the fire.

Driving to where he has hidden his daughter, he parks the car outside of the barbed wire that encloses the field and climbs the hill. First he pockets what of his caches he had left. Then he turns his attention to his daughter.

She is invisible within her burrow and remains silent when

he sticks in his hand. Unlike many young creatures, she has already learned prudence.

He locates her by the warmth of her quivering body. Grabbing her solidly by the scruff of her neck, he pulls her out. She tries to bite him then, and he permits the liberty. At the car, he stuffs her into the large cardboard carton he had picked up in Mountainair and straps the lid down with packing tape.

Almost immediately, the car becomes redolent with the odor of coyote urine, but he has lined the box with enough discarded newspaper to soak up the wetness. The stench he can live with.

He breathes into the air holes he has cut into the top, hoping that she will get some of his familiar scent.

"You won't need to stay in there for more than a few hours, little one," he says softly, "but I think a car ride would terrify you more than being shut in a box. We're going to see some old friends of mine . . . some very old friends."

She quiets then, although whether from fear or comfort he cannot be sure. Dumping more newspaper on the passenger seat, he straps the box into place. Then he gets in on the driver's side and turns them in the direction of Albuquerque.

The drive takes several hours, traveling mostly north and east. The road takes them through mountains and farmlands, through little towns that make Mountainair seem a major metropolis, and finally down through the Tijeras Pass and into the edges of Albuquerque.

A few miles' travel shows him that the city has grown considerably since the last time he tried to take a vehicle through it. After getting lost on unfamiliar roads and making several U-turns, he locates a cheap roadside motel.

The woman at the front desk doesn't ask about pets, and he does not volunteer any information. The Changer figures that they'll both be happier that way. In the room, he lets his daughter out of her soiled box and she promptly scoots under the table by the window—this being the closest to cover she can find, since the bed is built on a platform.

Taking pity on her, the Changer drapes a few towels over the table's edges and eventually her panicked breathing slows. Although feeding her so soon might be a mistake, he also knows that she is a growing child, so he calls room service and orders roast beef sandwiches and fries.

After he has tossed a sandwich and half the fries under the towel-hung table, he considers what to do next.

He needs to call the King, but he does not care to meet with him in this rather makeshift human guise. "John Anderson" was good enough for what he needed to do then, but not for the confrontation he plans.

Pulling the drapes shut and locking the door, the Changer removes his clothing. He has dwelled in New Mexico for a good many years now—although at least fifty have passed since he maintained a human identity. Doubtless he could use that form again and excite little or no comment. Even if he met with associates from those days, they would simply shake their heads and muse how much like Pablo that young man looked.

Still, he has not thrived by being incautious. Even though animals do not share the annoying human habit of keeping records, he has regularly reshaped his animal forms; to be less careful with humans would be foolish.

In any case, Pablo de Silva had his own history, a history he does not care to live again. A new form would be pleasant.

New Mexico offers him a delightful palette from which to work. The region is home to several groups of Native Americans, each with its own physical characteristics. There are also the Spanish—both those descended from the conquistadors and those of Mexican ancestry. And there are the Anglos, blond, brunette, or red-haired, with eyes of blue, or green, or hazel. Finally, there are a smattering of those of Asian or African descent. None of these groups is uncommon, so, effectively, he has the entire human race at his command.

His initial rush of delight at the possibilities ebbs as he considers his needs. He will need to keep this identity once his paperwork is issued, so he will need an appearance that is not overly noticeable. Dark hair, then, and skin that is neither too dark nor too fair. He considers what he has seen during his travels and begins sculpting.

The human male he creates is about six feet in height. Since the Changer will require physical presence when he is this man, he gives himself a strong build, muscular but lean.

The features he blends are taken from a variety of cultures. No one looking at him would be able to precisely place his heritage, but he could, with a shift of body language, pass for Hispanic, Anglo, or any of the local tribes.

Once the basics are completed, he works on the superficial details. First, hair: black as he had decided earlier, long, falling to the middle of his back. This last is vanity; having had a fur coat for so long, he feels ugly as a bare-skinned human. He reluctantly forgoes facial hair, deciding it might make him too noticeable, but permits himself slightly heavier than average body hair.

Hair completed, he shades his eyes light brown, almost a coyote yellow. The lines he etches in around them permit either menace or strength to be telegraphed with the faintest motion.

Finished, he surveys himself from head to toe, decides that he has precisely what he desires—a human male of strength and subtle power, who, despite these qualities, could vanish into a New Mexican crowd with minimal effort. After memorizing the form, as a final safeguard he designs alterations to the features and fingerprints. This way, if pursued, he can make subtle shifts that will protect his legal identity.

He showers and dons his now-ill-fitting clothing, then phones a number he has committed to memory.

"Pendragon Productions," a female voice says.

"I want to speak to Arthur or Eddie," the Changer says, his voice deep and just slightly gravelly.

"May I say who is calling?"

"Yes."

There is silence on the other end of the line as the receptionist tries to decide how to deal with this, then the line goes mute as she transfers the call.

"Pendragon Productions, Arthur speaking," says a baritone male voice.

"Arthur, this is the Changer."

"Changer? I didn't expect to hear from you."

"I know that, but I'm going to call my dues. Last I checked, I had about thirty years' credit to draw on."

"At least," Arthur agrees. "Fly on over. I'm at the same place as I was for the last Lustrum Review."

"Can't. I'm traveling with my daughter, and she doesn't shift."

"Hm." There are many unasked questions in that grunt, but Arthur is, if nothing else, politic. "Since you've phoned, I'm assuming that you're somewhere I can send a car."

"That's right." The Changer gives the address. "And make certain that it's someone who won't ask questions. I'm not in a mood to make idle banter."

"I'll send Vera."

"Good."

"It will be about a half hour or forty-five minutes before someone can reach you."

"Fine."

"Looking forward to the meeting with pleasure," Arthur replies.

"Right."

The Changer hangs up the phone and quickly resumes the John Anderson form. The latest shift has made him ravenous, and the she-pup is going to be hungry when she wakes up. He also needs another box. Somehow, he doesn't care to transport one that smells quite so strongly of frightened coyote.

3

Se non è vero, è molto ben trovato.
(If it isn't true, it is a happy invention.)
—ITALIAN PROVERB

NEW MEXICO CALLS ITSELF THE LAND OF ENCHANTMENT, and that is reason enough for a man who insists on calling himself Arthur Pendragon to set up residence there. He would have preferred the more eccentric, art-oriented cities of Santa Fe or Taos, but those cities lack major airports, a serious inconvenience for one who, in his position as king, must often travel.

Although part of his reason for residing in New Mexico is that it permits him to relive a persona he made famous in England, he actually likes New Mexico better than England. The British Isles' foggy softness had been enjoyable at first, but the brilliant sunlight and wide-open spaces of New Mexico's high-altitude grasslands remind him of the first land he remembers (as far as he knows, the land that gave him birth) and of several in which he had lived thereafter.

No, modern New Mexico might not be ancient Sumer or Egypt, but there is a pleasant sense of homecoming nonetheless.

Realities of the modern world being what they are, he will need to relocate within the next fifty or so years, but for now he has found a home. Perhaps next he will return to the Middle East, have altered the reddish gold hair and piercing blue eyes of this incarnation, shaved the curly beard, relinquish the cultured British accent, and resumed the burly-chested, dark-maned figure that had been his as Gilgamesh the Wrestler, the first king, one whose epic is the oldest recorded in human history.

For a moment, he wistfully wishes that he were one of those like the Changer who are not bound by human form. He would like to remain in one place, lazy decades stretching into centuries. However, he suspects that such might make him hidebound and dull. The need to continually outwit the humans who have spread over the world has kept him fresh and alive.

The Changer, though, no one would ever accuse that one of stagnating. Although he isn't like the satyrs, jackalopes, and yetis—the ones for whom modern science is a danger they do not dare confront—the Changer is in many ways wilder than those denizens of the untamed, isolated lands.

Wolf, coyote, raven, great cat: the Changer lives as a wild creature, rears his wild children, and reluctantly slouches into the meetings held every five years. Sometimes, he doesn't even bother to assume a human shape. Last Lustrum Review, he had perched on the doorway, dark-winged battle-bird, croaking an occasional "Nevermore" to those points on which he disagreed. Review finished, he vanished into the wilds once more.

He does live as a human from time to time, but those occasions rarely last more than a few decades. Then he returns to areas far from humans and dwells as a wild thing for decades.

Now the Changer is coming to Arthur for assistance—even the King would not use the word "help" where the Changer is concerned. He wonders what has stirred the old dog and looks forward to the challenge of assisting him.

Arthur rises from his polished-oak desk (this bought at an auction in New York City from himself the last time he needed to change personas) and crosses to the door of the office adjacent to his own. His knock is acknowledged by a male voice.

"Come in."

Arthur opens the door and enters an office as large and well-appointed as his own, even as it should be. Eddie has been at his side since the dawn of history, from a time when he was known as Enkidu the Wildman, a creature said to have been sent by angry gods to punish an arrogant king for abusing his power.

Of course, the gods had been disappointed. Enkidu and Gilgamesh had each found in the other the equal they lacked on the created earth. Rather than becoming enemies, they had become the closest of friends, and, when departure from ancient Sumer had seemed prudent, the excuse of Enkidu's death had been what Gilgamesh had used to send himself into voluntary exile.

Unlike what legend said, he had not searched for the secret of eternal life, for he already knew that aging passed him by. Enkidu had learned this sooner than Gilgamesh, thus his residence among the beasts, for they did not grow hostile when he did not journey into old age with them.

Gilgamesh and Enkidu also had learned that they healed much more quickly and thoroughly than those around them. Together, they had gone out into the world and left their mark on numerous cultures.

Arthur had the gift of inspired leadership. As Akhenaton he had tried to reform the theocracy in Egypt, as Arthur he had tried to found a society based on law, not might, in England. Many times, in many places, he had sought to change human cultures. His influence rarely lasted beyond his own reign.

For the last several centuries, he had turned his energy to a greater challenge, that of protecting the athanor from encroaching human civilization and its damning records. In this crusade, as in the others, Enkidu—now known as Eddie— had been at his side.

"Eddie," Arthur says, and his friend raises his head from the computer terminal at which he has been working. Dark, curly hair, and a perpetual five-o'clock shadow recall his original self, traits Eddie has maintained whenever possible. His build recalls a stone wall: thick and blocky, hard with muscle and square of jaw.

"Yes?" Eddie says. "You sound troubled."

"The Changer is coming here."

"The Changer? What does he want?"

"I don't know. He says he wants to call in his dues."

Eddie rubs his hand along his bristled jawline. "That's reasonable. Every year he brings his contribution to the treasury—sometimes more than is called for. We owe him service for that if for nothing more."

"I agree," Arthur says, "and there has always been his strong support of our rulership. Can you free yourself to attend the meeting? I've sent Vera to collect him."

Snapping off his computer, Eddie nods. "I would not miss it for the world. The Changer come for *our* aid. Old Proteus, sea-born, perhaps the oldest of us all."

"There is no proof of that," Arthur replies, slightly miffed. He has always enjoyed his seniority.

"No proof," Eddie says mildly. "True, but no lack of proof, either. He slips in and out of myths and cultures, refusing to be pinned down to any one origin just as he refuses to be pinned to any one shape."

"Or name," Arthur agrees. "The Changer. Most of us have names we use, a handful we return to as we return to certain callings. The Changer gives us no name to hold on to and remains an enigma."

Eddie stretches. "I could use a sandwich before confronting the ancient. How long do we have?"

"Easily half an hour," Arthur says, glancing at his watch. "Vera had to drive out nearly to Tijeras Pass to get him."

"Why didn't he just fly?"

"He said something about having his daughter with him."

"Daughter?" Eddie's bushy brows rise to his hairline. "How often has he claimed get?"

Arthur frowns thoughtfully. "That is a fascinating question, Eddie. I'd need to consult my records, but I could swear that this is the first time. She must be very special, this Daughter of the Changer. Could she share our gift?"

Eddie spreads his hands in a universal gesture of ignorance. "I don't know. Most of our children do not."

"Those of us who have children," Arthur says sadly.

Like so many of his kind, he is sterile. Even his celebrated daughters by lovely Nefertiti had not been his own. She had not been precisely unfaithful; rather she had been more than faithful, trying to give him heirs to carry on his dream. It had not made a difference in the end, and young Tutankhamen had been a weak reed who had forsaken the Aten.

He shakes himself, aware of Eddie's dark eyes gazing at him with kindness. Eddie has been burdened with a different sorrow. He has engendered children and it has been his lot to watch each die, of age, of illness, of accident.

Long ago, each had given up asking the question of whether their immortality was worth the price. Death is not a stranger to the athanor, only quiet, easy Death. When an athanor dies, it is in pain and suffering, body struggling to maintain a haven for life. Still, despite the phenomenal healing powers that are their heritage, athanor can die, they can suicide. That neither Eddie nor Arthur has pursued that option is proof enough that life still holds fascination.

"Let's get that sandwich," Eddie says, taking his arm.

"I'll be a moment," Arthur answers. "I want to check the records and learn what I can about the Changer's children."

His research confirms their earlier guesses. The Changer's biographical file lists no recorded children. Offspring from his numerous matings with various birds and beasts (of late mostly ravens and coyotes) must exist, but the Changer has never brought any to the Lustrum Review, never asked that any be recorded and recognized. This daughter, then, is a first.

Interesting.

He tells Eddie as they eat sandwiches and potato chips down in the warm, tiled kitchen.

"I'd better make a few extra sandwiches," the king concludes. "They should be here any moment."

As if in response, they hear the wrought-iron front gate opening and two cars coming up the gravel driveway. The door to the kitchen swings open a few moments later and Vera enters.

Dark-haired, brown-skinned, with high, rounded cheekbones and almost oriental eyes, she appears to be a classic Navajo woman in her mid-thirties. Even her speech is touched with an Athabascan accent: the even tones sometimes sounding flat, internal "r's" softened, the final "g" in a syllable often dropped completely. The only jarring element in this portrait is her large, grey eyes.

Grey-eyed Vera had not sprung full-grown from the forehead of her father as legend said, but such a tale might have helped a father explain the appearance of a rather too precocious young woman who was quite clearly his daughter.

Arthur had not known well the man who had sired Athena, later called Minerva, and currently known as Vera, but he had been one of the rare ones who not only was potent, but whose children carried his gift. He had died in the latter days of the Roman Empire, inadvertent victim of the persecutions of the Christians. His death had been slow and grisly; that it had ended up with his being made a Christian saint had doubtless been some small comfort to his daughter.

She had drifted from place to place, nation to nation, giving rise to a host of virgin saints and other such inspirational figures. That her celibacy was a matter of inclination rather than sacrifice did not bother her a whit.

"We cannot choose how people interpret our actions," she had said more than once, "and I will not behave as a slut merely because it would please some."

Arthur rather suspects that Vera's aversion to sexual congress is a reaction to her late father's promiscuity, but he does not care to address the point with her. That she might have inherited her father's prepotency along with his other gifts is a matter for quiet speculation when he and Eddie discuss such matters, but neither of them cares to bring up the matter with Vera. Her earliest identities had not been warrior maidens for nothing, and she has a tendency to take umbrage with a ferocity that recalled her legendary enmity for the people of Troy.

Instead they chose to let the grey-eyed girl take up residence with them, her formidable talents for organization and her solid common sense (on matters other than sexual congress) assets that help Arthur's organization to thrive.

At this moment, she looks less than tranquil. "I have directed the Changer to wait for you in the courtyard."

"You told an ancient to wait outside?" Arthur asks, surprised.

Normally, Vera is the soul of propriety; a fan of Miss Manners and Emily Post, she knows to the smallest margin precisely how much hospitality a guest is due. The Changer, despite his tendency in bird form to leave white droppings on polished doors and expensive carpets, has always been accorded the honor of a first place.

Vera looks momentarily uncomfortable, well aware of the breach of courtesy she has committed.

"He did not complain," she explains. "In fact, he seemed grateful for the opportunity to let his daughter out of her box."

"Daughter? Box?" Arthur actually stammers.

"His daughter," Vera answers woodenly, "is a coyote pup no more than a few months old. She is apparently terrified of everything and shows such by wetting copiously."

"Oh, my," Eddie says, chortling. "We should have guessed. The Changer hasn't been human for at least fifty years, and I don't believe he fathered any children during that incarnation."

"That we know of," Vera says stiffly. "It is not easy to know what that one has been doing. He has also acquired an old sedan with doubtful registration."

Eddie nods. "I can straighten that out."

"First," Arthur says, "let us hurry to greet him. If we must entertain him outside, at least the weather is pleasant."

When they enter the courtyard at the center of the hacienda, they find it tenanted by two coyotes. One is full-grown, grizzled grey above with a darker cross about his shoulders and a touch of white on his underparts. The other is a fat grey pup with hints of the coyote she will become. She had been cuddled next to her father but, upon their entry, she scuttles under a lavender bush. The thick blossoms and new foliage hide her very effectively, but if he looks closely, Arthur can see her eyes, still baby blue, peering suspiciously out.

With a surge of motion, the Changer takes a human form. The body is tall, dark-haired, and rather aggressively male—a fact that his present nudity does nothing to conceal. Perhaps out of courtesy for Vera, perhaps not, he reaches for the clothing draped on one of the teak patio chairs and dons it.

The jeans and shirt were clearly purchased for someone several inches shorter. From this, Arthur surmises that the Changer has used more than one human shape recently. Or perhaps he merely stole the clothing from some unlucky sod. The Changer has always been rather cavalier regarding other's property.

"Changer," Arthur says. "Welcome."

Occupied with buttoning his shirt, the Changer only grunts. Not a promising start for a conversation.

Arthur sallies on. "We made a few extra sandwiches when we were having lunch. Would you care to join us?"

"Thank you." The Changer now smiles warmly; he knows that offering food equals an offer of protection in many old cultures. It may do so no longer, but Arthur likes such archaic gestures. "Your welcome and your food are appreciated."

He takes a ham sandwich from the plate Arthur has set on the table and tosses it under the lilac bush, where it vanishes to a chorus of small growls. Then he takes a second and seats himself in one of the carved-teak chairs that are scattered about the patio. The others follow suit.

"How are you, Arthur? Eddie?" Somehow, the Changer's body language suggests that he is in charge of the little gathering. "Has the universe been kind to you of late?"

"Kind enough," Arthur says.

Eddie nods. "Pretty good. We had a bit of trouble with a clash between Katsuhiro Oba and Dakar Agadez, but that has been resolved satisfactorily."

"Who?" the Changer asks.

"Susano and Ogun," Eddie clarifies, using names with which the Changer is certain to be familiar.

"Gods of storm and iron," Arthur adds. "When they lack others to fight, they battle each other. How have you been?"

"Well enough until recently," the Changer says. He has inhaled his sandwich in a fashion that recalls a neater version of his coyote self. "And that recently is what brought me here."

He pauses. The others wait. There had been an anger in those last few words that did not invite casual rejoinders.

"A few days ago, my mate of these last five years and all of my family except for the poor creature under that shrub were slaughtered." The Changer's eyes narrow, and a dangerous light touches their yellow depths. "I have reason to believe that the killing was commissioned by one of our kind. I am here for three things. I want identification, so that I may move in the human world. I want to register my vendetta and its purpose with you. And I want to know where Lilith resides these days."

Arthur nods slowly. "I hear you and you have right to

claim the first two things that you have asked. Before I grant the last, could you explain why you want to know Lilith's location?"

"On the day my family was slain," the Changer says, "I returned from hunting in time to see the killers finishing their work. They rode from the site, my wife's pelt and that of my elder daughter behind their saddles. My babies were shoved in a sack—all but that one, who had been so terrified that she did not cry out and so saved herself."

The listeners do not need further details. In the long centuries of their existence, they have witnessed the cruelties of which humans are capable. Nor are they unduly judgmental, for they know well their own capacity for cruelty. The deaths of a group of coyotes at the hands of men who believed they were slaughtering "just animals" is a small thing on the scale of what humans can do to those they believe their equals.

The Changer also knows this, and so they know that this killing is not what has brought him from the wilds.

"I watched as they rode down the slope," the Changer continues, "and they were met by a car. A woman got out of the car and gave them money in exchange for the raw pelts. Her scent was carried to me on the wind and I knew that scent as that of one of our own—a particular one of our own.

"I have spoken to the rancher who did the killing. He said that the woman commissioned the killings—not just of coyotes in general, but of those coyotes. The name he gave me was 'Lil Prima' and the scent that I smelled was of the one who in ancient days was called 'Lilith.' "

He stops then, inviting their questions. Eddie begins.

"Did you get anything else?"

"Yes." The Changer takes Martinez's scrap of paper from his shirt pocket, but he does not relinquish it. "A phone number. And I saw the license plate of the car and memorized the number."

"If I can copy that phone number and have the license number," Eddie says, "I can do some checking."

The Changer gives him the information, then the slip of paper is tucked again into his shirt pocket.

"What do you plan to do if you find Lilith?" Vera asks, speaking for the first time since the Changer began his tale.

"*When* I find her," the Changer says, and his emphasis is enough to remind them all of his age, of the nightmare of being tracked by one whose shapes are nearly infinite, "I shall ask her what her purpose was in killing my family. I shall find out if she intended my death as well. Then I shall take retribution."

None gathered in that courtyard had expected anything less, but to hear those words spoken by that deep, husky voice strikes an atavistic fear in each.

"And if we recommend against it?" Vera says, nobly asking the question that Arthur should not.

"You are not my masters," the Changer says. "My support for Arthur's reign is out of appreciation for the loyalty he can inspire in others, not out of sworn obedience. You cannot turn me from my purpose—I can forgive human stupidity, for they do not know what they do. When an athanor challenges me, I must answer that challenge."

Silence falls then, broken only by the faint sound of the coyote pup digging a bed for herself beneath the trembling shrub.

"Lilith," Arthur muses at last. "I will look into this. In the meantime, let Eddie help craft you an identity."

The Changer nods. "I will. And Arthur, if you warn Lilith, and my vengeance is thwarted because of this, I will come for you and all the admiration I hold for you will not slow my wrath."

Arthur is not a king for nothing. He squares his shoulders and meets the ancient one's eyes.

"I know this, and I accept it."

The Changer smiles, a bitter quirk at the corner of his mouth. "Trust me in this. I have not lived to my age by taking pity on those who stand between me and my purpose."

His dark gaze includes them all; then, words spoken and understood, he gives his polite attention to Eddie.

Rebecca>> Hi, folks! I've just finished feeding the critters. What's up?

Demetrios>> We've been discussing the new appeal. Did you stop to look at it?

Rebecca>> No. Felt like talking. Dear brawny Bron is still fussing

over what the latest fury over fur is going to do to business. All
he wants to talk about.

Demetrios>> Poor dear. Basically, the Moderator has suggested
that we converge on Albuquerque and the King for the Lustrum
Review in June.

Rebecca>> Go in person, you mean?

Demetrios>> That's right! The Moderator has promised assistance with travel plans.

Snowbird>> My family would have a long way to come. I'm not
sure the non-American branch could get through Customs.

Demetrios>> What about the Alaskan branch?

Snowbird>> Possibly. Private plane would be our best bet. I'll
e-mail the Moderator.

Rebecca>> Albuquerque! You can't be serious!!

Demetrios>> Why not? We have as much right to attend those
Reviews as anyone else. I'm tired of having to hide away.

Rebecca>> Bronson would never let me go.

Moderator>> Just caught up. Rebecca. If Bronson won't let you
go, isn't he admitting the failure of the King's system? Isn't he
saying that we pay our dues to remain prisoners?

Demetrios>> Yeah!

Rebecca>> I suppose I could try . . .

Moderator>> Snowbird. We can swing that private plane or
fueling for your smaller plane.

Snowbird>> We're kind of tall for one of those sardine cans . . .
Let me consult with Swansdown.

Loverboy>> Hey! If we all get together, we can have a party!!
I'm so tired of private do's. Babes!! ;)

Moderator>> Did you know that Dionysus now resides near Albuquerque in Santa Fe?

Loverboy>> Party! Party!

Demetrios>> Keep your horse's ass in check, you idiot! This matter has serious implications.

Loverboy>> Party! PArty! ParTY!!

Rebecca>> Demi has a point. There are so many worldwide
issues we cannot address as we are. Human society has developed the means to destroy the world—and is destroying
large chunks of it. Perhaps they *need* to know that others share
this globe with them. Perhaps they would learn prudence.

Moderator>> Very thoughtful, Rebecca. The King must see that

our energies could be better used than on covert operations.
Humanity *needs* us.
Loverboy>> Party!! Whoo!! Babes!!

"Arthur?" Some hours after the initial conference with the
Changer, Eddie stands in the doorway of Arthur's office, his
computer tucked under one arm as once he carried his lord's
standard. "Do you have a moment?"

"Of course." Arthur flips off his own computer. "How
are things with the Changer?"

"As well as could be expected. He has incredible patience
and focus when working toward a goal . . . none whatsoever
for anything else. He's taken the puppy . . ."

"His daughter," Arthur corrects sternly.

"Right. Down to the *bosque*. I gave him 'can't miss it'
directions."

Arthur frowns, thinking of the Changer and a baby coyote
trotting through the wooded stretch along the Rio Grande,
amid the joggers and cyclists. He didn't want to consider
what might happen if anyone offered to cuddle the "cute
doggy."

"Was that terribly wise?"

"How would I stop him?" Eddie asks reasonably. "He's
not an easy one to cross. In any case, it's well after dark.
You've been working too late again."

Arthur glances at the clock, realizes that this is true, and
pushes back his chair.

"Can we talk in the kitchen?"

"It might be better if we don't," Eddie says, shutting the
office door behind him. "It's not the most secure place."

Arthur nods. "Secure from whom?"

"The Changer, maybe from Vera, maybe just because
what I want to bring up is supposition rather than anything
logical."

"I've grown to trust your suppositions, Eddie. If I had
listened to them more carefully in centuries past . . ."

"Arthur, you have a gift for self-recrimination. Stow it and
listen."

The great king does so. After all, Eddie is right.

Eddie takes a seat in a chair ergonomically designed for

perfect comfort and immediately leans forward, eschewing the chair's sympathetic lines.

"I think that the Changer is wrong. I don't think that Lilith was responsible for the death of his family."

Arthur cocks an eyebrow. "The evidence against her is pretty powerful. I've checked the license number. The car was rented to an L. Prima for the dates concerned. The phone number matches with her unlisted cell phone. And, the handwriting on that note matches some of hers I have in our files."

Eddie fidgets. "So there's a lot more than the Changer's 'catching her scent' to go on, isn't there?"

"That's right. It isn't enough for you, though. Why?"

"Maybe I'm too suspicious, but Lilith is of the ancient."

Arthur picks up a pencil and starts drumming on the desk. "True. She claims to be the oldest female human-form— Adam's original bride and all that rot. Even if you discard that nonsense, cross confirmation makes her about the same generation as you and me."

"And she's sly," Eddie continues, "and malicious. And known for her enmity to the traditional family."

Arthur sighs. "She claims that she never got over Adam's claim that the female was subordinate to the male."

"Whatever the reason, she's built quite a reputation for herself over the decades."

"There is a point to this?"

"You know there is, Arthur." Eddie takes the pencil from the King's hand. "And that drumming is driving me crazy."

"Sorry. Go on."

"To put it bluntly, I can't imagine that a sly ancient like Lilith would leave so clear a trail. It doesn't make sense: her own current name, phone number, a sample of her handwriting, a car easily traced to her. She's too good. If she was going after someone like the Changer, she'd be more careful."

Arthur begins to twiddle a pen, then sets it down. "You have a point. Caution is as natural to her as breathing."

"I've checked her current situation," Eddie says. "She's living in Santa Fe, running a gallery and helping Tommy establish his new identity."

"That's right, he's recovered and public now, isn't he?" Arthur sighs. "Is he doing music again?"

"Of course. 'Tommy Thunderburst,' part-Navajo, part-French. He's soulful as ever. Lil sent a copy of his 'demo' tape—bitter, acid, loving. I don't really care for contemporary music . . ." (by contemporary, Eddie means anything later than the eighteenth century) "but I could see the appeal of this."

"So why would Lilith be going after the Changer now?" Arthur muses. "She has a busy couple of decades in front of her."

"Precisely," Eddie says. "That's why I can't believe that she is the one behind the killings."

"The Changer does," Arthur replies. "And he won't believe anything she says. Lying is second nature to her."

"And so he will confront her and kill her," Eddie says, "and then there will be repercussions."

"For us," Arthur says, "because we permitted ourselves to be swayed by such flimsy evidence."

"Yes."

"And for the Changer, for slaying her without just cause."

"Yes."

"Who would do this?"

"I don't know, right off, but you know that many athanor grow bored. Such a game might amuse a few or . . ."

"Or?"

"Or someone desires to unsettle your kingship. You know that not everyone is happy with your policies. Some say that you play the humans' game of using information technologies more insidiously than they do themselves—and for far less pure intentions, since you *know* of our existence and use the threat of human revelation to control our actions."

Arthur huffs. "I do not! I simply advise prudence. Humans are no longer isolated societies to be manipulated by the powerful among us."

"Easy, friend." Eddie chuckles. "I agree, or I wouldn't be working with you. So do most athanor, or you would not have their support. Your talent for leadership is not merely charisma."

"Thanks," Arthur says, still piqued.

"But there are those who have not appreciated your efforts

these past two centuries. The most vocal have been eliminated, usually by their own actions. Only the subtle and creative remain.''

"There are Katsuhiro and Dakar," Arthur reminds him. "Neither is subtle."

"I think you underestimate them," Eddie says, "but I agree that they do not have the manipulative spirit I sense."

"A trickster then?"

"Perhaps." Eddie frowns. "Or perhaps the Changer himself."

"He would not slaughter his own family!" Arthur protests.

"Perhaps not."

"And he is not sophisticated enough to have gathered unlisted phone numbers and the like."

"How do we know? The Changer lives much of his life outside of our supervision. Just because he has not registered a human identity does not mean that he has not had one."

Arthur rubs his face with his hands. "I suspect we should consult Lovern on this one."

Eddie nods. There is something of a rivalry between Arthur's right hand and the sorcerer, but Eddie recognizes the talent of the man once called Merlin.

Not wanting Eddie to become affronted, Arthur hastens to clarify: "Lilith is a sorceress herself, although of a different type. Moreover, Lovern can craft a truthstone for us to use . . ."

"On the Changer?"

"Yes, and perhaps to loan to the Changer so that he can confirm or deny Lilith's innocence in a more objective fashion than just by interviewing her."

Eddie leans back into the chair's embrace. "That's a good idea. Where is the wizard now?"

"On sabbatical in Finland," Arthur replies promptly.

"Contact him," Eddie says. "Then you can consider how best to explain to the Changer that while we aren't calling him a liar, we aren't exactly certain that he is telling the truth."

"Oh, my," quoth Arthur. "That should be fun."

Caras vemos, corazones no sabemos.
(Faces we see, hearts we know not.)
—SPANISH PROVERB

THE JOURNAL ISN'T PAYING CHRIS TO INVESTIGATE Arthur Pendragon, so he waits for his day off to meet with Bill. A college student majoring in computer engineering, Bill Irish has frequently saved Chris hours of unproductive research through his singular talent for rapidly locating pertinent information.

"You know," Bill says as he comes in the front door of Chris's house, "I thought you were touched in the head when you asked me to check out an Arthur Pendragon."

Despite his name, Bill Irish is anything but. A Jamaican American, he possesses light brown skin and warm brown eyes. His shoulder-length, curly hair is habitually drawn back into a fashionable ponytail. At six-foot-one, he is several inches taller than Chris and lean to Chris's solidness.

"Come into the living room and show me what you have," Chris invites, pouring them both glasses of cola.

Accepting his, Bill sprawls on the sofa and unfolds a printout. "Pendragon Productions is registered with the state as a not-for-profit corporation," he begins. "No employees other than the three officers are listed."

"Not unreasonable," Chris says. "They may be broke."

"Someone has money," Bill contradicts. "Motor Vehicles

lists four vehicles for Pendragon Productions: two sedans, multipassenger van, and a trendy four-wheel drive. All are recent models and none are inexpensive. Arthur owns a large house in an expensive area. There is no mortgage—he paid for it up front and then did extensive remodeling. His credit record—as well as those of Zagano and Tso—is perfect. Wherever Mr. Pendragon gets his money, he is well-off.''

"Is that his real name?" Chris asks.

"As far as I could tell," Bill says. "He's a naturalized American citizen. His place of birth is listed as England."

"Maybe that explains it. Anything else?"

Bill shrugs. "Not much. Pendragon Productions seems devoted to rather ineffectively crusading for various causes. It doesn't fund-raise, and it doesn't spend much money. Tso and Zagano both live on the grounds of Pendragon's estate."

"Idle rich?" Chris tugs at his short mustache with his lower teeth. "Do you have a listing of Pendragon's pet causes?"

"Yeah. I extracted them from that nightmare of a webpage. Most are quite noble: social causes, environmental activism, government corruption, that sort of thing."

"Do they do their own investigation?"

"Not that I can tell—mostly they link up others' work."

"Weird. I'll see if I can get an interview with Pendragon."

"Is it worth the hassle?" Bill asks. "Mr. Pendragon seems like just another New Mexico crank to me."

Chris grins. "The *Journal* likes stories about idealistic local characters. In any case, I want to find out if Arthur Pendragon is quite as noble as he seems."

"And if he isn't?"

"Then maybe I'll have a story for the front page!"

❁◩❁

Sitting coyote-form in the courtyard of Arthur's adobe hacienda, the Changer scratches behind one ear and reflects on the events of the past several days. He and his daughter have been asked to stay at Arthur's place, ostensibly so that his paperwork can be done properly. He suspects deliberate delays, but that does not bother him overmuch.

His time has been well spent learning new dialects of Spanish and English, as well as current events so that he will not betray himself in casual conversation. His daughter, too, is thriving. A visit from a veterinarian has ensured that she will be protected against a host of potential ills.

Moreover, his hosts have heard his warning; they are not foolish enough to believe that he will not carry it out. Nor could they be absolutely certain that they could stop him.

Shapeshifters are notoriously difficult to kill—the true ones, at least. Not that he is invulnerable. Far from it, but over the centuries, he has memorized routines to enable emergency shapeshifts. For example, should someone shoot him at this moment, he would shift into a small, darting finch. Much of the damage would be healed in the change and a finch is much harder to hit than a coyote . . . or a man.

Such a change would arouse questions, of course, but the Changer can live with that. Caution is his chosen first armor. The defenses are secondary—or even tertiary.

Whining joyfully, his daughter comes out from under the lilac bush where she has dug her shallow earth. In the past several days, she has learned to recognize him by scent, rather than merely by shape, and consequently has become bolder. She still prefers him as a coyote, though.

Coming up to him, she drops a length of braided rawhide at his feet. Vera purchased it for her at a pet store and, although momentarily annoyed that his daughter might be being treated as a pet, the Changer has permitted the pup to play with it. Her satisfaction with Vera's choice is evident in the rawhide's increasingly chewed appearance.

Giving in to the pup's desire to play, the Changer grabs one end in his teeth and provides resistance as she tugs at the other. Her throaty, puppy growls vanish as footsteps come toward the courtyard and she retreats under the lilac bush.

Even before the Changer turns, he knows Vera by her scent.

"Why don't you turn into a puppy sometime?" she asks, seating herself on the edge of the patio table and tossing a chunk of cheese into the lilac bush. "She needs something her own size to wrestle with."

Not deigning to reply, the Changer gives the woman an ironic gaze. What does this virgin know about raising pups?

He does not tell her how to perform her duties in Arthur's business. Why does she try to tell him his as a parent?

"I thought you might like to know," she adds after a pause, "that Lovern has just arrived at the airport."

The Changer wonders who Lovern is. The human-formed tend to shift names as he shifts shapes. Recalling a couple of these tags and their scents is enough for him. He scratches again, then retrieves the untouched piece of cheese from the lilac bush.

Dropping it at Vera's feet, he shifts human in one surge. Politely recalling that nudity has a tendency to unsettle the woman, he reaches for one of the robes that, since his arrival, have been hung in odd corners around the hacienda.

"Please," he says, belting the dark blue terry cloth with a matching sash, "do not encourage my daughter to eat any food she comes across. A common way to kill coyotes is with poisoned baits. If you teach her to accept food other than what she hunts or what I give to her, you may be responsible for her death."

At first, Vera is indignant. Then her expression softens.

"I didn't think," she admits. "And I apologize. I won't do it again and I'll make certain that the others know as well."

"Thank you." The Changer shapes a smile. "Remind me which one Lovern is."

Vera looks momentarily startled. "Mimir. Merlin."

"That one." The Changer whistles coaxingly to his daughter. She comes out and he tosses her one end of the rawhide string. "Gilgamesh has summoned him?"

"*Arthur* has," Vera says, her slight emphasis on the name reminding him that etiquette demands that each be called by their given name of the moment. As the etiquette is based in protecting identities, the Changer accepts its wisdom.

"Arthur," he repeats. "Has it anything to do with me?"

"Yes," Vera says calmly. "Arthur believes Lovern could aid you. Also, your vendetta has interesting implications."

"I do not need that sorcerer's help to deal with Lil."

Vera does not comment for a long moment, watching instead the Changer's game of tug-of-war with the pup.

"Perhaps not, but Arthur gives full value for your dues."

"Were you sent to prepare me to accept the wizard?"

"No," Vera says sharply. "I came of my own accord. Arthur is the first among equals here, not my master."

"First among equals." The Changer's soft laugh is almost a growl. "The old Round Table dream once more. Perhaps it will work better this time. I doubt it, but it's a nice idea."

Vera says nothing, whether because she agrees or because she is affronted, the Changer does not know. Tersely, she excuses herself and departs.

Watching her almost masculine gait (no soft roundness to *those* hips) the Changer reflects on what he recalls of Mimir aka Merlin aka Lovern. There are many such memories, but all are colored by one from the earlier years.

Mimir was not among the ancient or, if he was, his early centuries had been spent in places isolated from the small, loose-knit athanor community in the Mediterranean basin. Being fond of a certain aura of mystery, Mimir had never confirmed which was true. The Changer cared little. His instinctive feeling for Mimir had always been that the man was a liar—or if not a liar, what later years would call a showman.

This impression had persisted until the day that he first had learned what Mimir was willing to do to increase the knowledge at his disposal. It had been during a battle that would afterward drift into legend as Ragnarokk, a battle so terrible that no human could believe that it had happened, but in order to remain sane must believe that it was yet to come.

The Changer had been winging over the battlefield, a black raven with a wingspan of over eight feet. Around him, like ebon leaves stirred by the power of his wings, natural ravens soared, their deep voices quorking derisive comments on the bloody chaos spread as a banquet beneath them.

The sides were well-matched. Those who would be remembered in legend as the Aesir and Vanir included those then called Odin, Tyr, Heimdall, and Freya. Others have been forgotten, as that battle was their last.

Arthur was there as well, but he was not called Arthur then. He who had been Gilgamesh, Akhenaton, Rama, was known at this time as Frey, the golden prince of the Vanir.

Merlin was also among the forces of the Aesir, but he was not yet associated with Arthur. That would come later, after the debacle of Ragnarokk. At this time he was called Mimir.

Later, legend would name Mimir one of the Jotun, the enemies of the Aesir, just as Arthurian legend would give Merlin an incubus as a father. There has always been that about Mimir/Merlin, for all his wisdom, that is dangerous and untrustworthy.

The opponents of the Aesir were not the evil creatures that legend later counted them. They, too, were athanor, but they held a different philosophy than the Aesir/Vanir alliance.

Whereas the Aesir, following the council of Mimir and Odin, were largely content to deal with growing humanity as something like equals, interacting as councilors and guardians, remaining behind the scenes if they meddled at all, the Jotun could see no reason for this stealth.

Advised by the trickster Loki, they gloried in their difference from the human race. Where Odin and Mimir emphasized the similarities between many athanor and humans, the Jotun noted the differences.

The battle that had spread out beneath the Changer's wings had been a living icon of this difference in philosophy. The Aesir fought mostly in human form, wielding weapons such as a human might wield. The Jotun shifted into fantastic, inhuman forms. There was Fenris Wolf and Midgard Serpent; there were giants of fire and of ice—and all of them had been athanor.

The Changer had striven alongside the Aesir, for his tendency toward caution led him to feel that the Jotun's desire for open domination of humanity would eventually lead to trouble. Compared to the relative infertility of his kin, humans, even with their single births and high infant mortality, whelped young in litters. Anyone who has ever observed a plague of mice or rats knows that those who breed quickly overwhelm in the end.

Still, he had not interfered in personal combat. From above the battlefield he had watched as Thor and the Midgard Serpent had torn into each other. The latter was his sea-born brother. He had been pleased to see Jormungandr win this contest. Thor was a braggart and a drunkard.

And as he had dipped wing in congratulations to his brother, he had noted an odd figure standing in the shade of a great elm near the fringes of the battlefield. It wore a silver-grey robe with highlights of leaf green and runes of power embroidered into the fabric. The hood was raised, bulking strangely around the shape within. The cowl hung so low about the face that even his raven eyes had difficulty making out the face it sheltered.

Yet raven eyes, especially the raven eyes of the Changer, can be more keen than those of a normal raven or, indeed, those of any man. They penetrated the darkness of that cowl and saw that within not one but two heads sprouted from the scrawny shoulders of the figure within the robe.

The heads were not identical. Both were grey-haired with the grey that denotes wisdom, even among their unaging kind. The skin of one head was smoother than that of the other, bore fewer lines, fewer traces of weathering, fewer signs of grief or joy.

At a beckoning gesture from the robed one, the Changer had soared away. He was one of the ancient and not to be summoned like a pet or a servant, even when the summoner was Mimir, who even then was called one of the great sorcerers of their kind.

Returning to the battlefield, he shifted into an even larger version of his raven-self and plucked Loki from the field just when that one's aid might have meant the death of Frey. From a great height, he dropped the trickster on a heap of rocks and believed him dead. Later, he would regret not having checked more thoroughly.

In the end, two heads or not, the counsel of Mimir was insufficient to protect Odin from his own death on the battlefield of Ragnarokk.

In recent years, Odin had taken to wearing his hair long and straight, cloaking one side of his face. Some said that he had lost an eye to an assassin and sought to conceal the damage. Others whispered darker things. Cunningly approaching from that blinded side, the Fenris Wolf swallowed the Aesir warlord whole.

After Ragnarokk had muddled to its bloody end, the Changer had swept from the skies, leaving his fellow ravens to feed with the wolves on the bodies of the slain. As an ancient, he took part in the conference to reset the balance of power.

Even the human legends of Ragnarokk do not claim a clear

winner. Instead, legend says, the survivors stepped back from the affairs of humankind and the children of Lif and Lifthrasir populated a new Earth beneath a new sun and moon.

The reality was a little different. Loki was presumed dead (although this was later proven untrue), and the most powerful of his allies were either slain or, as was the Changer's brother, Jormungandr, severely wounded. The Aesir were little better off.

Odin was dead, but Mimir remained. He raised up Frey, who had been stunned but not slain by the flaming sword of Surt, hailing him as a new ruler for their people, a champion of ideals, and one who could work both with humans and athanor.

Mimir discoursed with eloquence as was his wont, but, even more than that eloquence, what swayed the dissidents was the frightful rawness on one shoulder near to his neck. The rawness resembled the stump of a tree when the trunk has been shorn away. Those who knew what had dwelt beneath Mimir's hood feared, with a base, primal fear of black sorcery, what he had done to himself.

Following Mimir's nomination, Frey was accepted as ruler of a freshly forged Accord. Then the battle-worn and battle-scarred survivors had returned to their homes.

Rumors continued to spread, though, rumors that became accepted as fact. Soon everyone knew why Odin had worn his hair straight and long over one side of his face, knew what had been the price that he had paid for the counsel of Mimir: counsel that had won him his battle and his cause, but cost him his life.

Sprawled in a teak patio chair, the Changer remembers this and considers the possibility that Mimir has learned more wisdom over the centuries. Certainly Arthur has thrived and while there have been many wars, there have been no other Ragnarokks.

He will meet with Lovern, hear his council. Such is no great difficulty for him. After all, he hasn't finished acquainting himself with the changes to New Mexico and, even if Arthur thinks that the knowledge remains secret, the Changer has learned that his prey now dwells a mere sixty-five miles away in the city of Santa Fe.

✿◉✿

Arthur is anxious as the moment arrives to bring the Changer and Lovern together. He has not been a ruler of men and athanor these past centuries without learning to read something of their feelings, even when those feelings are masked by manners.

Clearly, the Changer does not bear Lovern any great respect or even admiration. Lovern, in turn, regards the Changer with that slight edge of insecurity that he brings, even this late in life, to his meetings with those athanor he does not overawe. Fortunately, there are few enough who have not learned to flatter the sorcerer. It is just Arthur's luck that the Changer's insouciant disregard for just about everyone extends to Lovern.

The five residents of Arthur's hacienda assemble in the courtyard, a move that gives a home-turf advantage to the Changer, since he has been residing there since his arrival.

Viewing the damage the coyote pup has done to the shrubbery and to the outdoor furniture, Arthur is grateful for the Changer's choice of residence.

The Changer is waiting for them in human form, his black hair loose around his shoulders. As part of crafting the Changer's human identity, Eddie had helped him order suitable attire. The former dog coyote now wears a dark green cotton shirt open at the neck and blue jeans, the knees of the latter begrimed with the marks of puppy paws.

Sitting relaxed in one of the chairs, his daughter crouched between his bare feet, her nose wriggling as she catalogs the newcomers' scents, the Changer looks scarcely less civilized than he does as a coyote—and far less so than he does as a raven. As often before, Arthur wonders how much of this is pose, how much is the ancient's naturally protean nature.

When Lovern seats himself across from the Changer, the contrast is marked. Like the Changer, Lovern wears his hair long, but his hair is silver and gathered in a neat ponytail at the nape of his neck. His tidy beard and mustache are the same shade of silver-grey and his eyes an icy blue. Although his attire is casual, his off-white button-down shirt and khaki trousers are custom-tailored. Needless to say, he is shod.

The wizard wears several pieces of jewelry: a loose chain, a wide bracelet on his left wrist, several rings on his fingers. One of these, Arthur knows, holds a truthstone set low in its open silver band so that it can touch the wearer's hand.

Truthstones are amulets of transient power and, undeclared, are considered a great rudeness. Arthur is willing to take this risk to confirm the Changer's story. Lovern agrees, for he has always used his magic as would best suit his needs without concern for what offense he might offer.

Given what the wizard is capable of, this truthstone is a mild enough affront. The Changer might even agree.

Vera, seated to the Changer's left, is charged with making certain that if he does take affront, the violence is minimized. Warrior maid, warrior saint, she is well suited to the job, although her hands are currently busy with weaving a pouch from beads, needle, and thread.

Eddie is, as ever, bodyguard to his King. His light sports shirt and khaki trousers could conceal nothing, but his wrestler's shoulders and heavy arms remain weapons that cannot be taken from him.

Their casual circle of five—six if one includes the puppy— is shielded from eavesdroppers by one of Lovern's spells, a neat little thing that replaces what is said with other words that will match the lip movements. Thus, not even a lipreader could garner the truth of what is being said.

Clearing his throat, Arthur turns to the Changer. "I've filled Lovern in on the basics. However, I was wondering if you would tell him your tale yourself."

The Changer nods. In that dry, throaty, almost growl of a voice, he recounts his family's death and his investigations thereafter. Lovern listens, nodding sympathetically and asking an occasional question. He is too good to let on whether the truthstone reveals any falsehood, but since he does not speak a prearranged phrase to inform Arthur of deception, Arthur assumes that the Changer's honesty (on this matter) is confirmed.

He feels vaguely relieved. It isn't that he precisely likes the Changer, but he respects the ancient—and he had hated to contemplate what would have happened if he had been forced to challenge the shapeshifter's story. Now all that remains is telling old Proteus that Lilith may not be the enemy he seeks.

Eddie takes his cue from Lovern. "Changer, I've been researching the information you brought us, and while it does seem to point to Lilith, I'm not certain that wily bitch would have left so clear a trail."

The Changer frowns. "My late mate was a bitch—Lilith is a witch and a black one at that. Perhaps she believed that I would be slain with the rest."

"I can't buy that," Eddie says, brushing a hand through his dark curls, his attitude casually brave. "She knows that you shift shape without preparation—you're not restricted by a sorcerer's rituals. Unless slain instantly, you would escape."

Vera turns her solemn eyes on the Changer. "What type of rifles were the ranchers using?"

The Changer shrugs. "I don't pay mind to such things. Hunting rifles, I think. Fairly light. It doesn't take much to kill a little canine like a coyote."

Vera frowns. "Surely, that wouldn't be enough to kill you, even with a shot to the heart or head."

The Changer neither confirms nor denies this. Wisdom dictates that only the braggarts give any idea of what their vulnerabilities might be. Arthur does not think that his silence is an indication that the Changer has detected the truthstone, just that silence is part of the ancient's perpetual defense.

Vera continues, "Lil could not be certain you would be the first one found by the ranchers. In fact, they were lucky to get both of the other adults."

Nodding, the Changer accepts this. Had his mate not stayed to defend the pups, and the yearling female been a bit more paranoid, both might have survived.

"So you are suggesting that Lilith was not the one who killed my family. Who then?"

"We don't know," Arthur says, bluntly, "but we certainly would like to."

"I'm not letting Lilith off so lightly," the Changer growls, and the pup echoes the menacing sound.

"I don't expect you to," Arthur agrees. "I only ask that you confirm her guilt before exacting retribution."

The Changer's gaze, ironic, unsurprised, turns to Lovern. "And I suppose that the sorcerer is about to offer me the means to do so."

Lovern nods, somewhat stiffly. The Changer's tone had been perfectly correct, but his inflection on the word "sorcerer" held something like a suppressed chuckle.

Arthur sighs. "Yes. Lovern has a few suggestions to make."

King and councilors had agreed that immediately offering a truthstone might tip the Changer that one had been used on him. It is too much to hope that the Changer will not suspect, but if proprieties are observed, perhaps he will choose not to be offended.

Like the gentleman he is, Lovern smiles at the Changer. "I could interview Lil for you. We are both initiates in the sorcerous arts. She may speak more openly to me."

The Changer shakes his head. "I'll speak to her myself."

"Then perhaps I could accompany you," Lovern says. "I could act as witness."

"That won't do," the Changer says. "You're too closely associated with Arthur. I won't have the King dragged, even by association, into my revenge. I wouldn't have waited here at all if it hadn't been for my daughter."

His rough voice softens with unexpected affection. "She couldn't fly with me."

Eddie leans forward. "Then you know where Lil is?"

"I do." The Changer grins. "Learned it here, but that phone number and license plate would have led me. I may not have your skills, but money can buy those who do."

"True enough," Eddie says, "and that is all the more reason to be suspicious. Why would Lil leave such a trail?"

"Yes." The Changer picks up his daughter and strokes her ears, letting her gnaw on the knuckles of one hand. "I agree. I don't want Lovern with me for the reasons I've given, but I wouldn't mind a witness when I talk with Lilith. It may protect both of us in the long run—if she's innocent."

This is a bit of good luck for which Arthur had not dared hope. He makes a quick mental review of who is available.

"How about Eddie?"

"Nope. He's like Lovern, too much one of yours." The

Changer's speculative gaze comes to rest on Vera. "Minerva—I mean Vera—might do."

"She would?" Arthur says, surprised. "Why? She's on my staff as well."

"Yes, she is," the Changer says, "but she has not been so for long enough to acquire that intimate association. And she has a reputation for supporting justice . . . on most occasions."

Vera colors. Her one romantic flirtation had ended disastrously when the man in question—a fellow immortalized as Paris son of Priam—chose another woman. While she had not reacted with the fury of her fictional counterpart, the experience had caused her to prefer judgments that were less subjective than those found in the interpersonal arena. In ages since, she has frequently served on the tribunal that deals with the transgressions of her peers.

"I'll go with the Changer," Vera says. "That will save us the time and trouble of searching for another escort."

"Thank you, Vera," the Changer says, "for your help."

He sets his daughter down, his body language suggesting that he considers the meeting over. Arthur clears his throat.

"There's one other thing we can do for you, Changer," he says quickly. "Lovern can create a truthstone for you."

"Oh? Aren't those things considered in bad taste?" the Changer asks, looking with amber-eyed innocence at the King.

Arthur tries furiously not to color. "They are. Its virtue will be short-lived and its warning will be most easily understood in relation to a direct question, but it could take some of the indecision out of your meeting with Lil."

Scratching behind one ear, the Changer rather resembles his canine daughter. "I'll take one. When will it be ready?"

Lovern frowns thoughtfully. If he deactivated it now, the one in his ring would be potent for some hours more, but he does not think that he should alert the Changer to its existence.

"A day," he says, "perhaps two."

"I will leave as soon as the stone is ready," the Changer says. "With Vera as a guide, I need not waste more time."

This time when he rises, he is clearly weary of conversation. Arthur does not attempt to hold the feral ancient.

"We will keep you apprised of the situation," the King says, allowing those words to stand in the place of a formal dismissal.

"Thanks." The Changer bends and picks up his daughter. "I'm taking her to the *bosque*. She needs to learn to walk on a leash if I'm going to be taking her out into the human world."

A few nods of agreement answer him, most relaxed because the interview has gone much more smoothly than they had hoped. Eddie, however, hears the edge in the Changer's voice.

"You plan to keep her in the human world?"

"Of course," the Changer says. "She's too young to survive in the wilds and, if you're right and Lilith is innocent, then I may have a much longer search in front of me."

Arthur frowns. "I don't suppose that you would consider turning the preliminary investigation over to us, would you?"

The Changer's smile is more a baring of fangs. "No. Someone has involved me. I plan to stay involved."

"I thought," Arthur says when the Changer is gone, "that we were making things better. Now, for some reason, I have a feeling that they have just gotten much, much worse."

"You're just being pessimistic again," Eddie says, but his tone holds no conviction.

Vera rises. "I'd better go and check the hours of Lil's gallery and Tommy's show schedule. I'd hate to take the Changer to Santa Fe and find them on the road. The ancient is quite likely to put that pup in a carrier and hop the nearest plane."

"Or camp in Lil's bedroom," Lovern agrees. "I had better prepare the amulet."

"Aren't you just going to give him the one from your ring?" Arthur asks, curiously.

"No." Lovern grins sardonically. "I don't know how much attention he pays to such things, but I don't care to have the issue of our testing him raised after the crisis is past."

"And we"—Eddie turns to Arthur—"need to go and review today's messages. Just because the Changer has descended upon us doesn't alter the fact that we have duties to perform. Anson is just back from Nigeria and may be up to some new mischief.''

''Tricksters!'' Arthur almost spits, he himself being the antithesis of these chaotic, creative types.

Eddie is more tolerant, at least of Anansi, who is a particular friend. Their shared fondness for professional wrestling has bridged the gap between their lifestyles.

''On a less individual front,'' he soothes, ''we have a formal protest from several of our kinfolk who reside in South and Central America, noting that if the athanor do not act to affect the environmental abuses in those regions, they will intervene.''

Arthur rubs his palms against his eyes. ''I almost wish I could let them. We'll work out a compromise.''

''Are we adjourned then?'' Vera asks, already halfway to the corridor toward her office.

''We are indeed,'' Arthur says. ''At least for now everything is under control.''

He taps the teak chair on which he had been sitting.

''Knock on wood.''

5

*"For the female of the species is more
deadly than the male."*

—RUDYARD KIPLING

Demetrios>> I've been thinking about this summer trip to Albuquerque.

Moderator>> Not getting cold feet, are you?

Demetrios>> The opposite. Isn't the weather really hot in Albuquerque in the summer?

Moderator>> Fairly.

Demetrios>> I'm not sure that summer is a good time for some of the theriomorphs to go there. The sasquatch and the yeti have lots of fur . . . and my legs aren't exactly hairless.

Moderator>> Wear slacks.

Demetrios>> That will do for me, but what about the others?

Rebecca>> I've been "listening." Demi has a point. I don't think I could *stand* being bundled up at summer temperatures. And humans wear a lot less in the summer! Wouldn't we stand out more if we were wearing long pants and shirts and hats and all??

Loverboy>> Babes in miniskirts!! Hot pants!!! Shorts!! :)

Demetrios>> Yeah, bud. Think of what you'd look like in shorts! They couldn't miss your horse's legs.

Loverboy>> That isn't what they'd be looking at, not once they got a look at my . . .

Moderator>> Sorry to interrupt, but this *is* a "G"-rated site.

Watch your language. There are ladies present.

Loverboy>> Prude! :(

Monk>> The Moderator has a point. So does Demetrios. I think we had better move the date to later in the season.

Moderator>> Not too late! If we do that, then those in colder climes may miss because we won't be able to fly them out.

Demetrios>> How about Halloween? That would be appropriate.

Moderator>> Well . . . Denver often has snow by then. I may need to use their airport.

Rebecca>> How about some time in September? We should have good weather.

Demetrios>> Daytime temperatures can still get pretty high, as I recall, but given the altitude, it does cool off at night.

Moderator>> I can work with September. It gives me a bit more time to get things into gear.

Loverboy>> I can get it into gear anytime!

Demetrios>> Rebecca, how are things going with Bronson?

Rebecca>> Not so good. He's still pretty adamant. Won't even discuss it, really.

Demetrios>> Oh. Sorry.

Loverboy>> If Bronson won't give his bride a GOOD TIME, I'd be happy to oblige. Huh baby?

Logged off: Rebecca

Loverboy>> What do you think, babe?

Demetrios>> She's logged off.

Loverboy>> Some girls!

Demetrios>> You really need to consider restraining your urges if you're going out in public. All we need is you getting arrested on an assault charge.

Loverboy>> Not you, too! I don't recall *you* being so prudish in the days of yore.

Demetrios>> These aren't the days of yore and there aren't likely to be days like those again if we don't pull this off.

Loverboy>> Maybe I should just stay home. :(

Monk>> Sulk if you want, satyr, but, remember, we've got our future in our hands. If we back out, hope dies with our retreat.

Loverboy>> Pretty poetry doesn't win dames, not anymore.

Monk>> No, but our moderator's plan may put us in the position to do so once more.

Loverboy>> Position . . . heh, heh . . .
                    Forced log-off: Loverboy

"It's beautiful, isn't it?" the Changer says after he and
Vera have been driving for about a half hour. His hand rests
lightly on his daughter, who sleeps on his lap.

Vera is startled, both by the comment and that the Changer
is actually making conversation. "Yes, I think it is," she says
at last. "I think it's the sky that wins one first. The horizons
go on forever—like over an ocean. Clouds, sunsets, thun-
derstorms . . . They all seem bigger here and yet somehow
more intimate than they do at sea."

The Changer grins. "Almost makes you understand those
stories about Father Sky and Mother Earth f— . . . meeting
and engendering all creation."

Vera realizes that the Changer's statement as he had first
framed it would have been far more earthy, that he has edited
his words out of respect for her tastes. She smiles warmly.

"Yes, it does, doesn't it? Have you ever lived out here?"
Her hand leaves the wheel to gesture at the surrounding
terrain. The Changer nods.

"Not specifically here for centuries, I think. I was raven,
then. Wings are good things when there is so much emptiness
between meals and water."

Vera bites her lip, aware that her next question violates
etiquette. "Don't answer if you don't care to," she begins,
"but are there certain animals you prefer taking the shape
of?"

The Changer stretches, long arms brushing the roof of the
Ford Explorer. His daughter rouses enough to make a few
little noises and flip her brush of a tail over her closed eyes.

"Yes, I do," he says after a time. "The survivors appeal
to me more than do the victims or the great predators. I also
prefer those who mate monogamously and raise families.
Years ago, after losing a beloved mate, I spent a year as a
grizzly bear. I thought that the respite from dependence, from
fear of loss would be a pleasure. Yet, by the next spring, I
could hardly wait to assume a more social form and go courting. I like having someone to care about."

"Then you actually love your . . ." She pauses, looking
for a word. "Wives?"

"Each one," the Changer agrees. "Furred, finned, or feathered."

"But . . ." Vera gestures wildly with the hand not occupied by the wheel. "They are so short-lived, even compared to humans. How can you love a being that will die in an eye blink?"

"Love," the Changer answers, his rough voice holding something that is almost a chuckle, "doesn't come with preset time limits. Only athanor live without dying. A human or, for that matter, a coyote or raven or wolf or eagle, selects a mate in the blind hope that the other will continue to survive. Death could come the next day or in half a century. From what I've observed, the former can be kinder."

"And your children?" Vera asks. "Do you . . ."

"Preserve them?" the Changer offers, and when she nods, continues. "No. I do them a parent's duty as is defined by the natural ways of that species. For some that is a season, for some—like the coyote—that may extend into two years. Then I let them go."

"And when they die?"

"If I know, I mourn. What father wouldn't? But it is a poor father of any species who would keep his children imprisoned merely to keep them safe. Parents give life; they must also realize that for that life to be truly given they must let their children go."

Vera shifts gears, for the great climb of La Bajada is beginning. Before modern roads, this stretch was so formidably steep that at least once a miracle had been needed to achieve the ascent. Today dynamite and asphalt have made travel routine, but even modern vehicles respect the great hill.

"Were you born knowing this," she asks, deciding to take advantage of the Changer's talkativeness, "or did you learn it?"

The Changer laughs. "I learned. Long and hard that learning was, but I learned that the only way I could love was to let go."

"And the little one on your lap?"

"When she wishes, she, too, may go her way. I will try to take her to a place unfrequented by humans, but I will let her go." The Changer's hand ruffles his daughter's downy grey baby fur. "She is a pup now, and my parent's duty to her holds."

"Yet wild creatures often lose their mothers," Vera says. "Aren't you somehow acting against nature in protecting her?"

Vera's eyes are on the road, but she can feel the fierce gaze the Changer levels on her and deep inside she shivers.

"My daughter," he says, and there is a slight emphasis on the "my," "lost her mother, but not her father. Both parents in a coyote family raise the young—as do older siblings. I wear a human form, but I am still her father."

"I'm sorry," she says. "I didn't think. You seem so . . ."

She stops, aware that she had been about to be tactless once more, wondering where her much-vaunted wisdom has gone. The Changer, however, has caught the drift of her sentence.

"Human?" he says, and, to her relief, he chuckles. "I am old Proteus, Athena. A shape is a shape, nothing more. I own all shapes and so am no one shape. I try to respect the custom of the shape I am wearing, that is all."

"I am human-born," she says, by way of apology, "and all my shapes are human shapes."

"A logical bias on your part, then," he says, accepting the apology. "Is that Santa Fe below us?"

"Yes," she answers, relieved at the change in the conversation. "It is. Blends in quite well, doesn't it?"

"Remarkably, for a human city of that size," the Changer agrees. "I don't believe I have been there for fifty years."

"You'll find it much different," she says. "That's all I ever hear from the people who have lived here for ten or twenty or more years—how changed it is."

"Change," the Changer says, "is natural. What many forget is how much a part of that changing they themselves are. Where will we find Lil?"

"Her gallery is off the Plaza in the older part of the city," Vera answers. "We should be there in about a half hour."

"I can hardly wait," comes the reply, and when Vera glances to one side, she sees that the Changer is not smiling.

Despite Vera's warning, downtown Santa Fe astonishes the Changer. When last he had been here, the streets had mostly been dirt or gravel, the stores largely devoted to the daily necessities of the people who lived and worked in this sleepy little capital city. Now, most of the stores are art galleries, jewelry shops, or expensive boutiques. The majority of the people who stroll the narrow sidewalks are clearly tourists rather than residents, or even legislators.

"Amazing," the Changer comments. "If it wasn't for the Palace of the Governors and a few other buildings, I wouldn't recognize the Plaza at all. As for the side streets . . ."

"Lil's gallery is off San Francisco Street," Vera says. "I'm going to put the truck in a parking garage. Will you leave your daughter there?"

"Certainly."

Strolling along the narrow streets, neither one spares attention for the kachina dolls, velvet skirts, and silver jewelry displayed in the windows. Tourist season has not quite begun, so they can walk side by side.

"Down there," Vera says, gesturing. "You can just see the sign."

The Changer grunts. Swinging out over a doorway halfway down the next block is a carved oval sign painted red and gold, embellished with a single word: "Prima!"

After the brilliance of the New Mexican sun, the gallery's indirect lighting is welcoming. Glass cubes displaying jewelry and sculpture in their interiors are scattered with artistic perfection about the room. Paintings and hand-woven rugs cover the pale cream walls.

Music, contemporary, but with hints of compositions far older in its instrumentation, throbs like an excited heartbeat from concealed speakers. The subliminal impression is that here is a place where treasures are to be found.

"She hasn't lost it," the Changer mutters. "Supreme manipulator."

"No," Vera agrees, and she might have said more but they are interrupted by the tapping of shoes on the polished wooden floor.

"May I help you?" says the sultry voice that claims the honor of womankind's first seduction and first disobedience.

The words are clearly routine, nothing more, for after the first few Lil's inflection alters as she recognizes Vera and, quite possibly, the Changer.

Her scent is the same, and by that the Changer knows her. Her appearance, however, is as different from the shape he had first known her to wear as could be and still be human.

Then she had been short, voluptuous, darkly tanned, with a fall of night black hair to her feet and eyes like jet. Now, she is tall, slender, elegant, and golden blond. Her eyes are brilliant green and her skin peaches and cream. She wears a stylish dress of mint green; her jewels are jade and silver.

There is no doubting who she is. When the Changer sees her he knows that if human males had hackles, his would rise.

"Vera!" Lil greets the other woman. Her accent is French and her tone mockingly friendly. "How delightful to see you and our ancient brother."

She turns that hard, emerald gaze upon him. "*Bonjour*, Changer. When did you decide to come slumming? Last time I heard, you were still doing it doggy style in the mountains."

Her taunting has the perverse result of relaxing him. He bares his teeth at her in a coyote grin.

"I came to learn if I need to hurt you, Lil. Consider my personal attendance an honor due to your great age."

She gives no sign of fear. "And is this honor for any particular reason, or have you simply decided that this is someone's day to suffer?"

Vera intervenes. "Someone has murdered the Changer's family. All the evidence points to you."

"Evidence?" Lil pulls out a cigarette as long and slim as she is and lights it, scenting the air with cloves.

"Phone number, handwriting, car," Vera says.

"Even description," the Changer adds, "now that I see you, rather than scenting your distinctive bouquet on the breeze."

"Why would I kill the Changer's family?" Lil asks. "We don't love each other, true, but there is no vendetta between us."

"There is now," the Changer says, "one that will continue unless I get proof that you did not arrange for my family's deaths."

"I didn't do it," Lilith says bluntly. "It would be senseless."

"Would you say that before a truthstone?" the Changer asks, causing Vera to wince. She prefers honesty as much or more than most, but certainly there are more tactful ways to introduce the subject!

What Vera doesn't know is that the Changer has already been using the truthstone. It rests in one of his trouser pockets (a pocket his hand has not strayed near since their arrival in the gallery), part of its surface touching his skin through a hole he had clipped in that pocket earlier that morning. Manners can make only so much of a demand on him.

"*Oui*, you can use a truthstone to confirm my honesty," Lil replies calmly. "I have nothing to hide—at least not on that point. And I have too much respect for your power, Changer, and for your temper, to spite you on such a small matter of etiquette. However, if I permit you and am proven innocent, I do expect an apology."

"Formal and direct," the Changer agrees.

He pulls the truthstone from his pocket and holds it flat on his palm. Wanting to avoid any suspicions that the Changer's own honesty had been tested by means of a similar amulet, Lovern had used a broad oval piece of agate as a spell receptacle. Tan and brown, with slim lines of red, the pattern in the stone suggests a landscape rendered in the abstract.

"Pretty," Lil says. "How does this one work?"

"By heat and alteration in the hues of the stone," the Changer answers. "So you will be able to see its assessment."

"How nice." Her tone is almost a sneer. Seeing some tourists gazing through her window, she crosses and with an apologetic smile flips over the OPEN sign to CLOSED. "Make certain your questions are direct, Changer. These stones work best with as few ambiguities as possible."

"Yes." He pauses. "Did you hire a rancher to kill eight coyotes, seven of whom were my get and one my mate?"

"*Non.*"

The stone remains cool, but the red lines brighten.

"It agrees with you," the Changer says. "Let us cross-check. Were you in the Salinas District eight to ten days ago?"

"*Non.*"

Again coolness and the flash of red.

"Did you have in your possession a rented Chevy Lumina eight to ten days ago?"

"*Non.*"

Again, the stone concurs. The Changer frowns. He looks at Lil, who is also frowning.

"I apologize, Lilith, for my suspicions."

"I accept," the immortal witch says with a graciousness that is only slightly mocking.

"Has it occurred to you that someone has tried to set us up so that I would kill you?"

Lil nods. "*Oui*, I did so wonder."

The stone on the Changer's hand flashes red and stays cool. He chuckles and drops it into his pocket once more.

"Why would anyone want to do that?" Vera says, breaking the silence she had maintained during the interrogation. "Do you have any enemies in common?"

"Not that I know," the Changer says, "but we must."

Lil takes a long drag on the cigarette that has been smoldering between her two fingers. "They must have believed that you could be aroused into an insane rage. Lucky for us both that you stopped to see Arthur."

The Changer nods. "The killer may have expected me to shift shape and follow the car that came to meet Martinez. They couldn't know that one of my pups had been missed and that I would stay to care for her."

"If you hadn't," Vera says slowly, "then you would have followed the car here, encountered Lil, had an argument at cross purposes, and then . . ."

"One of us," Lilith says, arching a stylish brow, "may have slain the other. Let us not give the Changer too much credit for his strength. In my own places, I am formidable."

Vera tenses, wondering if the Changer will take offense, but the ancient merely nods.

"Quite so," he says. "I respect your power as you do mine. We cannot predict the outcome, only that violent conflict, whether resolved quickly or not, would have been the end result."

"An extended conflict," Vera adds, "would have drawn others in: Arthur in an attempt to mediate, close friends for each of you. It could have grown ugly. I owe your daughter a new chew toy, Changer. Her instinct for self-preservation seems to have prevented at the least murder, at the most, civil war.''

"And which," Lilith says slowly, "was intended?"

The Changer shakes his head, long hair sweeping about his shoulders, fierce yellow-brown eyes lit with fire from within.

"I don't know," he says, "but I most certainly intend to find out, and no one, but no one, not Arthur nor Lovern, nor the strongest among us shall stand between me and that one's punishment when I find out."

Lilith chuckles, a throaty, catlike sound without mirth.

"Amen to that," she says, "and pity the poor bastard when you find him."

She laughs again. "I might even applaud."

¤🞊¤

In a stone *tupa* beside the sea in Finland lives a woman of cool beauty. Her long straight hair is the white-blond of winter ice and her eyes are as blue as the center of the sky. She calls herself Louhi, after the Mistress of the far Northland from Finnish legend, but she has had many names.

She lives in Finland these days, in a stone cottage by the shore, because, despite the modern age and its machines, Finland still has a tradition of superstition and witchcraft. The locals, recalling her name and its dark antecedents, court her and shun her as they might have a witch from the elder days. This pleases Louhi and so for her neighbors she binds winds and looses them, makes love charms and small curses, and otherwise is left alone.

The omens and auguries that she has been reading in a pool of water, in the dregs of a glass of wine, in the toss of knucklebones, please her less. They speak of delay and disappointment—though ultimately success is still in the stars. She lets this soothe her.

Brewing a mug of mulled wine, she recalls how Sven Trout (*that* a name woven from bitterness, for sure!) had come to her. He had changed his appearance, but she knew him still. Illusion, costuming, even shapechange could not fool her gifts for long. Nor had he insulted her by attempting any deception.

She had permitted him to flatter her, to make her gifts of jewelry and a *kantele* made in the old way, but even the richness of his gifts had not warned her what he wanted from her. The amulets and charms he had wanted her to craft—*that* she had expected. The lust with which he eyed her slender figure beneath its wool skirts and embroidered felt vest—*that* she had expected. What she had not expected was the offer to help overthrow the reign of King Arthur.

"I know that you despise him, Louhi," Sven had said coaxingly. "His policies of concealment and caution constrain your every action. A sorceress of your potency should be praised and feared from horizon to horizon, not isolated in a stone cottage in *Finland*."

Louhi had smiled at him. "*Ka!* Perhaps I like Finland."

"Perhaps you do," Sven replied agreeably.

"You may recall that I have often cultivated my solitude."

"As on the isle of Aeaea," he answered, nothing of mockery in his tone.

"But perhaps I weary of this banter. What do you offer me?"

"If I succeed, I will make you my partner in ruling our people," he had said. "Wife, consort, queen, vice president—whatever title you prefer, lady."

She had smiled slyly at him. "Yours is not the prettiest proposal I have received in a long life."

"I have little sorcery," he had answered bluntly. "Some small shapeshifting, some few tricks. Most of my gift is for guile. Were I speaking of ruling mere humans, that would be sufficient, but to contest Arthur I must have a sorcerer of Lovern's ability on my side."

Louhi had known flattery when she heard it, but she also knew truth. Lovern had his gifts, but she had her own. She had even been his student once—and had bested him, too, making him her prisoner.

That they had both enjoyed aspects of his sojourn in her keeping did not change the fact that they remained rivals in the art. To take his place ruling their immortal lot . . .

"I am interested," she had answered. "Speak on. Tell me what advantages you have."

Then Sven had told her how he had found his way to contact Lovern's most potent sorcerous tool—the duplicate head he had grown back when he was Mimir, advisor to Odin. The Head did not have Lovern's skill in spell-casting, but, implanted with the Eye of Odin, it could see possible futures and—more importantly—the road one must travel to reach them. The Head was also a repository of vast knowledge, knowledge it never forgot.

"The Head resents its creator," Sven told her. "I have promised it freedom and, if possible, a body of its own in return for its assistance in overthrowing Arthur. Your skill in shapeshifting others—even against their will—is well-known. Would you be able to give the Head a body?"

She promised to look into the matter and so, with great ceremony and greater magic, they swore a binding oath.

Immediately upon Sven's departure, she began researching how to give the Head the body it (perhaps foolishly) craved. Over time, she devised a complex enchantment that would work, but an essential ingredient was the blood of a natural shapechanger.

Her own and Sven's blood, when tried, were not potent enough. Indeed, after experimentation with donors willing, unwilling, and unknowing, she came to the conclusion that only the Changer's blood would be powerful enough.

This knowledge does not intimidate her. Indeed, sipping from her mulled wine and looking out over the wind-tossed waves, Louhi reflects that perhaps knowing that the Changer must be drawn into their conflict had been the final point that had soldered her into her peculiar alliance.

Some legends gave her father as the Sun. Others did not mention her lineage. Her current birth certificate gives a man who died in the Second World War. Her own suspicion, one she has held close and dear, is that her father is the Changer himself.

She had tried get him to acknowledge her, back when the world was much younger. He had gazed at her from eyes that, then, were emerald green and tossed back hair as golden as light.

"What purpose would an acknowledgment serve, even if your suspicions are true?" he had said. "Whether or not I am your sire, you have done well with your inherited gifts.

Life is a gift freely given. Take it and do well with it.''

He had shifted then, becoming a boar with golden bristles, and had departed. Later, she heard that he was living as an eagle in some isolated part of Asia.

She had moved to an island in the Aegean, resolving that if her father could treat her that way, then all men were pigs. For a long time after that, most of the men she met were pigs.

Or at least they became so.

¤◼¤

Seated on a bench alongside the Santa Fe River, Vera and the Changer recover from their visit with Lil Prima.

"Do you have any idea what you would like to do next?" Vera asks.

"Actually, I do," the Changer says. "I've been thinking about the person or persons who set me on Lil's trail. Perhaps they were too clever for themselves. Perhaps we can learn something from the trail they did leave."

"Trail?" Vera asks.

"Someone rented the car," the Changer says. "Maybe the agent recalls who."

"That's a long shot," Vera says doubtfully.

"Do you have any better idea?" the Changer asks.

"No."

The Lumina had been rented from an Avis counter out at the small Santa Fe Municipal Airport. The car-rental desks are to the far left, just beyond a coffee machine offering complimentary coffee for travelers on Mesa Air.

A brown-haired woman in a tan suit that seems to have been coordinated with the building, right down to the stylized cloud pin on her lapel, sits behind the Avis counter. Her name tag reads "HAZEL DUNN."

When they approach, she sets down the novel, (*Honor Among Enemies*, the Changer notes in passing, by someone named David Weber), with which she had been filling the slow time until the next flight.

"May I help you?" Her accent is Californian, her smile brightly professional.

"Yes," Vera says, efficiency incarnate. "We're trying to find out who rented a Chevy Lumina from Avis last week."

The woman frowns. "May I ask why?"

"The driver," Vera improvises facilely, "may have been a witness to a hit-and-run my brother here was in. We were hoping to track her down and see if she remembered anything."

Reassured that they were not trying cause trouble for Avis or Avis's former client, Ms. Dunn taps some instructions into her computer. Perusing the information, she smiles.

"Yes, here it is. An 'L. Prima.' "

Vera makes a note. "Did she give an address?"

Ms. Dunn nods. "It's a gallery on San Francisco Street here in town. There's a phone number, too."

When these are duly recorded, the Changer steps forward.

"Tell me, were you the one who rented the car to Miss Prima? Do you remember anything about her?" He smiles charmingly. "I'm rather worried about approaching a perfect stranger, you see."

Ms. Dunn looks thoughtful. "I was the one who rented her the car. I remember being surprised that she wanted such a big car for just a drive into town. In fact, I offered to call a taxi for her. She told me that she was planning on taking some clients on a drive and needed a bigger car—her own was something small and sporty, a vintage Jaguar, I think."

"Rich then," the Changer says, probing.

"Very," Ms. Dunn agrees. "We ask for a credit card for security. Ms. Prima wanted to pay cash in advance for a week's rental."

"A week?" The Changer's tone holds just the right amount of awe and astonishment to promote confidences.

"A week," Ms. Dunn confirms. "She paid it, too."

"So you didn't ask for a credit card?" Vera says.

"Had to," Ms. Dunn shrugs. "Company policy."

At this point, the Changer gently nudges a holder, spilling brochures all around. In the confusion, Vera tilts the computer screen toward herself and makes a few quick notes.

When the mess is picked up, the Changer and Vera make their exit, apologizing for the trouble and promising to let Ms. Dunn know how the investigation into the hit-and-run turns out.

"Did you get what you wanted?" the Changer asks when they have left the airport.

"What I wanted?" Vera asks.

"I could tell that you wanted something from the woman's computer screen," the Changer says, "but I wasn't sure what. That's why I pushed over the brochures."

"Oh," Vera says. "Yes, I did. I wanted 'L. Prima's' credit-card number."

"Will that help us?"

Vera pauses, remembering that the Changer has been out of human society long enough that he may have missed the gradual dominance of the credit card over cash and checks.

"It will indeed," she says. "The impostor may have been lucky enough to disguise herself as Lil, may have done her research into phone numbers and addresses, but it would have been a lot harder for her to have Lil's credit card."

The Changer nods. "I was wondering about the car Miss Dunn mentioned, the Jaguar. I wonder if Lil actually has a car like that or if it might be a slip on our quarry's part."

"Interesting," Vera says. "We can call and ask her."

"Can't we just drive back and ask now?" the Changer says. "I don't want to wait until we're near a phone and this is a bit sensitive to discuss over a pay phone."

Vera grins at him. She's having a surprising amount of fun indoctrinating the ancient into the latter twentieth century.

"There's a phone in the car," she says. "I guess you didn't notice. We can call from there."

The Changer shakes his head at this and shakes it once more as he sees the slim, relatively inconspicuous receiver Vera removes from its holder on the dashboard. His gaze on the puppy, who is enthusiastically digging beneath an ornamental desert willow, he listens as Vera punches buttons and then to the faint series of beeps and rings that follow.

"May I speak with Lil Prima?" Vera says. She pauses, evidently while Lilith is brought to the phone. "Lil, this is Vera. We've done some further checking and have a couple of questions for you."

A pause. The Changer can just hear Lil's confident, "Shoot."

"Do you have a vintage Jaguar?"

"The car? No. I drive a Porsche. Tommy has a van and a motorcycle."

"Okay. How about a Bank America Visa, Platinum." She rattles off a string of numbers.

"That'll take me a minute to check." Lil gives a sardonic chuckle. "I have lots of plastic."

"Check away," Vera says.

Lil comes back after a moment. "No, I don't. My Visa's from Bank of New Mexico. My MasterCard's Bank of America. Have you got a lead on the bitch who tried to set the Changer on me?"

"We might," Vera says, choosing not to correct Lil's terminology. "I'll let you know when I know more."

"Good. If someone wants my round little ass, I want to know who it is."

"I understand."

A few more caustic pleasantries and the call ends. The Changer whistles for his daughter and turns to Vera.

"So the trip wasn't a complete waste of time, even if Lil wasn't my target. Ah, well. I don't know why I ever thought that the job would be that easy. Things rarely are."

The coyote puppy lopes up and puts her dirty paws against her father's pant leg. Her protest at being returned to the car is ignored, and she rolls into a ball to sulk. Before they are out of the parking lot, she is asleep.

"We'll head back to Arthur's," Vera says, "and see what we can do about chasing down this credit-card number. The Jaguar is a more distant lead. We don't have our people register their cars with us. Still, if the credit card doesn't work out . . ."

"It's something," the Changer sighs. "And it might have been nothing substantial, just a small deception, like our story about the brother and the hit-and-run accident."

"I know," Vera says. "I hate admitting that we may need to give up."

The Changer's expression shifts to something dark and angry. "I won't give up. In any case, I don't think that whoever did this is going to stop with one failure. We'll hear from them again. We just need to be alert for the marks of their work."

"And then . . ." Vera begins.

"And then," the Changer interrupts, "I go after them. What else is immortality good for if it isn't for doing a job right?"

"First step," Vera says, seeking to chase the anger from his yellow-brown eyes, "is getting back to Arthur's and checking this number."

"With a stop for puppy chow along the way," the Changer adds. "We can't forget the really important things."

The sleepy wheeze of the puppy agrees with him.

Late that evening, Arthur comes out into the Changer's courtyard, where most of the household is gathered eating a snack of *sopaipillas* and honey left over from dinner. The Changer's daughter alternates between munching on bites of her new puppy food and begging for *sopas*, having already begun to suspect that what is good for her might not be as much fun as what the rest are eating.

"I have a mixed report on the credit card," the King says, snagging the last of the *sopas* from the basket and liberally covering it with honey.

"What is it?" the Changer asks, politely waiting until Arthur has taken a seat.

"It was issued to a Colorado manufacturing company. It hasn't been registered as stolen." Arthur's small smile reflects his pleasure at his hacking. "However, that doesn't mean that it hasn't been. The account is one of those they have for members of their sales force. They issue the cards at need, rather than one per member . . ."

"Cheapskates," Eddie mutters.

"Maybe," Arthur says, "or maybe they just don't want to keep track of a bunch of separate accounts. In any case, since the card isn't registered to a specific staff member, I need to see if I can find out who had it last."

"Find out everyone who could have had it," the Changer suggests. "Our quarry might be another member of the staff who snagged the card for an overnight."

"I bet it is a forgery," Eddie says glumly.

Arthur nods, a trace impatiently. For all his "Round Table" philosophy, a part of him still rebels at suggestions that aren't worded with proper deference. The Changer may see some of his pique or perhaps he merely wishes to keep the King cooperative.

"Thank you, Arthur, for once again working late while the rest of us loll about."

Arthur permits himself to be mollified. "Where's Lovern?"

"He's out at the Isleta Casino playing poker," Eddie says. "Said something about looking for portents in the cards."

"Can he do that?" Vera asks, stifling a yawn behind a honey-sticky hand.

"Who knows?" Eddie answers. "Maybe he can. Maybe he just wanted a night out."

"He may want a night out," Vera rejoins, "but he didn't have the day we did. I'm going to get some sleep."

"Me too," Arthur says. "Colorado's on the same time we are—I can get answers in the morning."

"Changer?" Eddie says, always courteous.

"I know how to sleep when I can," the Changer says. "Don't stay awake to amuse me."

The others depart then, sleepily. Only the puppy, snuffling after pastry crumbs, has any energy. Her father begins unbuttoning his shirt, steps out of his jeans. Standing nude in the cool, spring moonlight, he feels an ache of loneliness for his mate. Five years is not forgotten in a few days, not even by one such as he.

He shifts then, becoming coyote to the delight of his daughter. They romp for a while, then, tail to nose, flank to flank, they fall asleep beneath the shadows of the lilac bush.

Treason doth never prosper, what's the reason?
For if it prosper, none dare call it Treason.

—SIR JOHN HARRINGTON

THIS TIME IT IS A THREE-WAY CALL: SVEN, THE HEAD, AND Louhi.

"Hello, all!" Sven says cheerily. "Greetings from the land of sand and mountains."

"Hello, Sven, Head," Louhi says, and her voice is as crisp and as breathtakingly beautiful as a flower encased in ice.

"Hail, fire-born, wisewoman. What tidings bear you to your bound brother?"

Sven glances at his notes. "The Changer has come to Arthur's estate. He brought a coyote pup with him—probably my assassins missed one of the litter."

"That," comes Louhi's voice, "may be all to our good." The tinkle of her laughter is not kind.

Sven nods. "Yes, I had thought of various ways we might use the little bitch. Lovern has been summoned to Arthur's side. But, knowing you two, you've learned *that* already. Less good news is that apparently Arthur suggested to the Changer that Lil deserved more than a quick slash across the throat. He braced her, but our hoped-for battle didn't happen."

"They both remain unharmed?" Louhi asks, piqued.

"That's what I said," Sven says testily.

"Pity. We need his blood. You have promised it to us. If you fail to obtain it . . ."

"Oaths bound with bands of bright blood," the Head reminds, "when broken are broken with the same."

"Don't threaten me!" Sven says indignantly. "I've been busting my balls . . ."

"To minimal effect," Louhi says.

"Shit on that! I've brought the Changer from the wilds to where we can reach him. I'll force Lovern to bring the Head to Albuquerque. Give me time!"

"From your website," Louhi says, "I see that you are setting back our timetable several months."

"It seems like the best option," Sven says sulkily. "We need the theriomorphs to assure a vote of no confidence. Our only other choice is a direct coup. That didn't do much good last time."

"Ragnarokk was long ago," Louhi says.

"Ragnarokk ended up bringing Arthur to prominence," Sven snaps, "when too many of those senior to him died and the rest lost their taste for politics. I myself had to hide for centuries until the old grudges had softened a bit."

"Scion severed from sire," the Head adds, "was imprisoned deep within the whale's road. Wisdom was won at wondrous price."

Louhi isn't particularly impressed by their reminders, but then she hadn't been born when that great battle tore their people apart. "The plan was to have the vote of no confidence occur at the Lustrum Review this June when neutral parties would be present to hear us plead the theriomorphs' cause and our solution. Now we will lose that opportunity."

"Not if you still attend the Review," Sven says quickly. "Your interest in shapeshifting makes you a logical person to present the theriomorphs' case. The monsters will still be able to lobby over the website. We may do even better when we press the vote if the discontent has some time to brew."

"I believe I understand your convoluted logic," Louhi admits. "If a protest against current policy is raised but Arthur sticks to his guns and *then* we manipulate circumstances for the vote of no confidence . . . Yes, it could work nicely. Many of the neutrals will come over to our side if they perceive a real abuse."

"Not everyone," Sven reminds them, "is happy with Arthur's restrictions. I've just recruited some *tengu*. They're shapeshifters and so can pass as human, but Arthur's non-interference policy restricts them to only limited meddling."

"And *tengu* adore meddling," Louhi says dryly. "You'd better watch that they don't meddle with *you*!"

"I will and I have," Sven says confidently.

"Then for now we bide," Louhi says. "I will visit Albuquerque for the Lustrum Review. If you get the Head brought there before then, we may be able to free him from his confinement. Then he can assist with the rest."

"Merlin's magic minus me," the Head states confidently, "is minimal."

Sven winces. As they say their farewells, he breathes a silent wish that when the Head is no longer captive to Lovern's will he will give up his annoying fondness for alliteration. He suspects it's an empty hope.

But then, everyone is entitled to a dream.

✿✿✿

Spring in New Mexico is a season of winds: winds that sweep across the sandy grasslands around Albuquerque creating clouds of tan grit, knocking down fences and street signs, and otherwise making venturing out-of-doors unwise.

Unwise, that is, for those of humankind. Ravens enjoy the wild air currents, soaring on them with impudence, spotting with glittering brown eyes the trash bag ripped open or the cellophane bag torn from a hand, the tortilla chips within scattered.

It is with these busy scavengers the Changer flies one afternoon when Arthur's hacienda becomes too full of people for his feral soul. His daughter, replete with puppy chow and scrambled eggs, sleeps under the lilac bush. She is noticeably fatter than she had been when they arrived: a round, pudgy puppy, no longer a runt, but still not apparently a coyote.

The Changer is not thinking, just flying, enjoying the aerial game of snatching windblown tortilla chips from the dirt of the vacant lot. There are another half dozen ravens with him, unmated juveniles, all learning to survive before they complicate their lives with responsibility for territory, eggs, and mates.

One young male is a particular clown, a perfect, elegant acrobat, capable of soaring dives and wide-winged recoveries that the Changer would be proud to have mastered. It is with this one that the Changer falls into competition.

Resisting the urge to reshape his wings for slightly better maneuverability, the Changer targets a large triangular tortilla chip scudding like a sail without a ship beneath the wind's encouragement. His playmate targets this one as well, performing a daring barrel roll that permits him to come in just under the Changer's breast feathers and seize the prize.

The youngling rides the wind higher, his plumage lit with purples and blues by the brilliant sun, his triumphant croak muffled by the tortilla chip grasped in his beak.

Then his breast explodes in a burst of scarlet, blood splattering wide enough to coat the Changer's right wing, momentarily crippling his own power of flight.

The shapeshifter loses altitude, thick, clawed legs extended to take the shock of a forced landing. The young raven's corpse hits the ground next to him, a few crumbs of tortilla chip still flecking his gaping beak. Eyes that had been brilliant moments before are dulling now, but the Changer has no time to waste in sorrow. He must get to safety.

There is not much cover in the open lot over which the ravens had sported—a few scraggly cottonwoods and elms, a low clump of squat junipers and four-wing saltbush, tufts of blue grama and Indian rice grass. The terrain itself is flat, with only the tiniest dunes sculpted by the winds.

Those winds give the Changer some courage. What felled the young raven was clearly a rifle, probably nothing more than a twenty-two. Even an excellent shot would have difficulty bagging a raven taking wing when the winds are strongest.

Long experience has taught him caution about changing shape in the presence of an unknown, a caution that modern technology has only reinforced. He believes he can achieve safety while remaining a raven and that airborne he has the greatest chance of spotting his foe.

Shapeshifting slightly, just a ripple through the feathers of his right wing, removes enough of the young raven's blood that he can fly with minimal difficulty. Waiting for a violent blast of wind, the Changer again takes flight.

Dark wings spread, he lets the gusting air carry him aloft, beating those wings hard to gain the most favorable currents. His new vantage at first grants him little more than a view of the remaining ravens fleeing from a playground become killing field. Later they may return to dine on their fellow's corpse. Then again, they may not. An urban raven needs to be more cautious than the norm.

Soaring higher, subconsciously braced for another shot, the Changer scans the ground for sign of his enemy. A glint shows him the twenty-two, leaned against the trunk of one of the elms. He is so busy searching for something the size of a human that he nearly misses what comes screeching toward him from above.

It is a golden eagle, a type of bird found in New Mexico, although uncommon near cities. The Changer has no doubt that it is his enemy, eschewing the rifle for more personal means.

The eagle is larger than the raven, equipped with a wicked hooked beak and curving talons that show the raven's claws as small and pitiful by comparison. It is also the stronger flyer, but the raven is the more flexible.

Dodging the eagle's first dive so closely that he loses a few feathers, the Changer heads for the cover of the scraggly elms. The eagle pulls up short, soars to gain altitude once more. Between green gaps in the wind-tossed leaves, the Changer can see it circling in a lazy, energy-conserving fashion that conspires with the winds.

Momentarily, the Changer toys with the idea of shifting human and turning the rifle's power on its owner. He dismisses the idea as foolish. Not only isn't he sufficiently skilled, but the sight of a naked human standing in a vacant lot taking potshots at an eagle is certain to attract attention.

Although he is safe for now, the Changer is not complacent enough to believe that he will remain so. His opponent has already shown a willingness to shapeshift without regard for potential witnesses. Without knowing who he faces, the Changer cannot guess what shapes his opponent possesses.

The eagle dives once more, pulling up short of the treetops, his screeching taunting, calling a coward the great black bird who perches just out of reach. A natural raven would take some comfort in knowing that for the moment it is safe, but the Changer hears the mockery in the eagle's cries and the feathers at his neck fan out in anger.

He strides up and down the length of the branch, prudence and fury warring within him.

There . . . There . . . Just a few wing strokes away is the one who slew his family, who has dared assault him. To let this opportunity to know his enemy pass would be madness indeed and an invitation to assault him further.

Walking to the end of a branch, the Changer takes wing when the eagle's circuit offers him the best clearance. Furiously striving for altitude, he rises above the eagle.

The mind within the golden eagle's body is not the small, instinct-driven mind of the hunting bird, but the Changer well knows how the instincts of the body can shape the thoughts of the canniest mind. An eagle knows itself to be without peer in the skies, and so the rising of a solitary, black-winged scavenger bird does not trigger the panic that it should.

Almost lazily, the eagle alters its course, seeking the wind that will carry it above the arrogant raven. The Changer, however, is neither merely a raven nor prone to overlooking the effects of body on mind. He channels the raven's instinctive territoriality, the same instinct that bands ravens together to harry owls and hawks.

True, he does not have a flock or a mate to assist him, but the Changer thrusts that doubt from him. His harsh, deep-throated ''cr-r-ruk'' summoning assistance from his kind, the raven/Changer comes in behind the eagle.

His beak may not be curved and scimitar sharp, his feet may be clawed, not taloned, but with a four-foot wingspan and startling aerial dexterity, a raven can effectively harass an eagle. Moreover, his calls have summoned the ravens who fled the gun. They return to challenge this, to them, unconnected threat.

For the first time, the golden eagle realizes its danger. Its attempts to rise above the raven, where it can bring its natural weapons into play, end as it flees. Heading toward an artificial canyon formed by a cluster of apartment buildings, the eagle dives.

It vanishes into an alleyway. By the time the Changer has

soared over the same space, it is gone. He longs to dive after, but in those narrow spaces the raven's greatest advantage would be lost. Nor does he dare to shapeshift, not when his enemy has chosen the turf.

Quorking angrily, he rises to where he can survey the complex. His fellow ravens are scattering now, returning to their scavenging, pleased at having driven the eagle away.

The Changer watches for a long while, but either his enemy has patience as great as his own or he has departed in some subtle shape that his aerial observer cannot recognize. Nor does anyone return for the twenty-two.

When dusk falls, the Changer takes the risk and lands near the weapon. He approaches it cautiously, hopping and flapping his wings as a raven does when testing if something is truly dead or perhaps only shamming.

The rifle, unsurprisingly, does not move. He considers. The weapon might provide a clue, most probably would not. Leaving it here is the best course of action. Any form he could take to carry it would attract attention.

He settles for knocking the rifle over and scratching dirt and elm leaves to cover it. Then he takes wing. Ravens do not commonly fly at night, but he doubts that anyone will notice the anomaly—any, that is, but his mysterious enemy.

Given how he feels, he would welcome another confrontation.

He is anxiously awaited at Arthur's hacienda. When he emerges from his room, human-form once more, his daughter flings herself into his arms. The others are scarcely more decorous. Eddie, Lovern, Vera, and Arthur all wait in the courtyard, openly relieved to see him present and intact.

"Changer!" Arthur beams. "We had all but given up on you!"

"So I gather," the Changer replies, looking around the arc of smiling faces. "How did you know to worry?"

"We didn't . . . don't, not precisely, or we would have sent help," Arthur says confusingly. "Dinner is long past, but we saved something for you if you wish."

"I do, but only with an explanation as the sauce."

"It will," Arthur promises. "Bring the kid if you want; we can talk in the kitchen."

Gathering up the puppy, slightly bemused at her adoption by this august group, the Changer allows himself to be swept off into the kitchen. The puppy is set on the terrazzo tile floor and given a beef bone to worry. The others take seats around an oval table surfaced with hand-painted tiles depicting a herd of horses galloping around the table's circumference.

Eddie sets out a cold chicken and trimmings which the Changer begins to demolish.

"You must have had quite a time," Arthur comments.

"I did."

"Could you tell us about your day before Lovern tells you about his?" Arthur asks. "I'm very interested in those events in light of today's other occurrences."

"Sure."

Vera listens, frowning, making occasional entries into a notebook computer. Lovern sits impassive, nodding from time to time as if he finds some deeper meaning in the incidents.

Only the puppy does not listen, content to chew on her bone, polishing the tile floor with its greasy knob, and growling softly as she strives to crack the end.

"So the rifle may still be there," Vera comments as the Changer finishes his story.

"That's right," the Changer says. "I couldn't very well carry it in any but human form and I lacked both clothing and a desire to make myself vulnerable."

"We should try to retrieve it tonight," Vera says. "I already know Lovern's part of the story. I'll go."

"Be careful," Lovern cautions. "Our enemy may very well expect some such action."

"I will," Vera says, "but I'd welcome a chance at the bastards."

"Let's hope you don't get one," Lovern says dryly. "They seem formidable."

"Perhaps too formidable for Vera to deal with alone," Eddie says. "No insult intended, but whoever this is has given both the Changer and Lovern a run for their lives."

Vera nods slowly. She hasn't acquired her reputation for wisdom for nothing. "You're right. Should I wait until morning, or is someone free to come with me?"

"If Arthur can spare me," Eddie says, "I'll go."

Arthur makes a gesture of agreement as old as his first kingdom. "Go, then, both of you, but be careful."

"We will."

While they talk, the Changer looks around the kitchen, admiring the indirect lighting, the thick, rough-hewn beams from which polished iron and copper cook pots hang. Painted tiles border the wall above the countertops: bright red chilies whose shape suggests a red dragon, round yellow onions, fat turnips set on their points like shields. Even here, Arthur's decorating reflects the dream of Camelot.

When the Changer retakes his seat, his daughter drags her bone across the floor and comes to sit on his bare feet. Her subvocal growls as she chews are channeled through his flesh to mingle with his blood.

"So, I gather that Lovern also had an adventure this afternoon," he says. "Tell me about it."

Lovern's thin, nervous fingers shred a paper napkin. When he speaks, his words are breathy and hesitant.

"I went out to Old Town this afternoon, shopping for fetish carvings and other oddities. The trip was made on impulse. I told no one but Vera—Arthur and Eddie were busy with some problem that had cropped up. So I just went out, I didn't even take a car. I felt like walking, and I knew that if I got tired, I could call for a ride back."

"I don't recall where Old Town is from here," the Changer admits. "Is it a long walk?"

"Long enough. As I said, I felt like walking."

The Changer nods. He knows the impulse, but he suspects that for Lovern, the desire to travel under his own power is differently motivated. In ancient days, Merlin's magic had been inhibited by iron. Although cars contain less metal than once they did, traveling within one might make Lovern ill.

"So you walked to Old Town . . . and?"

"And I walked around, bought some fetish carvings, talked to a silversmith about a commission, had lunch, visited the Albuquerque Museum, did some other shopping. And all the time I was walking, I kept a touch of awareness watching my back."

"And?"

"Nothing. Peaceful. Sunshine and nothing more."

Lovern finally notices the mutilation he is performing on the napkin and stops.

"Finally, I took my packages and headed back here. The wind was blowing quite a bit, though, and I finally decided to duck into a shop, borrow the phone, and call for a lift.

"I called and got Vera. I wasn't far from a small park, so we agreed that she would pick me up there."

"Poor Vera," Arthur interjects, "is going to start insisting on being paid by the mile."

"So, after getting a cup of hot tea, I went into the park," Lovern continues, "and took a seat at a picnic table. One of my purchases had been a book of local Pueblo Indian legends, so I started reading.

"I wasn't exactly comfortable, but the legends were interesting, and my tea was warm. Still, I don't know how I could have been so completely distracted. I didn't sense the rattlesnake until it was coiling to strike."

The Changer raises an eyebrow. "A rattlesnake in a public park? Unlikely."

"Exactly, unlikely, not impossible—rather like a golden eagle attacking a raven over a vacant lot."

"From the fact that you're still here, I assume that you got out of the way before the snake could strike?"

Lovern flushes dark red. "Actually, I didn't. I was wearing hiking boots under my trousers. The rattlesnake's strike came in low—I think it was compensating for the picnic table—and it caught me in the ankle. Its fangs couldn't penetrate both my pants and the padded boot."

"Lucky for you," the Changer says. "Very."

"I thought so," Lovern answers, "although at the time, I was more interested in killing the damn reptile. I had a walking stick with me . . ."

He pauses and the Changer mentally translates that to "wizard's staff."

"The end was shod in silver and I brought it down on the snake's back while it was trying to dislodge its fangs from my boot. I'm no Hercules, but I'm strong enough that I should have broken its back. Instead, I only succeeded in making it thrash harder. But it wasn't until it began to sink into the ground that I realized that I was dealing with a magical being."

"A shapeshifter?" the Changer asks.

"The thought did cross my mind," Lovern answers. "In fact, I briefly entertained the idea that it might have been you."

The Changer raises his eyebrows, but doesn't choose to comment further. He and Lovern have been allies but never really friends. The fault is his own—he has never forgotten the black sorcery of which Lovern is capable.

"I dismissed the idea almost immediately," Lovern continues hastily. "As I said, it just came in a flash. At the time I was more interested in keeping the damn thing from getting away.

"No one else was in the park—I suspect the increasingly windy weather was keeping everyone indoors—so I sent a small charge down my staff. It went right into the rattler. There was a flash of white light that would have seared my eyes if I hadn't been wearing sunglasses. Even so, I was blinking away spots."

Lovern grins ruefully. "I don't mind telling you that I was terrified that some other attack would come while I was blinded. When my vision returned, this remained under my staff heel."

Taking a folded bandanna from his shirt pocket, Lovern carefully unwraps what appear to be a few pebble-sized pieces of broken greyish white stone. As he nudges them into rough order, the Changer realizes that they are the remnants of a stone carving of a rattlesnake on its belly.

It is crudely done, the coils compacted together, the scales and the bands of the rattles suggested rather than carefully detailed. The head remains intact: triangular, slit eyes set high on the sides, fangs just visible.

"A fetish carving," the Changer says. "One that suggests the old symbolism—see how the shape of the coils recall a lightning bolt? I suspect that this rattler might have delivered more than poison."

"My thought exactly," Lovern agrees. "And that explains why it released so much energy when I attacked it. My charge overloaded what it could contain."

Replete with chicken and out of the wind, the Changer is of a mood to worry this problem. "So our enemy is a sorcerer and a shapeshifter."

"Perhaps," Arthur says cautiously. "Our enemies could be many—a sorcerer, a shapeshifter, a warrior."

"Or," Lovern says, "a bit of each. We could face a cabal. It wouldn't be a large group. We surely would have heard rumors if a large group gathered against the King."

"The King?" the Changer says. "Only you and I have been attacked."

"Perhaps," Lovern says urbanely. "But we could consider the attack on your family an attack on Lil if, as we have hypothesized, you were meant to assault her."

Arthur interjects, "Changer, could the eagle that attacked you have been a sorcerous construct?"

The Changer muses. "Perhaps. I did not consider it at the time, perhaps because of my own tendency to shift shape to deal with difficulties."

Arthur makes a note. "How about an illusion?"

The Changer bristles. "I can tell the difference between an illusion and a real eagle."

Arthur holds up a hand, neither apologizing nor relenting. "We are collecting information, Changer. Given the wind and the gathering darkness, I felt it was a possibility."

"He asked me the same thing," Lovern says, "but I had the broken fetish to show him."

The Changer nods. "I don't think that it was an illusion, but you're right. The circumstances were not ideal. I was worried about another shot from the rifle—that was real enough. It felled the bird I was flying with."

"That bird saved your life," Lovern says. "You mentioned that it was more graceful than you."

"True."

"My guess is that your attacker made the mistake of thinking that it *was* you. You were close enough that your aura would have overlapped the natural bird."

The Changer nods. "I had considered that."

"I'll hazard a guess that whoever attacked you had the bullet enchanted for accuracy—that way he didn't need to worry about the wind."

"Can that be done?" Arthur asks.

"It can, but it's costly, like most amulet magic—doubly so if the material was iron. If it was silver, though . . ."

Arthur walks over to a telephone. "Let me see if I can

reach Eddie and Vera. If they haven't left the spot yet, maybe they can pick up the bird's body.''

While Arthur makes the call, Lovern continues to muse aloud.

''Whoever our enemies are, they have certainly expanded their options by using amulets. That may be their undoing as well.''

''I'm more interested in knowing how they found both you and me,'' the Changer says. ''Are they watching this place?''

''Probably,'' Lovern says. ''They can't see inside—I've checked my wards—but we cannot counter what they do on the outside. I could scout for magic, but there are plenty of technological devices that would do the job just as well.''

''Great.''

Arthur comes and takes his seat. ''I caught them just before they left. They took their time approaching the rifle in case it was a trap. They'll do the same with the dead bird; then they'll come back. So far, they haven't had any trouble.''

''Good.'' The Changer yawns. ''I hate to admit it, but the food and warmth has made me sleepy. I won't be much help checking out the rifle. I should get some rest so that someone is fresh in the morning.''

Arthur nods. ''Not a bad idea. If anything crucial is learned, we'll let you know.''

The Changer rises, bends, picks up his daughter by the scruff of her neck and her bone with his other hand.

''I'm sleeping outside, as usual. Coyotes hear all sorts of things that humans don't. Lovern has warded this place, but whoever we face got that rattlesnake through his personal wards.''

''Good point,'' Arthur says.

''Good night.''

''Night.''

The Changer walks outside, his daughter stirring sleepily in his grip. He tucks her into her burrow under the lilac bush, places the bone beside her, and strips to the skin. When he shifts into coyote form, the wind seems less a harsh taskmaster, more a vibrant messenger carrying news of the night's doings.

The stars above are bright; Orion and other old friends

visible despite the city's ambient glow and the light of the crescent moon. Standing on the teak table, the Changer studies them, wonders if someone studies him in return.

Tilting back his head, he howls once defiantly, then again, mournfully, missing the answering chorus of his mate, his sons and daughters. The little one wakes, barks a sleepy echo.

Half-asleep, he hears the car returning. He wonders what their enemies think of these efforts to discover who they are. In his mind's ear he hears secret laughter.

¤◙¤

Back in his motel room, Sven Trout studies his reflection in the mirror and contemplates the prospect of reporting failure. When he is completely honest with himself (which is as rarely as he is with anyone else—being a firm believer in consistency in some things) he admits that he is rather intimidated by his peculiar allies. Louhi is too powerful for anyone to take lightly. Only the Head's absolute lack of mobility has assured Sven of maintaining the upper hand in their encounters (when he considers it, his ally lacks hands as well).

Sooner than he would like, if they achieve their goal, the Head will no longer be handicapped in any fashion. Will he still need Sven then? Sven hopes that, like his creator, the Head will prefer to rule from behind the scenes. If not, they could run into some rather serious conflicts of interest down the road.

Sven shrugs away his worries. The way things are going now, he isn't going to be able to get the Changer's blood, and if he fails, then the Head will lack what he needs to metamorphose . . .

Picking up the phone, he punches in the combination for the impossible connection and listens to the chime of silver and crystal. At the same time, he places a call to Louhi, but she doesn't answer . . . bitch!

"Felicitations, fire-born!"

"Do you sit up nights thinking up those?"

"In neither night nor night's nether-reaches is this one permitted sleep's surcease."

"Well, I guess you have to do something with all that

spare time." Sven clears his throat, suddenly a bit nervous. "I've called to let you know that both Merlin and Proteus escaped the traps I set for them today."

"Squared bones bouncing upon velvet, come up sixes oft as sevens."

"Yeah. You makes your throws, you takes your chances," Sven agrees. "It's nice that you see it that way. Still, I think that our larger plan is developing nicely."

"Coyote father forced from fastness, kings and courtiers cast into confusion. Soon the master of magicks must summon his scion to his side."

"Pity he won't graft it back into place," Sven mutters, "but that's too much to hope for. How long do you figure it will be?"

"Born of one's blood, second's sight, struck off, stored in a cistern, much I know, much I can only guess."

"Can't you prompt Lovern to get you out of there?"

"Breath I do not draw, thus breathless I await. Sorcerer's son, sorcery's scald, Bifrost stands in gold."

"I'm afraid I don't have any idea what you meant by that."

A deep sigh, perhaps with a hint of burbling about the edges. "Yes."

"Yes?"

"Yes. As son of sorcery, of Merlin's magic, his will twist I as smiths twist wrought iron."

Sven chuckles gleefully. "It really helps when you use the first person and cut out the kennings."

"Tough."

"I guess it was too much to hope for." Sven leans back against his pillow. "What shall we do next?"

"Arthur's aides are assured in his aura. Unsettle their sureness in the potency of their protector."

Sven says, "I can do that. Eddie and Vera went out tonight, pretty confident that they could handle whatever we might try. I think you're right. They need to learn some respect."

"Forget not Dionysus, Orpheus, insane singer whose persuasive powers we must employ."

"I haven't. I've been going to his shows, dodging the bitch, and slipping him some 'gifts.' Rehabilitated or not, he has a hankering for hootch and hash." Sven pauses. "Damn! Now you've got me doing it!"

"Fates far more fearsome follow failure."

"I know. I'm being careful and running after my lackeys, too. You've got it easy just sitting there, let me tell you!"

"You have done so." There is a plosive sound, like bubbles blown in milk, that might be laughter.

"I'll going to ring off now, get some sleep. Let me know if you hear from Lovern and what he tells you."

"As always."

"Bye, then."

Sven hangs up the telephone and stretches. He tries to warm some leftover pizza and singes it just a bit. That's always been his problem—going just a bit overboard. This time, though, this time, with Lovern's sorcerous creation to aid and advise him, with Louhi to provide him with the magical tools he needs, this time he'll get it right. It will be good to be the king.

7

A mouth that praises and a hand that kills.

—ARAB PROVERB

TO HER CONSTERNATION, VERA FINDS HERSELF COMPELLED by the Changer. The attraction is not sexual—at least she does not think so—but she finds herself watching him, seeking out his company, looking for excuses to talk with him. What she and Eddie retrieve from the vacant lot gives her such an excuse.

She finds him, as is usual, in the courtyard of Arthur's hacienda. Also, as is usual at these times, he is in the form of a coyote. He has explained that he does not wish his daughter to become too comfortable with humans, or to forget that she is a coyote, not a dog.

"Changer?" Vera says, standing awkwardly in one of the entries into the courtyard. "I was wondering if we might chat."

The dog coyote wags his brush and trots into the room off the courtyard that the Changer uses as a closet. A few minutes later, the lean, dark-haired man emerges from the doorway. His eyes are no longer yellow-brown, but pure coyote yellow—a small enough change but one that emphasizes that he is not human. In his hands he carries a bottle of apple juice and bowl. A bag of puppy chow is tucked under his arm.

"Good timing," he says, by way of greeting. "About time to feed the little one."

"She's growing fast," Vera comments, watching the puppy bury her face in the food. "And prettier. She's looking more and more like a coyote every day."

"I think she's going to look a lot like her mother," the Changer agrees, "and I always thought she was the prettiest little bitch I'd ever seen. Clever, too. A good hunter and a better mother. Our children went out into life well prepared."

"You miss her," Vera says softly.

"Five years is five years, no matter how long-lived the one living them," the Changer says. "I've never been among those who discovered that great age meant that the years raced by."

"Maybe that's because you continue to live life at its simplest level," Vera suggests. "I've noticed that when life gets complicated the days seem to be spent before they are even lived. Plans, commitments, schedules—everything gets in the way of the day as it really is."

The Changer twists the cap off of his bottle of apple juice and takes a swallow. "I hadn't considered it precisely in that way, but I suspect you have something there. I must admit, a coyote or a raven or a dolphin doesn't worry much beyond meals, mates, and simple commitments."

"You've been a dolphin?" Vera asks, enthralled.

"I have. It was interesting. The pod is a family structure, and dolphins take joy in the weirdest things. Dionysus and I swam with the same pod once. He said that dolphins and whales had a mastery of song that he longed to know."

"And did he know it?"

"I'm not certain. He's a strange one. When he's happy, he's the most charming person I've ever met—the only male ever to tempt me. When he's depressed, he spares no one, least of all himself. I suspect that only Lilith could stand him long."

"I've never been very comfortable with Lil," Vera admits. "I know I should invite them over since we're in neighboring cities, but she makes me edgy."

"Lil and I have never been great friends," the Changer says. "She thrives on crisis and destruction. I'm a peaceful soul."

Something glints in his yellow eyes at these last words. Vera knows that he is thinking of their unknown enemies, of the vengeance he longs for, of the duty he must perform before he can again escape into the wild shapes he loves.

For a brief, heart-wringing moment, Vera wishes that the conflict would stretch out over years, over centuries so that this strange ancient would not vanish once more. She turns her gaze away, fearing that he will read her feelings in her eyes.

"Lovern has just completed analysis on the bullet taken from the young raven," she manages to say casually. "I thought you would like to know what we found out."

"I would."

"It was indeed ensorcelled: one spell for accuracy and another for force. Lovern says that spells of that sort have been invented and reinvented, shared and traded so many times that he may never pinpoint these precise ones."

"And then," the Changer says dryly, "they may not tell us anything more than that our enemy has learned a particular spell—or has an ally who has."

"Yes. The gun itself was unregistered, but it had a pawn-shop's mark. Eddie is going to try to learn if the owner remembers anything about the person who bought it."

The Changer frowns. "And that probably won't help either. Even a nonmagical disguise would be a simple enough precaution to take. Still, I don't suppose that we can leave any possible lead uninspected."

"No," Vera agrees. "After all, the assassin had no idea that he would be forced to leave the weapon behind. He might have been careless."

"Here's hoping," the Changer says, draining the last of his apple juice. "I'm getting very frustrated with waiting."

"We all are," Vera says softly. "I strongly dislike being the mouse in this game."

"It is easier to be the cat," the Changer agrees, "or the coyote. I'm going to take the little one for a run before it gets dark. After yesterday, I'm not going to make attacking me easy. Would you like to come along?"

Although uncertain as to whether he has asked her in order to have backup or because he wants her company, Vera feels her heart leap. She chides herself for foolishness.

"Let me see if Arthur needs me. Then, I think it would be nice to get out." She grins, pleased at her own composure.

They drive to a large, public park across the street from an elementary school. Although the students will not be dismissed for another quarter hour or so, a few cars are already idling by the curb. The area should be busy enough for at least the next hour, so that any enemy strike would need to be subtle indeed.

The Changer has kept his daughter on her red-nylon leash. Now, kneeling in front of her, he looks her squarely in the eyes.

"Come when I call you," he says sternly, then unclips the leash.

The puppy bounds off, rolling over her own front end in her haste, pausing to shake, then to bound off again, only to be distracted by a beetle.

"Did you ensorcel her just now?" Vera asks casually.

"When I looked her in the eyes?" The Changer chuckles. "No. I just put the fear of her father in her. She forgets from time to time that we are one and the same. The eyes remind her."

Even as he speaks, the Changer's gaze travels restlessly, marking possible threats.

"They do?"

"I have no sorcery," the Changer continues, "except for my changing of shapes. I must admit, that gives me quite a lot of power, as I can travel within all the elements but one and adapt to almost any circumstances. However, like our enemy, I need amulets to work spells."

"You're telling me quite a lot about yourself," Vera says, not knowing whether to be pleased or alarmed.

"You seemed interested," the Changer says, "and it's not anything that you couldn't deduce if you put your mind to it. I've noticed how fond you are of puzzles."

"Still," Vera cautions, "be careful of what you admit to whom. I could be one of your enemies."

"If you were," the Changer says, "I would disable you. Your knowing what I can and cannot do would not stop me."

Vera feels a thrill of danger and that damned attraction again. The Changer, his gaze shifting between the pup (now rooting under an ornamental boulder) and their surroundings, does not appear to notice.

"We're one large family," he says. "As such, we know rather too much about each other—especially those of us who have been around for a few millennia. Weaknesses and strengths alike—which can be one and the same. Take Eddie, for example . . ."

"Eddie?"

"That's right: Enkidu, Bedivere, Heimdall. Always a faithful follower—always faithful to one man and that man is Arthur. The bond isn't sexual, at least as far as I can tell. Simply, as the earliest legends suggest, something in Eddie was created for Arthur. He is happiest at his master's side.

"The times he has been most miserable have been when something has separated them. Sometimes it has been a family conflict—several of Arthur's wives have greatly resented Eddie—some of Eddie's wives have resented Arthur. Other times, Eddie has grown weary of being taken for granted and has gone off on his own for a few decades."

"He always comes back?"

"Or Arthur seeks him out. You see, Arthur is a born leader, but a leader cannot lead without followers. He is diminished without his faithful knight."

"I never thought of that," Vera says. "Arthur simply commands and others obey."

"Sometimes. Sometimes not. I must admit, since Arthur linked up with Lovern, his ticket has been hard to beat. Some have tried, as well you know. Before modern technology, our people often had several different governments. Now, however, between access to technology and high magic, any of those governments has been secondary to Arthur's."

"You've been thinking about this a lot," Vera says, impressed. She'd never considered what might have been going on in the mind of the silent coyote drowsing in the courtyard.

"I have," the Changer admits. "Lovern deliberately threw me a challenge last night when he suggested that our enemies might be out to undermine Arthur's reign."

Vera nods. "The idea has been mentioned to me. I have a bit of trouble believing it though. For centuries now, athanor governments have changed relatively peacefully."

"For centuries now," the Changer contradicts dryly, "the

majority of athanor government has been Arthur and Arthur's policies. The last athanor-against-athanor coup was in China in the seventeen hundreds. When, centuries later, Tin Hau grew tired of ruling, she made an alliance with Arthur in return for help relocating some of her people who were threatened by the communists. Even my brother now moderates his reign to conform with the Accord established by Arthur on land."

"Your brother?" Vera asks. "Oh! Duppy Jonah. He's the only one of our people you claim as kin. Isn't that true?"

"We are all kin," the Changer says, "but, yes, Duppy Jonah is the only one for whom I feel a sibling's bond. We were both sea-born long before humans rose onto two feet, long before dinosaurs ruled the lands."

Vera swallows hard. Some of the others are accorded the courtesy title "ancient"—Arthur and Eddie among them, but next to the Changer and Duppy Jonah, they truly are newcomers. Even her relatively vast age vanishes to nothing by comparison. She longs to ask questions, but she is too awed to interrupt.

"Perhaps someone seeks to overthrow Arthur's long monarchy. As much as I dislike considering that I have an enemy cruel enough to slaughter my mate and children to get at me, I like even less the idea of having an enemy who would slaughter my family to use me against Arthur. I will not be anyone's pawn."

The last sentence is nearly growled. Vera nods. "I don't like the idea much myself, and I don't have your apparent dislike of hierarchies."

The Changer grins at her. "I have nothing against hierarchies. I just prefer to choose my own position in them. With the current one, I consider myself a friendly ally."

"But not a subject?"

"But definitely not a subject."

Vera smiles, impishly. "Is this another of those strength/weaknesses?"

"Exactly."

"What do you see as mine?" she asks, surprised at the question, even as it leaves her lips.

"Do you really want to know?"

She hesitates. "Sure."

"You have several in common with the lot of us: arrogance, temper, a tendency to underestimate humankind. Otherwise, well, I think that one of yours is a direct opposite of mine."

Vera realizes that the Changer is being kind. By wording his response this way, he is admitting a weakness of his own.

"And that is?" she prompts.

"You are afraid of love," he says, "and I don't just mean the sexual kind—that much-vaunted virginity. I mean you are afraid to make that ultimate link to another. You fall into line in a chain of command; you are capable of loyalty far stronger than mine, but love in its many forms—not merely romantic love—you keep at bay."

He shrugs. "That isn't all a bad thing. Love is why I am where I am right now. It is why I am seeking revenge from people who may be more powerful than I am. My paternal love is why I am standing in a public park being buffeted by the wind when I'd much rather be making a new life somewhere else. Love restricts my actions, but love gives me strength as well."

"Love?" she says, hardly believing that she is hearing this from the fierce, dark, brooding figure beside her.

"That's right. Love makes me a creator—of children, of circumstances. It expands me in ways that I could not be expanded by my own power. But it limits me as well."

He glances at her, sees that she is listening without anger, and continues, "I think that's why Lil makes you so uncomfortable. You aren't destructive, but you see in her something that you could be. She negates, but you deny. From my way of seeing things, those qualities aren't all that far apart."

Children are streaming from the school now: running about, calling to parents, to friends. The Changer strides over to be closer to his daughter; Vera trails after, thoughtful.

She's too intelligent simply to reject his words out of hand, but she is not particularly pleased with them. How much truth had there been in that rambling speech? She had always believed that she loved—just that she chose not to have sexual congress. Could there be anything to what he had said?

Reminding herself that the Changer is no prophet, that he is a simple animal much of the time, that his drive to engender children is a base instinct shared by all beasts, Vera catches up to him. She certainly isn't going to confirm his opinion by rejecting him now when all he offered her was his honest opinion.

And she'll think about what he has said.

Really.

☼◻☼

Eddie sticks his head into Arthur's office. "Where's Vera?"

Arthur looks up from something he's been plotting on his computer. "She took the Changer and his daughter out to a park. Do you need her?"

"Not her specifically. I was going to run over to that pawnshop on Central—the one the twenty-two came from—and see what I can learn. I thought she might want to come along."

"You could call her and see when she's coming back."

"No, that's all right. I can probably be there and home again before she could bring the others back."

Arthur studies his friend. "You are still uncomfortable with the Changer, aren't you?"

Coming into the office, shutting the door behind him, Eddie slouches into the chair reserved for him. "I guess so, Arthur. He certainly hasn't caused any trouble, but he's so . . ."

"Wild? Strange? Unpredictable?"

"No. I mean, yes. He is all of those things, but so are many of our people. I simply dislike having someone who is not sworn to you residing under your roof—especially now."

Arthur strokes his beard. "He is one of our people, Eddie."

"By blood and gift, yes, but he is not one of *your* people."

"At least he is honest about that, my knight, unlike many."

"Yes, sir."

"Talk with him, Eddie. Consider it my request. The Changer has been known to us for many years, but you are correct. The Changer has never been of our court. Perhaps you can win him."

Eddie drums his heels against the floor. "I am tempted,

my lord. I, too, was once of the wild. There my potential would have been untapped. Perhaps I can make the Changer see this.''

"If anyone can sway him, it will be you," Arthur says fondly.

"Enough gossip." Eddie surges to his feet. "I want to get back from the pawnshop before rush hour starts. They're tearing up Lomas again. It's going to make a mess of late-afternoon traffic.''

"Good luck.''

Placing the cased twenty-two in the trunk of a modest sedan, Eddie drives over to Central. Once a stretch of Route 66 that passed through the heart of Albuquerque, this road has seen better days. The State Fairgrounds gives ample excuse for a number of seedy motels and questionable restaurants, but there are legitimate businesses as well.

The Golden Balls pawnshop, while sharing qualities with all businesses of its type, is definitely an upscale version. Floors are swept. A neat array of guitars, trumpets, and other musical instruments hangs on the walls. The long, glass cases displaying jewelry, watches, and knickknacks are clean.

The air smells of glass cleaner and pine incense, not at all a bad combination. A round-faced Hispanic woman looks up from her copy of the *Albuquerque Tribune* when he enters.

"Let me know if I can help you," she says politely and returns to her crossword puzzle. Eddie, who notices such things, sees that she is doing the *Times* puzzle in ink and is impressed.

Desiring to wait until the two other customers have left, Eddie browses at a case of silver jewelry. A silver pin of an owl, inlaid with jet and shell, catches his attention. Vera would like that for her collection.

Southwestern Indian art rarely depicts owls—these being considered birds of ill omen by Navajo and many of the Pueblos. Recently, more work is being done for the collectors and nontraditional subjects can be found. This piece, however, has a flavor of the old beliefs. The hunched shoulders and orange eyes look as if they hold secrets.

When the other customers leave, Eddie clears his throat. The shopkeeper looks up immediately. Given that many of her clients are probably embarrassed by their need for quick money, no doubt she is accustomed to the desire for privacy. Eddie's neat clothing gives no real indication of his relative wealth—especially in the Southwest, where jeans can be formal wear. In any case, with easy access to casinos, even the most prosperous might need a little quick credit.

"Yes, sir. May I help you?" When she stands, he sees that she is quite tiny, a doll of a woman. There is a toughness to her, though, and a confidence that suggests that either she has backup somewhere near or a very good alarm system.

"I wanted to look at one of the pins here."

She comes over, opens the case. "Which one?"

"That owl."

Without any reluctance, she hands it to him. Then again, her superstitions would be different. Although the Spanish and Indians have intermarried over the centuries since the Spanish first colonized New Mexico, the populations have remained distinct in many ways.

"Pretty," he says, turning it over in his hands, checking the set of the tiny rectangles of inlay, looking for the maker's mark and the certification of the silver's quality.

"It is," she agrees.

"A friend of mine told me about it," he says, continuing his inspection. "He saw it when he was here a couple of days ago to get a rifle—a twenty-two."

The woman nods. Perhaps bored by her crossword or eager to make a sale at this slow time of year she is inclined to talk.

"I think I remember him," she says, "red-haired, very fair. I told him he should watch that the sun did not burn him. He said he burns very easily. Is this your friend?"

"I think so," Eddie smiles. The red hair could easily be a disguise, so could the fair skin if the man has access to illusion magic or shapeshifting. Still, the description could help. "This is a pretty piece. How much?"

She takes it, checks a sticker discreetly stuck to the back. "Fifty-five dollars."

The price is fair. The person who pawned it certainly got much less.

"I think I'd like it. Do you take local checks?"

"Yes, sir. We like checks or credit cards. Cash, too, though not so much."

"Too tempting to thieves?"

"*Sí*. Your friend wanted to pay cash for the rifle and the bracelets he bought, and my husband put it in the bank *pronto*."

Eddie swallows a sigh. So much for hoping to get an address or credit-card number from her. He hadn't been sure he could, but he had been planning to try.

While Eddie is inside the pawnshop, Sven Trout sneaks over to Eddie's sedan. Taking a small velvet bag from one pocket of his denim jacket, he sprinkles some powder into the defrost vents. Then he takes a quarter-sized piece of carved limestone from another pocket.

Glancing at the door to make certain that Eddie hasn't come out yet, he unscrews the cap on the gas tank and drops in the limestone.

"Probably overkill," Sven reflects, momentarily regretting the loss of the expensive charm. Then he chortles, "But then, that's what I want, isn't it?"

When the mist first creeps up Eddie's windshield, he takes it for smoke and glances around to see which old oil burner is the source. He and Arthur have often joked that New Mexico has more old cars on the road than anywhere but Cuba.

No source for the smoke is visible, so he touches the car's wiper controls. The wiper fluid only seems to make things worse. Craning his neck slightly, he can see over the smeared area well enough to make the exit onto I-40.

As soon as he gets onto the expressway, he realizes that his problems are only beginning. Neither brakes nor accelerator behave as they should. He narrowly escapes being sideswiped by a pickup truck whose driver gives him the finger.

Traffic is compacting as the junction of I-40 and I-25, flippantly called the Big I by locals, rapidly approaches. Designed by someone with a very unrealistic idea of how traffic patterns work, the junction includes exits that enter into the fast lane, merge lanes that vanish with minimal warning, and some of the tightest cloverleafs in the city.

Cars enter the junction half-blind even under the best conditions. Eddie, struggling with a car that seems to speed up when he wants it to slow, to slow when he demands acceleration, to swerve right when he insists on left, is not driving under the best conditions. Only long experience with this stretch keeps him in a lane at all.

Coasting whenever possible, tapping brake and accelerator in reverse of what long training has taught him to do, Eddie strives to get to a shoulder from which he can call for help. He is just daring to congratulate himself for achieving his goal when a tractor trailer, its driver intent on making his last delivery and getting home for supper, decides that he can slip in front of the erratically moving sedan.

Eddie just barely sees the looming white form. Instinctively, he steps on the brake. The sedan charges forward. There is a squeal of brakes, a crashing sound. Then nothing.

8

*Make yourself into a sheep, and you'll
meet a wolf nearby.*

—RUSSIAN PROVERB

"HAS ANYONE SEEN EDDIE?" ARTHUR CALLS OUT INTO
the courtyard where Lovern, Vera, and the Changer are chatting.

"No," Vera answers. "He was gone when we got here. I
haven't heard his car come in."

"Nor I," adds the Changer.

"Damn," Arthur says. "Anson A. Kridd just phoned.
Frankly, I was hoping Eddie could deal with him."

"Have Anson call back," Vera suggests. "We heard on
the radio that there was a major accident at the Big I. Eddie's
probably tied up there. Or I can talk with Anson for you."

"No, I can handle the Spider."

Arthur retreats into his office.

Lovern is staring into the tea leaves in his cup.

"Call Eddie," he says to Vera.

"What?"

"Call Eddie," Lovern repeats. "I have a bad feeling about
this."

Vera cocks an eyebrow but picking up another line, dials
the number of Eddie's car phone.

"No answer," she says, surprised. "Maybe he isn't finished at the pawnshop."

"Maybe."

Looking quizzically at Lovern, the Changer starts removing his clothing, remembers Vera, and heads to his room.

"I'm flying over to the Big-I," he calls. "Omens are not to be dismissed lightly."

"There are accidents there all the time!" Vera protests.

There is no answer. A few moments later, a large black raven flies out of the Changer's suite. It croaks once and is gone.

¤✸¤

The Changer is not completely certain why he had felt so compelled to follow up on Lovern's "bad feeling." Certainly there is no great affection between himself and the wizard—indeed, he tends to distrust Lovern rather than otherwise. Despite such thoughts, he continues to fly toward the Big I.

It is easy enough to find, coming as it does at the intersection of two highways. Today, it would be difficult to miss, for traffic is snarled out from it in all directions.

He has to circle twice before he is absolutely certain that one of the cars below is Eddie's. The front end is crumpled against the rear of a tractor trailer. Two other vehicles—a pickup truck and a minivan—are also mixed into the pileup. The pickup has smashed into the back of Eddie's sedan and the minivan nose first into the concrete shoulder barrier.

Emergency workers are feverishly trying cut through the driver's side door to get to where Eddie slumps against the wheel. The Changer takes this as a hopeful sign. Certainly they would not be working so hard if Eddie were already dead. There must be at least some doubt.

Elsewhere in the chaos, others are helping the driver of the pickup from his vehicle. Blood courses from his ruined nose, but he seems to be walking on his own. The woman from the minivan leans heavily on a police officer, her hand covering one eye.

The man who had been driving the tractor trailer apparently has suffered nothing worse than a head cut. Holding a compress to his forehead, he is giving a statement to a police officer. The Changer perches on the cab of the truck to eavesdrop.

"I told you, Officer," the man says in a Texas accent. "He sped up into me!"

"One of the witnesses claims that you suddenly changed lanes without warning."

The truck driver, confident that no one will be able to gainsay him, shakes his head, then winces.

"I signaled, Officer," he says self-righteously, "Besides, how could anyone miss something the size of my rig?"

The police officer grunts. Obviously, he is far from won over by the driver's protestations.

With the rolling stride that marks the raven from the crow, the Changer walks to the back of the tractor trailer. The emergency workers have cut Eddie free now. He looks pretty bad—blood gushing down his forehead from a wide gash, eyes swelling shut, lips bruised and purple.

Ironic that both Lovern and the Changer have escaped death traps and that Eddie has been felled merely by accident.

Or was it an accident?

The idea excites the Changer so much that he hops from foot to foot. Perhaps Eddie's accident was not at all accidental. Only he will know the truth.

Impulsively, the Changer decides to follow Arthur's knight to the hospital and be on hand to question him as soon as he comes around. In his evidently critical condition, Eddie will certainly be refused visitors. However, no administration that has ever been designed could keep the Changer out when he is determined to get in.

When the ambulance departs, the Changer follows. In the congested traffic, raven wings easily pace the vehicle. As Eddie is being unloaded, the Changer lands and shifts into a field mouse. Running as fast as his tiny legs can carry him, he slips onto the gurney and hides between the padding and the frame.

Heart beating more rapidly than he had recalled was possible, the Changer trembles: waiting, listening, terrified as only a mouse can be.

¤▣¤

In his motel room, Sven Trout listens to the radio, waiting impatiently for the traffic report. When the block of music ends, an obnoxiously cheerful DJ segues into commercials. Sven listens to an ad for auto insurance, a concert appearance by a rock star whose popularity waned a decade before, a local restaurant, and a casino. At last the traffic report comes:

"Watch out for the Big I," a woman says over the sound of thudding helicopter blades. "There's been a collision between a tractor trailer and several other vehicles that's slowing down everything for miles in all directions. Emergency workers are on the scene now, but the congestion won't be eased until long after rush hour. Alternate routes strongly recommended . . ."

She goes on to talk about other tie-ups, but Sven is certain with that peculiar sixth sense that is his own that this first accident is the one he wants. Initially, he feels quite cheerful, then doubt sets in.

What if Eddie wasn't killed? Sven doesn't fancy talking to his allies and hearing their scorn if once again he has narrowly missed his goal. He waits for the earliest news broadcast. Fortunately, the wreck is a top news story.

"Rush-hour traffic was hopelessly snarled earlier this evening," the neatly coiffed anchorman announces, "when a tractor trailer and a passenger vehicle collided on westbound I-40, at the Big I. Miraculously, no one in any of the four vehicles involved in the accident was killed."

A video clip of rescue workers removing an unconscious Eddie from his sedan runs as the anchorman continues his narration.

"All involved were taken to an area hospital for observation. One man remains in the intensive-care unit in critical condition."

The announcer looks up and smiles. The clip behind him changes to one of girls jumping around a basketball court. "Elsewhere in the news, the Lady Lobos are doing well! Stay with us for . . ."

Sven slams his thumb down on the remote, cutting off the commentary. He cannot tolerate another failure. Eddie is almost certainly the patient in Intensive Care. Very well. He will pay him a visit. It doesn't need to be long, nor even in private.

He wonders if Arthur will be there. No matter, he can fool that stodgy bureaucrat—he's done so before. It will be harder if Lovern is also there, but Sven is willing to bet that the hospital will be restricting visitors. Perhaps there will be no one there at all. Perhaps Arthur will be nervously pacing in the waiting room while his undeclared rival neatly ends the life of his staunchest supporter.

Chuckling, his good mood restored, Sven contemplates his strategy. A shapeshift will be helpful, that, a tidy white dress, and a badge. He wishes that he had more time to design his costume, but as soon as Eddie is declared out of danger (which almost certainly will happen more rapidly than the doctors expect), Arthur will have him transferred home. In any case, Sven has faith in his acting abilities—deception is as natural to him as breathing.

He is humming as he tries on his new shape. After a few phone calls, he heads out the door. First a quick stop at a department store, then off to the hospital.

Sven looks around the hospital's neatly tiled environs with satisfaction. He had experienced no difficulty getting into the place, even into the Intensive Care Unit. Of course, he has made certain that he looks as if he belongs.

For one, he is no longer a youthful, flame-haired male. He has altered his shape to that of a kind-faced, somewhat over-weight, Hispanic woman, her permed hair drawn back into a neat knot. The relaxed dress code in the hospital has helped him to blend in as well.

No longer do nurses wear the stiffly starched white uniforms that recalled a nun's habit. Instead, neat white skirts or pants are topped with pastel blouses identical to what he had just purchased. His/her costume is completed by a clipboard and an intent, slightly vague expression.

No one questions her as she walks briskly down a corridor, glancing at the nameplates, apparently on an errand for some doctor. Crisis is replaced by fresh crisis in these white corridors; no one has time to worry about a helpful stranger.

Sven locates Eddie's room after several attempts. Waiting until the understaffed nurses' station is busy with calls, she slips through the open door. Hooked into monitors and an IV drip, Eddie rests unconscious on a hospital bed. He is alone.

Efficiently, Sven draws the privacy curtain, trusting that

no one passing by outside will wonder. Then she considers what her next move should be. She must be careful. If the monitors are unhooked, an alarm will go off at the nurses' station: the same applies to any slow attempt at suffocation.

In the hazardous waste trash disposal, Sven finds a hypodermic syringe, needle still intact. It is the work of moments to draw some air. A large air bubble into one of Eddie's major arteries and death should be quite prompt.

Humming, she selects the right spot.

"What are you doing?" says a male voice immediately behind Sven. At the same moment, the hand holding the needle is hauled back. Sven is forced to drop the syringe.

Sven cannot turn, but she can feel the warmth of a large body behind her. The arm that had forced the syringe away is now pinning her right arm to her torso. The other has twisted her left arm behind her.

Immobilized, Sven considers the question that had been put to her. "No particular good, if the truth must be known. Who are you?"

A deep-chested laugh comes from her captor. "I believe that only I am in the position to make such demands. Who are *you*?"

Sven has managed to catch a distorted reflection of her captor in the metal tube holding up the IV. It is male, dark-haired. She suspects the Changer.

"You're naked!" she squeals indignantly, not daring raise her voice too loud, but hoping to be overheard nonetheless.

"So I am. I am also stronger than you and have you in a rather awkward position. Tell me who you are!"

Sven rejoices that she had added perfume to her disguise. This, combined with the restrictions of a human nose, is clearly keeping the Changer from making an absolute identification. Still, the longer she is his captive, the more likely he will be to figure her out.

"I'm your worst nightmare," Sven says, and shapes a hissing rattlesnake that surges out of the woman's clothes.

The other shifts instantly (it must be the Changer, damn his eyes!), becoming a mongoose that seizes the rattler before it can coil to strike. Sven shifts into a komodo dragon and lunges for Eddie. Unfortunately, he has underestimated his size.

The komodo dragon is swift, but short, and his heavy tail lashes out, knocking one of the monitors to the ground. Alarms go off. Shouts come from the direction of the nurses' station.

Sven knows the complications that being caught in a questionable shape can create. The Changer, clinging to the back of his blunt head, refuses to let go.

Panicked, Sven shifts into another reptilian form, this one a slim, swift garter snake that eludes the mongoose and slithers under the curtain and out the door. Staying close to the walls, the garter snake ducks under an equipment cart and waits, its cold heart beating uncomfortably fast. The chill of the tiles seduces the reptile to torpor.

Although nearly exhausted, Sven becomes a tan spider. He doesn't like being an insect. Even the most venomous are too easily killed, but his repertoire of nonhuman shapes is limited and too many of them are large and menacing.

The Changer has not emerged from the hospital room or, if he has, he has done so in a form that Sven cannot see. The latter possibility terrifies him until he decides that the Changer would not leave Eddie until he is certain that the other man is safe.

Carefully, Sven spiderwalks down the wall, then leaps to catch a ride on a passing gurney. When he is clear of the ICU, he locates a locker room and steals a pair of pants, a set of sneakers, and a shirt. The outfit isn't the fashion statement he would have preferred, but he is willing to settle— especially since he can tailor his human form to accommodate the clothes.

With the Changer on his trail, he cannot linger. Eddie can wait. They all can wait. The end result will be the same.

¤�‫¤

In Eddie's hospital room, the Changer quivers in mouse form beneath the beside table. He had barely had time to stuff the *faux* nurse's clothes into the laundry bin and shift before the staff arrived.

Now he listens while nurses and their aides reconnect the equipment, fretting aloud: "I don't know how he could have knocked anything over!'' the floor supervisor says. ''I'm certain he's been unconscious the entire time.''

''Spasm?'' an aide suggests timidly.

''I guess.'' The supervisor frowns. ''Let's get the restraints on him, then. We don't want a repeat.''

The Changer agrees, waiting until they depart. He longs to find Arthur, to turn the guarding over to another and see if he can find sign of the shapeshifter he has just found.

But he does not dare leave Eddie alone. The assassin might return, might invoke a sending of some sort. He shifts from mouse to raven and flaps to perch on the open bathroom door. From there, he spots the telephone.

Cocking his head on one side and suppressing a thoughtful ''pr-r-uk,'' he considers his options. The Changer flutters down, shapes himself into a man, lifts the receiver. A dial tone greets him. Well enough. The Changer presses the combination for Arthur's cell phone.

''Hello?'' Arthur himself answers. Oddly, his voice is soft, as if he is whispering.

''This is the Changer. I want you to come to Eddie's room. He's been attacked.''

''What?''

''He's been attacked. Can you come here?''

''They suggested I wait until visiting hours, said that Eddie would be groggy from surgery.''

''He's more than groggy; he's out. Come here anyway. If someone tries to stop you, tell them you heard someone say there had been a crisis and you won't rest until you see him.''

''I'll try.''

''How long until you're here?''

''Just a few minutes. I'm down in the lounge now.''

''Good. I'll be waiting.''

''Right. Changer, what are *you* doing here?''

Grinning, the Changer hangs up the phone and shifts into a raven once more.

Arthur arrives within the promised few minutes, escorted by the protesting floor supervisor. Hearing them approach, the Changer reluctantly returns to mouse form and hides beneath the bedside table.

''I tell you,'' the supervisor is saying, ''your friend is quite fine.''

"I insist on seeing for myself," Arthur answers, stubborn and imperious. The Changer can imagine him sweeping along, his beard jutting forward, his shoulders squared. "And if you attempt to stop me, I will be forced to report you to the board."

The supervisor stops talking, trying to decide whether this arrogant man might have the connections to harm her. Evidently, she decides that challenging him further is not worth the risk.

When they enter, the Changer hears Arthur's sharp intake of breath when he sees his battered comrade. To the Changer, who had seen him raw and bleeding, Eddie's present appearance is an improvement, but he can understand Arthur's shock.

The bruises that had just been forming at the scene of the accident are purple and swelling. Eddie's five-o'clock shadow has lengthened some with the passing of the hours, but it is not enough to hide the abrasions on his chin—and nothing can conceal his split lip. His forehead has been stitched. And these are the minor injuries.

Arthur must have been told about the broken ribs, the lung that had to be reinflated, the pints of blood soaked into the upholstery of the sedan. He must know about the perforated bowel that has been resected, about the looming threat of peritonitis.

He mutters something softly and the Changer is among the handful of those living who can understand the tongue of ancient Babylon: "*Oh, my liege man! Oh, my friend! If you die, I will have the blood and heart of the one who has caused this!*"

The King sits heavily upon the room's one chair, his gaze still fixed on his Eddie's pale face. Accepting the inevitable, the floor supervisor departs. Arthur rises after she is gone and closes the room's door.

"Changer?" he queries the air.

The Changer scampers out from under the bedside table, crosses beneath the bed, and takes human form on the other side.

"Here, Arthur," he says.

Arthur looks across, gestures to the curtain. "Pull that closed," he says, "so you will have a moment to shift if the nurse returns. Did they see you before?"

"No, I came in as a mouse, remained as such until . . ." The Changer frowns. "Until Eddie's attacker arrived. She was dressed as a nurse or technician—I can't read their heraldry—and was going to kill him by introducing air into his blood."

"She?"

"Female form at least. When I tried to stop her, I had ample evidence that she was a shapeshifter."

Concisely, he recounts the skirmish, not omitting any of the forms he had seen his opponent assume.

"The komodo dragon was an interesting choice," Arthur says, when the Changer is done, "though not a terribly easy one to pass off if she was discovered. Did she remain female throughout?"

The Changer frowns as he tries to remember. "I can't be sure. I was too busy fighting to sex reptiles."

"All reptiles, though," Arthur says. "Interesting. If Satan was real, we'd have a match."

"Sadly, that one is fancy," the Changer says. "The trail is cold by now, but if you will remain with Eddie, I will scout."

"Go!" Arthur says. "I am not stirring from his side. If that devoted nurse tries to make me, I shall gently request that she check my name against the hospital benefactors' list. Do you need help making an exit?"

The Changer shakes his head. "No, I'll run mouse-form until I get outside, then shift raven. I should manage."

"Be careful," Arthur says, his gaze already returning to his friend's face.

"Are you armed?" the Changer asks.

Arthur smiles, lifts his jacket to reveal the gun holster concealed by his immaculate tailoring. "I also have a blade in my boot. However, I will keep the nurse's call button under my thumb and be prepared to make a ruckus if anything happens."

"Modern tools"—the Changer nods—"will serve you better here than steel."

"I know." Arthur's expression turns sorrowful. "And so I try to tell our people, but at times like this even I long for the direct solutions of sword or fist."

"Today is not the day to alter policy," the Changer reminds him. "I will let you know if I find something."

"Call in every hour or ninety minutes, if you would," Arthur says, his sorrow masked by kingly concern. "We do not want you to be taken without our being alerted. To be honest, we have been worried since you departed and sent us no further word."

The Changer looks rueful. "I forgot about the telephone. I tend to, after a long time away from such things."

Arthur smiles slightly, watches as the man becomes a mouse.

"Good luck," he whispers.

There is no answer, not even a squeak. The mouse skitters beneath the nearest cover and runs.

9

The long habit of living indisposeth us for dying.

—THOMAS BROWNE

Rebecca>> So what are you?

Monk>> Is telling a requirement for being on this site? How would you know if I was telling the truth, anyhow?

Demetrios>> Don't be so rude to a lady! She didn't ask anything offensive.

Monk>> Sorry. I guess we have all become so accustomed to protecting our identities that I jumped at the question.

Rebecca>> You don't need to tell.

Monk>> That's all right. I'm a *tengu*.

Demetrios>> Pardon my ignorance, but what's a *tengu*?

Monk>> I'm island-born, originally from the mountains of Nippon—Japan. A *tengu* is a shapeshifter. Some have called us tricksters. I don't think that's precisely fair.

Rebecca>> A shapeshifter?? What kind of shapes??

Monk>> Something like a bird-ogre, birds of prey, humans.

Demetrios>> You can shape humans? Then why are you interested in our cause?

Rebecca>> You can be human? Wow!

Monk>> Fair question, Demetrios. Like I said, some people call us tricksters. I prefer to think of us as social commentators. For centuries we have been the enemies of those who would use religion against the masses. Corrupt monks—especially wandering ones who begged for food and shelter and didn't have to answer to anyone—were our particular targets.

Rebecca>> What's to keep you from going after them now?

Monk>> Well, for one, there aren't quite as many as there once were. Two, Arthur has authorized some of the warrior athanor to keep us in check. You see, we have minor illusion magic. He's afraid that if we use it people will begin to suspect that magic works.

Demetrios>> In Japan these days, they'd prob think it was a microtech gimmick. I think Arthur's overreaching himself.

Monk>> Me, too. I'd love to expand my range. The television evangelists or media-darling politicians are right up my alley, but Arthur keeps the bully types happy by making creatures like me fair game. If I live quietly—human or avian—I'm fine. Let me do what I crave and WHAPPO!! I'm likely to be smiling up the blade of Katsuhiro's most noble sword Kusanagi.

Rebecca>> NO FAIR! NO FAIR!

Monk>> I might ask what has you two involved in this Cause. From what I've learned, you're both leading pretty good lives. Certainly a desire to play tourist isn't enough to make you dabble in political upheaval at the risk of your lives.

Demetrios>> No, it isn't, though touring all in itself is tempting. I'm in it for the natural world.

Rebecca>> I'd like travel, but I'm worried about the trees.

Monk>> You overlapped but your answers are pretty much the same. What do you mean, about being it for the trees?

Rebecca>> I live in forested land here in Oregon. Logging's bad enough, but industrial pollution—acid rain, chemical runoff, tainted water—and other things, like the damming of rivers so that the fish can't make their spawning runs, are having serious repercussions. My husband, Bronson, says that even where we live (and we're pretty isolated) he can see changes. He's an old one. Remembers when the Indians weren't even Indians yet, when there were still mastodons. These aren't the natural changes of evolution. These are major catastrophes that humans are too short-lived to understand fully.

Demetrios>> We're going to overlap again, but I hope I won't repeat too much. Fauns—like me—were the mobile nature types. Greek myths speak of nymphs: dryads, naiads, oreads—the spirits of trees, water, even mountains. I'm not just getting religious on you when I say that they exist. Not everyone can see them, but that doesn't make them any less real. After all, how many moderns have seen a faun or a sasquatch?

The massive destruction of natural areas is driving the nymphs to extinction. They're an endangered species with no one but my kind to speak up for them, but how can we? If I go on the Internet and lobby, I sound like a kook. But if someone sees me and figures "Hey, if there *are* fauns, maybe there *are* the rest . . ."

Monk>> I catch your drift, both of you. This is serious stuff. And Demetrios, I've never seen a nymph, but Japanese Shinto is full of references to things like them—*kami*, they're called. If you say they're out there, I'll believe you.

Demetrios>> Thanks.

Rebecca>> Do you understand how important this is, Monk? We can't just stay in our woods and glens. We've got to get *out* there and do something.

Monk>> Yeah. I sure do see. I'll talk to my kin. We can attend the Lustrum Review. We'll speak up for you, so you won't just have to be reduced to words on a computer screen.

Demetrios>> Thanks, again!

Rebecca>> !! Thanks!! :)

King Arthur's hacienda feels empty when the Changer flaps into a tree in the courtyard. The lilac from beneath which his daughter emerges, her bushy tail wagging wildly, has lost its blossoms, its leaves darkening with every passing day.

How long have they been in Albuquerque? Ten days? He feels as if months have gone by, but the puppy bouncing and yapping around the base of the tree on which he is perched is proof enough that comparatively little time has passed.

Swooping to the patio table, he shifts coyote, then jumps to nip and nuzzle the rejoicing puppy. Despite his daughter's yaps and whimpers he hears bare feet on the tiled hall.

Glancing up, he sees Vera standing beneath the arched entry. Her hands are twisting wool around a distaff in a restless motion that, nonetheless, is marvelously skillful.

"When you've finished with the pup," she says, her voice calm, "come into the kitchen. You've got to be starved. We can trade information."

She doesn't command, but she doesn't request either. The

Changer wags his brush in acknowledgment, romps with the puppy a few minutes more, then goes into his room to shift shape and don some clothing.

Good to her promise, Vera is waiting in the kitchen. She sets a bowl of puppy chow on the floor for the coyote pup, who looks up at her with pleading eyes.

"Sorry, kid," Vera says, "health food first. You can see if you can cadge something from your father later."

"Perhaps," the Changer says mildly.

"I think that Arthur was sneaking her table scraps," Vera says, shoving a bowl of *chili con carne* and half a loaf of corn bread over to him. "She seems to expect them."

"That may just be her coyote nose telling her that people food smells better than kibbles." The Changer dips a spoon into his bowl. "Thanks for this. Shifting takes its toll."

"You're welcome. I had to do something while I covered the base here; otherwise, I'd go crazy with waiting."

"Where is Lovern?"

"Out, like you were, scouting for signs of Eddie's attacker. He checked in forty minutes ago. No luck. How about you?"

"Nothing new since my last check-in, nothing at all for all the night's work."

Vera sighs. "Arthur phoned to say that the duty technician told him that someone had stolen clothes from a locker. Our guess is that's how the woman you met got out."

"Sounds reasonable. I wish I had snatched something of hers we could use for divining, but, to be honest, I was too busy defending Eddie—and myself."

"So it goes," Vera says. "At least Eddie is still alive. Arthur figures that he'll have him home within a few days."

The Changer frowns. "I dislike the idea of a stranger in the hacienda. Is Arthur recruiting an athanor?"

"That's right. I have calls out to several candidates. It's a blessing that the Lustrum Review is coming up. Many people have freed up some time from their usual duties."

"But can Arthur handle the Review without Eddie's assistance?"

"He must. He has little choice. If he cancels the Review, too many athanor would see Eddie's accident as insufficient reason to suspend normal government."

The Changer wrinkles his nose, a gesture more canine than human. "I forget these things so easily. What . . ."

The telephone ringing interrupts him. Vera answers it: "Pendragon Productions."

"What's cooking, grey-eyes?" chuckles a warm voice. "This is Anson A. Kridd. May I speak with Enki-dinky-doodle?"

Vera swallows hard. "Anson, Eddie's in the hospital. He was in a car crash."

"No!"

"I'm afraid so. Arthur's with him, but he's pretty badly beat-up—broken bones, lost lots of blood, all the rest. His life isn't in danger, though."

"I'll be there by this evening."

"That's not necessary, Anson. He's not up to visitors."

"Shit. I'm not coming to visit. I'm coming to take care of him. Don't cross me, Vera."

"I . . ."

"I'll be there. Eddie's one of my best friends. I'm not going to leave him to anyone else."

"I have called . . ."

"I can do as well as whoever you've called. I'm no spring chicken, eh? I've cared for my share of injured people."

"I . . ."

"Good. I'll leave a message when I have my flight information. Is there room at Arthur's hacienda for me?'

"Yes, but . . ."

"Good."

The line goes dead and Vera sits for a moment staring at the instrument before setting it down. She looks across at the Changer to find him grinning, yellow eyes twinkling.

"I caught enough of that."

"Anson A. Kridd is coming here," she says, disbelief in her tones. "How can I ever tell Arthur?"

"Fairly easily. Tell him that you've found a qualified nurse for Eddie, someone who will mend his spirit as well as his body. One of the elders of his line."

"Yes."

"Then, when he's expressed his gratitude, tell him it's the Spider come to stay."

"*Ave Maria.*"

The Changer breaks off a chunk of corn bread and drops it to the begging puppy.

"It could be far worse, Vera. I do not share Arthur's dislike of Anansi . . ."

"Anson," she corrects mechanically.

"He is adaptable, versatile, and nearly always productive. Creators are often unpredictable—how could they be else? Creation in itself involves envisioning that which hasn't been done before. King Arthur is a good man, but he has never been very creative—an administrator, a facilitator, and, usually, a just ruler, but not creative."

"And creativity makes him nervous?" Vera asks.

"Certainly. Just like it does you"—the Changer's expression is kind, but unswerving—"as well you know."

"I know what *you've* said," Vera retorts, rising from her seat. "Well, I can't very well send Anson away. I'd better see what rooms to give over to him."

"Put him near Eddie," the Changer suggests. "That's where he's going to be anyhow."

"Eddie's in the same wing as Arthur and me—the one we use for permanent residents. I'm not certain there's space there."

"Can you move or would it be easier to move Eddie?"

Vera stares at him in disbelief. "Why should I move?"

"To make room for Anansi."

"You would have me move for a transient?"

"Sure. Shifting dens is usual."

"But we *live* here."

"And I lived southeast of Albuquerque. I don't see anyone suggesting I should move back."

For a moment the grey eyes grow stormy, as if Vera wants to suggest just that, then she starts to laugh.

"Changer. You are that, aren't you? Very well, to show you I'm not the stick in the mud that you think, I'll move out and give my suite to Anansi. I can move into one of the guest wings."

"I'll help you," the Changer says. "There's not much else I can do now."

Vera shakes her head, laughs again. "Very well, ancient.

I accept your offer, but the puppy stays outside. I don't care to have her marking my belongings."

"Very well."

Vera opens the door to the kitchen stair. "I'll head up and decide what I need to move and what can be locked in a closet until Anansi leaves. Join me when you've settled your daughter."

"Which suite is yours?"

"It's in the west wing. I'll leave the door open."

The puppy wants to play, so the Changer humors her, knowing well that such games are necessary to develop her hunting abilities and stimulate her intelligence.

When she finally drops off to sleep, he resumes his human form and clothing, and goes hunting for Vera. For the first time since his arrival, he takes a good look at the interior of Arthur's hacienda. It's a sprawling structure with four wings built around a central courtyard. Unlike many Southwestern buildings, it's two stories high.

The ground floor is largely given over to shared areas: meeting rooms, offices, libraries, kitchen, dining room, sitting rooms equipped with big-screen television, even a swimming pool, smoking room, and a two residential spaces as well.

Three different staircases lead to upper areas: one from the kitchen, one from the entry foyer, and one from the courtyard. This last ends on a catwalk overgrown with flowering vines which provides an irresistible temptation to the coyote pup. She often races up and down it, certain she can catch the hummingbirds and butterflies if she is up on their level.

After prowling downstairs, he mounts the entry-foyer staircase. Once upstairs, the sound of drawers being slid open and shut guides him to Vera's suite.

An open door reveals a room decorated largely with owls. There are metal and ceramic owls on the shelves about the room, glass cases with owls carved of wood and stone in the corners, and owls woven into the rugs on the floor. There are no stuffed owls, though, nor any living ones, but through the window the Changer sees a tall cottonwood tree which most certainly looks like a place an owl might nest.

Stepping to the doorway, the Changer politely clears his throat. Hearing him, Vera turns from rearranging the clothes in a tall polished oak dresser.

"Come in! Come in! You might as well get a look at all the trouble you're putting me to."

"Me?" He cocks an eyebrow.

"You," she insists, but her tone is friendly.

The Changer browses as he waits for Vera to tell him what he can do. Vera's suite is quite large. Compared to a raven's nest or a coyote den, it seems a lot of space for one person. There is a parlor, a bedroom, and a spacious bathroom. The walk-in closet off of the bedroom is large enough to be another small room. Sensing that Vera feels shy about his presence in the bedroom, he drifts back into the parlor.

A large loom holding a partially woven blanket dominates one wall. The pattern is somewhat Navajo—Wide Ruins, he thinks—but far more detailed than usual. Near the west window an intricately carved mahogany table holds an array of small, wide-mouthed glass jars, each filled with tiny glass beads. There is no television, but a compact stereo and a selection of discs is tucked unobtrusively in one corner.

"I'll bring that," Vera says, gesturing to the stereo, "and I'm trying to decide about the beads. I'm working on a project now, but I'm not certain if I'll have time to get to it while Eddie's bedridden. Anson likes to weave—he might enjoy having materials available."

"Kind of you."

Vera shrugs. "I don't have a lot in common with the Spider, but weaving is one thing we share. He made that hanging on the east wall."

She gestures. The Changer inspects the delicate, lacy thing. "Very pretty. Did you make your rugs?"

"Yep, and the blankets, and the wall hangings, and several of the pieces in the offices as well. It's one of my favorite pastimes, but I won't sell the stuff. I've a lot more experience than any human weaver, and they can't compete. Here in New Mexico so many of the poor folks rely on textile weaving for a living that I'm especially careful."

"That's considerate."

She checks if he is mocking her, decides that he is not, and smiles. "I try. We are responsible to both humans and athanor."

"Athanor?"

"Humans aren't stupid. Our crafts could provide a means

to tracing us. Even though I try to innovate, I realize that my preferences for colors, for certain shapes and patterns, even for certain materials, could lead an expert to me."

"So you keep your works for yourself."

"For a limited audience," she corrects, "and usually with the promise that they will only be displayed in private areas."

"Seems wise."

"I *am* known for wisdom," she says, laughing at her own joke.

Shutting the dresser drawers, she looks at the clothing stacked on the bed. "There. I've emptied several drawers for Anson and moved the clothing from the smaller closet. I'll lock the walk-in closet. No need to tempt him to play with my belongings."

"Do you really think that he would?"

"Changer, this *is* Anansi the Spider we're talking about."

"True."

They carry several boxes of clothing, toiletries, and personal belongings to the suite in the north wing that Vera has selected. It's smaller than her own, but large nonetheless, with a bath and curtained-off bedroom.

"Arthur," the Changer says, setting down a box and looking around, "once again has a castle."

Vera nods. "And for similar reasons. Like a medieval king, he must be prepared to offer hospitality to his subjects. Much of the hacienda stands empty, but he can entertain a good number here. Overflow goes into hotels. But here our people can be among their own if they wish."

"Very kind of the King," the Changer says. "I certainly have been glad of his hospitality. Where are his rooms?"

"He has one of the suites across the hall from mine," Vera says. "One that overlooks the courtyard. Lovern has the other, when he's here. Eddie has the one next to mine."

"I'm surprised that Arthur has rooms overlooking the courtyard. Doesn't the noise of the household bother him?"

Vera shakes her head. "Not at all. He likes having people about him. Eddie prefers some privacy—that's why he chose a suite overlooking the grounds."

"And you?"

"I like both company and privacy. I could have had rooms in an empty wing, but I would have missed the sound of people coming and going. Even when I've dwelt in a convent under a vow of silence there have been others about. I don't think I would make a very good hermit.''

"Apparently not," the Changer says. He unfolds the bed-spread embroidered with owls that had been one of his burdens and shakes it out over the bed. "There. Is there anything else I can help you move?"

"I think not," Vera says, "at least for now. If I need to get anything else from my room, I can ask Anson."

The Changer nods. "Isn't Lovern late reporting?"

Vera glances at her watch. "Not yet, but close. I hope nothing has happened to him."

"Me too."

As if on cue, the phone rings. Vera picks up the extension in her new room.

"Pendragon Productions."

"Lovern here. I've found nothing, nothing at all. Is there anything I can do before I come back?"

"No, nothing that I can think of. You might call Arthur and see if he needs anything."

"I'll do that," Lovern promises. "And you may expect me back at the hacienda within the hour if you do not hear otherwise. Is the Changer there?"

"Yes. He returned recently. No news."

"Damn. Tell him I would like to speak with him when I get in—if he will grant me some of his time."

"I will. Be safe."

"I will."

Vera sets down the receiver. "That was Lovern. He's had no luck either. He asked me to beg audience with you."

"I doubt," the Changer's expression is wry, "that those were precisely his words."

"Nearly so," Vera says. "He sounded worried, tense."

"He has reason to," the Changer says. "Of course I will speak with him. I'm curious what he might want."

Vera surveys the unpacking that awaits her. "I should get to this."

"Let me excuse myself then."

"No," Vera blushes, a faint rose that goes very well with her grey eyes. "I mean, why don't you keep me company?"

The Changer studies her, raises an eyebrow. "Very well. I'll stay for a time."

"Tell me," Vera says, almost nervously, "tell me about what it's like to live as a wild creature."

"Very well," the Changer repeats. He pauses, tries to find words for experiences that are wordless. "It varies from creature to creature, from place to place, but, I find a certain joy in the life."

Vera nods, shakes out a skirt, fits it on a hanger, finding a certain joy herself in the rise and fall of the ancient's deep, gravelly voice.

¤◙¤

"Hello, Arthur? This is Lovern."

"Hello, Lovern." The King's voice sounds weary but steady. So he had sounded at Camlan.

"I've finished my hunting. No luck. I was wondering if you needed anything."

"Not really. The staff here has decided to be kind to me. I've been fed—and the food here is not bad at all—and been offered a steady stream of coffee, juice, and desserts. Vera brought some books earlier, and I have my laptop."

"And Eddie?"

"Mending. They should let me take him home tomorrow or the next day."

"Well, good night, then."

"Night."

Hanging up the phone, Lovern shakes his head in disbelief. He is very tired, and he doesn't dare overlook any important factor. In the past, he has done so to devastating result.

Completely honest with himself in a fashion he would consider *lèse majesté* from anyone else—even Arthur—Lovern snakes his memories back across the years to the mid-1850s.

Those were the years when, although most were unaware, the sun was beginning to set on the British Empire. Although Lovern himself had not been born in England, for many centuries he had involved himself in the plots, peculiarities, and purposes of that island realm. When she had begun to extend her control across the oceans to other lands—including the one that had given Lovern birth—he had followed her actions attentively.

In many ways, the aggressiveness with which he had aided the British Empire's expansion directly correlated with his resentment toward that bitch Nimue, who had made him captive. Once he had broken free of her spells and forced her to hide from *him*, Lovern had wrought intricate personal wards and rebuilt his personal power base. Then he had set out to show . . .

Who?

Lovern stops in the middle of unlocking his car door. To whom had he been demonstrating his power? Certainly not to Arthur. The former king of England had been almost pathetically happy when his councilor had returned (although Eddie had been less so). Not to the other mages. Among them, Merlin was acknowledged as without peer. Who then?

Perhaps to himself. Perhaps he had needed to assure himself following his disgrace that he was worthy of his legend and of all that he had wrought.

For whatever reason, Merlin (then Richard Wilson) had gone with King George III's subjects to India, the jewel of the empire's colonial possessions. He had been present when Lord North first regulated the East India Company. Careful never to draw too much attention to himself, he had traveled from region to region, offering advice, casting small enchantments, spinning a touch of intrigue. Many a colonial administrator was unaware how many of his decisions had been influenced by his unobtrusive counselor until Richard Wilson (or Lovern's successive identities Francis Eldridge and John Rowan) had moved on.

Getting into his car, Lovern forces himself to remember the moment when everything went to hell.

John Rowan had been in Delhi when the Mutiny broke out and only his skill at illusion had kept him from being slaughtered with the other English. Making his way through a countryside given over to horrid violence—both Indian and British—he realized that the rebellion was too big for him to contain. For the first time since Nimue had made him prisoner he felt absolute, sickening terror.

For too long he had been a ruler, although a ruler from the shadows. He had forgotten how angry subjects can become, especially when their rulers begin to treat them as counters on a game board rather than living, breathing entities: people with families, loyalties, and opinions all their own.

Made forever an exile by the passage of time, John Rowan had forgotten how humans can become attached to their homeland, how weary they can grow of the intrusions of conquerors.

Too knowledgeable about the forces that create religion, the wizard had forgotten the power of faith: how faith transforms the teachings of a single man or small group, how a simple code of conduct can become what the followers believe is a sure road to the rewards of the afterlife.

Having been acquainted with Buddha, Jesus, and Mohammed, having known some of those whose mystique shaded and shaped the Hindu pantheon, John Rowan had overlooked the fact that to the followers of those varied teachings the codes of their religion, the tenets of their faith, were more powerful, more essential than any king, queen, or army.

Thus, the blood had flowed and many—Hindu, Buddhist, Moslem, Christian—Indian and British alike—had died. John Rowan had been listed among the dead. Under a quickly crafted, short-lived persona, Lovern had helped Lord Canning, the new Governor-General, with that brave man's policy of reconciliation.

When this had been done, still acutely aware of how his meddling had helped create the circumstances that had led to the Mutiny, Lovern had returned to England. To no one, not even Arthur, had he revealed the guilt and horror that suffused him at the thought that had he not meddled in India, the rebellion might never have occurred or, if the Mutiny had been inevitable, that at least it might not have been so bloody.

Instead he had taken up residence on an isolated Pacific island. There he had renewed his studies of magic and consolidated the notes he had made during his nearly hundred-year sojourn in India.

As the immediate horror of the Mutiny faded from memory, Lovern considered the good he had done during his time with the British: The power of the East India Company had been reduced; the vile practice of suttee had been abolished; a successful campaign against the Thuggee had been mounted; several educational institutes had been established. For all of this and more he could claim at least some credit; surely his time in India had not been a complete debacle.

After twenty or so years, Lovern once again felt confident of his abilities as a counselor to those in power. Queen Victoria's proclamation in 1877 as Kaiser-i-Hind, Empress of India, seemed public proof that the debacle of the Mutiny had not been of lasting harm to either India or England.

Slowing, Lovern drives up the long, twisting gravel road to Arthur's hacienda. In his private calendar of events, the Mutiny had been the worst thing ever to happen to him. Remembering it—and how he had survived it—he takes heart. All things pass. So it will be with these latest problems. And, who knows? He may come through this period of adversity stronger than before.

✡▣✡

Not quite forty-eight hours after the accident, Eddie comes to clearheaded awareness and, when he does, his first bleary-eyed vision is of King Arthur waiting at his bedside.

"Ar . . . thur?" Eddie's voice is hoarse.

"Yes, I'm here, Eddie. Right next to your bed." Arthur says, setting aside his computer. He pours half a cup of water from the pitcher on the bedside table. "Take a sip of this."

Eddie tries and sputters. Although the hospital has him hooked to intravenous pain medication and liquids, his square-jawed face is pale and ravaged beneath his New Mexico tan. The bandage on his forehead adds to the impression of weakness.

"Slowly, slowly, my friend." Arthur wipes Eddie's lips and then holds the cup up again. "Try now. Slowly."

This attempt is more successful. Eddie swallows a small amount, then a bit more until the cup is emptied, leaving only the smallest trail down his beard-stubbled chin.

"More?" Arthur asks.

"Yes."

After another cup, Eddie smiles. "I . . . feel like I've been . . . hit by the Bull of Heaven."

"Close," Arthur says, setting down the cup and wiping

Eddie's chin. "You ran your car into a concrete median divider off the Big-I."

Eddie's eyes widen in memory and fear. "Was anyone . . . else badly hurt?"

"No. Two or three other vehicles were wrecked. Our insurance company is dealing with their insurance companies." Arthur's rich baritone breaks. "But that's nothing. You're alive. How do you feel?"

"Like I've been hit by the Bull."

Both men laugh, Eddie wincing at the twinge from his broken ribs.

"What's the prognosis, Arthur?"

"You'll live, you'll heal. The doctors warned me there might be brain damage. You hit your head hard enough to give you a concussion. Assessing whether there was anything more serious was difficult until you came around—but now that we're talking I think that brain damage can be dismissed."

"I hope so."

Eddie's expression is grim and Arthur does not need to ask to know what he is recalling—the memory of one of their own who survived a fall that broke both his back and his skull to live as a shadow of himself for a decade longer.

"I know so," Arthur says firmly. "Broken ribs and right leg, enough bruises and scrapes to make even *you* proud. You lost lots of blood, too. The doctors were concerned because of how long you were unconscious."

Arthur manages a small smile to conceal how concerned *he* had been. "You came around, rather muzzy, several times, but went under again almost at once."

"I don't remember," Eddie says as if confessing a fault.

"Don't worry about it, Eddie. Sleep heals."

This platitude is truer for many of the athanor. Excessive sleep can be the cost for more rapid than normal healing.

"Can I have some more water?"

Arthur again holds the cup for him.

"When can I go home?"

"Not today. I'll work on tomorrow. I've been agitating for home care since you came in, and they seem quite willing to agree." Arthur's expression becomes wry. "Apparently insurance companies don't like long stays in hospital."

"Cheap bastards." Eddie grins, pleased that he will be able to return home. Then the grin vanishes. "I won't be able to care for myself—not at first—and you and Vera can't be spared, not with the Lustrum Review this month. Maybe . . ."

"Peace." Arthur holds up a hand. "Your nurse would have come last night, but couldn't get a plane seat."

"Who?"

"Anson A. Kridd." Arthur can't keep a certain resignation from his voice, but the joy that brightens Eddie's pain-worn face is reason enough to accept the Spider in his house.

"Anson! I knew he was coming for the Review, but this is great! Still, he won't be much help with administration."

"Jonathan Wong has agreed to come early as well."

"Good!" Eddie smiles. "I almost feel better about this."

"Now that you are conscious," Arthur says, "let us start the wheels of administration moving. When the doctor makes his rounds I shall convince him that another twenty-four hours is all that is needed for observation."

"Good." Eddie leans back against his pillows. "And, as much as I hate to admit it, I could move if there was a marauding army approaching, but not for anything else. My head is pounding, and I can feel the ache in my leg even through the drugs."

Arthur nods. Eddie has moved—and been moved—with worse injuries, but then, as he had intimated, the only other choice had been death. Without fear's adrenaline charge to numb the pain, moving him could slow the healing process severely.

Eddie looks at Arthur. Already he is drifting back to sleep, but proof that his mind has come through the incident undamaged is found in the sharpness of his gaze.

"How long have you been here?"

"Since soon after you came out of surgery."

"That was how long?"

Arthur glances at his watch. "About forty hours."

Eddie's eyes widen. "And you've been here?"

"Of course." Arthur pats his shoulder. "You needed to be watched over. Vera can manage a few days without me."

"But you must be exhausted!"

"The room is furnished with a nice recliner. I take catnaps

and catch up on work. If you stay in here another day, I may even get to that correspondence backlog.''

''Arthur!''

''Rest, Eddie. That's the fastest way to get me to my work.''

''It's not that!''

Arthur grins. ''I know, but don't worry. Modern technology is wonderful. Between my computer, the modem, and a telephone, I'm unable to escape everything I left in my office. Rest now.''

''I . . .''

''Rest.''

Eddie's eyelids drift shut, though not without some protest on their owner's part. Watching him, Arthur realizes that he has lost count of the times that one has watched over the other. So many lifetimes, so many wars, so many assassins, so many just plain accidents.

He wonders which one of them will hold the final vigil or if some merciful power will make it possible for them to die within the same breath. The thought is not a new one, nor is his belief that their deaths will be far from painless.

Ewig ist ein langer Kauf.
(Forever is a long bargain.)
—GERMAN PROVERB

"I'VE SPOKEN WITH THE KING AND HE HAS AGREED," Lovern says, thus beginning his meeting with the Changer.

They were heading to the airport to pick up Anson. Vera had planned on going alone, but the Changer had refused to let her do so, pointing out that Eddie had been attacked while driving.

"So they can pick us both off in one blow?" she had responded tartly.

"I am harder to kill than that," the Changer says. "At least I dearly hope so. In any case, the wizard wishes to confer with me. If he comes along, I believe we can impose on him for a ward of some sort . . ."

Lovern had agreed and so the three of them—or four, since the Changer's daughter sits between her father's feet—ease through traffic toward the Albuquerque International Airport. The Changer sits in the backseat; Vera drives with Lovern in the passenger seat beside her.

"What has the King given you permission to do?" the Changer asks. "And why should knowing that he has given his permission sway my views one way or another?"

"Well . . ." Lovern stops, irritated with himself. He is so accustomed to backing his own desires with the authority of

another that he has overlooked the Changer's own likely reaction to such a statement. Also, with that irritating honesty
he seems to be bringing to all of his self-assessments, he
admits that the ancient makes him nervous.

"Let me begin again," Lovern says, stroking his beard.
"Given the current situation—the attacks on three residents
of Arthur's hacienda, the murder of your family . . ."

"I know the situation," the Changer interrupts. "What do
you want of me?"

"I want you to come with me when I go to retrieve a
potent piece of sorcerous equipment from where I have hidden it."

"Why me?"

"I have hidden it where few others could go."

"Oh? Couldn't another sorcerer go there? Or couldn't you
cast a spell to enable another to journey with you?"

"No. Yes. I . . ." Lovern stops, realizing that the Changer
is baiting him. The yellow-eyed ancient leans back in the
bucket seat and lifts his daughter onto his lap so that she can
see out the window.

"Pray, continue."

"I've hidden something under the sea," Lovern says
bluntly. "Your brother and I are not on the best terms. Previously, when I have visited my item I have done so astrally;
thus, there has been no need to trouble Duppy Jonah. This
time, since I need to physically remove it, I will need to deal
with the Sea King."

"And when you first hid it?"

"I did so without his permission. Thus, the ill will."

"Unwise."

"I know so now. I had not realized that he could hold a
grudge for so long. Then, however, we had been on opposite
sides during a then-recent conflict."

"Ragnarokk."

"Well . . . Yes."

"I see. Legend speaks of Mimir's Head being kept in a
well. There is often a small amount of truth in such tales. A
sea could be said to be the bottom of all wells."

Vera clears her throat. "Gentlemen, we're just about to the
airport. Do you want to continue talking while I collect An-

son? I don't think I'll be in any danger. Security at these places is pretty formidable.''

"I shall defer to the sorcerer in this matter."

"Vera, if you don't mind . . ."

"I'll go," she says. "Lovern, drive the van down to the baggage-claim level. We'll come out there."

"And if the plane is late?" the Changer asks.

The warrior maid taps her cell phone. "I'll call if it is."

As soon as Vera is gone, Lovern resumes the discussion where they had left off. "Yes, I've hidden Mimir's head in a well. It's safe there and, more to the point, so am I. When you create something closely tied to your own essence, it can endanger you."

"Nimue must have wanted to know its location very badly," the Changer says. "I congratulate you on your fortitude."

Uncertain whether he has just been subtly insulted by the reminder of his captivity or truly complimented, Lovern chooses not to respond. "Will you accompany me?"

"And negotiate with the Sea King, my brother?"

"Yes. And help if our enemies attempt to prevent me."

"I dislike the concept of the Head, Lovern. I have since you created it."

"It has permitted me to do great services for the athanor."

"Perhaps it has, but from my first sight of it, it struck me as a corruption of all that is natural."

Lovern decides that silence is his best reply. The Head *is* a corruption of what is natural. That it has expanded his abilities greatly made that corruption acceptable to him. Still, the revulsion it would spawn if its existence was generally known is partially why he has kept it hidden for so long.

"Will you help me nonetheless? The knowledge I have stored in Mimir's Head will help—and I have enchanted it with a gift for prophecy. It may be able to tell us who our enemies are."

The Changer narrows his yellow eyes. "Why can't you ask it these things with it stored safely beneath the ocean? Surely you haven't forgotten how to make an astral journey."

Lovern flushes. "I have not. I am . . ." He takes a deep breath. "I am afraid, Changer. During the astral journey my soul is connected to my body by only a slim silver cord.

There are magics for severing that cord. Nimue knows some of these. Our unknown enemy may as well.''

A small smile of approval for Lovern's honesty curves the corners of the Changer's mouth. Almost embarrassed, Lovern feels himself warm at the ancient's regard.

"Lovern, let me think about your request. Here comes Vera with Anson. You would not wish your secrets discussed publicly."

The Changer loops his daughter's leash firmly around the door handle next to her, then opens the van's door from the inside. Stepping down, he crosses to where Vera walks beside a long, wiry black man with an incongruous little potbelly, his hair bundled into dreadlocks.

"Anson."

The black man, his dark eyes deep pools of laughter and sorrow, ducks a slight bow of acknowledgment. '' 'lo, Proteus.''

"Let me take your bags," the Changer offers, lifting two hard-sided suitcases from the metal carrier Vera has been wheeling. "You don't travel light."

"Or I travel very light," the Spider answers, taking the other two bags and leaving Vera to gather the carry-on, "since my luggage contains most of my worldly goods. Not all of us are as footloose as you."

The Changer laughs. "Not so footloose as once. I have my own worldly bond with me. 'Ware the pup. She's coyote. She's prone to nip or pee when she gets excited."

"Ah! Vera mentioned something about her."

Leaving the Changer to assist Vera in stowing the luggage in the back of the van, Anson climbs into the passenger section. Carefully, he extends a hand, wriggling the long fingers slightly. The puppy wriggles happily in response, her tail wagging as if she has just met her first and oldest friend.

Vera blinks in astonishment. "You have quite a way with wild things."

"Not with wild things, no," Anson says, letting the Changer take the puppy in his lap, then settling into the seat beside him, "with young things. They appreciate whimsy in a way that their elders have forgotten."

Lovern makes a sound midway between a snort and a sigh

as he pulls the van out into traffic. "Thanks for coming, Anson."

"Hello, wizard. Here early for the Lustrum Review? Got to getta word inna King's ear first, eh?"

"Perhaps," Lovern says dryly, refusing to be baited. "Perhaps not."

"And how's my buddy, Eddie?"

Vera answers, "Arthur says that he is awake and alert. There was some fear of brain damage, but that is past. Arthur is agitating to take Eddie home. I'm supposed to ask you if you mind tending him on an upper floor—he has a broken leg."

"Not a problem, Lady Grey Eyes. I can spin a web and bring him down into the public places if he wishes. I think he will heal faster in his own rooms—keep him from trying to work too hard, eh?"

"I think so," Vera answers. "He's going to be worried about not pulling his weight while we prepare for the Review. Arthur has already told me that we need to keep him from fussing."

Anson A. Kridd chuckles, a deep, throaty sound that makes the coyote pup lick his fingers and wriggle in delight. "I think I can do that. Oh, yeah, that I can."

The drive back to the hacienda passes quickly as Anson asks after various athanor. By silent consensus, the others agree to wait to brief him about their secret enemy until the group is all safely returned to Pendragon Estates.

When they arrive, the Changer glances over at Lovern and says a single word.

"Yes."

✿◻✿

Logging off his rebellion website, Sven Trout rubs his eyes and permits himself a feeling of pride. The postings he has been reviewing for the past hour are so very promising. His little cadre of monsters and outcasts are ready to agitate for their rights. It's almost a pity that he can't stick to his original timetable and have them descend on Arthur for the Lustrum Review.

Two weeks, though . . . That's not much time to make all the arrangements. No, although he burns with impatience, he must bide until autumn.

Picking up the phone, he taps the numbers for Louhi's spell. After a brief pause during which he can imagine the confused computers passing on an improbable signal, he hears two sets of clicks. Luck is with him. Half the time, Louhi doesn't answer the connection. He suspects that it's pure cussedness on her part, keeping him on his toes, forcing him to leave a message she can dissect at her leisure.

"When shall we three meet again?" Sven intones.

"How about right now?" Louhi's beautiful voice is unamused. "I'll bring the Head on."

Sven waits while she does this, her success announced by a new voice saying: "Felicitations, fire-born, and mistress of magics. Your bodiless brother has long yearned for congenial converse. The hoary-bearded hawk has strangely silent been."

Sven frowns, his free hand burrowing in a bag of tortilla chips. "You mean you haven't heard from Lovern?"

"So said I."

"Sorta," Sven mutters. "Any thoughts why?"

Louhi cuts in. "I have a few conjectures. Head, by the spell that you wish from me, I bind you to answer simply . . ."

"Ever shall I obey thee."

"How often in noncrisis conditions does Lovern normally contact you?"

"In isolation silent . . ."

"Just tell me, dammit, if ever you have hoped for a body!"

"Once a week, maybe less often."

"And during a crisis?"

"Daily, sometimes every few hours."

"And how long has it been since you heard from him?"

"Three days."

Sven whistles. "Well, now, that *is* interesting. What are your conjectures, Lady Lou?"

He can almost see her scowl at his flippancy, but her chill voice could hardly become chiller.

"If Lovern is refraining from contacting Mimir's Head, then I suspect that your failed attack has made him fear for his life. During the long years he was captive to me, he also did not contact the Head.''

"Long years of lengthy, lingering, loneliness encircled the sorcerer's scion, creeping close as salt in the sea.''

"I'm sure.'' Louhi doesn't sound particularly sympathetic. "The spell by which I bound Lovern did not include a restriction against astral travel, but he was aware (having taught me himself) that I knew how to attack an astral body. Therefore, he protected himself by inaction, much to my dismay. I had hoped to follow him to the Head.''

"Do you think he knows that you're in on this?'' Sven asks worriedly.

"No, I do not,'' Louhi assures him. "I'm not the only magic worker who knows how to sever a silver cord. My guess is that Lovern is simply being cautious.''

"Then, dare we hope that he's going after the Head?'' Sven grins in anticipation. "How long will he do without access to his most powerful tool?''

"I assume that is a rhetorical question,'' Louhi says. "He can do without the Head indefinitely, but I doubt he will choose to do so. My guess is that he is planning to retrieve it.''

"The Sea King shall seek to stop him,'' the Head says. "His sea of hatred for the sorcerer's trespass has not ebbed.''

Sven shrugs. "Lovern must have a plan to deal with Duppy Jonah. If his plan fails, then I will negotiate with the Sea King to gain access to the Head. We have been allies in the past. However, I would prefer to wait until Lovern has failed. The Great Durag and I are, by nature, antithetical. I don't want to waste what regard he has for me.''

"That makes sense,'' Louhi agrees. "How goes everything else?''

"Eddie is recovering, but Arthur remains at his bedside, so I haven't been able to get another shot at him. On the good side, the King hasn't been home since my little encounter with the Changer. Anson A. Kridd is en route—he may even be there already—to serve as Eddie's nurse. My reporter is slower than I'd like. I'll need to toss something else his way. Everything is on edge, but nothing has fallen apart.''

"Still,'' Louhi responds with more kindness than Sven had

expected, "this may be all for the good. Now that we are waiting until autumn to spring our coup, it would not do to have Arthur's power base disintegrate too quickly. If it did, we might find ourselves with rivals when we raise the vote of no confidence."

"I had considered that as well," Sven says quickly, although, in fact, he had not. "Yes, the last thing we need is an extra party. We want people voting for us and against Arthur—not spending their vote on some other candidate."

"Proteus's potent blood . . ." the Head hints.

"Yes, yes," Sven says. "I'll keep trying to get some. Still, the Changer's blood won't do us much good until you are out of your undersea prison. Don't worry, I won't just be sitting on my hands until autumn comes."

"That reminds me," Louhi says, "of something I've been meaning to ask. Do you intend to attend the Lustrum Review?"

Sven frowns. "I hadn't decided. What does our prophet advise?"

"And answer simply," Louhi warns.

"If you are present," the Head says slowly, "then perhaps you shall be dismissed as the maker of this mischief."

"I agree," Louhi says. "And I shall snub you. If we are both present, we will be able to hide in plain sight."

"I can get into that," Sven answers, "though I really hate the Harmony Dance."

"You would," Louhi says dryly, "although being both in Accord and in Harmony is your greatest armor."

"I know." Sven sighs. "I know. We will use Arthur's Accord against him in the end."

Louhi agrees. "That is the plan."

The Head makes a coughing sound, although, not possessing lungs he cannot truly cough. "Within hacienda halls, there are many mansions—or at least sundry suites. Should one of you reside within . . ."

"That is a very interesting thought," Louhi says. "Unhappily, I cannot imagine that Arthur would be comfortable with Sven's presence. He would be certain to set a guard on him. Lovern would take similar precautions with me."

"Still," Sven chuckles, "we are members of the Accord. He's going to need to be tactful about assigning guards. If one of us is there, our mere presence will keep Arthur a bit off-balance.''

"True," Louhi says, as if she is reluctant to accept Sven's point.

"It's worth the try," Sven insists. "Do you want me to try, or do you want to?"

"You," the sorceress says. "I would love to have the chance, but my mingling with the crowd would be uncharacteristic. You, on the other hand, are most predictable when unpredictable."

Sven chortles. "I shall. What fun! I've been getting awfully tired of motel rooms. Arthur's hospitality should be prime. Does that cover all our business?"

"For me it does," Louhi says.

"Yes," the Head replies simply, mindful of incurring the sorceress's wrath.

"I'll check in with you both later," Sven promises. He hears two clicks, hangs up the receiver, and stares up at the ceiling. Then, swallowing a fiendish laugh, he picks up the telephone and enters a new number.

"Pendragon Productions," says Vera's voice.

"Hi, pretty lady, this is Sven Trout. I'm calling to see if I can have a room at Arthur's place during the Lustrum Review."

He hears her swallow hard, then the faint tapping of fingers on a keyboard.

"Uh, yes, we have some space. A single room is all."

"Great! I'll be in on the twentieth."

"I'll put you on the list."

"*Adios*, kiddo."

He hangs up, as delighted as if the entire thing had been his invention. Not only is this going to be fun, but with the Changer under the same roof, little problems like acquiring a vial of his blood should be as nothing.

As he stands, rubbing his hands together, Sven's laughter fills the little room with mirthless glee.

✿▣✿

At Arthur's hacienda, Vera sets the telephone in its cradle and stares with disbelief at the Yellowman painting on the wall opposite her desk. The peaceful tepees offer her no answers, so she gathers herself and walks out to the courtyard.

The Changer is there with his daughter, Lovern, and Anson. When Vera enters she is greeted by cordial nods. The puppy drops a rawhide chew toy on her foot in an invitation to play.

Idly picking up the toy and tossing it into the no-longer-flowering lilac bushes, Vera says, "I've done it again."

"What, Lady of the Owls?" Anson asks. "What horrible thing may you have done?"

"Sven Trout just called asking for a room in the hacienda during the Lustrum Review. I checked and saw that we still had a few—more people are attending electronically this year—and told him that we did. He'll be here the twentieth."

Lovern and Anson both look concerned, but the Changer, intercepting his daughter before she can drop the toy on Vera's foot again, shakes his head in confusion.

"I'm afraid I don't remember which one of us is calling himself Sven Trout. Is it a new name?"

"New since the last Review," Vera confirms. She takes a deep breath. "It's Loki."

"Oh." The monosyllable gives nothing away.

"You did what you must," Lovern says comfortingly. "By policy, the King's hospitality must be open to all in the Accord except for both members of a sworn and publicized vendetta. In the latter case, the first comer has precedence. Sven falls into neither of these categories. He may be trouble, but it is long since he declared any enmity to the King."

"That doesn't mean it isn't there," Vera says, pulling out one of the teak chairs and sitting. "I wonder what Eddie would have done?"

"The same thing," Anson assures her. "If the King plays favorites, then he is in a mess. Who is to know whether Sven had a truthstone or the like to detect if you were lying? If that had been the case, then we would have had a pretty kettle of fish, not just a single Trout."

"Odd name for him to chose," the Changer says.

"Doesn't legend say that it was in fish form that he was caught after one of his transgressions?"

"Yes," Lovern says, "it does, but most of those involved are gone now. I don't remember what happened precisely."

Vera pours herself iced tea from the common pitcher that stands in the center of the table. "Odd, isn't it?" she says. "We live for so long, but despite our abilities we still can forget, still can fear, still can make mistakes. What good is longevity if it doesn't lead to something like perfection?"

"That is a question for the philosophers among us," Lovern says. "I have often wondered if there is any purpose to anything at all, whether instigated by humans or by ourselves. Perhaps we each work within our individual bubble of time and nothing much lasts. Certainly I have seen enough of what I thought would be permanent vanish into nothing."

"As we all have, eh?" Anson agrees. "Lady, did your sojourns within convents not give you some answers?"

Vera shakes her head. "No. Some of the devoted sisters had visions of heaven. Cynics might say it was just a mental aberration, but I know that these women persistently held to a higher ideal despite the contradictions offered by the world. I wasn't so lucky."

Anson turns to the Changer, who has been listening while playing tug-of-war with the puppy.

"How about you, ancient?" the Spider asks. "You have been around longer than even I. What have you learned?"

The Changer's face is veiled by the fall of his dark hair, but they can hear the smile in his voice. "I have learned thousands of shapes, many long gone from this earth. I have learned that change alone is constant. I have learned that, for now, death has spared me, but whether that sparing is from purpose or from chance, I cannot say."

"Is that all?" Vera's tone, surprisingly, is pleading.

The Changer sits up and gathers his daughter into his lap where she promptly begins gnawing at his callused hand. "Vera, I have worn so many shapes that I have lost all belief in a constant truth. What is right and just to the rabbit is antithetical to what the coyote believes. Neither is right. Both are right. The same can be said for any opposition. Rarely is one side completely wrong."

"What about Hitler's atrocities?" Vera challenges.

"I would not have cared to be one of those in the prison camps; that is why I am so rarely a prey creature. I cherish this life, despite its length." He meets her eyes. "However, consider, would the state of Israel be so strong now without the memory of Hitler's atrocities to bolster it?"

Lovern strokes his beard sagely. "Our people have the advantage of seeing good come out of apparent evil . . ."

Anson interrupts. "Or evil from apparent good. Consider how 'good' actions like the damming of rivers for irrigation and better food production lead to evil when the stagnating waters breed creatures like the snails that carry schistosomiasis flukes or malaria-bearing mosquitoes."

"And even that," the Changer adds levelly, "could be said to be good for the snail or the mosquito, although it has been a long time since I considered either of those shapes particularly advantageous."

Uncertain whether he is joking or not, the other three let this pass. A silence arises, broken only by the playful growls of the puppy.

Reaching across to stroke her, Anson says, "When are you going to give her a name, Changer?"

"A name?"

"We can't go on calling her 'the puppy' for much longer." Anson chuckles, as the pup looks up at him, long ears perked. "She is all ears, eyes, and tail now, but to these eyes she's clearly a coyote. And she knows when she's being talked about."

"True." The Changer studies his daughter. "In all my long life, I have never met this particular challenge. Animals know each other by scent, by established precedence."

"What did you call your coyote wife?" Vera asks curiously. "The one who just died. You were together a long time."

"Five years," the Changer agrees. "Long enough. I called her 'Mine' or 'Darling.' "

He laughs at Vera's expression. "She called me about the same. It wasn't really words. It was attitude. The pups were simply 'Ours' or 'Mine' as opposed to anyone else's. As they grew, I suppose we gave them names of a sort: Big Male, Second Male, Weak Male. Female pups often stay with their parents for eighteen months rather than six, but that didn't change things. The female who died with her mother was simply 'Biggest Girl.' ''

''Where did this one fit in the pecking order?'' Lovern asks, moving his handmade leather boot away from the puppy's jaws.

''Runt,'' the Changer says bluntly. ''She probably wouldn't have lasted the summer. Unless her larger siblings met with accidents, she wouldn't have been able to compete for food and would have stayed small. That would have made her vulnerable to owls or bobcats or even dogs. There are lots of things that kill little creatures of any species.''

Anson looks at the leggy young canine. ''She certainly can't be called Runt now.''

''No.''

There is a thoughtful pause as the athanor study the puppy.

''We could call her 'Goldy,' '' Vera suggests, then shakes her head. ''No, too much like a pet. She's your *daughter*.''

''Don't some humans use that name?'' the Changer asks, slightly puzzled. ''I'm certain I've heard it.''

''True,'' Vera agrees. ''Still, it doesn't seem quite right.''

''Call her Shahrazad,'' Anson offers, ''of the long tail.''

''Shahrazad?'' Lovern says in disbelief.

''After the lady who told the stories in *The Thousand and One Nights*,'' Anson says. ''She was clever and brave—as coyotes are supposed to be clever—and she lived a long and, ultimately, prosperous life.''

''She even had an uncertain start to that life,'' Vera adds eagerly, ''like this little one. What do you think, Changer?''

''Shahrazad . . .'' The shapeshifter tries out the name as if tasting it. ''I like both the sound and the portents. If the pup will answer to it, then let it be her name.''

''Another advantage,'' Lovern says, joining the game, ''is that it sounds like nothing else in English, so she won't become confused.''

''Shahrazad, daughter of the Changer,'' Anson says. ''Yes, I like it.''

The puppy, hearing the repetition and sensing that she is somehow at the center of it, happily wags her tail.

Tact consists in knowing how far to go in going too far.

—JEAN COCTEAU

THE FOLLOWING DAY, EDDIE COMES HOME FROM THE HOSpital amid, as Anson notes, "much rejoicing."

Later that same day, Jonathan Wong arrives. He is a small, rather rotund Asian man. Despite the general informality of Arthur's household, he is attired in a charcoal grey suit, white shirt, and muted red tie.

Anson, who has come first to the door, embraces him. Jonathan squeezes back with surprising strength.

"I am delighted to see you, Spider."

"More than the King is," Anson says. "I make him nervous, but he will be oh so happy to learn you have arrived. Do you want to go directly to his office?"

"That would be best."

Arthur greets Jonathan with a handshake. "How are things in Boston?"

"Quite good. I have closed down Yu Tz'u's enterprises and can concentrate on this life's law practice."

Arthur nods, knowing that it has been a decade at least since Jonathan gave up his identity as Yu Tz'u, Hong Kong exporter. Still, such slow carefulness is typical of the man once known as Confucius.

Born in southern Shantung, in the year 551 B.C., Jonathan

151

had become famous under the name K'ung-Fu-tzu. After his "death" in his early seventies, Confucius had changed his name and gone into another province. Unlike many athanor, he had never believed he was alone in his immortality. The same logical and analytical mind that had shaped a philosophical code that would evolve into the next best thing to a religion would not permit such arrogance.

Methodically, Confucius had begun looking for indications of other immortals. In one village he found a pet bird whose owner insisted that it had been passed down from family member to family member for six generations. He remained in that village for forty years. At the end of those years, the bird was still thriving, although those who had introduced it to Confucius were now all dust.

Leaving the bird (which had achieved the status of a local god and so was assured of good treatment), Confucius continued his travels. In time, he found what he sought—other athanor. Some of these were arrogant and brash, like the self-proclaimed "god" Susano of Nippon. Others were more interested in living quietly and well. Each gave him useful advice for surviving in societies where he would outlive those around him.

Armed with this advice and his own good sense, Confucius continued to dwell primarily in the Middle Kingdom and to prosper. Among athanor, his talent for rational judgment was something of a legend. Along with Vera, he had often served as a judge in athanor tribunals.

Remembering this, and details from Jonathan's other lives, Arthur is heartened. There is nothing like tending to daily business to distract one from problems.

✡◉✡

Despite Arthur's plea that they remain, the Changer and Lovern depart soon after Jonathan's arrival. The Changer now bears driver's license, credit cards, and a checkbook.

Before they leave, the Changer consigns the care of Shahrazad to Vera and Anson. "She shouldn't be too much trouble," he says, glancing at the pup with a forbidding eye. "We've been here for going on three weeks now. I doubt she remembers her wild home as anything but vague memories. Keep her in the courtyard and away from strangers, and all should be well.''

"She'll miss you," Vera says, stroking Shahrazad between her oversized ears. "I think she knows that you're going."

"She does," the Changer says, an impish grin about his lips. "I told her, just as I told her to stay here and obey you. Whether she heeds my orders . . . well, I can't promise."

"What parent can?" Anson agrees. "I certainly never have been able to make such promises for my children. Nor have they been able to do so for me, come to think of it."

He laughs and Shahrazad wriggles, her momentary unhappiness forgotten. Leaving her with her toys, the group drifts to the front door where a cab waits.

"Hurry back," Vera says as they depart, speaking as if to both, but it is the Changer that her grey gaze follows.

Anson notices, but, flippant as he can be, he chooses not to comment. Instead, he walks to the kitchen and gathers a couple of sandwiches left from making the travelers' care package. Then he hurries up to Eddie's room where his charge should be waking from his morning's nap.

Vera stands in the doorway a moment longer, then closes the door and heads for her office. Work is a good antidote for worry. And for other unsettling emotions as well.

✿◙✿

At Albuquerque International Airport, Lovern and the Changer check in, then walk to their gate. There, Lovern indicates a couple of empty seats. Crafted from wood, their washable fabric backs and seats adorned with brass upholstery tacks, they are modeled after Spanish Colonial designs.

"Shall we sit here?" he says. "We have almost an hour to wait until the flight."

"I think I'll stand," the Changer says. "Soon enough we'll be penned in on the plane."

Once seated, Lovern pulls out a book—a technothriller, the Changer notes—and the Changer strolls over to the window. Beyond the thick glass pane, ground vehicles bearing luggage, food, and fuel scuttle beneath the giant aircraft.

They remind him of egrets around a herd of elephants or remora around a shark. He amuses himself with this fancy, studying the machines and realizing that he hasn't the least idea how they work.

The Smith had tried to explain airplanes to him once, waxing enthusiastic about propellers and jets, flaps and rudders. Although the Changer himself has flown for almost as long as any creature on earth (the incentive to do so being one of the things that had urged him to alter his early millennia of existence), still the method by which things of metal, heavily laden with fuel and people, can fly escapes him.

He wonders if he has reached the limits of what he can comprehend. The thought troubles him, recalling something his brother had said centuries before humans diverged from the rest of the primates. The conversation had not been in words, but in memory the Changer casts it so, as if he is writing a play.

They had been sea creatures then, great plesiosaurs, sleek, swift, and deadly. The memory of these particular creatures had led somewhat to the legends of sea serpents, although the sea serpents themselves had done more.

Duppy Jonah is the name the Changer's brother currently uses among their kind. It means "Jonah's Ghost" and is the origin of the sailor's nickname "Davy Jones." Perhaps he uses the name out of deference to Arthur—rather than calling himself the Sea King as so many still do. Perhaps he uses it out of a cynical desire to emphasize his own recent diminished status.

Duppy Jonah had not been pleased when his sea-born brother had ventured more and more onto land. "I cannot understand why you should shape land dwellers. They are uncouth and graceless. They lack our dexterity and beauty. And they are so vulnerable."

"There is an entire aspect of the world that you are missing, brother," the Changer answers. "Warm winds carry smells and noises that tell me of things unknown beneath the sea. I feel my mind actually growing as I expose myself to them, as I comprehend more and more concepts. Just as when we first isolated ourselves from the mass, venturing onto land is an expansion of the finest type."

The words had not been there—no more than a coyote has a word for danger or a raven for fear. But, just as a coyote can know what danger is without having a word for it, or a raven can feel fear without articulating the verb, so had he and his brother, already aware that they differed from the greater number of living things around them, expressed the ideas of change and the resistance to change.

Time and again Duppy Jonah had ventured onto land over the unrolling centuries, had learned many shapes, but his allegiance remained to the deeps, and his descendants bore shapes that sometimes mingled elements from land and sea: mermaids, sea serpents, hippocampi. Others, like the selkies, learned magic, shed their seal skins, and went ashore in human form.

A perky young female in a blouse and skirt vaguely reminiscent of a military uniform begins the boarding process, pulling the Changer from his memories. With Lovern, he joins the line shuffling forward.

Once aboard, situated in first-class seating, they try to ignore the envious or resentful glances of the less fortunate passengers. Taking out his thriller, Lovern tucks the rest of his bag under the seat. The Changer debates having a sandwich and decides to wait until he sees what the airline has to offer. Closing his eyes, he begins to make himself comfortable.

"What are you doing?" Lovern hisses in his ear.

"Taking a few inches off my hips and shoulders, shortening my legs slightly," the Changer responds softly. "These seats may be roomier than those in back, but they're far from generous."

Lovern sighs enviously and opens his book, but he doesn't read. Instead he sits staring blankly at the page.

"I wish I could have checked the odds that this plane will come to difficulty."

"With the Head?"

"Yes."

"You use it for such small things?"

"Why not? It is an available resource." The wizard pauses. "Or was."

"And soon will be again."

"I hope."

Feeling rawly pleased with himself, Sven Trout drives to Santa Fe. His spy-eyes (more of Louhi's work) have confirmed that Lovern and the Changer have departed. A bit of cunning telephone work (if he does say so himself) has confirmed for him that they are heading to the Florida coast—a hopeful sign.

His early-morning dip into the offerings on his website had also been encouraging. Arthur may not know it, but the drums of change are sounding and, as with the trumpeting of Joshua's horn at Jericho, soon the walls will come tumbling down.

Awash in self-satisfaction, the miles melt under his tires. When he pulls into the gated community where Tommy Thunderburst resides, his euphoria has hardly diminished.

"Pity I can't bottle *this* feeling," he muses to himself as he crosses the lawn to Tommy's town house.

Neither his ring of the bell nor polite thumping on the door brings any answer. Pressing his ear to the door, he hears a dull bass thudding. Tommy is in then, just absorbed in his music.

Ten days have passed since Sven's last meeting with the immortal musician. Ten days during which, he hopes, Tommy will have learned the joys contained in the little package of powder. Ambling around the town house, Sven comes to where elegant French doors stand ajar. The sound of the music is louder here, just at the border of what might make a neighbor complain.

Stepping through the doors and into the living room of the town house, Sven pulls the doors shut behind him. It wouldn't do to have anyone interrupt them now.

Tommy sits hunched over a keyboard in one corner, his shaggy hair masking his face, his long fingers dancing over the keys. A drum machine provides the bass line and, apparently, he is listening to other instruments over earphones.

He could, Sven thought, have performed the entire operation in apparent silence thanks to modern electronics, but this is not Tommy's idiom. Instead sound leaks out around him and, with it, a trace of the wild charisma that accompanies his music no matter what style his compositions take.

Sven knows that waiting for Tommy to finish playing of his own accord is one of the more useless ways to spend time—quite equal with drying raindrops or bottling the wind. Therefore, he waves his hand in Tommy's face. When the musician looks up, Sven notices that the amethyst thunderbird is around his neck.

"Hey, you!" Tommy says by way of greeting. "You're *here*."

Sven nods. "That's right. I was in the neighborhood and decided to drop in. How are things with you?"

"Pretty good." Removing the headphones, Tommy rises, stretching to loosen muscles cramped from sitting crouched over the keyboard. "The album is going to be released this month. Lil says that the prelim reviews are good. The video's done, too. I've just been noodling."

"Sounded good for noodling."

"That piece is gonna be called 'She Ripped My Head Off and Ate My Mind.' It's for Lil."

Sven makes a noncommittal noise, uncertain whether Tommy means the song as tribute or insult to the woman who has been his keeper and manager for centuries. Tommy spares him the need for further comment by drifting into the kitchen.

"There's coffee here somewhere, and tea. Want some?"

Sven glances into the kitchen, notices the dirty dishes and pizza box with its shreds of dry cheese, and decides that anything he drinks here had better be boiled in his presence. He may be immortal, but he isn't foolish.

"Tea, thanks."

While Tommy fills the kettle and sets it on the gas range to heat, Sven glances around the untidy living areas. What he sees gives him something like hope. The room is messy, but not descended into squalor. In the heaps of cans and bottles, he sees no evidence that Tommy is taking anything stronger than caffeine—and even that in moderation. Either that means he has finally beaten his tendency toward addiction or . . .

"How're you enjoying the stuff I gave you?" Sven asks, picking his way around a heap of fried-chicken cartons and going to the sink to rinse a mug.

Tommy's expression is beatific. "Cool. Really hot. Makes me feel great. Even laid off it for two days and didn't crave it. And I passed a drug test like nobody's bizz."

"Great." Sven takes the tea bag Tommy hands him and drops it into his newly washed mug. "Have you told Lil about it?"

"Naw. She asked where I got the T-bird. I told her from a fan at the recording studio. She didn't ask anything else."

"That's nice."

"I thought so."

Uncharacteristically, Tommy fidgets. Sven lets him stew, wanting the musician to be the one to ask. He sips his cup of tea and toys with a lucite sculpture of a saxophone.

"Hey, uh . . ."

Sven looks at the musician, apparently incurious, though his nerves are singing crossroads. "Yes?"

"Do you . . . Do you have any more of that stuff you gave me? I'm almost out and . . . I don't *need* it. I mean I put it by for two whole days, man, but I kinda *like* it, if y'know what I mean."

"Of course I do," Sven says. "I might have some more."

"I have money."

"I'm certain you do. Why would I want your money?"

"What do you want?" Tommy's leonine features are petulant, like a child who expects to be told to clean his room before he can have a cookie. Given the state of the rooms Sven can see, it must be a long time between cookies for Tommy Thunderburst.

"What do I *want*?" Sven feigns hurt. "I just want you to live up to your potential without chemical meltdown."

"Yeah?"

"Absolutely."

Sven reaches into his vest pocket and pulls out a packet containing, with conservative use, another ten days' supply. He doubts whether Tommy, having convinced himself the stuff is free from negative side effects, will bother to ration his use.

"Here you are, Tommy," he says, handing over the

packet. "That's all I have right now. I should have more by the twenty-first. Are you going to be at Arthur's?"

"The Review," Tommy says, looking up from the pale blue packet with visible effort. "Yeah. I'm going with Lil."

"I'll be there, too," Sven says. "If you need more, speak to me there, but remember, be discreet. Lil won't understand."

"Right." Tommy sets the packet down on the piano. "Where are you staying, man?"

"Here and there," Sven answers. "I have a room at Arthur's for during the Review. You can't miss me."

"But what if I need . . ." Tommy swallows hard and starts again. "What if I have something for you? I thought you might want a copy of my new CD."

"Keep it for then," Sven says. "I don't have a player with me now, so I couldn't enjoy it."

Tommy nods. After a few more minutes of sporadic conversation, a conversation in which the packet of blue powder is a silent participant, Sven takes his leave.

He's whistling as he heads down the walk toward his car, seeing in his mind's eye slender fingers ripping open a cellophane envelope and spilling just a little pale blue powder onto the varnished black of the piano.

¤◙¤

From the Irish lace–curtained front window of her town house, Lil Prima watches the red-haired man strut down the walk and (ignoring the signs requesting otherwise) across the grass. He has changed his appearance considerably (although he keeps that flaming red hair) but she knows him: Loki, Loge, Set, Fire-born, Fire's Friend, Troublemaker, Trickster.

The directory provided by Arthur and his organizers notes that Loki is calling himself Sven Trout now, a name fraught with ill portents to her way of seeing things, but then, Loki whistling is ill portent enough.

Ill for whom, though? That is the question she wants answered as she turns from the window. Perhaps it is merely for Tommy. She knows that Tommy has a new drug, a blue powder that he either sniffs or packs close to his gums. She

knows, too, that the amethyst thunderbird he wears so faith-
fully is a potent charm against intoxication. For now, she has
not interfered with his use of either.

Vine-wreathed deity out of the north, Dionysus has been
associated with intoxication even longer than with music.
Music now substitutes for chemical stimulants, but the sub-
stitution has not made him immune to the lure of the external
high. Lil doesn't try to keep Tommy from either music or
dope; she simply moderates his indulgence in the latter until
he has exhausted what music can bring to him. A fall from
the heights is so much more dramatic than a stumble into a
ditch.

So does Sven merely desire Tommy's addiction, or is there
some larger plot under way?

She hasn't forgotten the Changer's unexpected visit or the
uncompromising fury in his yellow eyes as he asked his terse
questions. Had he remained convinced that she was responsible for those coyotes' deaths, she would have died that day.
She does not doubt this, just as she does not doubt that she
would have severely hurt the Changer before breathing her
last.

And on whose side would Vera have fought? Would her
sense of justice place her on the side of the wronged Changer
or on the side of the Accord's ruling that any conflicts between their kind must take place in secrecy lest the battles
of the few reveal the existence of the many?

Biting into one Cupid's bow lip, Lilith spits her own blood
into a shallow basin of polished Nambé-ware, then adds
warm water and scented oil. The metal—pewter sheened with
a touch of silver brightness—reflects back the pink of the
mixture.

Lilith is old, older than Arthur, whom she views as a useful
latecomer, older than most of the human-form kind. She publicly claims to be Adam's first wife, a claim she likes as it
sets so many on edge. Odd how, having made mythology
themselves, they are still captives to its power.

Blood, oil, and water have separated into distinct levels.
Chanting softly in an extinct language, she sweeps an elegantly manicured hand over the basin and gazes green-eyed
into the reflective surface.

The scrying ritual is usually reliable. She has employed it

to keep track of Tommy, jealous rage feeding immortal bitterness as she voyeuristically participates in his amours. He has never loved her. She is not certain if she loves him, but she knows that she desires him. His self-destructive nature is counterpart to her destructiveness. He is a willing victim who would sacrifice himself if no one else was present to lift the knife.

As maenad, lover, goddess, and, lately, manager, she has wielded that knife, taking part in his self-destruction, feeling a frisson each time, as if at the lowest point their souls might merge and each provide what the other is lacking.

That union has never happened. Time after time she has drawn him back just as he was dying, nursed and guarded him in a fashion that she had once believed was foreign to her nature. When he is strong once more, then begins his spiral downward and the quest for completion at the borderlands of death.

Today, however, she does not try to see what Tommy is doing. The answer she seeks is what connects three things: the death of a family of coyotes, an ancient shapeshifter, and herself. She has her suspicions, but certainty is always preferable.

The oil in the basin vibrates, concentric rings forming in the center and rippling outward. Then the blood separates from the water and pools atop the oil. When it spreads thin, the image it makes is of Sven Trout, his hair the same color as the blood, driving south on I-25. Two faces are faintly sketched behind him: a drowned man and a woman with hair the color of ice.

The entire image fractures as Lil seeks to bring these dim faces into focus. Blood drops steam into a noisome vapor, and the oil burns. Someone has a protective spell in place and does not care who is injured by its operation.

Quickly, Lil pulls back from the flames. She has a partial answer. Sven Trout and two others she did not recognize tried to frame her for the death of the Changer's family.

What to do with that knowledge?

Arthur would certainly be able to use it, but, no matter how grateful she is to him for leading the Changer into caution, she does not think that he deserves the information for nothing. In any case, who is to say that she would not approve of what Sven is planning?

Clearly he has some use for Tommy. That is as obvious as the amethyst pendant the musician wears about his neck. That Sven considers Lil a possible impediment to his plans seems equally possible, but, since the attempt to set the Changer on Lil, no harm has come to her. Therefore, Sven may simply have viewed Lil as disposable.

Rinsing out her scrying bowl, Lilith smiles. Sven has a use for Tommy. That purpose might drive the musician to new highs or new lows, either of which might provide the transformation of spirit she has been awaiting these past several millennia.

For now she will watch and wait. It could be that in using Tommy, Sven will be of service to her and, if not? Well, she hasn't survived to her current age without learning a few tricks, tricks that should be sufficient to extinguish even *that* fiery trickster.

✡◻✡

Clad in baggy shorts and a tee shirt printed with a palm tree, the Changer sprawls in sleep on a Mickey Mouse towel spread out on the sand of a private beach on the coast of Florida.

Lovern sits beside him in a low-slung beach chair. He is dressed in what from a distance would appear to be an ivory-colored beach caftan. It is actually a mage's robe hand-embroidered with signs and sigils of power in thread only slightly darker than the fabric itself.

The two athanor had arrived in Florida the night before and had driven to this place, a beachfront estate owned (through intermediaries) by Arthur. Long hours within metal planes and cars had given Lovern the equivalent of a magical migraine. A shower, a good meal (fresh fish caught by the Changer), and a long nap have restored him. For the last several hours, he has occupied himself with reviewing the spells and inspecting the amulets that he will use to descend into Duppy Jonah's realm.

Although Lovern would never admit it aloud, he is annoyed by the shapeshifter's nonchalance. Certainly, the Changer is *old*, but doesn't he fear anything? If Lovern had survived from the dawn of life, he would do everything in his power to cling to continued existence. The Changer, though, seems to act with animal caution, but no particular . . .

Lovern sighs. He begins chanting a mantra he had learned in Tibet. Envy toward an ally is a foolish thing and, no matter why, for now the Changer is an ally.

When he has composed his soul, Lovern loudly clears his throat. He has already learned that waking the Changer by touching him is not wise.

"Yes?" The Changer makes the transition from sleeping to waking as a cat might, fully alert, with no lingering grogginess.

"I'm ready to depart at your convenience."

"Are there any sandwiches left?"

"A couple, turkey and provolone, I think." Lovern grins as the Changer digs into the cooler. "Didn't anyone ever tell you not to eat heavily before going swimming?"

The Changer laughs at the joke. "I'll want the extra energy for the shift. How are you traveling?"

Lovern shrugs. "Human-form. I have magics for such."

"Cumbersome, but I guess you know best." Finishing the sandwiches and draining a bottle of water, the Changer starts removing his clothing. "I thought I'd go as a bottle-nosed dolphin. They're not unheard of in these waters, and I like them. Do you know dolphin song?"

"Some," Lovern says proudly. "I studied it in Haiti."

"Good." The Changer shakes the sand from his shorts and shirt, folds them and his towel, and stuffs the lot into the now-empty cooler. "Do we need to put this in the house?"

"Not a bad idea."

Lovern considers commenting that strolling around nude might not be precisely polite—Arthur *does* have caretakers who drop in from time to time—but he dismisses the idea. There would be a lot more trouble if anyone sees the two of them descending into the sea and not emerging. The spell he plans to ensure against that should cover the other contingency as well.

Besides, he suspects the Changer would ignore any chiding.

When the Changer returns, Lovern's spells are ready. Side by side, as if they were a pair of more usual bathers, they walk down the white-sand beach. Little licks of water splash about their ankles and knees, the lapping tongues of warm, salty cats.

"Ride the horses of Lir!" the Changer says, running forward and diving into the surf. A dolphin emerges, bobbing and leaping, whistling joyously.

"A pretty image," Lovern says.

He has waded waist-deep now, but his robe does not become wet; rather it moves freely within the water like a bit of seaweed or mermaid's hair. Atop the staff he clasps firmly in one hand, a cut-crystal sphere glows with lambent, orange light.

In a few more steps he is fully submerged and walking along the sandy bottom. A few curious fish dart up to his light and then away again. Crustaceans scuttle across the bottom waving their claws, whether in threat or greeting is difficult to say.

"They will tell their master," the wizard says to the dolphin who swims at his side.

The dolphin's whistle suggests their master knows already.

"It is difficult to be sure, isn't it?" Lovern says. "What are the limits of the Sea King?"

If the dolphin knows, his answering whistle gives away no secrets. Instead it queries how far must they travel to find where Lovern has secreted Mimir's Head.

"I can shorten the distance magically," Lovern says, "but, as I mentioned before, I fear I cannot remove the Head without Duppy Jonah's knowledge. I would prefer an interview with him before undertaking the task. It seems more mannerly."

The dolphin laughs and rises to the surface for air.

Their journey takes on a curiously timeless feeling, one familiar to the Changer from his sea-born existence. Beneath the sea, sound is muted, as is light. Fire is unknown. Even volcanos bubble, steam, and struggle rather than engulf. Air in all her manifestations but one is unknown. Zephyr, breeze, gale, tornado: All are mostly known for their effects upon the surface.

Breath within the lungs of dolphin, whale, seal, wizard, breath alone carries air into the realms where water is emperor.

Traveling beneath the water one easily forgets the world above, quickly recalls how the seas hold dominion over most of the globe and that, even where there is land, the stubbornest divisions are those caused by rivers and lakes.

So as the wizard and the shapeshifter walk slowly beneath the sea, the sun sinks beneath the waters and the stars come to flirt with the whitecaps. The moon wheels above, and the oceans feel her pull as does no other entity on the Earth.

This connection to space beyond the globe makes the creatures of the sea philosophical and contemplative. They *know*, in a fashion that land-born creatures can only intellectualize, that there is a universe beyond the gravity well.

Near noon the following day, the dolphin submerges after one of his trips to the surface, hurrying to rejoin the wizard.

During their travels they have reached deep ocean. Lovern no longer strolls through the sand at the bottom, but walks in a middle distance, his feet striding upon nothing of substance. If the long hours of maintaining his magics have wearied him, he does not show any sign. His bearded features remain serene, and the orange light atop his staff glows as strongly.

"When I rose to breathe this last time," the dolphin whistles, "I was met by Mother Carey's chickens. They say that their mistress would have words with us."

"Above?" Lovern asks.

"There is a place that has been prepared," the dolphin answers, and his whistles express mirth independent of the perpetual grin of his long jaw.

Lovern glances up and sees the dark shadow of something floating on the water.

"A boat?"

"Something like that," the dolphin agrees. "Mother Carey is Duppy Jonah's queen. You should not keep her waiting if you expect to avoid his wrath."

"I know . . ." Lovern bites off the rest of his sentence and begins to walk upward, as a man ashore might walk up a steep hill. "I had thought that Duppy Jonah himself might meet us."

The dolphin only grins and swims to the surface.

When Lovern arrives, he understands immediately why the Changer was amused. Floating on the waves, bobbing gently with every caprice of wind, is the wreck of an old tall ship—a Spanish galleon, he thinks.

The ship's masts are broken, their sails gone. The hull is pierced by several gaping holes. What remains intact is carpeted with barnacles, oysters, and other, less solid, clinging things. The deck is awash with seaweed and slime. All the metal fittings are green with corrosion or white with shellfish. Only the wheel stands as it must have once, wood smooth and solid, brass brilliant, glinting in the midday sun.

All along the broken side rails and on the stubs of the mast storm petrels and seagulls squawk. There are many varieties: white, grey, piebald in black or tan. They laugh shrilly as the wizard floats out of the sea and lands on the deck. Nor are the birds any more impressed when the dolphin becomes a naked man clad only in clinging black hair who climbs agilely aboard.

"Mother Carey's chickens," Lovern says, observing the seabirds with less than pleasure. "Where is their mistress?"

"Here," says a voice as soft and breathy as the sound of the sea caught in a shell.

They turn as one to find a mermaid seated upon the deck near the wheel. Her hair is seaweed green, her skin pearlescent fair, shimmering with many soft pastel hues. The scales of her fish tail glitter like emeralds but the fins are sea-foam white, as are her round breasts with their coral nipples.

She is younger than many of their kind, born after humanity had taken to sailing over the waves in masted ships. Some say that she was shaped by human myths, others that she is the source of them. It hardly matters. Call her Amphitrite, the Sea Witch, Meerfrau, or the pedestrian Mother Carey, none contests that she is the Queen of the Sea.

Nor is she Queen merely by virtue of her partnership with Duppy Jonah. Her claim is hers by right and none, least of all the sea lord who loves her, question it.

"Don't you like my chickens?" Mother Carey asks Lovern, in tones of thinly veiled malice.

"I find them noisy and dirty," the wizard says bluntly.

"I find them graceful and daring," the Sea Queen answers, "and far more helpful servants to me than yours are to you, I warrant. Who is the dark man in your shadow, standing like a liege man behind his lord?"

The Changer is too old to be enraged so easily, but he also does not suffer impudence. He smiles, and the yellow in his eyes hardens to amber. "Greetings, sister. Surely you are not so reduced in your abilities to not know the Changer when he enters your realm?"

Mother Carey giggles, her mood shifting as quickly as that of the sea. "I simply wondered at the company you keep, dear brother. This skulking wizard . . ."

"Is not skulking today," the Changer interrupts. "He has come here openly and sought audience with you."

"And I have granted it," she says, producing an ivory comb from somewhere about her person and combing out her green hair. "What do you wish, Lovern?"

Like Arthur, Lovern has had his difficulties with women— Nimue being only the most notorious of his failed relationships. He neither trusts them, nor, within his darkest soul, believes them to be fully his peers, a misapprehension that has cost him repeatedly in the past and, the Changer muses, seems about to cost him again.

"I had come to treat with Duppy Jonah," he begins, "but I believe you can speak for him."

Mother Carey frowns, not pleased with Lovern's dismissive approach. "I wonder that you have lived to your great age, wizard. Speak quickly and mind what you say."

The waters about the ruined ship have begun to grow rough, though the wind has not risen. The Changer contemplates the wizard and decides that the time to intervene has not yet come.

"I . . ." Lovern swallows and starts again. "I simply meant to acknowledge your supremacy, Mother Carey. I have come to beg safe passage through the seas for me and a thing of my making."

"A thing you stored beneath these waters when I was but a child?" she asks teasingly. "A thing that you never asked my lord for permission to store within his realm? A thing whose power has been masked and protected by the ocean's depth without any thanks from you?''

Lovern looks as if he wishes to challenge, to qualify her statements, but he merely swallows again and nods.

"Yes, ma'am."

Mother Carey's expression softens, and the Changer judges that this is the time to intervene.

"Lovern acknowledges his rudeness, sister . . ."

His words are broken off when the ocean to the starboard of the wrecked galleon erupts in a waterspout. The battered hulk tosses in the waves, but miraculously does not break.

When all on deck are thoroughly soaked and the seabirds are a shrieking white cloud above, the water peels back, shaping the petals of a lily. From the heart of that lily, the head of a serpent rises and regards them.

It is twice the size of the wrecked ship and bearded as a dragon, but far more sinuous. The Changer recognizes it as the shape his brother wore when he battled beside Loki at Ragnarokk.

"He may have acknowledged his rudeness," the serpent hisses, his breath a wind cutting sharp, "but he has not apologized: not to her for his manner, not to me for his abuse. Who does this youngling think he is?"

The air stills, not calm, but torpid, holding the faint ringing brassiness that heralds an approaching storm.

"He knows what he is," the Changer replies, speaking honestly for one he does not completely trust, "a wizard of power, a man of influence, an athanor who—although young as you and I count the years—has still lived millennia."

The great sea serpent's whiskers quiver in what might be fury, might be swallowed laughter: "And why are you with him?"

"He knew he had wronged you," the Changer answers bluntly, "and he hoped that my presence would soften your wrath."

"As it has," Duppy Jonah admits. "It is good to have my sea-born brother come home."

"For a visit," the Changer says. "I have a whelp I am responsible for in this life. Her mother is slain, her sisters and brothers as well. The same enemy—or so we believe—

has sought my life, Lovern's, and that of Arthur's man, Edward.''

"Enkidu?"

"The same."

"I have enjoyed speaking with that boy," Duppy Jonah says. "He has wrestled with me as heroes of legend were said to have wrestled with Proteus. That takes courage."

"It does," the Changer agrees.

"And he has the good sense to find my wife beautiful."

"That is only the truth."

From her place beside the wrecked ship's wheel the Sea Queen reaches to stroke the sea serpent's neck, her hand smaller than even the comparatively delicate scales on the monster's throat.

"And an enemy has sought this brave man's life?"

"He owes his life to luck."

"And the same enemy sought your life?"

"So I believe."

"Do you know who it is?"

"I do not, and the trail has run cold time and again."

"And this one"—for the first time during the audience the serpent's gaze turns toward Lovern—"believes that his black art may serve to reveal the assassin?"

"He does," the Changer answers. He feels Lovern stiffen at the charge of black magic.

"Why can he not visit his tool as he has for these long years? I have sensed his ghost-shape coming through my realms."

"He fears for his life."

Lovern's teeth snap as he bites back a protest.

"Many fears," Duppy Jonah muses. "He fears the assassin; he fears my wrath, and he fears not to confront either fear."

Amphitrite nods. "It seems to me that Lovern is wise, my love. Fear is the law of the sea. Even those who love the ocean—the sailors, the fishers, the sea creatures—fear the temper of the waves. We cannot fault the wizard for fearing."

"No."

The vast serpent considers Lovern in silence, then says, "We will not grant your boon for naught, wizard. Consider what your tool is worth. Meantime, we shall consider what we will charge for the passage you request and''—Duppy Jonah begins to sink beneath the waves—''there is the issue of back rent.''

He disappears, leaving a series of concentric ripples to mark the place of his going. The mermaid waits a moment longer.

''Our palace in the deeps is open to you now. The way will be found easily by the Changer.''

Then she dives over the side. At the moment of her departing, the galleon begins to sink, heralded by the indignant cries of the seabirds.

Still man-form, the Changer turns to Lovern.

''Do you go on?''

''What choice do I have?'' the wizard says bitterly.

''Going back, continuing your astral ventures, making a lifelong enemy of my brother.''

''I do not concern myself with the last.''

''You bluster,'' the Changer says. ''He is more powerful than Arthur. Only his tie to the oceans has made him less active in athanor business. If he so chose, he could undo Arthur's Accord in a moment.''

''Why . . .''

''We do not have time to discuss further,'' the Changer says. The water tugs at his chest hair with playful fingers. ''I wish to know if you plan to treat fairly with my brother.''

''I suppose that I must.''

''Wise of you. Cast your spells then, and I will guide you.''

Dolphin, again, and man cloaked in power, they enter the waters. The wrecked ship shudders as it surrenders to the waters' embrace. Its timbers crack, the hull breaks, and it is scattered onto the sand far beneath the touch of the sun.

12

*If thine enemy hunger, feed him; if he
thirst, give him drink: for in so doing
thou shalt heap coals of fire on his head.*
—NEW TESTAMENT ROMANS XII, 20

Demetrios>> They're building a freeway off-ramp near my place
to serve a new subdivision. There goes the neighborhood!

Rebecca>> Will it hurt your dancing field?

Demetrios>> About a quarter of a mile farther south. Will ruin
"my" field, though. Privacy will be shot. I'm thinking about
moving again. Pity. I've been here fifty years. Guess I shouldn't
gripe. Would have had to move in ten or twenty anyhow.

Monk>> Even the human-form have to move time to time. It's
getting harder to transfer assets, too. I understand that there's
going to be a workshop about it at the Lustrum Review.

Rebecca>> Of course, none of us would ever have to move if it
wasn't for this stupid policy of secrecy.

Monk>> I know. I go back and forth. Have you ever read Heinlein's *Methuselah's Children*?

Rebecca>> No. Don't go much for sci-fi.

Monk>> SF or Science Fiction, please! Seriously, Heinlein dealt
with the question of how the normal humans would feel if they
suddenly learned of people among them who were much longer
lived—and his "methuselahs" weren't immortals.

Snowbird>> Or "monsters."

Rebecca>> I think that it's wrong for you to classify yourself as

171

a monster, Uncle Snowbird. We're just different types of people: more fur, different-shaped heads, bigger feet . . .

Demetrios>> No feet. I mean, I have hooves. Still, Monk has a point. Humans don't even like different humans.

Snowbird>> I'm happy being what I am. Why shouldn't I call myself a monster? I'm certainly not a human.

Rebecca>> Demi, maybe humans would like us more if they knew how *really* different we are. Maybe if it wasn't just a question of life span, but all the other stuff. Look at all the religions on the Web. People *are* searching for Truth . . .

Monk>> Or maybe it would be like one of those movies where humanity unites once there is an outside danger. I don't really want to be cast in the role of the alien threat.

Demetrios>> So I move. Big deal. I've moved before. Lots of times. Lots of countries.

Monk>> I want to respond to Rebecca's comment about religions on the Web. Lots *are* "advertising" there—all flavors and textures. I've been trying to decide how some of them would react if they got OUR take on history and theology. I mean, Jesus wasn't one of US but so many of the other religions/mythologies owe something to US. What would that do to Faith?

Snowbird>> Really help—some would say "See, here's a guy who can tell us what Jesus was like; he knew him." Really hurt—some would say "If this guy was both Frey and Gilgamesh and now he's just a business exec, how can we believe in any God?" Not have any effect because for some faith is completely personal.

Demetrios>> I think it would threaten organized religions for a while. Some would go under. Old campaigners like the Catholic Church would hold on.

Rebecca>> As many reactions as there are types of people.

Demetrios>> The more I think about what will happen if we reveal ourselves, the more vast the implications grow.

Rebecca>> Are you losing belief in the Cause??

Demetrios>>Maybe a little. I have trouble believing we can change things for the better—or that we should. Do we really want all the attention we would get?

Monk>> Nothing important is gained without cost.

Rebecca>> We don't have to get attention. We can be left alone if we want to be.

Demetrios>> Sure. Tell that to any movie star who has tried to live a private life. Some of us are sure to become tabloid fodder. The human-forms and shapeshifters won't.

Snowbird>> True enough.

Rebecca>> Wouldn't it be better to be tabloid fodder with the facts straight than to be misrepresented like we are now? If I see another Bigfoot article!!

Monk>> I resent the comment that shapeshifters cannot understand your plight. We are all in this together. At least I thought so.

Snowbird>> Maybe the highway construction is just getting on Demi's nerves.

Demetrios>> Maybe.

She digs beneath the bush that no longer smells so fragrant, deepens her hole so that she can hide. Part of her knows that she is growing big for such hiding. She is not a ground squirrel, not a rabbit; nonetheless, part of her is fearful.

The Big Male is gone. His yellow eyes are still strong in her memory, along with his assurance. But he is gone, and she feels vulnerable. Mother vanished and never returned. The others who had squirmed and bit and played in the den and the sunshine with her are also gone. So is the Not-Mother Female.

The coyote pup called Shahrazad by well-meaning not-coyotes misses her father without knowing what missing is, only knowing that she feels less safe. Her nose has sorted the other humans. There is the Female and the others. She knows by scent they are males, but Arthur might be chagrined to learn that to her nose his majesty does not set him apart from either Eddie or Anson.

She also knows that one of the Lesser Males (her name for all males who are not the Changer) has been wounded. He does not move often and sweats sour when he does. That he is unfailingly kind keeps her from fleeing him as wild things often do from illness, but his hurt intensifies her lonely fear for her father.

The lilac bush sways alarmingly as she weakens its root-hold on the sandy earth. Shahrazad stops digging, tries the newly dug earth for size. She fits. It will do.

Wrapping her tail (just beginning to show the promise of an adult bush) around her nose, she tries to sleep. Even as she does, her oversize ears remain perked for the sound of one hoped-for, dreamed-for, prayed-for (if coyotes do pray), voice.

¤☒¤

Its curving walls are of coral, its towers decked with pearls, its pennants of seaweed: green, red, and pale gold. About it, drifting jellyfish glimmer with faint phosphorescence, animate candles or perhaps living embodiments of the stars' reflection on the waves above. Set on the top of a sloping hill of white sand, its gardens landscaped with anemones and angelfish, the palace of the monarchs of the seas is far more elegant than Arthur's hacienda in Albuquerque, New Mexico.

Following a glittering white narwhal, the unicorn of the oceans, the Changer and Lovern have come here, dolphin and man. The arched entryway to a great hall opens in a cloud of bubbles.

Brown seals, their large, liquid eyes infinitely sorrowful and almost human, join their escort, their lithe swimming slowed to match Lovern's stubbornly human pace.

The Changer maintains his dolphin shape, knowing from the presence of the seals that there is magic in this place to enable air-breathers to subsist on the oxygen trapped within water. He wonders if Lovern realizes this, decides that even if he did, the wizard would not trust another's magic over his own.

There is light here, light that is an intensification of the sea's own power to give its deepest dwellers lanterns to carry. It is pale and mysterious compared to the light of the sun, but rather than seeming weak, it makes the sun seem garish.

In this ocean light, the hoards of gems, gold, carved ivory and marble carpeting the sandy floors and hanging from the lacy coral walls, shimmer faintly. The shadowed faces of the broken statues regard them with ancient sorrow.

"Magnificent," Lovern murmurs, his tones so soft that doubtless he expects to go unheard. However, magic to enable conversation is in place. His words carry to the couple enthroned at the far end of the great hall.

"Thank you, wizard," says Duppy Jonah. "We are pleased."

The Sea King has changed from his Midgard Serpent shape and now is a triton to complement his wife.

Like hers, his skin is pale with pastel nacreous undertones. His long hair is dark green. Where she is slim and pliant, however, he is broad and powerful. Both monarchs embody their realm. She is its invasive, subtle self: death in a teacup. He is the hurricane, the crashing tsunami, the earthquake.

Like Poseidon, Duppy Jonah holds a trident in one hand—the traditional scepter of the ocean's lord.

Lovern is too old a conniver to show surprise at being overheard. When he reaches the supplicant's dais at the foot of the thrones, he bows. "Your Majesties, thank you for granting me audience."

"We are always pleased to receive embassies from the dry lands," Duppy Jonah replies, "and more so when my long-landed brother accompanies them."

The Changer cannot bow in his current shape, but he whistles his thanks.

Mother Carey's smile reveals teeth which are, unsuprisingly, like pearls. "We have considered the terms on which you will be permitted to bear from our realms in safety the thing which you have secreted in our keeping."

Lovern bows again. "I await your ruling."

"The Lustrum Review," Duppy Jonah says, "comes soon. Our desire is that you escort my queen to the Review. Seaborn as we are, we have never attended in person. Long ago my brother and I toyed with landed shapes, but only he exploited them."

"I," Mother Carey says sadly, "have never managed the gift. Even the shapeshift that permits the selkies to go between the sea and water is not mine. Although I cannot imagine forsaking the waters, I would like to go upon the land as land folk do."

"And I," Duppy Jonah adds, "would like to have my queen represent our Realm. For too long we have needed to trust to minions or to mechanical devices. As trusted as the former may be, they cannot debate policy with the full freedom of a ruler. The mechanical lacks intimacy."

Lovern strokes his grey beard thoughtfully. "I could work such magics, but they would take time to design."

"Take the time," Duppy Jonah says.

"Now?"

"Now. Do you think we would let you have your toy without first paying its ransom?" Duppy Jonah's gaze glints stormy and dangerous. "You secreted it here when you believed the Midgard Serpent beaten, its power no longer a thing to concern you. I will not permit a similar oversight to delay your workings."

"But the Lustrum Review begins in less than two weeks!" Lovern protests. "My lord Arthur will need my counsel before that time, especially with Edward wounded."

Mother Carey smiles, a shark's merciless grin. "You boast of your abilities, wizard. Are you saying that your talents are not equal to your boast?"

"I . . ." Lovern swallows further useless protest. "I am equal to the task, but the work will take some days."

"Take those days," Duppy Jonah says. "If harm should come to my queen because of your carelessness, I should swamp the lands with such storms that King Arthur would have no choice but to turn you over to my vengeance."

Lovern stiffens. "My magics would not fail her!"

"Indeed not," Duppy Jonah says, "nor will your watchfulness. My queen is not a creature of the land. I shall insist that you assign yourself guardian of her safety."

Darting a glance at the Changer, Lovern realizes that there will be no rescue for him from *that* quarter. The Changer simply drifts, grinning a broad, pleased, dolphin's grin.

"Am I to understand then," Lovern says with exquisite formality, "that the price you place on me is twofold? First, I am to design magics to permit Mother Carey to be as a land creature for a time, then I am to appoint myself her personal guardian during the time she remains on the land?"

Mother Carey nods. "I would prefer human form, Lovern, for most of those who will attend the Review will be as humans. Second, I will not require your constant attendance, nor will you be held account for every stubbing of a toe (a curious concept, that), but for my overall safety and care."

"I have duties to King Arthur," Lovern states. "If these

interfere, will I be permitted to assign another to escort you?"

"If that one is acceptable to me," Mother Carey says.

"And if you realize that the ultimate responsibility remains your own," Duppy Jonah rumbles.

Lovern considers, no longer stroking his beard, but nibbling at the tuft beneath his lip. After several minutes, he nods.

"If you will help me acquire certain elements and give me a place to work and a space of days, I believe I can do what you wish. The transformation would not be long-lasting, but I believe I can craft it so that Mother Carey could break it at will. Once broken," he hastens to add, "it could not be easily renewed, but then she can regain her natural forms."

Sea King and Queen exchange glances that speak of excitement, decision, and anticipated sorrow at their separation.

"We can give you those things," Duppy Jonah says.

"I would need for Mother Carey to grant me audience so that I might mate my sorcery to her particular needs."

"I will grant you that," she says, her voice thrilling with anticipation. Then her eyes narrow. "And the spells must do what we have asked, no more. If you seek to control me in thought, in belief, or in action, I shall wreak such vengeance upon you that what my good lord has threatened will be as nothing. Do you understand?"

Lovern nods hastily, knowing the power of a furious woman.

"Then we are agreed," Duppy Jonah states. "I shall have chambers made ready for you and place selkies at your disposal."

"One more request," Lovern says obsequiously. "Might I have leave to call my liege lord and tell him that I shall not return for some days yet?"

"You may." The Sea King grins. "We have tapped the phone cables that run through our realm. Useful tools, these. Speak to your lord."

A seal escorts Lovern to a phone, and the monarchs of the sea turn their attention to the Changer.

"We would be pleased if you would bide with us," Duppy Jonah says. "It has been too long since you visited."

With a single, eye-blurring surge, the Changer takes the

form of a merman, his scales blue-green, his upper torso like to that of the man he has been ashore, although with less body hair.

"I would be pleased to do so, brother," he replies. "We have a lot of catching up to do."

¤◙¤

Two days have passed since Lovern's call. At that time, the wizard had also requested a room be reserved for the Sea Queen. After some thought, Vera decides to give her the room that shares a bath with her own temporary quarters.

"From the little Lovern explained," she says to Arthur, taking a seat in his office beneath a piece of her own weaving, "I don't think that Mother Carey has ever been on dry land—at least not for long. Someone should be on hand to advise her about human customs, and as I am the only female resident of Pendragon Estates . . ."

"Very good, very good," Arthur says hastily, not wanting to be reminded of this imbalance in his establishment.

Vera has not seemed to mind, but some of the more militant females among their people have complained about the inequity. Some have even gone so far as to suggest that a representative sort of government needs to be set up. Only the fact that none of them particularly wants to be a representative or to relocate has kept that proposal from becoming law. It's certain to be brought up again this Review.

Arthur sighs. A king must be answerable to his subjects, but sometimes he longs for the days of absolute monarchy— and a much smaller, less opinionated group to reign over.

"Have you decided where we will put . . . Sven?"

Vera colors a very pretty rose beneath her coppery skin. She hasn't quite forgiven herself for letting the fiery trickster into Arthur's establishment, although Eddie himself has assured her that she had only done what she must.

"I thought that we'd put him in the room that shares a bath with the Changer," she answers. "The Changer does not like him overmuch, but I don't believe he dislikes him as actively as some of those who will be staying here."

"A good point. The Changer is tough, too. Sven would

need to behave himself with such a one in proximity. If annoyed, the ancient is as likely as not to take Sven's red head off.''

Vera relaxes a bit. ''That was what I thought. I had considered putting Sven with Katsuhiro, but I couldn't decide whether they'd hate each other or hit it off.''

''Either alternative is pretty frightening,'' Arthur agrees, drumming lightly with the rubber end of his pencil. ''It's a pity, as Katsuhiro is at least firm in his loyalties.''

''Except for this current rivalry with Dakar,'' Vera reminds him. ''Dakar hasn't requested shelter here, but I'm certain he's going to attend the Review in person.''

''Another problem to deal with when we must. Have the South American contingent made their wishes known?''

''Yes. They're staying in the Crown Plaza Pyramid. I think they're making a statement about their unhappiness with athanor policy on the ecological situation by not accepting shelter here. I suspect we'll be having a difficult time with them.''

''That's no surprise. My problem is that I cannot help but sympathize with some elements of their position.''

''I know.'' Vera glances down at her notebook. ''Lovern won't be pleased, but Louhi is attending. She's not staying here, though. She's requested a hotel room.''

''Lovern can put up with her attending. We all meet old lovers and old enemies at these things.''

''True. And Lil Prima says to tell you that Tommy will be glad to perform if you'd like. They're driving down from Santa Fe and staying in a hotel, but she says they can bring his gear.''

''That would be nice.'' Arthur drums a riff from one of Tommy's old pieces. ''We'll let him choose the selections. Perhaps we can have him play at the reception on the twentieth.''

''I'll call Lil.''

''Thanks.''

''Eddie has been handling the catering arrangements via telephone. Anson keeps him from overworking, but your loyal sidekick is miserable at being laid up.''

Arthur grins, knowing full well how sour Eddie's mood has been. ''I've been grateful to Anson. The Spider manages to maintain a good mood no matter what he's up against."

"Remember your gratitude," Vera says, "when next he annoys you. Is there anything else? I need to double-check some of the details on the Review agenda."

"It's stupid but . . ." Arthur pauses, uncertain whether to continue.

Vera cocks an eyebrow at him, surprised to see the usually decisive king hesitant. "Yes?"

"I was wondering . . ." Another pause, then the words come out in a rush. "What are we going to do about the puppy?"

"Shahrazad?"

"Yes. She's tearing up all the plantings in the courtyard. We need it for small meetings and as a place where people can gather. I know we have other conference areas, but . . ."

"We can't exactly cage her up," Vera says, her tone making this a suggestion.

"No." Arthur shudders at how the Changer would react. "Do you think we could get her father to keep her in his room?"

"Maybe. She'll ruin anything there. Shahrazad's not only a puppy, she's a *coyote* puppy. She's only sort of housebroken."

"Can you talk with the Changer about her?" Arthur asks, hastening to add. "It's not that I'm afraid to talk with him, but if I say something, it takes on the tone of a royal edict or a request from the head of the house. I don't want to offend him."

"No, that wouldn't be a good idea." Vera nods. "Yes, I'll talk with him when he gets back. Meanwhile, we can have the landscapers set up some small tables and benches in the external gardens. It's not as if you don't have other grounds."

"I don't suppose . . ."

"That we should put Shahrazad out there without her father's permission?" Vera draws herself up indignantly. "I should think not! If you were worried about the courtyard, you should have mentioned this sooner."

"I didn't know how long he would be staying away," Arthur replies lamely, "but you're right. Pity his current room doesn't open to the exterior of the house."

"It doesn't, and I really can't move him without first speaking to him. Do you want me to call him at Duppy Jonah's?"

Arthur thinks, then nods. "Yes, tell him that we've decided to empty the ground-floor rooms bordering the courtyard so that people can meet there. That makes sense, doesn't it?"

Vera smiles. "It does."

"Good." Arthur drums a satisfied tattoo, then sets his pencil aside. "I need to get back to setting up the video cameras before my meeting tonight. There are times I wish we could have servants."

Tucking her notebook under one arm, Vera starts out, "But that would mean that more people would need to know what we're doing here. The days when our own would do menial labor are long past. Those who don't have much money would rather serve mortals than humble themselves before other athanor."

"True."

"Still," Vera says, sticking her head back through the doorway, "you might try contacting the Smith. He loves gadgets."

"Good idea."

Each is so immersed in their immediate problems, needs, and responsibilities that neither spares a moment to think about their mysterious enemy. Eddie's accident and the subsequent attack had been a week before. There have been no problems since. Neither considers how very strange this is; even Eddie gives the date only a passing acknowledgment.

There is so much to do.

❖▣❖

Rather to Chris Kristofer's surprise, Arthur Pendragon refuses to be interviewed. His polite but firm letter intensifies Chris's desire to get the man's story.

With an avidity that endears him to his editors, Chis covers the city's public forums, especially those dealing with the issues raised on the Pendragon Productions website. In the second week of June, his perserverance is rewarded.

The issue under review is the Albuquerque city government's hopes that the contradictory aims of limiting water use and encouraging city expansion can be achieved. Officials wax eloquent on incentives for reducing residential water use, but Chris's "people sense" can tell that many attendees aren't buying the tidy arguments.

When the officials open the meeting to questions from the floor, one of the first to speak is a bearded man of medium height. His reddish gold hair just brushes his collar, and his clothing is expensive but understated.

"Even an idiot," the man begins in a British accent, "can see that no matter how many homes put in low-flow toilets and showerheads, no matter how many people tear out their bluegrass lawns and xeroscape, new construction eliminates the gains."

"I think you exaggerate, Mister . . ." the official on the platform hesitates.

"Pendragon," the man says. "And I think not."

"Perhaps someone else would like to speak," the official says desperately, glancing about the listening crowd.

"He's doing just fine!" someone shouts.

Mutters of agreement force the official to wait in silence as Pendragon moves to the front of the hall, where he coolly appropriates an overhead projector.

"These water-use figures," Arthur Pendragon begins, "were obtained from publicly available sources. I would be happy to share my sources and a copy of this handout after the meeting."

He begins detailing current household water use, then demonstrates how, even with the water-conscious guidelines for new landscaping and plumbing, new construction (including a planned golf course) will severely tax the water table.

Chris notes that although neither tall nor conventionally handsome, Arthur Pendragon looks like a man accustomed to being followed. His blue eyes glow as he makes his points; his gestures are economical and eloquent. The city officials dim into insignificant bureaucrats beside his charm.

When the meeting adjourns, Chris works his way through the throng to where Arthur is handing out flyers.

"Thanks," Chris says, accepting one. "I'm with the *Jour-*

nal. I was hoping you'd let me have an interview.''

"So sorry," Arthur says, "but I don't give interviews."

Chris drifts back, certain from the firmness of Arthur's tone that arguing would get him nowhere. Very well, if Arthur won't talk to him, there are other methods for learning his secrets. Not all of them are polite, and a few are of dubious legality, but since when has that stopped a crusading reporter?

❁◼❁

Crafting the spell that will enable the Sea Queen to reside on land takes ten days. During these, Lovern is hardly seen by any but those assigned to wait upon him and carry his messages. In addition to the selkies, Duppy Jonah has deputed two octopuses to assist the mage. These are athanor creatures, wise in their way, dexterous beyond humanity's best dreams.

"At first I felt as if I had Cthulhu at my side," Lovern confesses to the Changer during one of his rare rest breaks some days into the project, "but now I know I will miss them when next I do a work of this complexity. I call them Odd and Pod."

"Have they a language you can speak?" the Changer asks.

"The selkies translate, but we have worked out hand signals that do almost as well for smaller jobs. Odd is the quicker to comprehend, but Pod can perform multiple simultaneous tasks in a fashion I quite envy."

"And how goes the work?"

"Well, but it is complicated. Given the penalties for failure, I do not dare be sloppy—as I might in a jury-rigged spell for myself," the wizard admits. "Moreover, I do not wish to offend the Queen, so I have consulted her about how she wishes to look as a human." He sighs at the memory. "She was quite particular, but I believe she will be satisfied."

The Changer smiles understandingly, for he knows that Mother Carey's knowledge of human concepts of beauty is gleaned largely from statuary and paintings. She had consulted him and had fretted when she found that he could not take female form. Thereafter, she had settled for what the selkies could show her and for making reconnaissance swims to beach resorts.

Lovern continues, "I've called Arthur, and paperwork will be waiting for her at his Florida estate. Plane tickets, too. I'm to call when I can better estimate when I'll be finished."

The Changer flicks his merman's tail. "Then I should be away and leave you to your work."

"Bide," Lovern almost pleads. "Odd and Pod are fine assistants, but they cannot chat, and I am still out of favor with Duppy Jonah. The selkies treat me as their master's mood dictates."

"If I won't keep you from your work," the Changer says, "then I will stay. If I delayed you, then, brother or no, I should be out of favor with both King and Queen. Today, they have gone somewhere together. I believe they will miss each other greatly."

Lovern nods. Almost unwillingly, he, too, has been touched by the love between the two monarchs. "My spell is 'simmering' for lack of a better word. My assistants rest, but I am restless."

"Eat, at least," the Changer advises. "If you cannot sleep."

"Will you join me?"

"Certainly."

They adjourn to a garden where sea plants grow strange fruit and small fish swim freely. Here Duppy Jonah has stored a variety of human foods. The wizard transfers a plastic package of pickled three-bean salad and a small canned ham within his protective aura.

"I would give much for a hot meal," he muses. "My magics keep me dry and warm, but this dim-lit place chills my soul."

A fish held pinched between his slightly webbed fingers, the Changer shakes his head. "You should shift shape, then you would not be fighting your environment."

He pops the fish into his mouth (where the teeth are somewhat more carnivorous in shape than would be found in a mouth otherwise so human) as punctuation.

"I wear shapes," Lovern says, admitting more than he would in other circumstances, "but I strive not to wear the mind. The bodies can offer me freedom I would not otherwise have, but I dislike the sensation of otherness invading myself.''

"It is not otherness," the Changer says, "if you surrender to it. Then it *is* self."

"The one who hunted you in the form of a golden eagle surrendered to that otherness and so lost his prey. Had I been the hunter, I would not have made that error."

"Nor would you have flown with the eagle's full abilities, and the raven still would have bested you.''

"Perhaps. It is an interesting problem."

"Someday, if you wish, I will show you I am right."

"You and Duppy Jonah name each other brothers," Lovern says somewhat tentatively. "I have wondered why."

The Changer does not seem troubled by Lovern's bad manners. "He is the first one of our kind I recall. So am I to him. We are not drawn to each other as mates—both being essentially male—nor do we feel as parents might. Therefore, the only term that fits our mutual affection is 'brother.' It is a label evolved when such things became possible."

Lovern is intrigued by hints of times so long ago that even language might not have existed. "And how long ago did you meet?"

"Long, long ago." The Changer stares at the wizard with eyes that remain coyote yellow. "I have watched the Earth herself shift form, seen oceans recede, continents split, watched her shrug earthquakes in temper or merely to stretch.''

"That old . . . I had suspected but never was certain."

"You younger ones make too much of age. Age is not power, it merely is experience."

"Experience is a power in itself!" Lovern protests.

"Perhaps." The Changer snares another fish and chews it thoughtfully. "But for all my age, I cannot do magic as you do, nor can I command loyalty as Arthur does, nor can I weave as Vera does, nor create devices as the Smith does. My experience has only given me a mastery of shapes borrowed from other creatures."

"Can you shape creatures that are extinct?"

"I can."

"Have you never wished to?"

"I have, from time to time, as need demands."

"You are . . . fertile."

"Often."

"Have you never thought to restore a lost species to the Earth by taking a mate who could also take the shape?"

"No. Change is part of the Earth's life as much as of an individual's. It is not my place to halt change."

"But you could undo errors."

"You mean human-caused extinctions?"

"Yes."

"And would you also have me bring back the mastodons, the dinosaurs, the great sea creatures? Where would they live in this human world?"

"Humans would be delighted!"

"Only for a time. Then the novelty would wear thin. A poor man in Africa who sees his fields trampled by elephants and rhinoceroses does not delight in the creatures as does an American safe in his suburban lair, his welfare unthreatened."

"True." Lovern digs a last grape from a can of fruit cocktail. "You are quite thoughtful."

"I have had a long time for thought."

Lovern chuckles. "Then experience *is* a power—even if only in that it gives time for reflection."

"Perhaps." The Changer grins, his teeth still holding flecks of recently eaten fish. "But I have seen many who have lived long and reflected little."

An octopus jets into the garden, snags a fish with two arms, and signals to Lovern with two others.

"That is Odd, telling me that the enchantment is ready for its next stage. I beg your permission to depart, ancient."

"I grant it. Good luck with your workings."

"Thank you."

Alone in the garden but for the little fish and the plants, the Changer shapes a course of creatures not seen within the oceans for more millennia than the whole human race has known.

Would the human race welcome these? Would his own people? Returning to his merman's form, the Changer's expression is wry.

He doubts it.

¤✸¤

In darkness, in wetness, in cold, and in solitude, one waits. His only stimulation, other than the unpleasantness of his surroundings, are thoughts and memories.

Perhaps when Mimir had set his second head in this isolated place he had already divined something brainwashing experts in centuries yet to come would learn: A person left absolutely solitary comes to cling to whoever breaks that loneliness. Comes to cling, even to love, after a fashion, the only companion of all his days.

Such love had Mimir's Head felt toward the man who had once been called Mimir. This same man who had later been called Merlin, Ambrose Hawk, Richard Wilson, and many other names—the most recent of which is Ian Lovern.

This strange love had been colored by the fact that Mimir's Head was, if not precisely the child, most certainly of the making of this enigmatic wizard. The Head did not call Mimir Father, but he knew by the very blood that ran in him that he was of that other's engendering.

Had Odin, whose eye had provided the other elements for the Head's generation, lived past Ragnarokk, then this filial loyalty might have been diluted. But Odin had been slain, and soon after the Head himself had been imprisoned.

At first he had clung to his memories of his brief life in the world outside of the cold, wet darkness. He recalled sunlight and birdsong, the tramp of hooves on the turf, the warmth of a fire. All of these were recalled as by one muffled beneath a cowl, an experience that foreshadowed his current imprisonment, but they were sweet memories indeed when that phase was replaced solely by mental stimulation.

The puzzles the wizard set his creation became meat and drink, sunlight and birdsong, to the imprisoned Head. He sought to please his master, initially out of some vague belief that success would bring a reward, later because it was the only amusement he received.

Then came the day when the wizard, then called Merlin, changed. At first the change was a sense of cheerfulness or lightness of spirit. He was not unkind to his creation, but his visits were more brief, his questions more perfunctory.

Through careful gleaning, the Head learned that Merlin had fallen in love with a woman called Nimue, an athanor sorceress. For her, Merlin did what he had done for no other. He allowed her to see the Head, but once, but briefly, the astral audience shading everything pastel blue and silvery white.

The Head never forgot her. He dreamed of her, brooded over her, envied Merlin for his time with her even as he hoped that the romance would last and the lady be brought before him once again. Then came the day that Nimue, having learned all she could from Merlin, piqued because he would not give her the secret of the Head, turned her lover's own magic against him.

A faint astral scream was the Head's only warning before his solitude became absolute. Later, he learned that he had been alone for hundreds of years. Merlin had the painful comfort of Nimue's teasing visits, his own occasional piercing through to the outer world. The Head had nothing but cold, darkness, wet.

During that time he did not grow to hate Merlin. No. He pitied him. Hate came later when, having won his own freedom, Merlin did not set his tool free as well. Long imprisonment had damaged Merlin's pride, made him distrustful of any relationship where he was the weaker, but it had not taught him empathy.

Then did Mimir's Head begin to hate. He began to realize that to Merlin he was nothing more than a useful Thing.

The Head took his vengeance in small ways; he gave advice that, while not wrong, withheld some crucial bit of information. Meanwhile, he found ways to cause Merlin to set out small markers that led to the Head.

Had he possessed a heart, the Head would have hoped that Nimue would track him down. Still, the fiery trickster Loki was hardly less welcome. Now the Head had a companion other than his master. He welcomed every visit and when, after subtle prompting on his part, Loki brought Nimue into their circle, the Head's ambition grew.

The price the Head demanded for his participation was his freedom—and not merely from his cistern. He craved the freedom of a body of his own. The others agreed, research was begun, and ever so slowly the pieces were put into place.

Now, he could sense the tumblers in the lock that held him. After centuries of darkness, he would see the light; after centuries of cold, he would feel warmth. After centuries of patient hatred, he would have his revenge.

¤☒¤

Far from their palace where Lovern labors and the Changer waits, beneath the icy waters of the Arctic Ocean, Duppy Jonah and Mother Carey swim. They are humpback whales here, massive bodies well suited for this cold, cold water, tiny eyes seeing far more than a human might imagine.

Swimming around icebergs, beneath the fragmented ice sheet that covered the waters below, they revel in the crystalline beauty of this isolated part of the world.

"But even here," Duppy Jonah says, "even here we can see the marks of human carelessness."

What has drawn his wrath is frozen garbage, carried here by currents from who knows what distance. The organic parts have rotted or been eaten. Cans, bottles, plastic bags, metal drums slowly leaking poison, the faint taste of oil in the water all speak of humankind's continuing naive belief that the Earth's ability to absorb waste is infinite.

"They are not evil," the Sea King says, "not all of them, but I prefer the days when the ships were of wood and the trash that remained was somehow beautiful."

"I will do what I can to make Arthur understand that our continued isolation from humanity cannot persist," Mother Carey replies. "I will also meet with the South American contingent. From what I have gleaned, they are actively furious about what the 'developing' nations on that continent are doing."

"We let North America be taken without protest," Duppy Jonah agrees. "Now there are plains where once there were forests and the streams are saturated with fertilizers that fill the still waters with algae. True, some communities seek to mend what was done, but a patched sail is not the same as a whole one."

Mother Carey rolls with ponderous grace. "I shall have

them call me Amphitrite above. Mother Carey is too soft a name.''

''Too soft for any but sailors,'' Duppy Jonah agrees. ''They know the power of the Sea Witch.''

''And of the siren's song,'' she agrees, ''but the land-born have become forgetful. Look at the arrogance with which Lovern came here. You soon set him right.''

''I did and I am satisfied with what I have done. You also must use the threat of rising seas, hurricanes, and storms. Let Arthur recall that we have kept our peace by choice, not from inability.''

''I will.''

''And I'll miss you terribly.''

''Shall I stay then?''

''No. Go. Just come back to me.''

''I will.''

☼◙☼

By June 18, Lovern has prepared the spell that will permit Mother Carey, now Amphitrite C. Regina, to shapeshift from a mermaid into a human being. They gather on an isolated island in the Florida Keys to test the potion.

''It's in this vial,'' Lovern explains, displaying a container holding about a half pint of milky liquid. ''Drink it off, but sit down first or your tail shifting may unbalance you.

''Your human shape will last three weeks or until you shift it voluntarily. At that time, you will revert to mermaid form, so I suggest that you be near an ocean—and there aren't any bordering New Mexico.''

''Three weeks should be enough,'' Amphitrite says.

She and Duppy Jonah rest in the sandy shallows of the island's deepest cove. The Changer, now in human form, stands waist-deep, watching silently.

Amphitrite turns to her husband, who takes her in his arms and presses her to his chest. They speak, but whatever they say is covered by the polite susurrus of the waves against the sand. Then, still partially in the water, she seats herself decorously and drinks off the potion in a single, long draught.

"Rich tasting, like whale's milk," she says brightly. "When will the effects begin?"

"They have already," Lovern says, holding out a hand mirror scavenged from a wreck and polished bright. "Look."

The others do not need a mirror to see what is happening. Amphitrite's skin has lost its pearly tint, pale blues and pinks replaced by a golden brown tan. As if autumn is come to a woodland, her green hair becomes golden blond, highlighted with touches of red. Finned tail splits into legs, long and shapely, like those of a professional model.

Indeed, what she resembles most of all is a fashion doll come to life, but her sea-green eyes glow with an intelligence beyond any doll's—or most humans'. Standing with a steadiness that is surprising, given that she has never stood before, she views her nude body with unself-conscious pleasure.

"What do you think, dear?"

"I prefer you as an orca, a seal, a mermaid," the Sea King grumbles proudly, "but you shape a fine human."

"I think so, too," she agrees. "A bit top-heavy, but that is all to the point."

No one dares chuckle, lest her pun is unintentional, but Lovern stands taller with pride at what he has wrought. "You recall how to change yourself back?" he asks.

"I do," she says, "and I shall not forget the words, nor am I likely to speak Phoenician accidentally."

"Good." Lovern now includes Duppy Jonah in his steady gaze. "Now that I have fulfilled the first part of our bargain, will you permit me to retrieve my property?"

Duppy Jonah does not turn from his wife. "We will. Go where you will and take the Changer with you. I shall escort Amphitrite to Arthur's Florida home."

The Sea King moves into slightly deeper water and shifts into a striped dolphin, large enough to bear a human burden. Amphitrite, still graceful in the water despite her human form, swims to join them.

"Ta-ta, fellows!"

Watching the pair depart, the woman astride the dolphin, Lovern grumbles sourly, "What if anyone sees them!" Then he shrugs. "That is not for us to worry about. I *did* suggest that we have her test the potion at Arthur's beach and save this trouble.''

The Changer wades into deeper water. "It is no trouble. While we fetch your tool, they will make love before parting.''

Lovern interrupts a mystic hand gesture. "What? How?''

The Changer grins, shaping the bottle-nosed dolphin. His only reply is a suggestive squeal. Lovern completes the aborted gesture and soon his orange glow reappears around him.

Now that Duppy Jonah's permission has been granted, the wizard uses a variety of magical shortcuts to take them to where he has secreted Mimir's Head. If he hopes that in this way he will keep the Changer from knowing where they go, nothing in the shapeshifter's bearing tells him if he is wasting his efforts—or if the ancient cares at all.

At last they come to a trench so far beneath the surface of the ocean that light has never shone there. The darkness eats Lovern's wizard light so that only his hand on the staff and his face, as if disembodied, can be seen.

Long before they reached these depths, the Changer shifts into a giant squid, a vast thing even a sperm whale might fear. Silently, he jets along at the wizard's side.

At the edge of a nub of congealed lava, Lovern halts. With the tip of his staff, he taps the smooth surface. He mutters words as well, but the Changer pays no heed. His role is to make certain that one or both of them return from this place intact. Otherwise Amphitrite will be without escort—and he has much respect for his brother and much belief that if anything happens to his beloved, his vengeance will be terrible.

The rock opens and from it Lovern draws a hexagonal case about the size of a large hatbox. It gathers the available light into the gold and precious stones that encrust its surface.

Hefting the box, Lovern eyes the boneless monstrosity pulsing restlessly in the cold waters near him.

"This is it. We can go back now.''

The squid instantly begins retracing their route. Lovern follows, walking carefully lest he upset the contents of his box. As they make their slow way to shallower waters and finally to sunny places, it seems to Lovern that the box shakes in his hand, a rough, uneven vibration.

Were he given to fancy, he would believe that the Head within is laughing uproariously.

✡◻✡

Tommy Thunderburst is happily at work on the new piece for guitar and drums that he has titled "She Blew My Head Off and Ate My Mind" when Lil Prima saunters into his studio. As always, she is elegantly dressed, but something about the way her golden hair is coiled atop her head and the style of her shoes signals that she's been in a meeting.

"Hi, Lil," he says cheerfully. "Want to hear the new one? It's about you."

"Later, darling, later," she purrs, running her hands through his hair. Her fingers stop to toy with the silver chain holding the amethyst thunderbird, making his heart race lest she question him about it, but they pass it by. "I've just come to tell you that the videos for *Angel of Destruction, Demon of the Night* look really good."

"That's the set we did with 'Hell Cat' and 'Blue Suede Shoes'?"

"That's right." She strokes his shoulders approvingly. "The buzz on 'Blue Suede Shoes' is already starting."

She's particularly pleased with this last coup. The Presley estate has been very particular about permitting covers of the King's works, but Tommy Thunderburst has a special, unique—one might even say brotherly—relationship with Elvis Presley, one that nullifies such obstacles with the wave of a hand.

"Yes. I've coyly indicated that because of your extraordinary talent and charisma, the estate was willing to waive its usual restrictions. The story has already been picked up by the major fan publications. You're going to sell a lot of albums just because of curiosity."

Tommy diddles a few jarring chords, mentally files them away for inclusion in "She Blew My Head Off and Ate My Mind," and asks, "Won't radio play, like, hurt the curiosity bug?"

"No, I don't think so," Lil says. "The radio demos will only include 'Hell Cat' and 'Blue Suede Shoes.' That won't keep DJs from using the album to play 'Hound Dog.' Still, the fanatics will want to play Elvis's version side by side with yours and analyze the hell out of them. They'll want the CD.''

"Elvis will win," Tommy says bluntly.

"Of course he will," Lil agrees. "He's a demigod, or would be if this age acknowledged gods in any form. You're just starting, but why not borrow some of his mana for yourself? After all, you created him."

"Yes, I did." Briefly, Tommy looks sad.

Lil gently nudges his hand where it rests across the guitar strings. The faint sound pulls Tommy from his brooding. "And Arthur has expressed enthusiasm for your performing at the Lustrum Review next week."

"Cool."

"He said that the twentieth, during the opening reception, would be a good time. The South American contingent have invited you to perform at a reception they're holding the night of the twenty-first."

"Cooler."

"That might cause some trouble with Arthur," Lil muses. "From what I gathered during my chat with Isidro Robelo, Isidro and his allies are very unhappy with the level of despoliation happening on the South American continent. They feel that the tropical ecology can take less long-term abuse than the North American temperate zone."

"They'll have Rain Forest Crunch ice cream," Tommy says. "Cool. And probably mixed nuts, good coffee, and lots of orchids. Orchids are the sexiest flower. They remind me of you, especially the carnivorous kind."

Lil rolls her eyes, but she is pleased rather than exasperated. "Are there carnivorous orchids?"

"You dig my drift, anyhow. I'm not botanizing, I'm flirting." He grins at her, lion to lioness.

She licks her lips as she steps out of her shoes. "I thought you were composing."

"A song about you," he says, setting the guitar aside. "Inspire me."

13

*You should never wear your best trou-
sers when you go out to fight for liberty
and truth.*

—HENRIK IBSEN

ON THE BEACH, THE CHANGER IS INTRODUCING AMPHITRITE
to the concept of clothing, something which, like modesty,
she has frequently observed but never bothered with. Alternately giggling and frowning, she tries on the two dozen or
so outfits that Vera has express-ordered from a variety of
catalogs.

Lovern pleads tiredness and retires to where the gold box
waits. For the flight, he plans to stow it in a padded carry-
on bag that has been ensorcelled so that airport security will
overlook it.

Once inside the house, he carries the Head's box to a room
that overlooks the waterfront. From there he can keep an eye
on the two out front. Their essentially nonhuman nature is
obvious as they play with the clothing. Mixing and matching
skirts, tops, and shorts, they remind him of cinema aliens
who have observed human behavior but never really tried to
duplicate it.

The Changer has used human form repeatedly, but his
knowledge of female attire is limited. Amphitrite is enthusiastic but apparently puzzled by such things as brassieres.

195

Lovern feels apprehensive about the coming trip, but those worries cannot distract him.

For the first time in millennia, he undoes the locks on the golden box. Placing a wide plastic basin close by, he reaches into the viscous ichor. Grasping a handful of hair as grey as his own but matted and wet, he braces himself. Then, swallowing revulsion, he tugs the Head to view.

It is not a pretty sight, thus removed from the fluids that have sustained it. Long hair and beard hang lank, gathered into heavy locks that drip shiny ichor into the waiting basin. The skin is pale and translucent, the thready network of veins visible beneath. Its mouth is shapely, the lips full, pouting, and incongruously rosy. The eyes that open to regard Lovern are mismatched: one his own piercing blue, the other Odin's brown.

"Greetings, wise wizard, bringer from beneath the whale's road, ender of exile." When the red lips move, ichor dribbles out from between them, catching in the still-dripping beard.

Lovern manages a courtly smile. "Welcome to Florida, Head."

"Land of sunlight, sweet oranges, blue waters, broad beaches," the Head comments. "Starved for sunshine, this one would see what lies without."

Unable to refuse, Lovern pulls aside the drapes with his free hand. Amphitrite is pirouetting on the sand in a green-silk skirt and lacy white blouse. Her feet are bare, her fair hair a corona about her laughing face.

Lounging on the sand, the Changer is apparently offering her some advice, for she picks up something pink from a heap on the sand and pulls it on beneath her skirt.

"Bountiful beauty born of the waves," the Head comments, leering. "Amphitrite walks on wizard-won legs."

"How do you know?" Lovern asks.

"Crafted to ken what is hidden from others," the Head answers sensibly, "my maker's mark is as sun to these eyes."

He blinks away stray drops of ichor, spattering Lovern slightly. The wizard is too distracted to notice.

"Head, I'm taking you to Arthur's hacienda. An enemy has attacked several of us. I desire that you divine who this is and help me unmask him—or her—or them."

"Service is the source of my existence."

Lovern does not perceive the irony in the words. "I will keep you in my suite there, in a place well warded against intrusion. I wish that the Lustrum Review did not need to go on while this enemy is unidentified."

"Could the King cancel?"

"It wouldn't be wise," Lovern says, "not without more reason. The South American contingent, at the very least, would consider cancellation an attempt to stonewall their protests. That's the last thing Arthur wants to do, especially since he sympathizes with many of their complaints."

The Head hangs limply, his eyes actively watching Amphitrite and the Changer on the beach. They have given up playing with clothing and are tossing bread to the seagulls.

"My arm grows tired," Lovern says after a moment. "Since we cannot converse astrally during this crisis, I must rig something more convenient—a stand of some sort. The ichor sustains you, but without the ocean's cold to battle, you should be able to subsist for brief times outside of it."

The Head does not protest being lowered back into its container. It has new sights to mull over, plans to make. Lovern tops off the ichor from a container he prepared back in Albuquerque. Then, without a word, he snaps shut the locks and seals them with a charm.

After inserting the Head's box into the special traveling bag, he glances at a clock. About time to get those two ready to go to the airport. They'll be home in time for him to get briefed on preparations for the Review.

He feels fortified by the presence of his favorite tool. Surely he can handle anything that might come up, even at short notice. Hasn't he always before?

¤◉¤

Amphitrite looks around the Albuquerque airport terminal, her wide, sea-green eyes devouring every detail. Although she misses Duppy Jonah so intensely that she has already phoned him twice, she must admit that she is having a wonderful time.

Everything is so different—different even from the expectations raised by the photographs (carefully sealed against water damage) that the selkies have brought them. It is the little things she is not prepared for: the sound of shoes and boots against the floors, the feeling of cushioned seats (similar yet different from the giant sponges she and Duppy Jonah have employed for similar purposes), the taste of hot chocolate.

Using an ancient Mycenaean dialect interspersed with English, she questions the Changer endlessly. Some questions, she is surprised to learn, he cannot answer. He has been, he tells her, a wild thing too long.

Lovern could help since he is fluent in ancient Mycenaean, a tongue which had been the *lingua franca* among their people, much as English is now. However, he seems distracted and unhappy. Perhaps the box he refuses to let go of weighs him down.

For her own part, Amphitrite strives to put Lovern at ease by acting almost childlike in her eagerness to experience everything. She has eaten ice cream, but a float is a new experience, one she immediately resolves to share with Duppy Jonah. Lovern sees her pleasure and tells her that she must try a hot fudge sundae next.

She does have some difficulties in areas where the males cannot help her. A public rest room with self-flushing toilets terrifies her; a faucet that turns itself off frustrates her efforts to play with the hot water. Still, she assures herself, she is staying out of trouble remarkably well.

Perhaps the most difficult thing for her is controlling her imperious expectation that she will be obeyed. When a flight attendant ignores her request for a refill on her tea, she raises a hand to slap her until the Changer, his yellow eyes hard, restrains her and shakes his head.

Two wait for them at the gate. Amphitrite recognizes both Vera Tso and Anson A. Kridd, for she and Duppy Jonah make a practice of learning about their dry-land counterparts.

"And so here you are, safe and sound," Anson says heartily, "after a vacation in the sun, leaving us to do the work!"

He rolls his words without taking breath, a rich sound that reminds Amphitrite of the slow breaking of waves against beach.

Vera greets the others, then turns to Amphitrite and smiles.

"I'm pleased to see you again, Amphitrite. You're looking very well. Did the clothes suit you?"

Amphitrite refrains from saying that several outfits had not suited at all—the stiffer fabrics had offended skin accustomed to nothing more harsh than sea-foam.

"Many did," she says, gesturing toward the silk skirt and blouse she now wears. "I especially like the silks."

"Lovely stuff," Vera agrees, "but hard to keep clean. Do you like the colors or the texture?"

"Texture," Amphitrite says, "though the silk holds jewel tones like nothing else you sent."

Lovern clears his throat. "We don't have any baggage to claim. Shall we head out?"

"Always rushing," Anson says, leading the way. "The world will end in its own sweet time."

As they walk to the van, Vera politely chats about fabrics and clothes, but Amphitrite senses that her mind is not on the words. The dark-haired woman's gaze keeps straying to where the Changer strides along beside Anson. He is silent, so it could not be that his conversation is more interesting than her own.

Amphitrite notes Vera's interest and resolves to keep watch. If the Changer is in any danger, then she owes him her protection, for he is sea-born and her husband's own brother. If there is something else, then, well, he may still need her advice.

They are on the road when the Changer finally speaks. "How is Shahrazad? Well?"

"Nervous," Anson says honestly. "She didn't like having you gone away. She has also taken a fondness to shoes. Vera finally took pity on her and went and got her some shoes of her own."

"I went to Goodwill," Vera explains, "and bought some secondhand pairs—all leather. I washed them to get the worst of the polish and dirt off."

"The day that dirt harms a coyote is the day that coyote isn't fit for life," the Changer says. "Thank you."

Amphitrite watches closely. Vera's skin is coppery brown, but she is certain that the other woman blushed. Interesting.

When they arrive at the hacienda, Arthur is waiting for them, Eddie at his side. Eddie walks with crutches now, his heavily muscled shoulders and arms serving him well.

"Welcome, Your Majesty," Arthur says. "I am delighted to have one of the monarchs of the sea in my house."

Amphitrite replies graciously, "It has been long since you dwelt on English shores. I am pleased to visit you inland."

Eddie also greets her formally, but when those greetings are finished, he grins. "Don't you look wonderful! I didn't know that Lovern ever paid attention to female beauty."

"Don't believe it," she says. "He took to the design like a fish to water."

"Speaking of water," Arthur says, "you must be parched. Why don't you join us in the courtyard for a glass of iced tea?"

When they reach the courtyard, the Changer has taken the form of a grizzled grey coyote and lies on the ground permitting a young female of this species to chew at his ears and throat. Vera watches with amusement.

"His daughter?" Amphitrite asks.

"Yes. We call her Shahrazad. She's grown a great deal since they first came here. Soon no one will be able to doubt that she is a coyote."

"I could not doubt it now," Amphitrite says. "She looks much like her father, though tawnier. She has more white, too."

"Our problem is," Arthur says, pouring tea, "that many humans fear coyotes. They say they prey on their pets, their livestock, even their children. This hacienda has several acres of land about it, but, even so, if someone saw her and knew she was a pet, we might have difficulties with animal control."

"Then no one should see her," Amphitrite says, tasting the tea and enjoying the coolness of mint mixed into the brew.

"Easier said than done, especially now," the King replies. "We have many outsiders—caterers, florists, equipment rental—providing services for the Review. None will stay long, but their presence does increase the risk."

He raises his glass to Amphitrite. "Again, welcome." His smile reminds Amphitrite of the sun unexpectedly breaking though storm clouds. Smiling back, she feels that she is among friends.

✿▣✿

"Right over there, right over there! Yes, that will do."

Chris Kristofer sets down the stack of folding chairs and leans against the wall, trying to conceal that he is breathing hard. Unfortunately, Vera Tso proves to be as sharp-eyed as she is hard-driving.

"Are you all right?" she asks.

"Fine, fine!" Chris assures her heartily. "Just pinched my finger between two of the chairs. I'll start setting them up right away, Miss."

Their conversation is interupted by the entry of two more men, each bearing another stack of chairs. Someone calling from elsewhere in the hacienda draws Vera away.

Chris starts unfolding the chairs, arranging them to face the speaker's platform at the other end of the room. He hopes that Bill is having more luck with his own snooping.

Soon after the water-use meeting, Chris had told Bill about his determination to learn more about Arthur Pendragon. The college student had reacted with enthusiasm, helping to interview the neighbors, trying to gain access to Pendragon Estates, and following up a couple more cryptic e-mails assuring them that something big was going on.

The initial results had been disappointing. The neighbors knew next to nothing about three people who lived behind the high wall. Pendragon Estates proved impenetrable by the usual means. Salespeople, fund-raisers, and panhandlers were rejected without preference—none ever got past the heavy wrought-iron front gate. Chris even went so far as to acquire an electronic eavesdropping device, but met with nothing but static.

Then Bill had observed that Pendragon Estates was renting party supplies from a local merchant. The two investigators joined the crew for one delivery and triumphantly rode past the gate that had previously remained stubbornly closed.

Within minutes, Chris had acquired more information than he had during the previous month and a half. The hacienda at the center of the tree-shrouded grounds proved to have been restored with taste and apparently with no thought for expense. Clearly, it can house more than the three permanent inhabitants and more than those three are currently in residence. However, he can't tell if they live there permanently or are present for whatever event requires a truckload of folding chairs, card tables, glassware, and sundry other items.

Soon after the two professional movers have left Chris to continue setting up, Bill Irish wheels in a last load of chairs.

"C'mon," he hisses at Chris. "Coast's clear!"

Chris hurries over and looks down the hallway. He can hear voices arguing in the general direction of the kitchen. Unzipping his fanny pack, he takes out a small camera.

Bill tugs his arm. "I think the offices are this way!"

With Bill pushing his chairs in the lead, Chris snaps pictures of his surroundings. From the expensive rugs and knick-knacks, to the art hung on the walls, evidence of great wealth is all around him. Where are the servants who keep this place so gleamingly clean? In all his days of hanging around, he had seen no evidence of any coming or going. Did Pendragon keep separate servants' quarters, perhaps with wetback slave labor?

Confidently, Bill opens the door to an office near the entry foyer. "Take a peek," he whispers. "I'll keep watch. If someone sees us, we're just taking these chairs to the foyer."

Chris hopes the excuse will do. The office he has entered is decorated with examples of the most exquisite weaving he has ever seen—and he has a Southwesterner's jaded eye. He snaps a few shots as he moves across to the desk. It is singularly free of paperwork, and the computer screen is dark.

Damn.

"Nothing doing there, not without a lot more time," he says to Bill, emerging and shutting the door behind him. "It's a completely modern office. Let's stow those chairs in the foyer. We might have more luck upstairs."

Bill agrees. They hasten up the broad stairway with its hand-carved banisters.

"Money, money everywhere," Chris says softly, "yet nobody does a drop of work, no one is listed in anyone's database of prominent fortunes. I bet the IRS would love to see this place."

"Which way do we go?" Bill says.

"Pick a direction at random," Chris says, leading the way

down a corridor, trying doors, and finding them locked.

"This place is almost like a hotel," Bill offers. "What do you want to bet that the guests will be checking in tomorrow?"

"How about," says a clear, baritone voice with a slightly singsong accent, "today?"

Chris turns around slowly. Between them and the stairway stands a hirsute Asian man radiating a distinct air of belligerence. A suitcase rests by his feet.

"Who are you?" continues the stranger, his bristly beard jutting out aggressively. "And what are you doing up here?"

"We're deliverymen," Bill says quickly. "We're just checking out where . . ."

"You may be deliverymen," the stranger interrupts, "but I doubt that you should be here. Come! Let me make certain that you are trespassing before I beat the skin off of you."

There is no arguing with him. Chris and Bill obediently march down the steps into the entry foyer. Chris is mentally constructing excuses when their progress is interupted by an enormous broad-shouldered man with shining dark skin.

"Well, hello, Katsuhiro," the newcomer says in a deep, rumbling voice that is all the more menacing for its precise, rather British accents. "I thought I smelled your particular stench."

Their captor sneers, "I am Oba-san, to you, Dakar Agadez. Stop acting like the lump of iron that you are and let me pass. I have business with Arthur."

"So do we all," says Dakar Agadez, "or why else would we be here? I came to offer him my services in preparing for . . ."

For the first time Dakar notices the two investigators. Chris swallows hard, his carefully prepared excuses withering to nothing beneath the black man's deep, wild gaze. Terror rises within him, clouding his mind.

"What do you have here?"

"Two thieves I caught prowling above," Katsuhiro snarls.

"I should have known you couldn't deal with them yourself, that you'd go sniveling to Arthur . . ."

"YOU!" Katsuhiro roars something unintelligble. Dakar howls back. Within moments, massive fists are raised.

Realizing that they are momentarily forgotten, Chris fights

down his fear, grabs Bill, and drags him out the front door and across the grounds to the delivery truck.

When they are safely back at Chris's house, the two men review their experiences and the data they have gathered.

"I'll offer a theory as to what Mr. Arthur Pendragon is up to," Chris says solemnly. "There's only one thing that would pay for living so far beyond his apparent earnings *and* for doing business with ruthless thugs like the two we met."

"I bet I can guess," Bill says with a shiver.

"That's right." Chris lets the words roll off his tongue, imagining the breaking story. "Illegal drugs."

✿▣✿

Nattily attired in a crisp beige-linen suit, Sven Trout gets out of the taxi that has delivered him to the front door of Arthur's hacienda at about two in the afternoon.

After paying the driver, he pauses to admire the rambling adobe-brick building, its wide windows, wooden trim, and neatly tended garden beds proclaiming the best of the old and the new. There are several outbuildings as well: stables, storage buildings, a potting shed. No doubt most of these remain from when the hacienda was a working farm.

Straightening his bolo tie and picking up his suitcase, Sven strides to the front door and rings the bell.

It is answered after a moment by Anson A. Kridd, attired in a casual, floor-length caftan printed with bold stripes. He's munching a chocolate donut.

"Hello, Anson."

"H'lo, Sven. Come in."

Sven does so, not concealing his admiration for the lovely, understated decor of the front foyer. Wooden benches crafted along Spanish colonial lines are grouped around wool rugs to make cozy conversation areas in the vast space. More rugs hang on the walls. The mantel of the kiva fireplace set into one corner is decorated with several pieces of pottery by local artists. A baby grand piano fills the opposite corner.

"Very nice," Sven says. "Very. So, Arthur's got you working as doorman, hey, Anson?"

The black man smiles. "Worse, eh? Nursemaid. Eddie was

badly hurt a week or so ago. I came to take care of him.''

"Hurt?"

"Car wreck. Broken leg and ribs. He's hobbling, tiring himself terribly, trying to do all like before. The accident couldn't have come at a worse time than before the Lustrum Review."

Sven has lots of experience hiding his feelings, so he suppresses a satisfied grin and instead makes a nod that indicates acknowledgment and a touch of pity. He and Eddie have never gotten along very well, so showing more than general interest would be unwise. Indeed, he expects that if Eddie, rather than Vera, had been managing arrangements when he called for a room, the inn would have been full.

Anson gestures for Sven to follow and heads toward one of the openings radiating off the entry foyer.

"All the rooms upstairs were bespoken when you called," he says, the lilting rise and fall of his accent making the simple phrase poetry, "so you are on the ground floor. We have put you in a single room that shares a bath with another room. We hope you won't mind."

His words seem sincere. Sven reminds himself that despite Anson's close friendship with Eddie, he, too, has had his problems with Arthur.

"Who's my bathroom-mate-to-be?" Sven asks.

Anson chuckles. "The Changer and a coyote pup named Shahrazad."

The Changer! Sven's heart nearly skips a beat, and he hopes that his fair complexion doesn't reveal his flush of excitement.

"The Changer?" he says, and is pleased that his voice shows only mild interest. "He's in out of the wilds?"

"That's right."

Anson doesn't volunteer why. Sven, of course, knows why, and feels smug. His surveillance of Arthur's hacienda has been far from perfect, restricted mostly to the outer grounds, and comings and goings. When the Changer vanished at about the same time that Lovern did, Sven hoped that he would return, but this is his first confirmation that he had. He hadn't dared watch the airport too closely lest he be noticed at this critical juncture—many athanor could sense a fellow even in a shifted shape, and too many are beginning to arrive for the Review.

"Well, I hope he doesn't snore."

"It wouldn't matter," Anson says, unlocking the door to Sven's room. "The soundproofing is very good. Here is your key. It opens both this lock and the one to the bathroom."

"Thanks. What about on the Changer's side?"

"He has different locks. If you are using the toilet and want privacy, there is a latch you can throw."

Anson starts to turn away, then pauses. "Tonight, as you know, there is the opening reception so there will be a buffet. If you get hungry before then, there's stuff in the refrigerator."

"Great!"

"Most of us are helping with last-minute arrangements. That's why no one else has come to greet you. However, you are welcome to sit in the central courtyard."

"And if I want to pitch in?"

"I'll be in the kitchen. Come and find me there, and I'll put you to work." The Spider rubs his belly. "They've asked *me* to supervise the catering deliveries! Hah!"

Sven, who knows something of the Spider's legendary appetite, grins appreciatively. "I'll be there in about twenty minutes."

"Very good."

When he is alone, Sven goes into the bathroom he will share with the Changer. It is very nicely appointed with double sinks, a toilet, and a shower and tub. If it weren't for the painting on one wall, the eclectic fish-shaped soap dish, the softness of the towels, it could be a bathroom in a better hotel.

He tries the door to the Changer's room and finds it locked. Pressing his ear to the door, he strains to hear. Nothing.

Blood. He needs the Changer's blood. Now Fate has conspired to make him neighbors with his proposed victim.

Whistling softly a very old tune, Sven Trout trades his linen suit for a short-sleeved button-down shirt and blue jeans, then heads for the kitchen.

Anson is unpacking several boxes of ready-to-heat quiche. A lean but muscular dark-haired man with a coyote pup sitting on his feet is polishing a silver tray.

"Hello, Changer," Sven says cheerily.

Blood.

⚙️◉⚙️

Six hours later, the foyer that had been so empty and elegant when Sven arrived is bustling with activity. A cosmopolitan throng mills about, filling the benches, devouring the buffet supper, and listening to Tommy Thunderburst perform on acoustic guitar and piano.

Nor are they restricted to the foyer. The central courtyard rapidly fills, and the guests spill out into the gardens, where benches are conveniently placed. Fragments of conversation make a music of their own:

"Hello! It's been a long time!"

"Since the Wilson administration, I think. I've been living in Pakistan."

"Why ever would you do that?"

Tonight, Albuquerque's weather is perfect. The skies are clear and dark. The temperature is cool enough that formal wear is comfortable and remains crisply elegant.

"Welland! I'm so glad to see you. Are you still doing swordsmithing?"

"Pretty much as a hobby, these days. There's so little demand I have avoided drawing attention to myself."

"Would you consider doing some work for a friend?"

Drifting through the crowds, Louhi listens to snatches of conversation, greets old friends and acquaintances. There is no one here she has not known for at least two hundred years. Sometimes she finds this stifling.

"Patti Lyn, I have a hard time imagining you working on the stock exchange."

"Why, Jon? I'm no fool—like a couple I could name—believing that the old ways to power will still work."

"But you were always so hot-tempered!"

"If you think the stock exchange is silent but for the clatter of ticker tape, you need to update your image of the world. The world market is the last true battlefield and one with real long-term potential. Honestly, I have more to do with an immortal existence than cut off people's heads with swords."

Louhi passes Sven, who is absorbed in teasing Lil Prima. Lil looks stark and elegant, as if she had been poured out of molten gold and then had a skin stretched over her. Whatever Sven is saying does not amuse her. Her gaze, green as jealousy, is only for Tommy. Tommy's gaze is only for his guitar.

Near the buffet table, Katsushiro Oba and Arthur are busily discussing video cameras and computer modems. A few paces away, Dakar Agadez, hulking and black like wrought iron, argues contemporary African politics with Anson A. Kridd.

Louhi walks passed, hears a conversation that interests her.

"I don't need to look any further than those gathered here to see the real danger to the continued prosperity of the athanor. We've been living as humans for so long that the crafts that set us apart are being neglected."

"Do you mean magic, Oswaldo?"

"I do. I have had little help getting instruction, yet I have the talent. I would wager that among us we no longer have a dozen skilled generalists."

"You must be kidding!"

Eddie, leaning on his crutches, is flirting mildly with Tin Hau, who is calling herself Alice Chun these days, and writing novels set in ancient China. They had been married once, during one of the periods when Arthur and Eddie were not on good terms. Louhi suspects that there is still affection between them.

Now, in the courtyard, the Hero Twins (she forgets their current names) are debating the fragmentation of Eastern Europe with Vera and Patti Lyn Ansinbeau, who is best known as Morrigan.

Louhi drifts past and nods to Amphitrite, who is talking low-voiced about industrial waste and human expansion to Isidro Robelo and Cleonice Damita of the South American contingent.

Out in the garden, Louhi pauses to admire several pieces of sculpture, to chat with a tawny cat who knew Ramses the Great, to offer her opinion on Caribbean package tours to the Vagrant. Finally she sees the one who she has subconsciously been seeking.

He is in coyote form, grey, with a darker cross about his

shoulders. Beneath the ornamental junipers and cedars, a young female coyote is chasing a brace of jackalopes easily half her own size. Even at a distance, Louhi can tell that the older coyote is watchful of the little one's play.

She wants to go over to him, but he is in the company of Frank MacDonald, Old MacDonald, Francis of Assisi. Frank has no trouble speaking the languages of animals. Like Finn or Sigurd, his ears have been opened to their speech. He is a friend of the nonhuman, especially the nonmonstrous among the immortals: the Raven of Enderby, the Cats of Egypt, the Chinese nightingale, the Southwestern jackalope. It is like him to seek the Changer in such a noisy gathering.

Although Louhi can take many shapes, she only understands the speech of animals through spells. Not wishing to work even a simple bit of magic in such a gathering, she turns away and finds herself face-to-face with the one person she did not care to see.

Lovern looks very fine this evening. His long silver-grey hair is bound in a ponytail by a silver band; his beard and mustache are closer cut than she recalls from days of old. He wears a loose jacket and matching trousers of rough black silk. His tuxedo shirt is unruffled and white.

Louhi can sense the little emanations of power from the studs that close the shirt, from the cuff links, from the rings on the wizard's hands. Here, in his liege lord's hacienda, Lovern does not precisely flaunt his power, but where other adepts have left most of their amulets, as others have left their weapons, at the door, Lovern maintains his. It is a subtle reminder of his position in the King's esteem.

"Hello, Louhi," Lovern says, brilliant blue eyes seeking to meet her own. "You look lovely tonight."

There is nothing mocking in his voice, nor should there be. Louhi knows that she looks well, realizes with a strange pang that her pale platinum hair, fair skin, and blue eyes seem almost a match to Lovern's own. Her gown, however, is silver-shot velvet and her jewelry (but for routine wards) only adornment.

"Thank you," she says softly. "You were in Finland recently, were you not?"

"I was. It is still a land of mystery to me."

"Cold and ocean hold their secrets well," she agrees.

"I had thought about calling on you."

"You did?"

"Professional courtesy. I *was* in the land you had chosen for your own."

"Ah." She wonders if there might be more to his interest. Such courtesies might be extended within a city, but within an entire country? No, even a small country like Finland offers room enough for two athanor wizards.

"I was investigating Lappish songs," Lovern says, "but my singing voice is a weak instrument."

Louhi smiles, remembering Lovern's voice. Ages past it hadn't been very good. Encouraged by her smile, Lovern continues. "Still, I recorded many chants, made copious notes. Perhaps I will learn something new. There is always something new to learn, isn't there?"

He is definitely flirting with her. This puzzles her. Several hundred years have not made him forget his captivity in her keeping. Forget? No, never. Forgive? Perhaps.

She tries smiling again and sees Lovern relax further.

"Can I bring you a drink? The local wines are very good. New Mexico viticulture is the oldest in North America."

"I would like to try some," she says, knowing that she does not yet have the courage to speak to the grizzled coyote. "Perhaps I should come in with you."

"That would be very nice," Lovern says, offering her his arm. "Very nice, indeed."

Together they walk toward the house. Neither notices that a sardonic yellow gaze marks their progress.

¤◙¤

The next morning the Lustrum Review begins with a roll call of the athanor dead. It takes a long time, beginning with names so old that the languages within which they had originated are not only forgotten but unsuspected. In each case, the deceased is called by the name he or she had been best known. The mood when Arthur begins intoning the list is solemn, but by the end there is general fidgeting.

In this restless atmosphere, even the financial statements and routine departmental reports are greeted with an aura of relief. Following these, there is a short period of question and answer, then a refreshment break.

When the group returns from that break there is excitement in the air. Everyone knows that Isidro Robelo, the spokesman for the South American contingent, is going to bring up their pet issue.

In his place at the back of the room, the Changer leans against the doorframe. He knows the arguments that will be raised, partly because he has heard them before in other contexts, partly because Cleonice Damita has already lobbied him. Since he spends so much of his time in animal form, the automatic assumption is that he must be an environmental activist.

The Changer had not liked disillusioning that passionate woman with her feline manner, but his neutrality is precious to him. Were he to take an active role, he would be admitting, however tacitly, that he is a member of this Accord. As he sees it, the next step would have been trading votes on other issues, being nominated for elected offices, and other such insanity.

So he has politely refused to take part in any aspect. Still, he is interested. The issues may be the same, but the tools available for the task have changed.

Isidro Robelo rises to present his contingent's carefully crafted arguments. He is a handsome man whose first origin was in the Near East around the time of the Crusades. Many athanor consider him a newcomer. Isidro's dark hair and eyes, pointed beard, and coppery coloring could make him a representative of many races. Today, he looks like a Spanish don, but the Changer recalls when he looked equally convincing as a desert sheik.

Helping with his presentation is Cleonice Damita. She currently looks enough like Isidro that she passes as his sister. Actually, she was born in Mexico of an Aztec woman and a conquistador who was not as Spanish as he claimed.

Cleonice's father had kept an eye on her. When he realized that his athanor heritage had been passed on, he had taken his daughter from her homeland. She was about forty then, and her unaging was beginning to cause comment. Some years later, he had died in a street riot in Spain, never having been apotheosized, known to family and friends as a good man in a tight place.

The third member of the contigent is Oswaldo Barjak. Shorter and stockier, Oswaldo resembles a plump Mexican, especially in his bright *hurachas* and embroidered shirt. In fact, Oswaldo's heritage is far older. Born a Mongol, he had known Genghis Khan, and had served in his army of conquest.

The depredations of the Horde had made him swear off military life. For centuries, he has been a poet and scholar, known for great knowledge, odd flashes of passion, and a tendency to act the gentle clown. In the last century or so, he has begun a study of shamanistic magic.

Isidro and Cleonice produce photographs and progression curves supporting their claim that the plight of South America has serious repercussions for global ecology.

After they finish their introduction, Amphitrite rises and comments on the impact of global warming, deforestation, and unregulated dumping on the ocean environment.

Point and counterpoint, argument and rebuttal follow.

"Perhaps many here do not know," Isidro Robelo says, "or choose to forget, that the history of South and Central America have been actively shaped by athanor intervention."

Cleonice, her very presence a reminder of one of those interferences, takes up the point: "My mother's people told legends of Quetzalcoatl, the green-feathered serpent who also took the form of a white man. They said he was sent out into the world to reform it."

Ignoring Arthur's attempt to respond, Oswaldo Barjak expands on the point. "Inca legends spoke of Viracocha, the old white man who created men and women, and then educated them. They told how Viracocha walked away over the sea, but prophesied his return."

"That was just Vaiinamoinen!" Eddie protests. "He always was arrogant. That's why he didn't bother to alter his appearance to blend in with the local populace."

"And Vaiinamoinen's arrogance worked against the Incas," Oswaldo says, "for when Pizarro and his men came, the locals believed that he was Viracocha returned."

Cleonice adds, "As the Aztecs believed that Cortez was Quetzalcoatl come back."

Arthur gavels for silence. "Certainly you see that these very instances are reasons why we should not interfere in human societies! Vaiinamoinen meant well, but he did not consider the later repercussions of his actions."

Isidro Robelo shouts, "Yet no one stopped later interference that favored the conquistadors! Many Spanish chronicles recount how Saint Michael and his angels assisted Pizarro's forces against the cannibals of Puná. Then there was the 'miraculous' intervention of the Virgin Mary that smothered the fires when the Inca's forces attempted to retake Cuzco."

Oswaldo, who is rarely seen without a book in his hand, continues pedantically, "Modern historians explain these as either a ploy by the Spanish—who had been chided by their own king for the extremity of their actions—to demonstrate that God was on their side, or as the influence of the fanciful literary romances of the time on the style of the chronicler's reports. We know otherwise, don't we?"

Arthur shouts over the building hubbub. "Had I been in a position to do so, I would have stopped that action. I was not then. Now I am in a position to advise against similar action. Records of that interference—no matter how fancifully recorded—have been used as 'proof' that there was 'alien' interference in earthly affairs. I don't know about you, but that's a little too close to reality for me."

Isidro shakes his head. "I disagree. We are responsibile for our past actions and for mitigating what they have snowballed into now. Had South America been left to the Incas and the forest tribes, today's ecological crisis might not have occured!"

Jonathan Wong protests, "And how far back would you have us be responsible for the past actions of our kinfolk? I founded a philosophy. Arthur has left his mark in several legend-lines—including one that provided an initial impetus to monotheism. Does that mean he is responsible for correcting every religious war or for counseling Arthurian scholars? Let us be reasonable!"

Isidro tosses back his handsome head. "Perhaps if he had, those areas wouldn't be in the muddle they currently are!"

By the end of the scheduled meeting time, there have been further point and counterpoint, anecdotes galore, and furious clarification of perceived historical fact. Nothing is settled, but the question of what is meant by "interference" and the extent of its ramifications have been closely defined.

Arthur's voice is husky from shouting. Eddie is worn and pale. Despite the demands his injuries put on his body, he has insisted on remaining at Arthur's side. Vera is beside the King as well, her eyes stormy as the most volatile of the protestors insinuate that Arthur has ulterior motives for permitting current trends to continue.

The meeting formally adjourns at five that evening, but feelings are so high that there is no doubt that the discussion will continue wherever two or more of their number gather.

Other than the Changer, only one person in all that company expresses no opinion on the issues. Tommy Thunderburst, his guitar case hanging loosely from one long-fingered hand, waits patiently for Lil Prima to stop arguing with Frank MacDonald so she can drive him to the Crown Plaza Pyramid where the South American contingent are entertaining tonight.

Moved by some obscure impulse, the Changer walks over to Tommy. "So where do you stand on the matter?"

"It would be good if we could help," Tommy answers, "but can we? I mean, we can't always help ourselves. We're full of shit thinking we're the answer to the world's needs."

It is one of the longest speeches the Changer has heard from the laconic musician. "So you don't feel we should do anything?"

"Maybe, y'know, we should get our own house in order. All this arguing reminds me of the days when too many of us thought we were, like, gods."

The Changer nods. "And we're not."

"Hell, no, man! We're just not dead."

"Your hosts tonight might be surprised by your ambivalence."

"Why? I'm no green peacer."

"But you're a musician."

Tommy's gaze is clear and sad. "The single most self-destructive profession—least that's how it looks from this side. Oh, I don't mean the orchestra folks; they've got harmony of soul as well as when they're playing."

He pauses. "Least I think so. But I've never figured out

how rock 'n' rollers, most of whom are trashed off their asses most of the time, can get off telling the world not to spoil nature. I mean, if you don't tend your personal ecology, where do you get off telling others how to tend to Mother Earth?''

"Interesting."

"Hey, man, I know it. I mean, I've been there. Over and over again. You coming to the party?"

"Probably not." The Changer gives a rueful shrug. "I have spoken with more people today than I usually do in five years. I will stay here and wash dishes or something else helpful."

"Yeah." Tommy's eyes grow vague, and the Changer thinks he is forgotten. He is departing when Tommy says, "Remember what it was like when we didn't give a shit who knew we were different? Then we didn't do the dishes and eat catered banquets. There were giants in the earth in those days and we were them."

"I remember those days," the Changer says, "although I lived then much as I do now."

"There were servants," Tommy says, "and no press, no television. We did what we wanted."

"There were always uprisings and witch-hunts."

"Only for those who weren't careful. Lots of humans liked having heroes. Look at how they still pine for Arthur. Shit, the French even think de Gaulle will return. That's pathetic."

"Why?"

"Because we're really here. They don't got to dream about heroes. We're here. Magic and might, power and grandeur. I mean, we're *here*."

"So we are."

"Yeah." Tommy sighs. "I liked my last life. I was like a king again, with my knights and my buddies. I didn't need to fuss about all this shit. If I wanted something, it was mine."

The Changer shakes his head. "You will probably have that again. You could have it now."

"I need the crowd," Tommy says, only partially listening. "I can't just jack off in private. That means a persona who can get away with shit."

"I see."

"Here comes Lil. Guess it's time to jam."

"Yes."

The Changer gives Lil a polite bow as they pass. Shahrazad has been locked up for several hours now. Doubtless she could use a run. After everything he has heard these past hours, so could he.

¤◻¤

Arthur rubs his eyes with fingers that feel thick as sausages. Lifting a plastic bag of trash (after the afternoon's arguments, it seems emblematic of the wastefulness of all the Western World) he troops into the kitchen. Lovern is there loading trays and serving pieces into the dishwasher.

"I don't suppose you could summon up some brooms to do the cleanup, could you?" the King asks his court wizard.

"I've already activated the routine housekeeping spells," Lovern assures him. He has draped his silk jacket over a chair, but otherwise remains formally attired. "It's a pity that Odd and Pod, Duppy Jonah's octopus servants, aren't here. They have arms enough for washing up."

"Maybe the Changer could . . ." Arthur guffaws at the image.

"Don't laugh," Lovern replies. "He's tending to the outer gardens and has expressly requested solitude. I suspect that an anomaly walks among our shrubbery."

"I hope no one sees . . . whatever he is."

"He hasn't survived this long without being careful."

"True."

The King carries the trash out to the garage, coming back with some empty bags. Perching on a stool, he begins to sort recyclable materials. "I've put Eddie to drafting and printing a summary of today's meeting. He refused to go sleep."

"*That* I may be able to help with."

"Only with Eddie's permission. Vera is checking the guest rooms. Almost everyone went out to the South Americans' party."

"How's Eddie feeling?"

"Not great—not that he'll admit it. I wish that Garrett had been available to attend the Review."

Lovern nods, knowing that the greatest of the athanor doctors might be able to hasten Eddie's healing—or at least provide him with relief from the pain. Garrett Kocchui, however, is currently serving with a Red Cross emergency medical team and Eddie had categorically refused to have him summoned.

"Anyone else stay in?" Lovern asks.

Arthur nods. "The Smith—he's downloading the late e-mail from those of our people who were teleconferencing. Anson's helping him. Said something about spiders knowing webs."

"Amphitrite?"

"She went to the South Americans' party." Seeing the panicked expression on Lovern's face, Arthur reassures him. "She said to tell you that she released you from caretaking duties this evening. She has asked Jonathan Wong to look after her."

Lovern visibly relaxes. "Good. No one will cross him. We've all needed his expertise too frequently."

"That's why I didn't mention anything earlier."

Arthur finishes sorting the trash. When he returns from putting the sacks in the garage he says, almost diffidently, "Do you think the South Americans are right, Lovern?"

"About the ecological crisis?"

"That's right."

"Yes and no. Yes, there is a building crisis. No, I'm not certain that athanor can do anything about it. Individuals can alter their own behavior." Lovern shuts the dishwasher and sets it to run. "Or we can surreptitiously deal with problem areas."

Lovern pours a glass of red wine from an almost empty bottle. Sipping it, he starts wiping off the countertops. "The problem is, humans have developed tools and weapons that have a far greater dispersal than we can quietly effect.

"Today Amphitrite spoke eloquently about the effects of ocean dumping. What happens if we agitate to end ocean dumping and then an oil or chemical spill pollutes the same waters? Do we try to stop shipping?"

Arthur washes his hands, all too aware of the soap (at least the brand they use is biodegradable) washing away with the dirt and grease down the drain. "I sympathize with the South

Americans, but I understand what you're saying. I wish I knew what to command.''

Lovern finishes his wine. "Don't worry too much. Tomorrow afternoon the seminars begin. Let Jonathan talk about new advances in forgery. Let Patti Lyn lecture on future financial planning. Let Lil talk about the mixed blessings of investing in art and antiques. By evening, at least half of those who are so passionate now will be worrying about whether their stock portfolios will keep them in style for another hundred years or about whether they should update their identities. I've seen it happen time and again. We are all idealists until we get down to the nuts and bolts of survival.''

Arthur seems relieved. "Speaking of nuts and bolts, I'd better go and review the e-mail.''

"Don't stay up too late,'' Lovern cautions.

"I won't. I'm taking my laptop to bed.''

"Our guests have keys?''

"Yes, and the alarm code. We'll need to reprogram the security system and wards when they've left.''

"Right. Good night, Arthur.''

"Good night, my wizard.''

14

The trouble with our times is that the future is not what it used to be.

—PAUL VALÉRY

THE MEETING ROOM THE NEXT MORNING IS FILLED WITH A buzz of satisfied conversation. Even without listening closely, Vera, seated to one side of Arthur at the curved table in the front of the room (it rather resembles half a donut and is, in a sense, the current incarnation of the Round Table), catches fragments:

"I really think that the solution involves taking a direct hand in matters."

"Well, I certainly don't want to be responsible for more extinctions. I still feel bad about the passenger pigeons."

"Until last night I didn't realize how many of the things we take for granted come from the rain forests."

Clearly many of the athanor think that the issue has been settled in the informal discussions held the night before. Now she regrets not going to the South American contingent's party—if only so she could tell Arthur what had been said. A long time has passed since she cared about the opinion of the mob. Only when the Olympians (as they had jokingly referred to themselves) had been the reigning force in the Mediterranean basin had she been part of a ruling oligarchy.

Staying back at the hacienda, walking from guest room to guest room and leaving a basket on the doorstep with fresh soap, towels, a package of candy, and the next morning's agenda had been more to her liking. And had her absence been much of a loss? No one would have talked freely around her. Certainly Jonathan Wong has reported anything significant to Arthur.

During her rounds the evening before, she had sneaked periodic glances out the windows, trying to see what the Changer was about, but had learned nothing. All she knows is that this morning the gardens look untouched—not as if they had just been host to dozens of wandering conventioneers.

When the meeting begins, Isidro Robelo is recognized first, but his speech is hardly more than a rehash of the previous day's arguments. Vera hides a little smile, noting that Isidro is losing some of his audience and offending those who are not already of his party with his assumption that they will be swayed by mere repetition. Good.

Her gaze drifts to where the Changer leans against the doorframe. His eyes are mostly closed, his chin against his chest. To any who look his way, he may seem asleep. She wonders if this is so; the ancient cares little for athanor politics. Then Louhi is recognized. At her first words, Vera sees the Changer's eyes open.

"Eve's unwashed children," Louhi says in her cool, precise tones. "In the part of the world where I currently dwell, that is the story they use to explain what they call the *huldre* folk—the hidden ones."

"I don't know that tale," Dakar says, his voice gruff and deeper than usual. He's never been able to hold his liquor.

"Eve was washing her babies when God came to visit," Louhi says, as if recounting history. "She hid the children she hadn't tidied up yet. When God asked if he had seen all her children, she insisted that he had. God asked again. When Eve continued to insist that the tidy children were her entire family, God said: 'Very well. Those you have claimed will be seen by all, but those you have hidden will remain hidden.' "

Lil Prima's husky voice is heard commenting softly, "Eve always was a dumb bitch."

Louhi continues as if there had been no interruption. "I wonder if Arthur considers us Eve's unwashed children—a

disgrace to be hidden from the world. We have called ourselves by all manner of proud names: Aesir, Olympians, Il-
luminati, but truly, who is more a *huldre* folk than
ourselves?''

Laughter, sarcastic comments, beginnings of argument,
shouts to be recognized break out as Louhi finishes. Arthur
lets chaos dominate for a moment, then gavels for order.

''Silence! Silence!''

The roar ebbs to a dull hum. Arthur points the handle of
his gavel at Jonathan Wong, ignoring mutters of favoritism.

''Jonathan, you are recognized.''

The portly Chinese rises and faces the assembled company.
''Louhi has made a fascinating point. However, I wish to
remind her that the days when a Sargon or Moses or Momo-
taro simply could claim to have been found in a basket as a
child are gone.''

A deep voice rumbles from the back of the room: ''Sargon
the mighty king of Akkad, am I. My mother was lowly, my
father I knew not. The brother of my father dwelt in the
mountains. My city is Agade, which lieth on the bank of the
Euphrates.''

Even the murmuring stops then. The speaker, who now
quietly farms rice in Korea, rises and bows in Jonathan
Wong's direction. ''It *was* easier then,'' he says, and takes
his seat again.

Next Arthur recognizes Lil Prima.

''I agree with both Louhi and Jonathan,'' she says, her
small smile acknowledging that she is aware of the apparent
contradiction in her position. ''We are the hidden folk, but
we are hidden for a reason. Today, most nations record even
a foundling. Also none of us are children. Even those who
can shapeshift have better things to do than put in a twenty-
year apprenticeship for the sake of an identity. Thank God
(or whoever) for war and natural disaster! Without them, we
would be in a great deal of trouble.''

''Why must we hide at all!'' shouts someone from the safe
anonymity of the crowd.

The orderly meeting dissolves into argument. Frustrated,
Arthur hammers for quiet, then orders an adjournment. People flow from the room like the ebb of waters before a tsunami.

The South American contingent desperately try to get attention returned to their pet issues. Others are insisting that neither issue is as important as the matters raised in the seminars scheduled for the afternoon. Dakar and Katsuhiro are shaking fists at each other, blocking one doorway until the Smith, with calm disregard for his own safety, shoves them through.

Vera glances about, hoping to find the Changer. To her surprise, he strolls to stand beside her.

"More trouble than for many years," he says, surveying the almost empty room. "I wonder, could this somehow be connected to that event which first brought me here?"

His cryptic phrasing puzzles her only for a moment. Seeing her about to speak, he lays a finger against her lips.

"Enough said. Perhaps too much. I refuse to take sides in mere government, but if this is something more . . ."

She feels his growl, is too aware of the warmth of the strong finger against her lips.

"I will not speak to Arthur," the Changer says, removing his finger. "You, though, I can speak to unofficially and know that the words will go where they should be heard. Yes?"

"Yes, of course."

Her voice catches slightly, but she doesn't think the Changer notices.

"I will be back for the next portion of the meeting," he says. "Thank you."

As he leaves, she sees that he is already loosening his shirt. Shapeshifting, then. Spying almost certainly. She feels a momentary regret that he no longer strips in public.

¤◼¤

Fear that he is missing something crucial gives the Changer speed. He almost runs down the corridor to his room, unbuttoning his shirt as he goes. When he enters the room, Shahrazad pounces on him, whimpering her happiness that he has returned.

"I can't stay, little one," he says in English, "and you cannot come with me unless you grow wings and fly."

She does not understand, nor did he expect her to do so.

Frolicking, she tugs at the cuff of his jeans as he pulls them off, seizes one of his socks and vigorously "kills" it. Doubtless she associates his removing clothing with his shifting into a shape that will play with her. He regrets that he must disappoint her.

He is about to shift into the form of a common garden sparrow when he notices that Shahrazad has spilled her water dish. Picking the dish up, he unlocks the bathroom door. He may begrudge the time, but in this arid climate he cannot responsibly leave her without water.

As he turns the tap, he feels a sharp pain. Looking at his hand, he sees blood running from two of his fingers and the thumb. A quick shift closes the wound and, after setting down Shahrazad's dish, he searches for what has cut him.

Behind the cold water tap, he finds a piece of clear glass, wedged into place and nearly invisible. The tumbler, he notices now, is a different one than the one that had been there that morning. Perhaps Sven broke it and missed this one piece. He might even have swept the shard into its new harbor when wiping up the mess. The angle is consistent with such a scenario.

The Changer does not spare much thought for the accident, but drops the glass shard into the trash can before locking the door. When he glances out into the corridor it is empty. Stepping nude out into the hall, he closes the door firmly behind him and slips the key onto the slight shelf created by the molding around the door. It is not the best hiding place, but it must do. So prepared, he shifts shape into a sparrow.

There is the chance that someone will scent him, but he plans to keep upwind of anyone he is eavesdropping upon. He flies down the hall, through the open door into the courtyard, and into the sky above. Much precious time has been lost, but he still hopes to learn something that will lead him to his enemy.

✿◙✿

In the angry tumult that disrupts the meeting, Louhi hurries into the kitchen and up the steps to the residential areas.

During her conversation with Lovern the night before she had ascertained which room was his. Now, her heart pounding, her imagination fluttering with various excuses she could make to explain her presence in this area, she moves quickly, but without apparent stealth toward Lovern's room.

When she arrives on the appropriate corridor, the doors to all four suites are closed. She has seen both Arthur and Eddie downstairs, but there is a chance that one of them—or Anson—might dash up for something during this unexpected break.

Standing before Lovern's closed door, she focuses her astral sight. A faint aura, rainbow-hued, its power contained into such a narrow band that a less sophisticated practitioner might believe there was no ward at all, gleams along the door, crisscrossing it lightly at the panels.

She frowns. Were Lovern not in the hacienda, she might try working her way through the ward, but this close he is certain to sense any meddling. The Head must wait in his isolation a bit longer. Her desire had been less to gain actual entry than to see what awaited her.

Balked, but not defeated, she returns to the stair by which she had ascended. When she reaches the kitchen, she listens, but doesn't hear anyone within. However, when she steps out, the room is not completely empty. Vera stands filling a basin with water, her expression thoughtful. She turns as Louhi enters.

"Good morning," the sorceress says boldly. "Can you tell me which is Jonathan Wong's room? I want to leave him a note."

Vera is not convinced, but she answers politely. "He's in A-4, but you can't leave him a note short of tacking it on the door. The rooms are locked and the doors fit too snugly."

"Ah," Louhi nods solemnly. "Than perhaps I shall slip it into his pocket. Thank you so much."

She exits. Vera watches her leave and wonders what Louhi was really doing upstairs. She doubts that she could find out and, glancing at a clock, sees that the intermission is over.

Outside the window, a sparrow flits by.

☼◉☼

The morning session continues with a return to the South American contingent's proposal. By the lunch recess, much has been discussed, but nothing resolved. There have also been two fistfights, a broken chair, and a great deal of shouting.

"You would think," Eddie says to Arthur as they adjourn to the King's office for sandwiches and cola, "given our ages we would be less fractious."

"Why?" Arthur says wearily. "We are all accustomed to influence within our daily spheres. Even those with no fixed address, like the Vagrant, have resources beyond the folk they encounter in their daily routine. Such confidence breeds arrogance, and arrogance does not make for quiet cooperation."

"True."

"Now, let's review the order of the afternoon seminars. How did the sign-ups go?"

☼◉☼

After promising to meet Amphitrite and a *tengu* for lunch out in the garden, Sven excuses himself and heads back to his bedroom to see if his little trap caught anything. Unlocking his door, he checks a few routine indicators and is satisfied that the room has not been entered in his absence. Then he opens the bathroom door.

The glass shard is gone from where he had so artfully secreted it. When he fishes it from the trash, a pale pink trace marrs its clear edges. Not enough blood to do him any good, but proof that someone—presumably the Changer—was cut.

The ivory porcelain of the sink is unstained by blood and he curses softly. All is not yet lost. Opening the cabinet under the sink, he finds a small bucket tucked behind the extra washcloths and rolls of toilet tissue.

Rinsing the bucket in the tub, he unscrews the trap in the sink's piping. A flow of reddish water, slightly foaming from soapy residue, rewards him. The blood has been diluted, but perhaps it will be enough for Louhi to work her spell.

Setting the bucket carefully aside, he reassembles the trap. After washing his hands, he pours the bloody water into a wide-mouthed jar he had brought along for the purpose.

The room does not have a refrigerator, but there is an ice bucket which he fills from the bin in the courtyard. Once his prize is cooling, he glances at his watch. Still enough time to make his lunch date. He can get the bottle to Louhi tonight.

Locking the door behind him, he strides down the hall.

☼◉☼

The afternoon sessions are calmer than the morning's for two reasons: They are smaller and the topics are preassigned. From meeting rooms a dull buzz of voices, sometimes raised in question and answer, can be heard. The hacienda might be a small college. For now, the morning's arguments have been put aside.

Hanging by his hair above the gold, hexagonal box, the Head strains to hear what is going on in the world without.

Even this much freedom had been difficult to gain. Only the threat of absolute silence had won him this concession.

True, without complete immersion in the sustaining ichor, Mimir's Head is more vulnerable to the vagaries of the world without, but Lovern has rigged a field of sorts to keep away insects. A humidifier helps compensate for the dry air, and the Head feels that chapped lips and tired eyes are a fair trade for the sound of voices and birdsong. Even his pulled-upon scalp has ceased to ache.

Moreover, his gaze can wander about Lovern's room. He has yet to grow weary of color, light, motion, shadows, and the little details of daily life. He reads the titles of books on shelves, sees for the first time amulets and enchanted gewgaws he had helped to design, and his ambition to be free swells.

Once he hears a set of light footsteps pause outside of Lovern's door. However, no effort is made to open that door, and he is left to wonder if one of his associates had attempted to visit him. Perhaps the sound had just been Vera dropping off paperwork or one of the guests gone astray while searching for a specific room. No matter, even the conjecture is a pleasant change from the monotony of his dark, cold, aquatic prison.

The Head swings slightly in the breeze from a window he had asked Lovern to leave ajar. He imagines that he is walking, and his grotesque mouth twists in a smile.

¤▨¤

The Lustrum Review stretches on for a week. By the end of it, all around, tempers have gone from fervent to thin and frazzled to merely exhausted.

In Vera's room, Amphitrite sprawls on the bed. Vera sits next to her, rubbing moisturizing cream into the Sea Queen's suntanned skin.

"I can't believe you can *live* in this climate," Amphitrite says. "The air is so impossibly dry."

"New Mexico *is* arid," Vera admits, "a land of wind and sunlight rather than of water."

"I've been invited to visit South America and see these rain forests. Do you think I should go?"

"You might find the heat as extreme a burden as the dryness," Vera says honestly, "but you wouldn't need to worry about dry skin."

"I wonder. I would like to see more of the land than just this Albuquerque, but I miss my husband."

"Judging from the rash of spontaneous deep-sea storms," Vera chuckles, "he misses you, too. The human meteorologists are even more confused than usual."

"Can you put some more cream on the area between my shoulder blades?" In a more thoughtful tone, Amphitrite continues, "I forget that humans can now see even what goes on in the vastness of the ocean surface."

"Not in the depths," Vera agrees, "not yet, but on the surface. Weather satellites, military satellites, broadcast satellites . . . Not much on the Earth's surface cannot be seen. Fortunately, much that is seen is still not understood."

"Yet Arthur believes that we can hide in plain sight."

"We have thus far."

"There have been more advances in human technology in

the last two hundred years than in all the time before."

"That, of course, is a matter of debate." Vera grins impishly. "As we have heard over and over again this last week."

"Especially over the meaning of the term 'advance,' " Amphitrite agrees. "Leaving that aside, humans can see more, record more, analyze more, communicate more swiftly and over longer distances than ever before."

"And so can we," Vera reminds her. "These abilities once were the provenance of the rare wizards among us. Now they can be possessed by any of our people."

"As long as they have money."

"True. I suspect that Arthur views the good of the whole as sufficient reason to supply those who cannot purchase what they need for themselves."

" 'Good' being defined as keeping our existence secret."

Vera snaps the top closed on the moisturizer bottle. "Yes. As we both know."

"And have heard debated over and over." Amphitrite squeezes the other woman's hand apologetically. "I am sorry. I wasn't challenging you. I simply . . . I miss having Duppy Jonah to talk with about such things. Telephone calls are not the same."

"So I've heard."

Rolling onto her stomach, Amphitrite cradles her face in her hands. "Haven't you ever been in love?"

Vera frowns, her gaze fixed on the plastic bottle in her hands. "There have been a few times that I thought so, but, no, I've never been in love in the way you love Duppy Jonah."

"Few," Amphitrite says honestly, "love as we do. We have weathered our storms, learned that we are equals despite his great age and my relative—to him—youth. Still, I think there are shorter-lasting loves that are no less powerful: Eddie and Tin Hau, for example, or the many among us who have loved mortals despite the knowledge that they would die before us."

"I don't know if I could stand that knowledge," Vera admits. "There are legends from my birth land of goddesses who loved men and wished them immortality only to see them wither into grasshoppers or sleep forever."

"All the world has such legends," Amphitrite responds. "Some told from the point of view of the mortal, some from the immortal. Scholars tell us that they are allegories for the risks taken by all who love. Remember, even in human unions, one partner will usually outlive the other. Even among our folk, accidents and battles end lives."

Remembering the litany that began the meeting, Vera nods. "Yes. I know. Why are you talking about this?"

Amphitrite smiles, sits up, puts on a brassiere, then a silk tank top. "It is well-known that lovers delight in talking about love. I thought you might welcome the opportunity."

"Me!"

"I have seen how you watch the Changer, how you find small reasons to seek him out. I thought that perhaps . . ."

"No!"

"I apologize, but I don't think that I am wrong."

"I have kept an eye on him," Vera says defensively. "He is a wild thing in this house. With the Review taking so many violent turns, I worried about such a potent, unallied presence."

"Wise of you, but then you are known for your wisdom."

Vera rises, obviously uncomfortable. "I'll leave this bottle of moisturizer in the bathroom."

"Thank you for your help. I am much more comfortable." Amphitrite stretches, then reaches for her panties and skirt. "I will consult with Lovern before I decide whether or not to take up the South Americans on their invitation."

"Good idea."

"See you at dinner?"

"Of course."

Vera departs rapidly. Amphitrite laughs softly as she finishes dressing. There is time to call Duppy Jonah before she is needed. He will be terribly pleased to hear that his brother has an admirer.

She wonders if the Changer would be as pleased.

✧✧✧

The Lustrum Review ends that evening with the grand ritual of the Harmony Dance. No one, not even the Changer or

Lilith, recalls precisely when the Dance came into existence, nor has it remained the same over the unfolding of the millennia.

It occurs once every five years at the conclusion of the Lustrum Review, and such is the artistry of its design that the number—or the humanity—of the dancers does not markedly affect the performance of its complex choreography.

In some ways it resembles an English country dance, for the assembled dancers take places in two lines facing each other, but the line is not straight. Instead it curves like a lazy snake so that all but the outermost lines have at least one line in front and one in back.

The music changes from era to era and according to the customs of the country in which the Review is meeting. This year the composition is indebted to fiddles, chimes, and a light percussion like very small hailstones striking a copper roof. There is also an undertone of thudding monotone drums.

Needless to say, the entire Harmony Dance is greatly dependent on magic, but, appropriately enough, it is not the magic of any one individual. Rather, it is the magic created by the gathering of the athanor. The Dance signifies their desire to live in accord with each other, and it is not unknown for blood enemies to dance a measure or two with each other in the most supreme elegance and kindness.

It is more than just a dance, however, for Harmony is the greater element that binds them all together, the force that rejuvenates them. Even those, like the Changer, who are not signatories to the Accord are within Harmony. To be outside of Harmony for an athanor is to be as good as dead.

This year, as for some years past, immediately prior to the Harmony Dance those who wish to renew their oath of fealty to Arthur and Accord come before him in his office. The swearing is brief and dignified. King Arthur does not lord over his subjects, but rather accepts the responsibility that they are consigning to him. Even the South American contingent comes to swear—and some of the weariness slides from Arthur's features.

As the athanor gather on a broad, clear section of the grounds outside of the hacienda (it cannot, in all fairness be called a lawn as there is no grass but only a covering of fine crushed gravel the color of old emeralds), a pale white mist rises from the ground and cloaks their activities from any who might by chance be out this early-summer evening.

"Lovely," Amphitrite comments to Jonathan Wong.

"Lovern's work, though I believe that Lilith, Louhi, Oswaldo, and several others have given their aid. Once the Dance begins it will be sustained by Harmony itself."

"I've never been to one of these," the Sea Queen admits, "though we have our own Dancing beneath the oceans for those within Harmony who cannot come to land."

Jonathan Wong's expression becomes wistful. "I have always wished to see how the Sea Dance is done."

"Come next year," she invites him. "You would be welcome."

"Thank you."

With a gentle tintinnabulation, the music begins. Everyone bows to their opposite, even the jackalopes who take care that their antlers do not scratch and the *tengu* who have, in this moment of privacy, assumed the shape of long-nosed Japanese monks with awkward-seeming wings.

Then the fiddles strike up something light and cheering, a fast-moving tune that makes even the most solemn smile and those who had thought themselves tired discover new exuberance. The dancers side right and left with their opposites, turn to offer the same courtesy to those to either side, then the entire figure uncoils into something like a spiral, groups of four making a star with their right hands, then spinning out to join an entirely different set of four.

Turning out of the second star, Amphitrite finds herself dancing opposite Vera. The grey-eyed girl has piled her black hair high on her head in the traditional style for Navajo women. She wears a dress of dark red velvet with buttons made from flattened coins the same color as her eyes.

Vera smiles greeting and reaches out to take Amphitrite's hands. Spinning around once, they reach out and grasp the hands of those on either side, Lilith and the Smith, as it turns out.

Their four goes once quite around, like children playing ring-around-the-rosy, then joins hand with another four, making a circle of eight. Their circle of eight opens to encompass a circle of four, one of whom is a young coyote pup, prancing gaily with the rest.

"That's Shahrazad!" Vera exclaims in surprise, then she is whipped away to become the center of a circle made up of eight others. In the general company, it seems full right that a coyote should dance, and so Vera forgets to be surprised.

Nor does the Changer, human-form for this event, make any comment. He bows to the pup when they pass in a form and she wags her brush with glee and picks up her paws most elegantly. Implications are things for the morrow.

When the chimes blend with the fiddles, the Dancing becomes less expansive. Small sets are danced, sometimes in groups as small as two, sometimes alone. However, even in these sets, the Dance emphasizes the Harmony of the whole, the actions of the individual varying only slightly from those of the dancers in nearest proximity. Thus, although the motions of the dancers on the outermost rim bear no similarity to those in the center, a continuity can be perceived.

Were one watching from above, one would see the exquisite balance of the dancers, each swirling in his or her own orbit, each, like stars in a spiral galaxy, each kept in place by the greater force of the whole.

One does watch from above, by means of a magical mirror it has activated. Hanging by its hair, its skin tormented by the dryness of the air, Mimir's Head watches the celebration of community it has been denied even as Harmony pulls it into temporary congruence with the whole.

It weeps, but its tears are red as blood and its thoughts are filled not with a longing to be one with the group below, but with the longing to destroy it.

15

The head is always the dupe of the heart.
—LA ROCHEFOUCAULD

THE MORNING FOLLOWING THE HARMONY DANCE, SVEN Trout drives his latest rented car to the hotel where Louhi is staying. Boldly assuming his welcome, he goes directly up.

Louhi answers the door clad only in a wrap of woven silk the silver-green of winter ice. The weave of the fabric is so fine that it clings to the roundness of her breasts and even to the hollow of her navel. Sven feels himself stiffen in admiration.

"Good morning!"

"I thought it must be you," she says, not inviting him in but instead studying him thoughtfully.

"Is this a bad time?" he asks with a leer.

"Any time a man interrupts a lady is a bad time." She sighs breathily, causing interesting corresponding motions in her breasts. "I suppose I must speak with you sooner or later. Come. You can wait in my parlor."

Not one of those who needs worry about money, Louhi has taken a suite. An unfolded newspaper and a plate with a few crumbs on it show how she has passed the morning.

"Wait here," she says, pointing to the sofa. "I will be with you anon."

She exits into the bedroom. There is the pointed sound of a door locking. Sven chuckles and picks up the newspaper.

When the shower starts, his gaze becomes dreamy and he puts the paper aside. The trend of his thoughts can be read in his anatomy.

When Louhi emerges from the bedroom, she is dressed in a midcalf-length broomstick skirt of light cream-colored cotton and a matching embroidered blouse. Her feet are bare, but around one ankle she wears a bracelet of pearls and jet. Her wrists are adorned with intricately carved bangles of cinnamon wood, and from her ears hang Venetian glass pendants.

Sven is familiar enough with her magic to suspect that one or more of her pieces of jewelry are enchanted and puts aside certain fantasies, albeit regretfully.

"I suppose you've come to ask about the blood that you gave me," Louhi asks.

"That I have, lovely one."

"There isn't enough for my needs, nor can I work with it in such a dilute form."

"Damn."

"Did you attempt to get any other samples?"

"I did. I didn't have much luck. I couldn't very well leave more glass in the bathroom . . ."

"No." Louhi's sour expression shows how little she thought of that gimmick.

"I couldn't very well ask him to bleed into a jar!"

"No."

"I set a trip line outside of his door, a thin filament that would break on contact."

"And?"

"He never caught on it. That damn bitch . . ."

Louhi arches an eyebrow.

"The coyote puppy," Sven clarifies, "broke it. The Changer didn't take part in any of the pickup games the rough-and-tumble types organized, and, even if he had, I suspect he would have simply shapeshifted to heal any damage."

"True." Louhi's expression is unsympathetic. "So what are you going to do? You have promised the Head his body. I have done my part and designed the spell. You are the one who has thus far been found wanting."

"I've tried!"

"We are not children here that such an excuse is acceptable. I managed brief contact with Mimir's Head during the Review. He is delighted to be out of his prison, but his impatience grows."

"Tough. He's going to keep waiting."

"And if Lovern returns him to the ocean's keeping?"

"He won't. I plan to keep harrying the household. Harmony be damned! I don't care if anyone gets killed if I can keep Lovern nervous." Sven grins maliciously. "In any case, I don't think that Duppy Jonah has forgiven him his trespass. Wherever the wizard next stows the Head, it won't be underwater."

"Don't you realize that the more of those games you play, the more chance there will be of your being taken?"

"I have already made provisions against that." Sven looks around the room. "Can I call room service for something? Breakfast was rather slim at the hacienda this morning."

"Certainly."

After placing his call, Sven continues, "Several *tengu* attended the Lustrum Review. A few I have been courting in my persona as Moderator; a few others came to support Katsuhiro Oba if his feud with Dakar Agadez flared."

"No luck there."

"Not for them, but for me. They were pretty bored and testy. One 'Monk'—his Japanese name is a tongue twister—I had a pretty good read on from the chatroom. I didn't let on that I was the Moderator, of course, but I did let on that I thought that the stuffy sorts could use some shaking up."

Louhi smiles. "And, since *tengu* are already inclined to think that way . . ."

"Don't overlook the artistry of my manipulation . . ."

"He took to the idea."

"Precisely. Monk and his fellow *tengu* will be performing the trickster parts. If they are caught, their 'confessions' will lay the groundwork for September's Event."

"Very nice. Meanwhile, you will be free to take on other tasks."

"Like getting the Changer's blood." Sven chews his lower lip. "I thought that we were going to get our vote of no confidence right at the Review, but Arthur calmed them down. He even had the South Americans eating out of his hand by the end.''

"Too many of our people are too centered on their own needs," Louhi says, fully aware of the irony of her words.

"Yes. It's probably good that the vote didn't happen. There would be no reason for anyone to support *me*. In September, things will be different.''

"They had better be," Louhi says. "You've made some big promises.''

"Don't worry, darling," Sven replies. "The Head will have his body. I will have my throne, and you will have the Changer's attention. One big happy triumvirate.''

"You sound so certain.''

"Why not?"

A knock announces the arrival of Sven's meal. He goes to the door, but when he begins to sign the bill to the room Louhi clears her throat. He fishes out his wallet and pays the man in cash.

"That was cheap of you," he says, lifting the cover off of his plate of *huevos rancheros*.

"I've extended you enough credit," Louhi says. "Now I want some results.''

❖▣❖

The morning following the Harmony Dance, nearly all of the hacienda's guests take their leave. After the last load is driven to the airport by Anson, the remaining residents gather in the courtyard for lunch.

"I'm going to take the pup away from the city," the Changer announces. "No purpose is being served by our remaining here.''

Arthur and Eddie nod agreement. Lovern frowns. Perhaps only Amphitrite, sitting beside her at the teak table in the courtyard, notices Vera swallowing a protest.

"Do you think it is wise?" Lovern asks. "I will be escorting Amphitrite on her South American tour. This leaves Arthur rather thinly protected.''

"Arthur's safety is not my business," the Changer replies calmly. "As far as I can tell, he has not been threatened. You have, Eddie has, I have, but Arthur and Vera remain untouched.''

"For now," Lovern intimates darkly.

"That is not my business. My daughter is. She is growing too large to live in a courtyard and far too unguarded with humans. I will not encourage behavior so counter to survival.''

"We still don't know who planned the attacks!" Lovern protests.

"Nor do I see any evidence forthcoming," the Changer says in a low growl. "Despite the trouble we took to bring that foul Head here, it has been little help to you.''

"There are magics to guard against scrying."

"I know. I have often wished I possessed them."

"I'll offer a trade—an antiscrying amulet against your remaining here a month longer.''

"No. An amulet would not shift with me; therefore, it would be of limited use.''

"But . . .''

Arthur gestures regally with one hand. The gesture is slightly diminished in that he holds a sandwich.

"Enough, Lovern. The Changer has bided with us over a month. He is right. We have eliminated possibilities, but we have not found a solution. I am of the opinion that the attacks were an attempt to unsettle this household before the Review.''

"By whom?''

"Perhaps the South American contingent. Our being unbalanced would have worked to their advantage as they made their appeals.''

"But stooping to near murder?''

"Such tactics have been used before. They will be again.''

The others had listened in silence. Now Eddie cuts in, "Nothing has happened since the Review began. I agree with Arthur. Our enemy had set a time limit of the Review. Now that it is past, all should be well.''

"Sycophant," Lovern mutters.

"Excuse me?" Eddie asks stiffly.

"Nothing.''

"If you are so worried," Eddie says, his tone making quite clear he had heard, "why don't you stay here?''

"I must escort Lady Amphitrite to South America," Lovern replies, "as well you know. The consequences of harm to her are such that I cannot leave her unguarded."

Amphitrite smiles prettily. "My husband is quite protective. I cannot answer for his temper."

"Can't someone else go?" Eddie says, clearly enjoying toying with the wizard.

"Who?"

"How about Anson? He's quite a world traveler. Has a few tricks up his sleeve, too."

"That's what I fear," Lovern says darkly.

"Vera? Certainly you aren't going to say that she is less than competent."

"True, but she did not give her oath to the Sea King. I did."

Eddie rubs his hands together briskly. "Then you're in a bit of a bind, aren't you?"

The Changer scratches under his chin, enjoying in an abstract fashion the squabbling his simple announcement has generated. Vera turns to him.

"When are you going?" she asks. Her voice is quite steady.

"Tonight, I think," he says. "There is no need to delay. If someone can drop us off, we would have several hours to find a place to hide until day."

Arthur nods. "That won't be a problem. I can drive you myself if no one else is available."

"Good." The Changer's tone does not acknowledge that he is aware of the great honor which has been offered.

"But where do you want to go?" Vera presses. "Surely not back where you were before?"

"No," the Changer says. "I have been considering my old hunting grounds and comparing them against current maps. There are large portions of the Sandia Mountains that are either park or reservation land. That should do. With summer coming on, I would prefer not to be out in the plains."

Lovern looks hopeful. "So you are going to stay close to Albuquerque."

"For now. Shahrazad would be endangered in ranch lands. She isn't afraid enough of people to avoid traps and poison."

"The Sandias begin the eastern edge of Albuquerque,"

Arthur comments. "If you're looking to keep her away from people, wouldn't it be better to range farther?"

"Yes." The Changer's yellow eyes narrow. "But I haven't forgotten our enemy—even if he has forgotten us. I want to be near enough to join you if you get a lead."

Vera brightens perceptibly. "Then we can visit you!"

"I'd prefer not." The Changer's tone is not cold, but nonetheless his words wilt the smile from her face. "My goal is to teach my daughter to be a wild thing. If I have my way, she will never interact with humans again."

Conversation moves to other things. With Anson's return, the party breaks up. Vera goes to her office and shuts the door firmly behind her.

As the Changer walks toward his room, Lovern follows him.

"Changer," he says when they are alone in the hallway.

"Yes?"

"I saw Shahrazad at the Harmony Dance."

"So did I."

"You realize what that means." When the Changer does not answer, the wizard forges on. "She is athanor, not just coyote."

"I know." The Changer's expression is sad. "But a long time may pass before we know if she is anything other than a potentially long-lived coyote. Why do you think I want her to know how to live wild?"

"True, but . . ."

"No 'buts,' Lovern. She must know how to be a coyote. Otherwise, she has nothing but her life, and life, as we all know, is a very fragile thing."

✿▣✿

In the forests of Oregon, Rebecca Trapper sits and stares out of a window set in a frame of earth, hidden from view by misdirection and a light screen of brush. She does not appear to see the towering pines or the clouds that scud above their tops. Nor does she look upon the crystalline waters that cascade from the waterfall that conceals a hidden exit from their home. Her usually warm, brown gaze is blank and empty.

"Becky?" Bronson Trapper's voice is rough yet tender. He shambles into the room, bringing with him the scents of leaf mold and mink musk.

Rebecca does not answer, nor does she move when he comes and places a huge, hairy hand on the silky black fur of her head.

"Becky?"

She turns slowly then, looking up at him as if the effort to move her head is almost too much.

"What's wrong, sugar bug?"

"It's over. That's all."

"The Review?"

"Yeah."

Bronson considers her response. He had followed this Review via the new computer modem and satellite-dish link to the live video; it had given him a more comprehensive coverage than had been available even five years earlier.

The pictures on the video monitor had reminded him somewhat of when his second cousin (or was that third?) had lived nearby. Viola had the rare gift of scrying and had summoned up segments of the Review in a pool of water spread with oil. They had used the then-new telephone technology to comment on the action. When Viola had married a Tibetan yeti, the scrying had ended. Bronson had not really missed it.

As technology had caught up with magic, he had taken to recording the Review, skimming the meetings via tape and fast-forward, then sending his comments in. He'd done the same this year, but now that he considers the past week, he remembers that Rebecca had barely budged from her computer while the meetings were in session.

"Are you unhappy with any of the results?"

"A little." Rebecca's gaze returns out of the window. "I thought that Arthur might have to change some of his policies. In the end everything stayed the same."

Bronson frowns. "I wouldn't say that. The new committee to distribute funding for ecological issues is quite a monumental change. I never thought I'd see Arthur agree to make anything like that official rather than merely voluntary."

"That was a good thing," Rebecca agrees. "Do you think

that the Sea Queen's presence influenced the King's decision?''

Bronson considers. ''Yes, I do. Her rather forceful presentation that no landmass is as isolated as land dwellers would like to believe made an impression even on *me*.''

''And she was pretty, wasn't she?''

''If you like skinny, bald, blond creatures''—Bronson chuckles—''which I don't particularly.''

Rebecca turns from the window, rising all in one movement, surprisingly lithe for a creature of her height and bulk.

''Bronson, the members of my chat group have been talking about taking a trip to Albuquerque in September. I want to go.''

''What? Why?''

''Because Albuquerque is where Arthur is. We wanted to go for the Review but decided that we really couldn't pull it off in the summer. Too many of us need to wear heavy clothes to cover our . . .'' She searches for a word, her expression bitter. ''Our inhumanity.''

''Nonhumanness,'' Bronson corrects sternly.

''Arthur acts as if we are inhuman—somehow less than those who can wear a human shape. Would he have listened to Amphitrite if she had shown up with a fish tail and eaten raw herring?''

''Probably. The sea is a powerful force. Its monarchs are not to be taken lightly.''

''Still, she chose to wear human-form. Even the *tengu* and the Changer himself wore human-form. The time has come for Arthur to face that some of our people are not human.''

''None of us are human, Rebecca.''

''You know what I mean.'' She begins to pace, clenching and unclenching her long-fingered, simian hands. ''Arthur and his ilk pretend that they are humans—just the better, longer-lived models. They ignore those of us who threaten that illusion!''

''I do not call the help we have received from Arthur's government 'ignoring,' Becky. We would not have this land nor the electronic equipment you so treasure without his assistance.''

''Gilded bars for a cage!'' Rebecca retorts. ''If the humans learn of us, then the jig is up for the rest of them. I watched all the submeetings, the ones you skipped. Over and over again the theme was concealment lest we be discovered. If they're worried about creating electronic records or financial trails, how much more do they fear people with fur or hooves or horns!''

'' 'They'? They are us. We are one type of people: the people of myth and legend, those who live outside of human time.''

"No! We're the *huldre* folk, just like Louhi said. We are hidden from view. We're Eve's unwashed children, the people that everyone denies. I, for one, am tired of it!''

Bronson looks at her, his heavy brows drawn down over jetty eyes. "And so you want to go to Albuquerque.''

"Yes.''

"And what will you do once our hiding is over?''

"Live like a normal person.''

"But we are not normal people. We are tall, massive, covered with fur. We have heavier bones. We climb trees like monkeys. We live for centuries—except when we are slain by action or chance. You cannot deny what we are, Rebecca. We are not normal people.''

She stares, having rarely heard him speak so passionately.

"Then,'' she says, more hesitantly, "we will show them that shape and size don't matter. What matters is the mind.''

"You believe that you can demonstrate this . . . even though humans still divide themselves with barriers of race or creed or nationality?''

"Yes!'' She raises her chin defiantly. "Of course. How can they deny the evidence of their own eyes?''

"Easily.'' Bronson scratches beneath his furry rib cage. "They do it all the time. Get out on that precious Web of yours and look at something other than the opinions of your isolated chat group. Take a look at the splinter religions, the hate groups, the news reports from areas where humans are busily slaughtering each other. Do that for a week and then tell me with the same confidence that humans are ready for sasquatch and satyr, fauns and *tengu*, sea serpents and jackalope.''

"I want to go to Albuquerque,'' she says stubbornly. "I've hardly been anywhere but these forests.''

Bronson frowns. "We go to visit the Olsens.''

"Same old forests, just in Washington State."

"I took you to Alaska to visit Snowbird's family."

"That was cold. I want to see cactus. I want to feel really hot sunshine. I want to talk to people up close, not just through the computer or telephone."

"You see the Olsens, Frank MacDonald, and the Vagrant every year. The Smith comes by, too."

"A handful of people out of billions! They're all athanor. I want to know what a crowd is like. I want to know something *different*! Bronson, I'm two hundred years old—almost as old as this country—and instead of seeing my horizons increase, I watch them getting narrower with every technological advance."

"Two hundred years," Bronson smiles, "and each day as long as any other day for anyone else. Yes, I know. I forget that what seems like peace to me may seem like stagnation to you."

Rebecca frowns, uncertain if she is being teased. "I know you are older than I am . . ."

"Much. My grandmother carried my father to this continent in her arms when there was still a land bridge over the Bering Strait. I remember migrations across this continent when I was small. My father died then; my mother, too. We may have had more freedom, but life was much more dangerous."

Bronson takes her hand. "Come and walk outside with me. You've been too much indoors."

She starts to pull away, to return to the comfortable terrain of her depression and sulky mood, but the unbearable tenderness in his expression touches her.

"All right."

They walk outside. June is turning into July with an end to pale greenness. The trees are in heavy leaf now. Birdsong speaks of territories defended, young calling, not of courtship. Far above the lake, an eagle screams and dives.

"I've known that eagle longer than I have you," Bronson comments. "Twice I've removed bands from his leg to protect his secret. I think fifty years had to pass before I was certain it was the same bird. Just goes to show that we don't all know each other on sight."

"Some do," Rebecca says tentatively. "Right? I've heard

that some athanor can identify others of our kind by scent or by some indefinable aura.''

"That's true, but just as not all of us have magic or fur or whatever, not all of us have that talent.''

"We differ so. Are we really all one people?''

"Yes. No matter shape or size or gift, we are all in Harmony. Harmony is what gives us our long lives and greater resilience. The Harmony Dance, more than any other single thing, proves that we have something in common.''

"But *we* don't get to Dance.''

Bronson strokes her furry rump. "Really?''

Rebecca blushes. "There was something extra that night, wasn't there?''

"Yes.''

"What's it like when you're alone?'' Rebecca asks.

"You must know. You didn't always live with me.''

"But I lived with my family. Then after the accident . . .'' Her eyes cloud with tears as she recalls the flash flood and mud slide that had wiped out her entire family when she was seventy-five, "I lived with the Olsens until I met you. They always held a celebration. I've always had other sasquatch around. You've been absolutely alone.''

"That's true.'' Bronson considers. "I think there's always a tingle at the edge of the mind, but for many years I didn't attend to why it was there. I was just more likely to celebrate with a glass of honey mead and reflect over my good fortune that I had survived another few years.''

They walk for a time in silence. Bronson remembers other places. Days when mammoths and dire wolves walked the continent, when humans were a fragile novelty, not a threat. Until Rebecca came to him, he had always been something of a loner and had never really been lonely. Perhaps that was Nature's compensation for a people that seemed to breed more males than females and very few children. Perhaps had just learned to consider solitude the norm. Whatever the reason, Rebecca is not him. She is clearly lonely, and if he does not help her, he may lose her.

"Rebecca?'' he says, decision made. "If you want to go to Albuquerque, we will, but it must be on my terms.''

"We will!'' She stops. "What are your terms?''

"We will take care to conceal ourselves. We will warn

Arthur of our coming, not take him by surprise. I want you to remember that he is not an enemy—no matter what role your chatroom has cast him in.''

''We haven't!''

She protests, then, grinning, runs a few steps and grabs a low-hanging branch. Lithe as the apes she vaguely resembles, she swings back and forth. The tree shakes slightly in protest.

''Bronson! You're wonderful!'' She jumps down and hugs him tightly.

''I'll want to read the plans your group is making and offer suggestions,'' he warns.

''Of course!''

''And we'll need to start researching appropriate clothing . . .''

''I've done a little already.''

''And think about how we're going to avoid being noticed for our height.''

''That's harder, but I'm certain we can come up with something.''

''I don't want to depend on some wizard for our security,'' Bronson warns. ''Debts to that type are never a good idea.''

''Fine!''

''You're happy, aren't you?''

She turns a cartwheel, comes up and squeezes him again.

''Oh, you can tell, can you?''

Her joyful laughter fills the air, blending with the cry of the immortal eagle soaring out over the bright waters of the lake. Bronson feels his chest tighten both in response to his wife's beauty and with the faintest touch of fear.

❁❂❁

Sitting in her office, mechanically responding to queries in her e-mail, Vera jumps when the knock sounds on her door. For a moment she considers not answering. Then she feels a sudden thrill of emotion. Maybe it is . . .

''Come in!''

She swivels her chair, unaware that a touch of rose has risen to her coppery cheeks, knowing that her breathing has quickened and struggling to slow it. When she sees that her visitor is Amphitrite, she feels unreasonably disappointed.

"I hope I'm not interrupting anything too important," Amphitrite says.

"No, just answering routine queries—mostly for copies of the sessions or for the resolutions. Nothing that won't wait."

Her heart has stopped thudding now, but irrationally, Vera struggles against a sense of expectancy. She gestures toward one of the taupe chairs.

"Make yourself comfortable."

"Thanks." Sitting, Amphitrite toys with the end of one blond lock. "Want to go to South America with me?"

"Me?"

"You." Amphitrite leans forward. "I know a great deal about the world under the waters, but I know very little about the politics of the land. Their very passion for the issues distorts the South American contingent's presentation. I would like to have a more objective point of view along."

"But you will have Lovern."

"He is *not* objective. Although he stays in the background, Arthur's policies are his policies."

"I'm on Arthur's side, too," Vera reminds her.

"As are Duppy Jonah and I, but there is a difference between agreeing that someone is the best ruler and agreeing with all of that person's policies."

"True."

"And, honestly, I am not overly fond of Lovern. For too long I have known him mostly through his public role and through my husband's resentment of his trespass into our realm."

Vera taps a few keys, sending off another burst of electronic information. "The sea is a big place. Lovern may have felt Duppy Jonah's control extended only to what he could govern at a given time."

"I am certain that he did," Amphitrite says. "I was small fry in those days. Duppy Jonah was the Midgard Serpent, however, and recently defeated. Lovern took advantage of that. Had he been chivalrous to a defeated foe, I might feel differently."

"I can understand your point of view."

"You are of Arthur's party," Amphitrite continues. "You

know the full reasons for his stance on certain issues. I would feel better advised if you were along."

"The South Americans might not like it."

"Tough. I am a reigning monarch. I am entitled to whatever entourage I choose. Besides, they may enjoy the opportunity to indoctrinate you."

Vera smiles a bit wryly at such arrogance coming from what to all appearances is a blond beach bimbo.

"True."

"And I thought that you might enjoy an excuse to get away."

"Why?" This last comes out more defensively than Vera had intended. She softens her tone. "I mean, now that the Review is over, things will quiet down. I can return to my weaving."

"I thought that the absence of a certain person might haunt the hacienda."

"You mean the Changer?"

"Yes."

"I told you . . ."

"I saw your expression at the lunch table. Anyone with less self-control would have shouted aloud in protest. You managed to keep silent, but I saw, just as I saw your eagerness when you thought that you might have excuse to visit him."

"I . . ."

"Why do you so struggle to deny it, Vera? The Changer is a powerful entity and, whatever his shape, he is all male. I knew your father. There are certain similarities."

"Are you saying I'm looking for a father figure!"

"I am not. What I am saying is that often we are attracted to those who possess qualities we have admired in others."

"I did not precisely admire my father."

"You did not admire his womanizing, but you must admit that there was much to admire otherwise."

"I cannot deny that." Vera crosses her arms over her breasts and frowns. "Why are you harping on this? Let us hypothetically say that I am attracted to the Changer."

"Hypothetically."

"What would I do? He is happiest as an animal. I am human-form and have always been so. I cannot be a raven or a wolf or a coyote. I am a woman—a woman of many appearances, true, but just a woman.''

Amphitrite nods. "That is a difficulty. However, unless you broach the subject, he will not even consider it."

"Am I so unappealing?" Vera looks sad. "It has been long since any paid me court."

"How long since you invited it?" Amphitrite counters. "Among our people, your celibate status is accepted. Even the great womanizers have given up the conquest."

Remembering a few long-ago courtships, Vera manages a smile.

"And," Amphitrite continues, "you do not mingle much with human folk. Look at you now—living in this hacienda with two of the great misogynists of our people."

"Eddie likes women!"

"I meant Arthur and Lovern. Perhaps misogynist is too strong a term, but neither of them has had the greatest luck with their womenfolk."

"They don't trust those of our kind—not after what happened between Louhi and Lovern."

"Huh! I think he deserved it. He flaunted his power. She merely turned the tables."

"Whatever. Are you saying that if I want the Changer to consider me, I should start courting *him*?"

"Yes. And be prepared for potential rejection and a reawakening of interest by many of our own people."

"I'm not sure . . . If I thought . . . Then . . ." Vera gnaws thoughtfully on one pinky nail.

"So come to South America with me," Amphitrite prompts. "You'll have time to think and the comfort of distance."

"Comfort?"

"On another continent you won't be thinking up excuses to go up into the Sandias."

Vera blushes. "I had been thinking I hadn't ridden on the Tram for a long time."

"Exactly. Give yourself some space. You may find out that this is just pheromones run wild. Or you may decide that the potential gain is worth the risk."

Vera logs off her computer. "When are you leaving?"

"Tomorrow. Lovern's shapechanging magic has a time limit."

"Tomorrow."

"The Changer leaves tonight. Nothing is to be gained by staying here."

"Tomorrow." Vera nods sharply. "Very well. Tell your escort I'm going along. I'll tell Arthur and Eddie. Anson is staying for a while longer. He can help cover my jobs."

Amphitrite smiles a perfect, pearly smile. "Thank you!"

Vera rises to see her to the door. "Thank *you*, Amphitrite. Thank you."

When the door closes behind the Queen of the Sea, Vera glances around her comfortable office. Somewhere outside, Shahrazad yips. She restrains an urge to go out and check if the Changer is with his daughter. Amphitrite is right. She does need to confront her feelings—at least to herself.

Maybe even to someone else.

Ogni debole ha sempre il suo tiranno.
(Every weakling has his tyrant.)
—ITALIAN PROVERB

THAT EVENING, WITH AS LITTLE CEREMONY AS WHEN THEY
had arrived, the Changer and Shahrazad prepare to depart
Arthur's hacienda. Shahrazad is at least richer by a name;
the Changer has gained only a host of troubling conjectures
and a few outfits.

"If you don't mind," he says to Arthur, "I'll leave all the
clothes here except for the stuff I'm wearing."

"No trouble at all, my good fellow," Arthur responds.
"We have lots of closets. Why don't you stash your things
in the guest room you were using?"

The Changer nods. He has already done so. The clothes
he wears are simple: jeans, a lightweight shirt, socks, and
sandals. One pocket of the jeans holds a folded plastic bag,
another some money.

"Why don't you wait for me in the front foyer?" Arthur
suggests. "I'll go pull the van around."

As soon as the Changer enters the foyer, Shahrazad trailing
at his heels aware that some adventure is about to begin,
Amphitrite drifts in to join them.

"Have a good time, brother."

"Thank you."

She kneels and rubs Shahrazad behind her ears. "And you be good, little one."

Shahrazad wags her tail enthusiastically.

"And don't forget your aunt."

The Changer frowns. "That is precisely what I am hoping she will do. Despite my best efforts, she is too tame."

Amphitrite rises, light as sea-foam on a wave. "Perhaps she is clever enough to know enemy from friend."

"Then she is smarter than most of us."

"True."

They share a laugh. The thump of crutches is heard, and Eddie comes in to join them. His leg is healing nicely, but he is being careful with it. The only thing worse than a broken leg is an eternal limp from a badly healed break. The Smith knows this and warned Eddie during his visit. It has been millennia since the fall that shattered his leg and hip, and he still limps.

"Ready to head out, Changer?"

"I am."

"I'm sorry we didn't learn who killed your family."

"So am I."

"I hope that the visit was not a complete waste of time."

"Not at all. I learned who did *not* do it. That narrows the field somewhat."

"Than you are not giving up?"

"No."

Anson slides down the banister and bounces lightly when he lands. "You didn't expect him to, now, did you? He's not one to forget a wrong—at least not a wrong so large."

The Changer only smiles politely, but something in his yellow eyes glints agreement.

"What are you doing next, sister?" he asks Amphitrite, pointedly turning the conversation from himself.

"Going to South America with Vera and Lovern. I want to see these rain forests and mountains and endangered creatures."

"Ah."

Anson briskly rubs his long-fingered hands together. "And if South America is not enough, Lady Queen, give me a call and I'll take you to Africa. You want to see problems? There I can show you problems!''

Amphitrite smiles at his enthusiasm but doesn't overlook the sorrow in his dark brown eyes. ''I would if I could, Sir Spider, but my magical lease on legs will not last much longer. I've used ten days already. This will be a quick trip.''

''The offer stands. Perhaps another day, eh?''

Through the nearly opaque panels bordering the front window, they see the van pull up.

''There's your ride, Changer,'' Anson says, offering his hand. ''Good luck.''

''Thank you.''

The Changer shakes hands all around and, with a glance commanding Shahrazad to follow, departs. As he watches the van pull away, Eddie comments, ''I wonder if he noticed that Lovern didn't see him off?''

''Or Vera,'' Anson adds.

''He noticed,'' Amphitrite assures them. ''What I wonder is if he cared.''

Unlike the Sangre de Cristos farther north, the western face of the Sandia Mountains is largely without plant cover. Even in the height of summer, grey stone is visible. The Sandias' height is frequently underestimated. So round, so stony, so barren, the mountains seem intimate, but in reality they crest five thousand feet above Albuquerque. As Albuquerque is situated at five thousand feet, the Sandias are no small mountains.

Arthur steers the van easily through traffic.

''Are you certain that you want to go here?'' he asks. ''The city now ends practically at the base of the mountain.''

''The mountain itself is Forest Service land,'' the Changer reminds him, ''and the Sandia Indian reservation claims still more. Plenty of room to support two more coyotes.''

''How shall I contact you if there is news?''

''Mark well where you drop us off. I will return there every other day. If you would leave me a message, leave it there.''

''Will you and Shahrazad be safe so near the road?''

The Changer's smile is almost mocking. ''Why should we stay near? I can take a swifter shape and cover distance quickly. Shahrazad will remain in whatever grounds we claim.''

"Quite. I overlooked that possibility.''

Without further conversation—on Arthur's part because he is a little miffed at having been taken so lightly—on the Changer's because he has nothing more to say—they go on. Arthur concentrates on driving the van up the twisting road toward the crest, the Changer on watching.

"Up ahead will do," the Changer says at last. "There, where there is a wide spot on the shoulder of the road.''

Arthur parks there and the Changer grunts satisfaction. When the van stops, he opens the door and Shahrazad leaps out.

"Don't stray," he calls after her. Immediately, she slows and begins sniffing the roadside debris.

"Thank you," the Changer says to the King, extending his hand. "You will know where to leave a message?''

"I have noted the mile markers," Arthur says, accepting the handclasp, "and I will make other notes when I leave.''

"Good. If you want me quickly, tell me so.''

"I will.''

The Changer nods farewell. Arthur watches, sees the two step into the evergreen forest. Then the shadows swallow them and even his ancient eyes can see them no longer.

Rebecca>> He said Yes! He said Yes!!

Demetrios>> He? who? what?

Loverboy>> "Yes" is my favorite word!

Rebecca>> Bronson said we can go to Albuquerque!!!

Demetrios>> That's great!! I think we'll have at least a dozen attending. I've been talking to some of the other fauns, and at least two want to give it a shot.

Loverboy>> Fuzzy lady, is the hubby coming with you??

Rebecca>> Two other fauns! Great! And I know that the Olsens are coming and some yeti cousins of ours who emigrated to Alaska ages ago and us, and, of course, the *tengu*.

Demetrios>> I wonder if Frank MacDonald would come?

Loverboy>> Why Saint Frank? He's human-form.

Demetrios>> But he is sympathetic to the plight of athanor animals. They have, if possible, less say than we do.

Rebecca>> Yes, Loverboy. Bronson is coming. Demi, I like Frank.

Shouldn't the Moderator be responsible for invitations like that? I mean, isn't this his project?

Loverboy>> :(Fuzzy lady's hubby is coming! Where's the fun for me? Will Arthur let us get near the human babes?

Demetrios>> Maybe the Moderator should talk to Frank. Who is he anyhow? I've been trying to figure it out.

Rebecca>> That's not polite.

Demetrios>> Satyr, don't you ever think of something other than babes?

Loverboy>> Who cares about stuff like the Moderator and the guest list? We're gonna have a PARTY!!

Demetrios>> Sweet Springtime! I wish we could leave you!

Loverboy>> Can't buddy! I've got my invite, too. And you're not the only one who's bringing friends!

Demetrios>> Oh, no!

Loverboy>> We're *all* gonna have a party!

Very early on the morning after the Changer and Shahrazad have returned to the wilds, Arthur and Eddie drive Amphitrite, Lovern, and Vera to the Albuquerque International Airport.

"What is your destination?" Arthur asks.

"Belém, Brazil."

"Belém?"

"A coastal city of a million or so on the Atlantic Ocean," Vera clarifies. "It isn't far from the mouth of the Amazon."

"Reasonable."

When they enter the airport, the three members of the South American contingent are waiting near the ticket counters. Isidro and Cleonice are as poised and darkly patrician as ever. Oswaldo has a book held loosely in one hand.

They greet Arthur and Eddie with brisk American-style handshakes and welcome the other three more warmly.

"Our jet is fueled so we can depart immediately," Cleonice says. "I'll pilot first, then Isidro will relieve me."

"I guess that's a hint we should be leaving," Lovern says, setting down his bag to shake Arthur's hand. "We should see you in a week or so."

"Have a good trip. Be safe," Arthur answers.

He hugs Vera and then, after a moment's hesitation, Amphitrite.

"Don't overwork Eddie," Vera warns.

"I won't."

"And I won't let him," Eddie chuckles.

"And you both come to visit my husband and me," Amphitrite says. "You have been too long a stranger to a greater part of the planet."

"We will," Arthur promises.

When good-byes are finished, the travelers walk briskly to a gate reserved for private departures. Isidro insists on carrying Amphitrite's bag. At a glare from him, Oswaldo reluctantly shoves his book under one arm and takes Vera's light carry-on. Lovern is permitted to tow his own suitcase (by far the largest of the three pieces of luggage) himself.

Seats on the plane are roomy and comfortable. Each of the visitors is offered a window seat, but Lovern, sensitive to his responsibility for Amphitrite's safety, forgoes the honor and seats himself next to the Sea Queen.

Isidro seats himself next to Vera. Oswaldo happily takes the seat behind Amphitrite. His book is open almost before he has his seat belt buckled. Cleonice vanishes into the cockpit, where she can be heard running preflight checks.

"Well, this is much more comfortable than the commercial airlines," Lovern says appreciatively.

"It is indeed," Isidro agrees. "I am surprised that Arthur does not maintain a jet of his own."

"He considers it a waste of money with the airport right here," Vera explains. "These days, the commercial airlines can serve his needs."

"I suppose they would be sufficient" Isidro says acidly, "since all the world comes to his humble door."

Vera frowns. Isidro smiles ingratiatingly and explains, "In our poor third-world nation, we need a jet to reach the 'first-world' nations with any convenience. We also maintain a smaller plane for intracontinental flights. That is what we will use to take you on your tour tomorrow."

"Good," Amphitrite says, turning from watching the bustling ground crews. "I have been worried about Lovern's spell expiring before I can see your continent's beauties."

"We have kept that in mind," Isidro promises.

With solid thuds, the jet's outer doors are closed. Two short, broad-chested, brown-skinned, dark-haired people—a man and a woman—come walking back and take seats.

"These are part of our flight crew," Isidro explains, "Rahua and Manco. They are of Inca descent, adapted by centuries of evolution to high altitudes. Our copilots are also Inca."

"Hello," Vera says, pleasantly.

"Neither of them speaks English very well," Isidro says. "Spanish and Portuguese are more immediately useful, though we are teaching them English as well."

"*¡Hola! ¿Como está?*" Vera says.

"*Bien,*" Rahua answers shyly. Hawk-nosed Manco only nods with a touch of *hauteur*.

Cleonice comes on the radio, asking them to prepare for takeoff. When the plane has reached cruising altitude, Rahua and Manco bring out a selection of juices, fresh fruit, and pastries.

"We will serve a more substantial lunch later," Isidro says. "Would anyone care for coffee? We have some fine Colombian."

"I would," Amphitrite says. She has been staring out the window at the unfolding panorama of brown land. "I believe that hot drinks are the one thing I will miss about land living when I return to the ocean."

Lovern smiles. "I felt much the same when I resided in your palace, lady."

As they enjoy breakfast, Isidro begins what clearly is a lecture. His dark eyes are brilliant with passion, his voice that of a trained orator.

"The continent called South America is the proud possessor of the biggest river, the longest mountain range, the driest desert, and the largest forest in the world. The continent holds the greatest variety of life-forms on any landmass. It blends the cultures of several European nations with the remnants of many Indian cultures—at least one of whom, the Inca, built to rival the pyramids of Egypt.

"Yet when the wonders of the world are spoken of, no one mentions South America. The Nile is a poor second to the Amazon, but is spoken of in greater awe."

Lovern mutters, "I don't think that's precisely true."

Ignoring him, Isidro sweeps on. "Elephants and giraffes are certainly marvelous, but the capybara and rhea are as wonderful. The last of the dinosaurs still walk our land: caiman alligators, anacondas, and, within human memory, the doedicurus. Jaguars and other exotic cats prowl the jungles, gigantic fish and electric eels fill our waters, but South America remains forgotten."

Vera nibbles on the edge of a cherry-filled Danish. "In any case, I wouldn't think you would *want* people to know more of your wonders. Wouldn't that encourage immigration and exploitation? If you want an unspoiled continent, anonymity is your greatest ally."

"It might be," Isidro says, waving his own pastry like a baton, "except that ignorance of wonder leads to easy destruction. If nothing is at risk but monkeys and orchids, people don't care. Even local residents need to examine South America with new eyes."

"I can see your point," Amphitrite says, "and looking at the wonders of South America is precisely what we are here to do."

Isidro leans back in his seat, sets his pastry down, motions for a servant to fetch more coffee.

"Yes, you are. I hope that this will be a memorable trip and the beginning of great things to come for us all."

The air voyage takes many hours but, although he did not sleep much the night before, Isidro does not nap. Even when he takes over piloting, his eyes shine with the fervent belief that long-sought-after desires will soon be realized.

✿◙✿

After the activity of the previous month, the hacienda seems very, very quiet. Leaving his private suite, Arthur trudges down the kitchen stairs seeking companionship. The kitchen is empty, too, but there is conversation from the courtyard. Getting a beer, the King goes to join his much diminished-court.

Eddie and Anson are sitting at the patio table playing a game that Arthur remembers from his days in Egypt. Then it was called *sekhet* but there are many variations throughout

Africa—*mancala*, *awalé*, *woaley*, *aju*, *ouri*—each slightly different from the other, even as they all differ from their nearest European cousin, backgammon.

Arthur, then called Akhenaton, had played *sekhet* on boards made of ivory with markers of gold. The board that Anson and Eddie are using is a long rectangle with six cups at each side and a seventh cup at the end. The entire board is made of polished wood and the markers are smooth pebbles. Nothing but the skill of its crafting makes it valuable.

Walking to where he can watch the play, Arthur observes silently for a few rounds.

"What variation are you playing?"

"Nigerian *ayo*," Anson says, looking up with one of his brilliant smiles.

"Ah."

Arthur pulls up a chair, leans back, sipping slowly on his beer and trying not to think about work. The easy pace of the game, the slight rattle of pebbles against wood, soothes him.

"I never thought that I'd admit it," he says during a pause in play, "but I miss that coyote pup."

Eddie nods, drops pebbles into various cups, counts his take. "Me too. Maybe we should get a pet."

"Animals are so short-lived." Arthur's words are not quite a protest, more a reminder. "They age so swiftly."

"There are turtles," Eddie says, "like the one that Salome had in Vierek and Eldridge's novel."

"Turtles don't wag their tails or yip when they see you coming."

"Parrots?" Anson suggests, dropping pebbles into cups in rapid succession and chortling at the look on Eddie's face. "I've often considered a parrot. I would get one, I think, if I didn't travel so much."

"That's a better thought," Arthur admits. "I'd need to check what types are legal to own in the United States."

"Or we could ask Frank MacDonald if there are any athanor animals in need of a home," Eddie suggests, warming to the idea. "I know that he keeps track of many of them. An immortal animal wouldn't offer the same emotional risk."

"True." Arthur sips his beer. "Of course, that extends our responsibility for quite a long time."

"Nothing comes without cost," Anson reminds him. "Nothing at all."

"True."

The phone rings just as Anson and Eddie are counting up their score. Arthur rises and answers it.

"Pendragon Productions."

"Are you a big man?" a shrill voice giggles. "Are you the biggest of the big? Tallest of the tall? Most important indeed?"

"Excuse me? I believe you have the wrong number."

"Number! You're number one!" More giggles, these so shrill that the receiver vibrates in Arthur's astonished grasp. "Hail to the King! Kingy thingy! Hip-hip hooray!"

Arthur cuts off the connection.

"What was *that*?" Eddie asks, brown eyes wide with wonder.

"Prank caller," Arthur says frowning. "I think."

"Press the code for last caller," Anson suggests.

Arthur does so, checks the readout. "Tabular Risa. No one I know."

"Nor I," Eddie says.

Anson shakes his head. "Sounds sorta like *tabula rasa*—a blank slate, an empty mind."

"Or 'no one,' " Arthur adds. "Interesting. I'll make a note of it. We *do* get some strange calls. Even with this number unlisted, sometimes people learn of Pendragon Productions and decide it would be fun to taunt the 'King.' "

His sour expression makes quite clear what he thinks of this.

"And we *did* just hire a great deal of outside help," Eddie offers. "Caterers, rental furniture, even hotel accommodations."

"True."

Anson glances up from counting his *ayo* stones. "Twenty-three. I think you've beaten me, Enkidu."

"I have—at last," Eddie agrees, tumbling his twenty-five pebbles back into the reserve at the end of the board. "Arthur, why don't you play a round? I'd like to stop while I'm winning."

"I'll need a refresher on the rules," Arthur says, "but that would be smashing."

Anson rubs his long fingers together briskly. "At last, I have a chance!"

Eddie snorts. "You won three out of our last five games!"

"Don't try to cheat, Spider," the King warns.

"Cheat? You wound me, Majesty." Anson laughs.

Arthur pulls his chair closer and listens to Anson and Eddie's recounting of the rules. When dusk falls, an automatic light flicks on. None of them notice the eyes watching from one of the upper rails of the balcony, *tengu* eyes in a long-nosed face, eyes that are filled with gleeful laughter.

✿◻✿

Sven Trout ambles into the *Prima!* gallery just after noon on a sunny day. The tourist season has begun, but at this moment the pristine gallery spaces are empty—perhaps because the art on display is not the clichéd Western and Indian work tourists expect. Perhaps because an empty shop is more intimidating than one filled with gawking others.

Lil Prima, dressed in an ankle-length patchwork skirt and a scoop-necked ivory blouse whose décolletage shows her rounded cleavage, saunters over to meet him. Her blond hair is twisted up, and she looks vaguely, intimidatingly, French.

"Hello, Lil," he says.

"*Bonjour*, Sven." Her smile is perfectly correct. Only a glitter in her green eyes reveals some distrust.

"I decided to stay around for a few days and do some touring. I haven't seen Santa Fe since the wagon-train days."

Lil cocks a shaped eyebrow at him. Although they are alone in the gallery's white spaces, such talk is in poor taste. How is he to know that she does not have an assistant in the back?

"I hope you are enjoying your visit."

"I am. It's changed, though. I can hardly believe that this is the same mud village."

"Santa Fe has always been the capital."

"A courtesy, you must admit."

"*Oui.*"

She waits, her gaze fixed and level. Sven remembers certain meetings long ago. He has desired Louhi, but she is cold, his desire the thrill of a conquest. Now, as he looks upon Lilith, he wonders that he could have lusted after the other woman.

Here before him stands a woman who can suck out a man's soul and give it back to him wrung free of anything nonessential and somehow more purely his own for the loss. The embrace of her arms and her legs had bound him to her, but he had struggled only to stay within their prison. Her eyes had been brown then, her hair dark as night, her figure voluptuous. When she had put him from her, he had fled, knowing that if he did not, he would be her prisoner forever.

He swallows a sound suspiciously like a whimper. A glitter in those green eyes tells him that Lil knows quite well the train of his thoughts. Bitterly, he knows that she let him go because he could not do for her what she did for him. He wonders if even Tommy fills her lust for creative annihilation.

"I . . ." He swallows the sentence, begins again in a stronger voice. "I heard Tommy play at the Review. Impressive."

"He has recovered at last from his previous incarnation," Lil answers. "I think he will be a success once I learn how to use the new media successfully. Last time, our ventures into video were less than a *tour de force*."

Sven nods, recalling a parade of horrible movies, movies that captured the image of the pouting, dark-haired, blue-eyed singer without capturing his charisma.

"Somehow," Lil continues, "I must find a way to record his image as successfully as we have recorded his voice. Today, a singer without a good music video cannot break into the market."

"Tommy told me that you had a video for this new album."

"We do, but it relies heavily on animation and computer-generated effects. I want to bring *him* alive for his audience."

"Quite a challenge."

"What else is left to us?" She shakes back her blond hair, making her breasts bounce, and Sven swallows hard. "I certainly do not care to crusade for wildlife or ecology. The world has destroyed itself in ice several times in my memory. To believe that this ecosystem is permanent is foolishness."

"So you go for more immediate pleasures?" Sven says, thinking of a few pleasures rather carnal and immediate. He imagines ravaging her here on the gallery floor amid the staring faces of her sculptures and paintings. Let the tourists watch! They'd probably dismiss it as performance art.

"I do," she answers, and her inflection is so provocative that for a moment he believes that she has agreed to his fantasy. "I enjoy managing Tommy—both in art and life. It has given purpose to an existence that was getting too lengthy."

"I was wondering if you'd mind if I gave Tommy a commission," Sven says, ambling over to a sculpture as if to admire it, but in reality wanting the pedestal between his crotch and her line of sight. Thank fashion that baggy trousers are in!

"A musical commission?" she asks.

"Yes, a song-and-dance number."

"*Intéressant*." She doesn't ask for more details. Doubtless she will enjoy trying to get them out of Tommy. "*Certainement*, you can speak with him. I can't make him take the commission. I'm merely his manager, not his muse."

She looks vaguely sad as she makes the final statement.

"I'll speak with him, then. Where can I find him?"

"We have a couple of town houses on the northern edge of Santa Fe. I'll give you directions."

Sven swallows. His anatomy is under control again.

"Are you free for lunch?"

"I ate early."

"Dinner?"

She licks her lips and his rebel member stiffens again.

"What do you have in mind?"

He resists an urge to shout, "Fucking you!" and answers suavely, taking a turn around another statue.

"Why don't you pick the place?"

"I have expensive tastes."

"That's fine. You're worth it."

"Dinner, then. Eight o'clock." She stretches luxuriously, making Sven wish her skirt were not quite so long. "Now, I'll get back to my cataloging."

"I could pick you up at home," he suggests hopefully, "seeing that you live nearby."

"I'll meet you," she answers. "I have a client coming by later. Call here at about four, and I'll tell you where."

"It wouldn't be any trouble," he says. *If he could just get her in his car. She may be a witch. She may be among the first, but if he could just get her in his car . . .*

"No," she purrs. "It will be better this way."

"Right," he says, not believing it. "Right."

Still throbbing from unrequited lust, Sven contemplates finding a prostitute before going to visit Tommy. Reluctantly, he decides against it. Not only isn't he precisely certain just where the Santa Fe red-light district is located, but even one of the athanor needs to fear the specter of AIDS. Their more potent immune systems are still vulnerable to the AIDS virus, as the recent deaths of several promiscuous womanizers has proven, and Garrett Kocchui, their own Aesculapius, had issued dire warnings based on his studies of the virus.

Sven sighs, contemplates condoms, risk, and masturbation, eschews all and, drives out to Tommy's town house.

He raps on the door and is surprised when it is promptly opened by Tommy. The singer is clad in faded black jeans, the amethyst eagle pendant, and nothing else. An acoustic guitar hangs by an embroidered strap around his neck.

"Hey, man." Tommy holds the door open wider. "Cool."

"Hey yourself," Sven replies, momentarily envious when he discerns the faint red marks of a woman's fingernails on Tommy's shoulders and, as the musician turns, back. There's a bite mark on his left biceps as well. "How's it going?"

"Cool. Isidro Robelo gave me a couple recordings of some Andean music. Neat. Haunting. Lots of pipes, drums, and chimes. Reminds me of when I was young."

"Pipes? Like syrinx?"

"Yeah. Good lady, that. Don't wonder that she didn't go for Pa Faun, though. Rough rider, him. Split a little thing like her in two."

"Still, did she have to suicide?" Sven has never really understood any behavior so counterproductive to survival.

"Guess she did," Tommy says, closing the door and leading the way down to his music-strewn living quarters. "She did."

"You're right."

Taking his customary seat on the couch, Sven decides to get down to business before he loses Tommy's surprising alertness.

"I want to commission you to write some music for me."

"Yeah?" The guitar rests on Tommy's knee, but he only idly strokes the strings. "What?"

"I've been thinking about the Harmony Dance."

Tommy's expression grows tranquil. "Yeah. Me too. Wish it wasn't just every five years."

Sven suddenly comprehends the reason for Tommy's unusual attentiveness and alertness. The Harmony Dance, with its supernatural music, must knit his self-destructive soul back into something resembling wholeness. Some years, when Tommy is already far gone into drugs or drink, the force of Harmony must not be enough to heal him. This year, however, with his newly rejuvenated body almost untouched, when, due in part to Sven's own meddling, intoxicants have less of a hold on him, the Dance must have filled him with an abundant vitality.

Quickly, Sven changes his tactics. It would not do to ask directly, as he had been about to do, for music to a Disharmony Dance. He must be more subtle.

"I wish the Dance happened more often, too," Sven says, seeing his way with that preternatural clarity of invention that has long been his gift and his bane. "Wouldn't it be great if we had a Dance that would bring each individual into Harmony with him- or herself?"

He doesn't mention that doing this would, almost by definition, weaken Harmony with the whole. Very few can carry both self-interest and altruism in their hearts simultaneously. Only saints manage complete altruism. Among their people both the saints and demons have long gone the way of the dragons.

"That would be cool," Tommy agrees, his eyes sad. "A Harmony with the self. Yeah. I wish . . ."

"Don't you think that if anyone can compose such a piece it would be you?" Sven says, dangling the bait. "Music is the universal language, and for all that good King Arthur and his merry minions appoint a new trade tongue every century or so, we are a people of many natal speeches.''

''I know,'' Tommy says, and the language he speaks is a northern Greek dialect only suspected by scholars.

''Music could make us each hear our birth language speaking softly to our souls,'' Sven says, warming to his topic, forgetting his hypocrisy. This is another of his gifts. He always believes his pitch when he is making it. ''A song to sing to the heart. A dance to lighten the feet and reveal the inner passions. What a beautiful thing that would be!''

''Beautiful, man!'' Tommy agrees. ''A medicine for the wounded soul, one that doesn't have any side effects. I wish I could write that song.''

Sven leans forward, intense, his sharp features like a greyhound's scenting a rabbit. He runs his hands through his fiery hair. For this moment even his unrequited lust is forgotten.

''If you can't do it, no one can, Tommy. Time and again you have composed songs to touch the soul. The Elysian mysteries are still spoken of with reverence. Your last life is rapidly becoming deified.''

''But those are all songs of sorrow,'' Tommy protests. ''The king dies to feed the land. Love is unrequited. Shoes are tread upon. Man, I can't make the whole world sing! I'm a mess!''

''You're not trying to make the whole world sing, Tommy, just a few lonely souls cast adrift in time.'' Absently, Sven compliments himself for the artistry of that last phrase. ''You're trying to reach a people who know the fragility of life and still strive on. You're trying to reach those who cannot even call bedrock solid because too many of them have seen bedrock shift. You're trying to reach your own people!''

''My people.'' Tommy tastes the words.

''Your people. Not fans, not poor mortals, but athanor who do our best in an increasingly uncaring world.''

''Yeah!'' Tommy's shoulders straighten. He strikes a vibrant chord on the guitar in his lap. ''My people. A song to strengthen the self between the times when we're all drawn together. Sven, that's beautiful!''

Sven smiles shyly. ''The Harmony Dance has always had a deep effect on me.'' (That's why he avoids it as often as possible.) ''Even when I'm far away I feel its pull.'' (Even when dead drunk or stoned or in bed with a dozen women or serenaded by the screams of a tortured prisoner—he's tried all the ways he can to break that damned Dance's pull.)

"I'll do it, Sven," Tommy promises, his fingers already drumming on his leg. "Can I get Lil to help? She's got magic that I don't."

Sven considers, decides that Lilith's predatory nature might well provide the final ingredients needed for the mix.

"If you must," he says, as if reluctantly. "She is a powerful woman, but she is not always gentle with those weaker than herself."

"Yeah." Tommy lifts off the guitar strap and picks up a syrinx. Holding it beneath his sensual lips, he blows a few notes. "Still, if I need advice, she's close by."

"I trust your judgment, my friend," Sven says. He glances at the clock. "Can I borrow your phone? I need to call to confirm a dinner date."

"Sure," Tommy says.

Sven can tell that Tommy has already half forgotten him under the pull of his new composition. He walks into the kitchen and dials the *Prima!* gallery. If he's at all lucky, it'll be a hot time on the old town tonight. If not, well, condoms are cheap.

17

Dulce bellum inexpertis.
(War is sweet to those who have not experienced it.)

—ERASMUS

SHAHRAZAD CROUCHES LOW IN THE SHELTER OF A LONG-needled ponderosa pine, her gaze fixed on a ground squirrel chewing on the end of a peeled twig. Something in her remembers lessons about stalking, patience, staying upwind of prey. Despite those memories, she grows impatient and springs forward.

The ground squirrel doesn't even need to drop its twig in order to retreat into its nearby burrow. Shahrazad digs after it, but the little rodent is safe.

Disappointed, her paws still sore from following her father long miles the day before, she trots over to where the Changer dozes beneath a scrub oak. He smells tantalizingly of mice and rabbit. When she nudges under his jaw in an appeal for him to regurgitate a share for her, he growls.

An aching shoulder where he had struck her and thrown her to the ground the day before reminds her that she must not defy him. Unhappily, she tries a few berries from a nearby juniper, but, although they are sweet in a resinous fashion, they do not satisfy her hunger.

Somewhere, she knows, there is a place with plenty of food. Even the puppy chow she had disdained in favor of

ham or bread or scraps stolen from the trash would be welcome now. Mournfully, she whines, wishing that wild things
were not so unwilling to let her eat them.

The Changer rises and shakes himself. He is not indifferent
to his daughter's plight. Indeed, at three months she is young
to be expected to feed herself without his help. Still, hunger
will add immediacy to her lessons.

After Arthur had dropped them by the roadside, the
Changer had led Shahrazad deeper into the woods. The rise
of a few thousand feet in altitude had not troubled either of
them greatly, but he did not care to add to Shahrazad's troubles by taking her to the crest. Instead, he had kept them
within about seven thousand feet, good hunting grounds this
time of year when the lower lands are feeling the summer's
heat and dryness.

However, the pup has forgotten more than he realized of
her early lessons. The month spent living easy at Pendragon
Estates had whetted her talent for scrounging rather than
hunting. Therefore, he takes her away from the roads, hiking
trails, and ski areas, away from anywhere she might be
tempted to supplement her poor hunting skills with carrion
and trash.

Sadly, although carrion is a coyote's due, even as it is a
raven's, he does not wish her to depend on it. Ranchers often
poison any carcass they come across, preferring to risk the
spread of disease by its slow rotting than to tolerate that any
coyote might live. Roadkill does not carry the same penalty,
but he does not wish Shahrazad to acquire the habit of relying
on carrion. She may not always live on Forest Service land.

As he sees his duty, he must teach her two lessons. One,
to hunt and forage, the other to beware of humans. Both of
these have been greatly undermined by the kindness of Arthur's household. Somehow, he must tap the fear she had felt
after her mother and siblings were killed.

Shahrazad watches the Changer with hope. Now that he is
on his feet, perhaps he will take her to where food can be
had. Vaguely she remembers a field's edge where mice were
easily taken. Wagging her brush and dragging her belly to
the ground, she comes close enough to nudge him.

This time he doesn't growl, but nudges her in return. Dawn
is coming, the moon setting. Unlike many predators, coyotes

are not nocturnal. Favoring neither night nor day, they can hunt whenever is most favorable. Since the pup is hungry, he will give her a lesson now.

The day before, after they had arrived in this area, he had briefly shapeshifted into a raven in order to scout. He had marked a dense thicket of brush as offering good hunting.

Leading Shahrazad into the thicket, he tells her to wait at the edge. Already she has learned to stay without protest. Swiftly, he finds mice. Positioning Shahrazad by a den with hot scent, he begins to flush prey. This time she waits until a mouse runs toward her and snaps when it comes into range.

She is surprised to find the warm body squirming in her jaws, but not surprised enough to let it go. A crunch and a swallow and it is gone.

The mice become wary quickly, but not before Shahrazad has caught another. As the sun warms the mountain slopes, the Changer takes her to a small meadow where grasshoppers are beginning to appear. Later in the summer they will be plentiful enough to provide a substantial portion of her diet, so he teaches her to hunt them now.

By midday, even her growing belly is full. They shelter in a manzanita copse and curl close together, each watching where the other cannot, each with an alert nose to the wind.

¤◙¤

The telephone rings. Arthur reaches for it with trepidation. Were it not business hours a few days after the Lustrum Review, he would let the answering machine take it. As he had feared, a cackling laugh assails him even before he can politely say, "Pendragon Productions."

"Arthur King! Arthur King! Oh, he's the Thing, that Arthur King."

"Who is this?" he asks sternly. Efforts to trace the calls have been useless.

"A friend. Your Jiminy Cricket. Voice of your conscience. You pompous ass, you!"

More laughter. Then several voices begin in chorus: "Arthur King, Arthur King! He's the Thing, that Arthur King! He doesn't use his ding-a-ling, but bears a scepter and a ring.

He's the king of everything. That's his Thing, that Arthur King.''

Arthur slams down the receiver, ignores the phone when it rings again.

"Damn!"

He storms from his office into Eddie's, not bothering to knock. Eddie looks up from his computer terminal.

"Arthur?"

"I'm not answering my phone anymore."

"More of those calls?"

"Yes."

"Still no source?"

"None."

"Did you call the cellular carrier?"

"Yes. They wouldn't tell me much. The account was taken out just a few days ago by a business called Tabula Rasa.''

"Did the owner give a name?"

Arthur bares his teeth. "Nemo Nada."

"No-one Nothing, owner of Blank Slate." Eddie shakes his head. "Didn't the phone company think that at all strange?"

"I didn't even ask. This is New Mexico, Land of Enchantment and People with Weird Names.''

"That's true."

"I'm going to set my answering machine to take all calls, but I'm afraid that my prankish friends will just fill the memory with their prating.''

"Are they getting any better?"

"No. Now they've come up with a nonsense rhyme."

"Did you write it down?"

"No."

"Pity. We might be able to analyze it and make some educated guesses as to who is making the calls.''

"Someone who can make rhymes with 'king' and possesses a juvenile sense of humor.''

"Still, we might be able to deduce whether it is one of ours or merely a human who has gotten hold of your name and number.''

"True," Arthur agrees reluctantly. "Well, I still won't answer it.''

Anson knocks and, at their joint invitation, comes in.

"You know, I've been helping Eddie with his work, Arthur, looking over the mail from the Review, taking over some of Vera's jobs since she's out on vacation."

"Thank you." Reluctantly, Arthur is coming to appreciate that the Spider has more to offer than a sense of mischief.

"I don't think you'll like what I just downloaded."

He sets a printout on the desk where they can both read it: "Arthur King, oh, Arthur King! He's the Thing, that Arthur King. He doesn't use his ding-a-ling, but rules by scepter and signet ring. His chamber pot is first-class Ming. He's our main man, that Arthur King. Sing it now! Let's all sing the hymn to glorify Arthur King. Ring the bells. Let the song take wing. Let everyone praise Arthur King."

Arthur swallows and speaks in a voice that is preternaturally calm. "Goodness, they've expanded what I heard on the phone. How creative of them."

"Not much to indicate who wrote it," Eddie admits. "Anson, was this sent just to Arthur or mailed out in general?"

"I checked my e-mail and it isn't there—not yet at least."

Eddie checks his account. "Nothing here. We'd need to do a wider sample, but maybe, just maybe, they are limiting themselves to taunting Arthur."

"I never thought that would be a relief," Arthur admits, "but it is. Can we find out if anyone else has received it?"

"Not without telling them what to look for," Eddie says, "and I don't think you want that."

"No!"

"Use my computer to check your private account," Eddie suggests. "See if they have that address, too . . ."

Arthur does so, scanning the messages with trepidation. "Nothing here. Yet."

"Then it may be someone who has learned of Pendragon Productions." Eddie frowns. "That doesn't narrow the field."

"True."

"I don't suppose you would talk with them?"

"I've tried. All they do is make rude statements."

"Then maybe staying off your phone *is* the best course. They may get bored."

"That's what I'll do. I hope I won't miss any important business."

"What is there that can't wait," Eddie says, "for a few days? If nothing else, athanor possess time and to spare."

"True," Arthur says, "and if you and Anson would continue to review the e-mail and tell me what I must deal with, we will rob these pranksters of their pleasure."

"Done," Eddie says.

Anson nods. "Catchy bit, though. Better hope it doesn't get out. It could become a national anthem."

"Spider . . ." Arthur begins, indignantly, then, realizing he is being teased, forces himself to relax. "Let's not try it just yet, okay?"

"Okay, boss," Anson laughs a deep round belly laugh. "That's okay with me."

¤🗙¤

The mansion in Belém is a fine, elegant building that recalls Portuguese tastes in architecture. Stuccoed white with arched windows and doorways, with flowering vines climbing up pillars to second-story terraces, it might have been from another century if not for discreetly concealed modern improvements.

A manservant, less stocky than the Incas who had attended them aboard the jet but still obviously Indian in his heritage, answers the door and bows deeply as he ushers their group into the entry hall.

"How wonderfully cool!" Vera exclaims.

"Air-conditioning," Cleonice says, almost apologetically. "Without some way to reduce the humidity we could not hope to preserve our papers and more delicate equipment."

Isidro deftly guides them from the hall into a parlor whose long, glass windows look out over a garden that is such a riot of color that it takes a careful look to sort the individual flowers and birds from the general mass.

"We maintain a botanical garden of sorts. Take care that you don't go out into it unattended. Many of the plants have spines or toxic chemicals in their leaves."

"What if we don't touch anything?" Amphitrite asks.

"I suppose if you watch out for ants you should be fine.

We try to keep the population down, but ants . . . Out in the rain forest they outmass every other animal.''

''Don't you mean outnumber?'' Amphitrite says curiously.

''No,'' Isidro smiles like a benevolent teacher trying to discourage an eager student. ''I mean outmass. There are lots of ants: the *tucandera* whose sting can kill a child or leave a grown man in agony, the *suava* or leaf-cutting ant who can strip a tree or a field of crops, the red fire ant that . . .''

''Stop!'' Amphitrite pleads. ''You're making my skin crawl. I don't think I'll go out at all.''

With a glance at Isidro that seems to chide him for his excesses, Cleonice turns to their guests.

''We thought that you might be tired after the long flight. Our thought was that we would let you rest, perhaps take you around Belém if you had the desire, then tomorrow we would fly a small plane out to show you the rain forest.''

''We're surrounded by it now, aren't we?'' Lovern says.

''That's right. The mouth of the Amazon River isn't far.''

Vera yawns. ''Your plan sounds good to me. After a year in New Mexico, I've lost my liking for humidity.''

''I rather like the dampness,'' Amphitrite says, ''but I could use a rest. I'm still unaccustomed to moving about without the water's support.''

''And I will follow the ladies' preference,'' Lovern says gallantly, ''although I may take a wander in your gardens. I'll keep your warnings in mind.''

''Don't be startled,'' Oswaldo says, looking up from his book for the first time since he arrived in the parlor, ''if you hear something large moving around. We have a few tame anteaters and several monkeys and macaws. The anteaters will most probably avoid you, but the rest may come begging.''

''That's good,'' Lovern says. ''Do you have any treats?''

''I can get you some,'' Oswaldo says, levering himself out of his chair reluctantly. ''Come along to the kitchen.''

Early the next morning when dawn's comparative coolness still touches the air, they drive out to the private airfield. The visitors are still somewhat overwhelmed from the whirlwind tour of Belém the night before. Quietly they board the small plane to which their hosts proudly conduct them.

The amphibious craft's silver hull is touched up with decorations in green. Its name, *Caiman*, is written in a curling script alongside the nose. The interior, while not roomy, is comfortable, with one seat on either side of a narrow aisle.

"We'll take the pilot and copilot's seats," Cleonice explains, "and leave Oswaldo with you in the cabin. I'm afraid we aren't well equipped for steward services, but I've had the staff pack us a basket with drinks and snacks."

"Sealed against the ants, I hope," Amphitrite says, her playfulness not quite hiding her apprehension.

"Always," Oswaldo assures her.

Takeoff is handled with smooth professionalism. Rapidly the airfield and Belém itself are swallowed by the spreading green jungle.

"If we had left earlier," Cleonice says, via the cabin radio, "we could have taken you to where howler monkeys greet the sunrise. Still, I believe we have wonders enough on today's agenda."

"Are we going to the Xingú National Park?" Lovern asks, betraying that he has done some research.

"Not today," Oswaldo answers. "Today we are going to areas where just about no one lives. The Xingú National Park was created as a refuge for the native peoples. We are taking you to places where no people live and which are, oddly enough, in greater danger because of that."

Vera, not looking away from the verdant panorama spreading out beneath them, offers, "Because no one lives there, there is no one to protest if the lands are abused."

"And no one," Oswaldo agrees, "to act. The lands are often sold for a few thousand dollars to speculators who often fail in their ventures, at the cost of a great deal of ecological devastation. At least when the Indians lived in the lands, they made war on invaders."

There must be a listening device of some sort in the plane's cabin, for Isidro adds, "To be fair, the depths of the rain forest may not be in as much danger as some ecologists say. The lands are too wet, too persistently humid, to be inviting. Much of the clear-cutting is occurring further inland, near Rondônia, for example."

"And elsewhere," Cleonice adds. "The damage may be overestimated, but it exists nonetheless."

After two hours flight time, Isidro announces. "We're going to come down on that broad spot in the river. Don't worry—the area isn't as small as it looks."

After the *Caiman* has splashed to a landing, Oswaldo produces an inflatable boat large enough to carry them all ashore.

Cleonice looks wistful. "I'd like to come along, but someone should stay with the plane."

"I thought you said it was deserted here," Lovern says, looking at the tangled jungle with suspicion. Ever since his time in India, he hasn't particularly cared for places where plants dominate.

"Unpopulated," Isidro corrects, "but not deserted. There could be a few stray Indians or some ambitious *garimperios* searching for the next big strike. Whenever possible we leave someone with the plane and maintain radio contact."

"Wise," Vera says, and that rather ends the matter.

With Oswaldo in the bow and Isidro in the stern, the boat is paddled ashore. Lovern leaps out to help Oswaldo pull it ashore.

"The rain forest," Isidro says, lecturing even before his feet hit the shore, "is home to countless varieties of plants, including many types of orchids. Some of these are rather disappointing to any but the *aficionado*, but others are lovely enough to make a poet's heart sing."

Vera, wiping sweat from her forehead, nods. Amphitrite, unsurprisingly, is unaffected by the humidity, but Lovern looks sour and wilted.

"Beyond charming poet's hearts," Oswaldo adds with a self-depreciating smile, "there are plants with medicinal value. As the fanatics are fond of saying, perhaps the cure for cancer is being burned away so that some farmer can grow cattle for the American hamburger chains."

Isidro nods solemnly. "But we have not brought you here to inundate you with details you could learn by a quick trip to the library. We want you to see for yourself the surrounding beauties. Lovern, won't you stop scowling long enough to admire this princess earring?"

He indicates a red flower that dangles from its parent plant. It does not take much imagination to envision this floral beauty swinging from the ear of a dusky-hued jungle princess.

Lovern steps toward the flower and almost immediately crumples as if he has been hit solidly in the gut. He staggers a few steps then falls to his knees, and from there to the damp ground. When Vera and Amphitrite move to assist him, Oswaldo pulls a handgun from the bag he has been carrying.

"Please stay where you are, ladies."

They halt. Oswaldo's round face is no longer vague and jovial, but filled with ruthless purpose. There is no doubt that within the poet the Mongol warlord has smoldered.

"We would prefer to have you alive," Oswaldo continues, "but people die by violence every day in Brazil. You came into the country without official notice. You can die without official notice as well. One of the problems of our particular Accord is that Arthur will be reluctant to search too publicly for you lest he endanger the secrecy to which he is so devoted."

Vera grabs Amphitrite's hand when the Sea Queen rages forward a few steps, but she cannot still the other's words.

"You dare! I sympathized with you! Know that the seas will never be safe to you again."

"I am prepared to take that risk," Oswaldo says, "as are the others. Your sympathy is not enough, Your Majesty. We came to the Review with heartfelt pleas and ample evidence of our serious need. Instead of help, we got a committee. We must do more to draw attention to our need."

"Killing us will not give you what you desire," Vera says coldly. "It will only get you removed from the Accord."

"We do not plan to kill you."

"And Lovern?"

Oswaldo does not remove his gaze from them, but asks Isidro, "How is the wizard?"

"Out." Isidro rises from where he has been binding Lovern's wrists and ankles with cold-iron manacles. "And disabled. The plane ride almost certainly weakened him more than we realized. Your shamanistic charm has dropped him into a coma."

"What do you plan to do to us!" Vera exclaims.

Isidro lifts Lovern into a fireman's carry over his shoulder. "We are going to strand you here. If Arthur will agree to certain of our policies, we will notify him where you can be found. We will even come to retrieve you ourselves.''

Amphitrite spits at him. ''Bring a gun or three, or I will have your eyes!''

''I will so remember, Your Majesty.'' Isidro's slight bow is mocking. ''If he does not agree, you will be left here and Arthur can deal with the fury of Duppy Jonah and of all those who have come to respect and admire Vera.''

''And what is to keep us from taking vengeance on you once we are free?'' Vera asks. Her face is full of cold fury, reminding them all of the pitiless maiden goddess who would not forgive Troy her slighting by one nearly forgotten prince.

''We are prepared to accept some risks,'' Isidro says. ''Our Cause is greater than ourselves.''

Oswaldo nods and gestures with his head toward the shore. ''Take Lovern to the boat. Cleonice is waiting.''

''And I'll bring back the supplies,'' Isidro agrees.

Vera and Amphitrite are too aware of the delicacy of their situation to attack Oswaldo once he is alone. Even if they managed to fell him, they would still need to deal with both Isidro and Cleonice. Lovern, incapacitated as only an iron-bound wizard can be, has become hostage to their good behavior, as they will be to Arthur's.

When Isidro returns, he has two small packs slung over one arm and a gun in his free hand. From one pocket he takes a piece of rope.

''Over to that tree,'' he says, gesturing to a tree. ''Put your backs to it and your hands toward each other.''

''Why?'' Vera says angrily.

''Because I will shoot you in the foot if you do not.''

Amphitrite glances at Vera, who shrugs. They walk to the tree and stand as ordered.

''I will tie your hands,'' Isidro says, looping the packs over a branch, ''in such a fashion that you should be able to work free within a few minutes. I merely take this precaution so that Oswaldo and I will be able to make our departure.''

''Bastard,'' Vera mutters.

''Aren't we all,'' he agrees. ''There are knives and other survival tools in the packs, including lightweight hammocks. I do not suggest that you sleep on the ground. Moreover, there is a short guidebook listing the most dangerous plants and animals, along with a description of various things that you can eat. If in doubt, I suggest that you try something else.''

''My husband will kill you,'' Amphitrite says coldly.

''Your husband never leaves the water,'' Isidro answers, ''and we are prepared to avoid his domain.''

''Good luck,'' Vera growls.

''Enough talk,'' Oswaldo says shortly. ''We need to get back in time to make our calls. The longer we delay, the longer these ladies need to remain in discomfort.''

''I am just finishing,'' Isidro states. He gives the rope an experimental tug. ''There. That should do just fine.''

Oswaldo speaks into the radio. ''We're on our way.''

''I understand,'' Cleonice says.

The two men sweep genteel bows and retreat. In the near distance, the sound of the *Caiman*'s engine creates an uproar among the waterfowl. Neither Vera nor Amphitrite pays any attention. Their fingers are busy with the ropes.

✿◙✿

In Belém five o'clock has just struck. Cleonice, Isidro, and Oswaldo have returned to their estate, showered, and dealt with all the little problems with servants and such that always crop up when one is away from home for an extended period.

''Do you think Arthur will ransom Vera and Amphitrite?'' asks Oswaldo, his ruthlessness vanishing as the poignant image of the two women stranded in the rain forest touches his poet's soul.

''I certainly hope so,'' Isidro replies. ''Our entire valiant gesture could be misinterpreted otherwise. Still, this is war, and in war there are casualties. If we will not take risks, who will speak for the voiceless ones of Mother Earth?''

''Yes, yes,'' Oswaldo says, suddenly weary of the other's revolutionary rhetoric. ''When will you call Arthur?''

''I thought that I would try now—they are four hours behind us. We should find Pendragon Productions open for standard business hours. Cleonice is dropping our message bottle in Duppy Jonah's waters even as we speak. I want Arthur to realize that the Sea King's anger is of our making.''

"Wise."

Isidro lifts the telephone receiver and places the call to Pendragon Productions in Albuquerque. After a delay and several rings, the King's recorded voice says: "This is Pendragon Productions. No one is available to take your call, but if you leave a message, someone will get back to you."

The beep sounds and Isidro hangs up.

"Well," he says in response to a questioning glance from Oswaldo, "I couldn't very well leave a message saying 'We have stranded Amphitrite and Vera in the Amazonian rain forest as a means of making our continued dissatisfaction with your ecological policies heard. We also have taken your pet wizard prisoner. Our number is . . .' "

"No," Oswaldo says, grinning slightly. "I guess you couldn't."

"I'll try again in a few minutes. Perhaps they are at an early dinner or something."

Several hours later, the phone has yet to be answered.

"Damn!" Isidro slams down the receiver.

Oswaldo sets down the book of Borges's verse from which he had been reading. "Do you have Arthur's private number?"

"Of course not!"

"How about Eddie's?"

"No."

"Too bad." A few minutes later Oswaldo again sets down his poetry volume. "How about leaving an e-mail message?"

"For something as important as this?"

"I was just making a suggestion."

"I want to hear Arthur's voice when I tell him."

"Childish. You might as well say you want to see his face."

"No. I don't want to do that. He's still Gilgamesh the Wrestler under that effete exterior."

"Maybe. Maybe not. People do change."

"I don't want to be the one to find out he hasn't."

"Very well."

Eight hours later, Oswaldo is asleep with his book in his lap. Isidro scowls at the phone.

"I suppose I should just wait until tomorrow. Certainly

they'll be answering the phone then." He shoves Oswaldo awake and repeats his statement.

"Certainly." The tail of the word is lost in a smothered yawn.

In Albuquerque, New Mexico, Arthur Pendragon notes that the Pendragon Productions phone has stopped ringing. He smiles. He's beaten the bastards at their own game. It feels good. He returns to the baseball game he has been watching, relaxing as it heads into extra innings.

¤🔲¤

Out in the North Atlantic, a blue bottle, stoppered with a cork and sealed with heavy red wax, rises and falls with the swells.

Set in the red-wax seal is an amulet made from moonstone and gold, an amulet that emits a siren song meant for only one person, a person who is certain to be swimming in those waters, for his love and his wife is visiting those shores. The moonstone gleams like a particularly solid reflection of the starlight in the dark heavens above.

A great bull elephant seal, eight thousand pounds of rubbery flesh, amazingly graceful for all that mass, swims nearby, tasting the faint freshwater taint of the Amazon as morose lovers throughout time have savored some fine liquor to soothe their bruised hearts. The amulet's call reaches out to him and, surprised to find his solitude so broken, he heeds it.

He does not locate the bottle instantly. Even within a limited range, the ocean's waters are still vast. When at last he finds it, he swims over to the bottle, nudging it with his heavy, trunklike nose.

Immediately, his mournful thoughts leave him, for the amulet informs him that the bottle contains a message intended for none but him. His first thought is that the communication is from Amphitrite, but he banishes that hope instantly.

She would telephone or, if that would not work, command Lovern to do her bidding and make sorcerous contact. In any case, she lacks the sorcery to create what he senses here.

Shifting shape into a handsome triton, Duppy Jonah unstoppers the bottle, unconcerned about the effect of the salt water on the contents. Whoever has sent this will have proofed the missive against water. A spill of what appears to be heavy parchment falls into his webbed and finned hands. Unrolling it, he reads glowing violet and silver letters:

Arthur's minion has failed to protect your consort— even as the King's policies have failed to preserve the planet that is our joint heritage. Amphitrite lives, but is lost. If you join us in our efforts to change the world, we shall return her to you.

Isidro Robelo
(for the South American Contingent)

A typhoon of fury rises in Duppy Jonah's broad chest. Howling in primal fear and rage, he stirs the ocean with his hand. Unheeding of the consequences, he releases a swirl of fury that will beat itself out as an impossible *pororoca* within the broad mouth of the Amazon River.

Then he dives. He must speak with his land-born counterpart. Things have gone too far.

18

God gave burdens, also shoulders.

—YIDDISH PROVERB

RESTING IN HAMMOCKS STRUNG BETWEEN BROAD-LEAFED tropical giants, Amphitrite and Vera awaken on the first day following their marooning. Thus far, they have stayed near the spot where they were left. The minimal supplies left by their captors had not inspired a desire to roam.

In addition to the promised guidebooks there had been the hammocks, a first-aid kit, two machetes, a box of electrolyte-replacement powder, some water-purification tablets, two filled canteens, and two neatly packed meals.

The meals more than anything else had encouraged them to remain where they were, for they seemed to speak of a limited expected duration to their stay. After the two athanor had untied themselves and made certain that they were indeed stranded, they had inspected their packs. Their first step was to string their hammocks—Isidro's stories of the native ants were still vivid in their imaginations.

Their anger had been intense, but not to the extent of making either of them foolish. Dakar Agadez or Katsuhiro Oba might rage at injustice. Practicality and responsibility were more typical traits of the women once hailed as a goddess of wisdom and the Queen of the Sea.

As dawn is announced by a booming chorus of unseen howler monkeys, some of this calm is giving way to worry.

"How long do you think it will be until someone comes for us?" Amphitrite asks.

"I don't really know," Vera admits. "Isidro . . ." She spits at the name. "Isidro planned to contact Arthur. I had thought we would have heard something by now."

"Maybe I frightened them," Amphitrite says, not looking at all unpleased by the thought, "when I threatened them."

"Maybe." Vera doesn't look precisely dubious, but she sounds far from certain. "Still, Arthur may have insisted on coming himself—or at least sending an emissary like Jonathan Wong to handle negotiations. Even if Isidro called Arthur as soon as they returned to Belém, there could be a delay."

Amphitrite frowns. "I hope not too much of a delay. Lovern's spell will grant me these legs only for another week or so. I'd hate to be stranded as a mermaid . . ."

Vera swings upright in her hammock. "Can you change back and swim to the ocean for help?"

"I can change back," Amphitrite says, "but I have no idea how far we are from the ocean or if there are any blockades. A waterfall, a series of rapids, or even an unusually shallow or marshy stretch could leave me, well, like a fish out of water."

Neither of them smiles at this feeble attempt at a joke.

"Can you summon a sea creature to carry a message to Duppy Jonah?"

"I'm not Aquaman," Amphitrite says sourly. "In the ocean we have our servants and sworn followers, but we do not command everything that swims."

"Sorry. I didn't mean to offend."

"No. It was a good idea."

"Is there any water left?"

"Just a swallow. We're going to need to purify more."

Vera grimaces. "I can't stand the taste of those tablets."

"Better than amoebic dysentery," Amphitrite says, "as you reminded me. At least I'm not as thirsty here as I was in New Mexico."

"True. I wonder how long these packets of electrolyte solution will last? Should we ration them?"

"I don't know. I'm not terribly well informed about the

limitations of a land-based life. How much danger are we in?"

"I'm sweating a lot—or maybe the humidity is just so high that I never dry off. We are hardier than the usual mortal, of course, but . . ."

"What you're saying is that you don't know."

"I'm afraid so."

"Then let's use half of what is recommended as a daily supplement. How many days does that give us?"

"A little over a week."

"After that we'll have an entirely new set of problems," Amphitrite says, thoughtfully gazing at her legs. "And I cannot imagine that Duppy Jonah will remain patient for that long. I typify the ocean's more tranquil, food-giving nature. He is storm and tempest."

Vera smiles. "Do you really believe that?"

Amphitrite shrugs. "Why not? It provides something like a division of responsibility. Of course, mermaids have also been accused of luring sailors to their doom. I'm not completely without my menacing aspect."

"I'm amazed," Vera says. "On land, most of us have given up identifying with anything larger than self-identity."

"Oh, really?" Amphitrite says dryly. "After meeting Arthur, I cannot precisely believe that."

"His self-identity," Vera answers, floundering, "is King."

"As mine is Queen."

"But he has," Vera chews her lower lip, searching for a term, "updated? his image. He now sees himself as an administrator rather than a monarch."

"I hadn't noticed."

Vera shrugs. "It's not worth arguing about."

"No, not really, but it does illuminate a particular problem we have. How is Arthur going to respond to this issue? Will he act as a friend or as a head of state? If he acts as head of state, we may not be ransomed at all."

"Yes." Vera looks shamefaced. "I had been hoping that you wouldn't think of that."

"I am a queen. And Duppy Jonah and I have followed politics for a long time. If Arthur ransoms illegally taken hostages, then he creates a precedent of astonishing ramifications.''

"True. And if he does not . . .''

"Then Isidro and his allies must either back down or act in a fashion to show that they are not to be trifled with.''

"The easiest way to do that,'' Vera says bluntly, "is by killing one or both of us.''

"If I die, Duppy Jonah's fury will be merciless,'' Amphitrite says. Her tone is neither smug nor self-satisfied. She is merely stating a fact.

"There is no one to avenge me with such wide-ranging repercussions,'' Vera says calmly. "Perhaps friends will refuse to treat with the South American contingent, perhaps someone will declare a vendetta, but that is all.''

"Which means that you are in greater danger than I am.''

"I expect so, but you are limited in the amount of time you will be mobile on land.''

They sit in thoughtful silence for several moments. A pair of green-and-yellow-feathered macaws flash across the glade. In the distance, they can hear monkeys scolding and, faintly, something that may be the cough of a jaguar. After a time, Vera picks up the conversation as if there had been no interruption.

"Staying here seems increasingly foolish. We make ourselves more vulnerable to both our enemies and to you being stranded when Lovern's spell is exhausted.''

"We could build a raft or a canoe and try our luck on the river,'' Amphitrite suggests. "Even in this form, I swim well.''

"I swim adequately, but there are piranhas and alligators in these waters.''

"There are ants on the land—as well as jaguars. To avoid the water-dwelling menaces, we merely need to stay aboard. I'm not certain we would have such luck with the land-bound ones.''

"No.'' Vera wipes sweat from her face. "Do you know anything about making boats?''

Amphitrite smiles. "Boats and I were born in the same age. I have always taken an interest in them. Did Isidro give us anything to make fire with?''

Vera checks. "There are matches in the first-aid kit.''

"We could make a dugout then, but perhaps a raft would be better. Let me take a look at what is growing in the vicinity."

"Do that. I'll see what I can do about making us some weapons with more range than these machetes. Can you use a bow?"

"No, but I can use a spear."

"Very well. The hammocks were wrapped with some cord. It isn't exactly what I'd choose, but I think I can make a serviceable bowstring. Still, two spears would be my best start. We'll need to make do with fire-hardened points. I'm not certain if the materials for chipped-stone heads will be available, and I certainly don't have the sinew to lash them into place."

Amphitrite looks at her with wonder. "I had forgotten that Minerva was a goddess of war as well as wisdom."

"Damn straight," Vera says, almost happily, "and Joan of Arc learned a trick or two from me as well. I may have been reserving my skills for self-defense, but I'm far from helpless."

Keeping a respectful distance from the thorns and toxic saps of the jungle plants, Amphitrite begins her survey. Humming under her breath, Vera builds a small fire, then cuts two lengths of wood and begins sharpening them.

A plan, no matter how faint its chance of success, heartens both of them as waiting had not. For the first time, they even forget that anyone might be seeking to rescue them. Still, in the depths of her heart, Amphitrite feels the roar of the sea and knows that it rages for her.

✡◉✡

Things feel as if they are getting back to normal that morning at Arthur's hacienda. The King comes down to the kitchen, dressed casually in khaki trousers and a cotton button-down shirt, and finds Eddie seated at the counter watching the news and eating a bowl of cold presweetened cereal. A cane, rather than crutches, leans against the stool alongside him.

"Yuck," Arthur comments, rooting in the refrigerator and

coming up with a carton of vanilla yogurt. "Whose turn is it to grocery shop?"

"Yours," Eddie says without looking away from the television screen. "You don't want the Spider grocery shopping. Trust me."

"I do. His appetite is phenomenal. I wonder how he keeps from getting fat?" Arthur pats his thickening waist morosely, then glances at the television. "What's so absorbing?"

"The weather report. There have been freak storms all through the North Atlantic, especially along the coast of Brazil. An unexpected tidal wave wiped out several fishing boats and at least one cruise liner."

"Damn!" Arthur stops stirring granola into his yogurt to watch the screen on which pictures of rescue operations are now being shown. "Duppy Jonah?"

"I'm worried that it is. Have you checked your messages?"

"I . . ." Arthur sighs. "No, I haven't."

"I think you had better. I checked mine. *Nada*."

Carrying his breakfast with him, Arthur goes into his office. The red light on his machine is blinking. He presses the button, bracing himself for the shrill voices of his tormentors. What he gets is far worse. A voice, deep and rumbling as waves beating on a rocky shore, growls:

"Call me, damn you, Arthur! I want to know what Lovern did with my wife! I'll try your private line. Call me."

The rest of the messages are perfectly mundane.

"Duppy Jonah," Eddie says, from the doorway into the office. "And he sounds very unhappy. Did he try your private line?"

"I don't know." Arthur covers his embarrassment by chewing a spoonful of yogurt and granola. "I didn't answer that one either. The office phone rang repeatedly last night."

"Might have been Duppy Jonah. Are you going to call him?"

"As soon as I look up his number," Arthur says. "I wonder what the hell has happened?"

"Something to Amphitrite, apparently. If it's any comfort, I doubt that she's dead."

"I'd guessed that," Arthur says, "or we'd have more problems than a few tidal waves."

"Right."

Arthur is reaching for the phone when it rings. Without hesitation, he picks up the receiver. Right now the pranksters would be a relief. He needs someone to chew out.

"Pendragon Productions."

"Arthur?" The voice is unctuous. "This is Isidro Robelo."

"Yes."

"Have you seen the news this morning?"

"Yes."

"This call is to claim responsibility for the catastrophe."

"You?"

"Yes, Majesty. We have taken both Amphitrite and Vera. They are hidden where you will be unable to find them without our aid nor will they be returned to you unless you agree to put your full support behind our policies."

Arthur switches to intercom mode so that Eddie can listen.

"Your policies?"

"Yes. We want financial and magical support to preserve this continent and other places on the globe."

"I thought that this was discussed at the Review," Arthur says, schooling his voice to neutral calm with centuries of experience. "A committee was formed to explore the best means of reaching those objectives."

"A committee!" Isidro makes the word sound like an obscenity. "We cannot wait for a committee to make recommendations."

"What makes you think that we will comply?" Arthur's inflection leaves no doubt that the "we" is royal.

"Vera and Amphitrite will remain our captives until you comply," Isidro answers. "You must comply."

"You have not mentioned my wizard, Lovern. Does he live?"

"He does, and we intend to return him to you as an indication of our good faith."

Arthur forces himself to chuckle derisively. "And perhaps because keeping a wizard captive is difficult?"

"We *can* keep him. We did take him, and Oswaldo is an initiate of the craft."

"Return Lovern as you wish. I am neither accepting nor rejecting any of your offers."

Isidro clears his throat. "We have said we will return him to you. He will arrive this evening. Do not take this as a sign of weakness on our part."

"Certainly." Arthur's tone becomes friendly, his British accent more pronounced. "And, do tell me, have you considered the personal risk you are taking in holding Amphitrite?"

"It is an acceptable risk." Isidro's words are firm, but Arthur thinks he hears a slight quaver.

"I just wanted to make certain. I suppose we will speak later."

"And our terms?"

"Really, Isidro. Are you trying to rush me?"

"Vera and Amphitrite may not have much time."

"You should have thought of that yourself, my good man. Good-bye."

Arthur hangs up the phone, glances over at Eddie, and grins weakly. "I hope I handled that right. Now I'd better call Duppy Jonah."

"Do." Leaning heavily on his cane, Eddie limps toward his own office. "I'm going to review the e-mail and my messages to see if any word of this is out. I'll wake Anson, too."

"No need to do that yet," Arthur says, starting to punch in numbers. "We may need someone well rested later on."

"True."

The phone begins ringing, the sound distant and echoing, but the connection when it is at last answered is sharp and clear.

"Yes?"

"Arthur Pendragon, here. Is this Duppy Jonah?"

The Sea King's voice is deep and wild. "So you've returned my call at last."

"We've had some trouble with the phone lines," Arthur fibs. "I stopped answering until it was straightened out. I've heard from Isidro Robelo."

"So have I."

"He has not only taken Amphitrite. He has also taken Vera."

"What is that to me?"

"A relief? Your lady is not alone."

"And what of your precious wizard?"

"He is being returned to me. According to Isidro, he will be back in Albuquerque by this evening."

"Alive?"

"As far as I know."

"Pity. He will not live long thereafter."

"Duppy Jonah . . ."

The Sea King interrupts. "The wizard has broken faith with me."

"You don't know that. Even a wizard can be overwhelmed and held captive."

"Yes, I know." This last is said grudgingly.

"If Lovern lives, he may be a source of valuable information for us. Isidro spoke oddly—there was something in the way he spoke of the ladies that makes me wonder if he knew precisely where they were."

"Oh?"

"Just a feeling. I want to interview Lovern, see if he knows anything."

"If you can trust what he says."

"I don't think he will toy with me."

"You are too trusting, Arthur."

"Perhaps." Arthur is relieved to hear that Duppy Jonah's great voice no longer booms and crashes, only rumbles. "I was wondering if you would cease inciting the waves until we are certain that Amphitrite is indeed unfindable."

"Why? Those fools should think before toying with me!"

"Innocent people are being hurt."

"They can stay off of my waters. It is not their element, it is *mine*!" The roar and crash returns. "Pity is not part of my nature. Ask the bones of the drowned dead if you doubt me."

"I do not, Duppy Jonah."

"Get me my wife or accept that I will mourn her in tempest, typhoon, and tsunami!"

The connection goes dead. Arthur looks at the gluey mass of yogurt and granola sitting beside his phone. Somehow, he doesn't have much of an appetite any longer.

✿◧✿

Slumped in a seat on the custom jet that has landed at Albuquerque airport, Lovern frets at his impotence. Wrists and ankles are encircled by tidy bands of cold iron concealed beneath his clothing. He suspects that there is more iron in the jaunty fedora Cleonice has just placed on his head.

"We're taking you from the plane to a van. The driver has instructions to drive directly to Arthur's house. In case you are considering trying to work some vengeance on us, you should know that along with your food you swallowed a small charm that will make sorcery very difficult for you even when you have removed the iron jewelry you now wear."

Lovern cocks an eyebrow, trying hard to seem nonchalant. "You've gone to a great deal of trouble over this."

"We respect your power. We do not doubt that if we took fewer precautions, you could do us harm."

Lovern does not bother to disabuse her. Magical power is a much more fragile thing than the uninitiated would believe. He suspects that Oswaldo, the adept among the South American contingent, demanded these extremes in part to increase their respect for his own abilities.

Manco calls to Cleonice in Quechua, the language of the Incas. "The silver bird is fueled. We can depart as soon as you get rid of the greybeard."

"Good," Cleonice responds in the same language. Then in English. "Come with me, Lovern."

For a single moment he considers answering her in Quechua, then decides that would be childish. Why give her information that might, just might, come in useful later?

Instead he mutely follows, shuffling slightly as if the iron on his ankles hurts him. Cleonice leaves him at the gate.

"Your driver is over there," she says, gesturing to a long-jawed fellow in a cowboy hat and jeans. His tee shirt reads "Two Hearts Van Lines" and is printed with a picture of the sacred hearts of Jesus and Mary. "We have already paid him and given him your luggage."

"Thank you." He offers her a jerky bow. "I do not see the hanged man. Fear death by water."

"What nonsense are you speaking?"

"It's poetry. Ask Oswaldo." He turns away without further comment, leaving her staring after him in puzzlement.

The drive to Arthur's hacienda is without event. The driver is cordial but not intrusive. Lovern struggles to make conversation, knowing that he must drag himself from the depression that seeks to claim him.

When he arrives at the front door of Arthur's hacienda, the driver refuses a tip, saying he has been amply paid. He sets the bag on the front doorstep and goes away with a polite cheerfulness that strangely warms Lovern.

Arthur must have watched for the van to drive away, for the door swings open before Lovern can raise his hand to knock.

"My wizard!"

"My liege." Lovern looks at Arthur, his normal cockiness falling prey to despair despite his best efforts. "My liege, I have failed. The Sea Queen and Vera are lost and . . ."

"You have been a victim, not a failure," Arthur says heartily. "Who would have believed that Isidro and his allies would break their oaths so lightly? We will punish their arrogance, but first we must decide if we can rescue our people."

Lovern lets himself be led into Arthur's office. As he had expected, Eddie and Anson are already there. Also, to his surprise, is Jonathan Wong.

"I thought we might need legal advice," Arthur explains. He takes a seat behind his desk as he once might have mounted a throne. "Lovern, can you report?"

"Certainly," he says, "but while I do so, would someone remove these from my wrists and ankles?"

He shoots back his cuff, revealing the iron bracelet. Anson immediately rises and kneels beside him.

"Locked, eh? I can pick it. Do you have a paper clip?"

Arthur opens his desk drawer and tosses him one. "Is that all you need?"

"Oh, yeah. These locks are just meant to keep Lovern here from taking off the bracelets all by his lonesome. Anyhow, what good is a skill if you need fancy tools to use it, eh?"

Lovern watches as Anson unbends the paper clip and sets to work, then focuses on the present.

"The day after we arrived, we were taken into the rain forest, ostensibly to tour. When the plane landed, the three of us—along with Isidro and Oswaldo—went ashore. I was led into a magical field that knocked me out. That's all I remember.

"From what I overheard later, I gathered that Vera and Amphitrite were left in the rain forest."

Eddie raises his pencil for attention. "Why didn't they just imprison them?"

"Partially it's symbolic—they are endangered by the rain forest as the rain forest is endangered by human action. Partially, it is because they did not want either Vera's or Amphitrite's deaths to happen directly by their own hands. A loss to Harmony will not be dismissed lightly."

"Then the threat to kill them is empty?" Arthur asks.

"No. I don't think so. Isidro is a fanatic—he has always been so, whether for *jihad*, the Allies, or this. He has killed for ideals in the past. This time, he can claim with some truth that he wanted the ladies to get to know the rain forest intimately—that the sojourn was part of their education."

"Then he is thinking about the future."

"In an odd way."

"Do you think he is sane?" Arthur asks.

"In the legal sense of being responsible for his actions?" Lovern glances at Jonathan. "If he's crazy, he's crazy like a fox. All of them are. They know full well that our people would not condone a usual hostage situation, so they have created an unusual one. My guess is that their version of events will be that Vera and Amphitrite became lost in the rain forest."

"And if we say other?"

"My guess is that our silence will be part of the price for the ladies' safe return."

Jonathan Wong nods. "That is logical. If we let it become widely known that we made concessions to regain the hostages, then we are vulnerable to similar tactics in the future. Isidro and his associates may be counting on our realizing that silence is in our own best interests."

An iron bracelet thumps to the floor. Anson chortles and moves on to the next.

"And what if we do not treat with them?" Arthur says. "It is against my policy to endanger the whole to regain the few."

"Then," Lovern says, shaking his wrist as Anson removes the second bracelet, "I believe they will both die and the lands will be awash with the wrath of the Sea King."

Eddie nods. "I agree. Amphitrite's death is what we must fear. If we get her back alive, Duppy Jonah will be appeased.

"I'm not saying," he adds hastily, "that we should forsake Vera. Not at all, but Duppy Jonah poses the greatest danger to ourselves, our secret, and innocent others."

"True." Arthur muses. "We need to send an emissary to him asking for time. Who will he speak with?"

"The Changer," Lovern says immediately. "I saw real affection between them when we sojourned beneath the waves."

Anson finishes unlocking one of the ankle bands and glances up. "I agree. The Changer can also travel by land or sky or sea as a creature of them all."

"Then he must be sent for," Arthur glances at a calendar. "As I count the days, he will be checking for messages tonight. It is already evening. Someone should leave right away."

"Let Anson and me go," Eddie says. "I know the area, and he can post the message and drive."

"Done," the King says. "Stay there until the Changer comes. He may agree to return with you immediately."

"Very well." Eddie leans on his cane and pushes himself up.

Anson removes the last bond and grins at Lovern. "There you are, magic man. Soon you'll be back to power, fast as you can."

"I hope," Lovern grumbles. "And thank you."

"The rest of us," Arthur says, after Eddie and Anson depart, "will try to find ways to stall both Isidro and Duppy Jonah."

Jonathan Wong sighs. "I wish Vera were here. We could use her wisdom now."

"So do I," Arthur says with a trace of bleak humor. "After all, if she were here, then we wouldn't be in this mess."

Swansdown>> We have a private plane. It's very useful out here. We figured that the family would fly down to Albuquerque in that. The Moderator has said that he can arrange discreet refueling caches along the way.

Rebecca>> Don't you do everything with dogsleds out there?

Swansdown>> :) You have a somewhat antiquated notion of Alaskan life. How long since you visited?

Rebecca>> I guess it's been a century or so.

Swansdown>> Technology has changed our lives a great deal, my dear niece. My little daughter Dawn speaks seven languages fluently thanks to audiotapes and satellite-dish programs—and that's even though she's never met anyone but a few Eskimos.

Rebecca>> I wonder if Bronson would get us a plane?

Swansdown>> Ask! He's a bit conservative, however.

Rebecca>> But wonderful! He's a survivor.

Swansdown>> As we all are, my dear, as we all are.

Rebecca>> Are you excited?

Swansdown>> About the trip or the proposed revolution?

Rebecca>> Both.

Swansdown>> The trip, definitely, a bit scared, too. I'd be happier if we were going in winter, not in autumn. I understand we'd never get the fauns and satyrs, then. As for the revolution? Arthur needs to face facts. Just like you, I think he overlooks the possibilities modern technology offers—he only sees the threats. Still, he has been a steady monarch.

Rebecca>> Static.

Swansdown>> However you choose to see it, my dear. I really must log off. I hear Snowbird and Dawn arriving. They'll need help unloading.

Rebecca>> This has been nice, Aunt.

Swansdown>> Indeed it has. Do consider coming for a visit after the Albuquerque trip.

Rebecca>> I will.

Dear Aunt Swansdown, Rebecca thinks. *It's easy for her to be so content. She's a shaman and one with not a few*

*charms. Her curses are legendary. I bet she has the locals
cowed.*

The young sasquatch considers checking her e-mail or
looking in at the Moderator's chatroom. Neither satisfies her
completely. Instead she drifts out into the living room. The
tables, beautiful things she made out of slices cut from giant
forest trees and polished with beeswax, are covered with
books and magazines on New Mexico.

She picks one up and looks into the face of a Pueblo girl
of about twelve. What would that girl think if she met Rebecca or Bronson? Would she feel that her horizons had just
opened wider or would she be terrified at the knowledge that
monsters far more solid than her people's kachina gods walk
the Earth?

Rebecca cannot decide. Outside she can hear Bronson
humming to himself as he stretches mink pelts on drying
racks. He has been much encouraged to learn that even if the
first-world fur market is falling off, furs remain popular in
other countries.

The athanor eagle screeches and dives for a fish just a few
feet outside of the concealed window. The spray catches a
few rays of sunlight and sheds rainbows that gladden her
heart.

"Bronson," she calls out, "can I bring you anything?"

"Coffee," his gruff voice answers, "and a look at your
smile."

¤◪¤

"Coffee?" Eddie asks Anson. "The pot in the kitchen was
fresh, so I filled a thermos."

"Did you think to bring cream and sugar?"

"Of course. I know you of old."

"Then definitely, and if you reach behind my seat, you
will find a box of doughnuts." Anson chortles. "I knew we
might have a long vigil, so when I went to get petrol, I got
supplies."

Eddie leans back and snags the box. They had arrived at
the turnaround on the shoulder of the road a few minutes
before. Anson had scouted and reported that he couldn't tell
whether or not the Changer had already been there.

"How can you tell when the tracks of any wild thing *or* human-type person might be his?" he had said reasonably.

He had cached their message beneath the rock that had been appointed for this purpose and returned to the van.

"How long should we wait?" Anson asks, brushing powdered sugar off the front of his shirt.

"Until dawn, I think," Eddie answers. "Arthur can reach us by the car phone if there is a change in the situation."

"Hopefully, we will not need to wait so long." Anson stretches, cracking his neck and popping his shoulders. "I had wanted to watch a talk show tonight."

"Did you set your VCR?"

"I forgot."

"Let's call and have Arthur do it. He'll be horrified that we're thinking such mundane thoughts in the midst of a crisis, but that will be good for him. He sometimes forgets that all the world does not prioritize as he does."

Anson places the call and, after he has hung up, he grins at Eddie, his white teeth the most visible part of his face in the gathering darkness.

"He was horrified, as you said, but he promised. I wonder how you have worked with such a serious one for so long. You are not nearly so dry."

Eddie sighs. "I don't know about that. There are times I think I am even more staid than Arthur. He leads. I serve. I'm not certain how much glory there is in such a life."

Anson reaches for another doughnut—his fourth. "Is there anything else you would rather do?"

"I want a challenge," Eddie says, "a new land to discover, a good fight to win."

"And you do not find the challenge that, say, the South Americans offer, one that stirs your blood?"

"Not really." Eddie rubs his hand along his jaw. Anson can hear the rasp of the whiskers. "I'd love to be an astronaut, but the physical exam is the one thing I cannot risk. I'd pass it—that's certain—but there is too much chance they would find anomalies in my blood."

"Too true."

"Even mercenary work is no longer a place for anonymous service. I've thought about looking into the Foreign Legion, but fighting isn't what I want. I want a challenge."

"No one to love?"

"Not now."

"That Vera—she would be a challenge. Could you teach that virgin to love like a woman?"

"That's rude, Anson! She's entitled to her choice." Eddie chuckles. "In any case, she's a tough lady."

The Spider smiles. "I was just looking for a challenge for you, my friend."

"How do you fill your time?"

"Africa has many problems, many wars, much political maneuvering. It is an entire continent of puzzles to be solved."

"You don't speak up for Africa as Isidro and Co. did for South America."

"The problems there are people problems, in large part. I enjoy those types of problems, but I do not think that they can be solved by outside intervention."

"Except by yours."

"I am not an outsider. I was born there. Many tribes still tell the stories of how Anansi the Spider brought the people gifts from the Creator. Other stories make Spider the creator of all. It is very heartening."

Eddie reaches for a doughnut. "You've eaten most of these!"

"My appetite is also legendary. Don't worry. There's another box."

"And my legend is almost forgotten except by scholars." Eddie sighs. "Enkidu the Wildman is viewed as a prototype for Tarzan and Mowgli. Most modern treatments of Arthurian legend leave Bedivere out completely in favor of a love triangle that didn't happen quite that way. Forget the rest. I have always been a shadow."

"You are sad, eh?"

"Discouraged. More coffee?"

"That would be very fine. I have decided, Eddie. However this all turns out, you are coming to Nigeria with me. Lovern will owe us favors immense. If he can give a mermaid legs, then he can work a charm so that you will be as dark as me."

"But Arthur . . ."

"Arthur will manage. Think about it as much as you like. In the end, I will not give you a choice, huh?"

Eddie laughs. "Tell me about modern Africa. Even for athanor there are only twenty-four hours in a day. I've been remiss regarding the Dark Continent."

"Ah, you will regret asking this, my friend," Anson reaches behind his seat, his long arm bending at what seems impossible angles. He comes out with a box of chocolate-frosted cupcakes. "I have stories, and stories about stories."

"And we," Eddie says, reaching for a cupcake, "have a long wait in front of us."

Two hours past midnight, Eddie and Anson are playing a lazy game of foreign-language hangman by flashlight when there is a thump on the roof of the van. A moment later, a large raven, something white in its beak, flaps onto the hood where it stares back at them like a distorted hood ornament.

"Anomaly." Eddie shakes his head. "Ravens don't fly by night."

"This one does," Anson says, getting out and opening the back door of the van. "Come in, Changer."

The raven flies in and lands on the floor. Dropping the folded sheet of paper, it croaks hoarsely. Then with a blur of motion, the strong, lean, human form of the Changer is sitting cross-legged before them, clad only in his long, dark hair.

"Your note says that Arthur needs to speak with me." His voice is gravelly, his speech hesitant, as if during his few days in the wild he has forgotten how to use his voice.

"That's right," Eddie says. "We have big trouble."

Economically, he outlines the situation, helped by the fact that the Changer does not interrupt, only listens, his yellow eyes widening slightly in reaction to the enormity of what Isidro and his allies have dared.

"And Arthur wishes me to speak with my brother, to beg forbearance." The Changer frowns. "I must have full freedom to make whatever deals I wish."

"Arthur can tell you what is beyond his power to grant."

"Tell him what I have said."

"Aren't you coming with us?"

The Changer tilts his head, as a bird might when orienting on a sound. "My daughter is alone out there."

"I see." Eddie chews his upper lip. "I had forgotten that she doesn't fly. Can you leave her for a few days?"

"No, she is too young to support herself, even if her education had not been retarded."

"Can one of us fetch her?"

"I hope not. I have been trying to instill caution."

"How long will it take you to get her and return here?"

"Until midmorning. I can get to her fairly swiftly, but the return will be slow."

"Is there any road closer?"

"No."

"Then midmorning it will have to be."

Unlike Arthur, who might have argued, both Eddie and Anson have been fathers. They know the responsibility that the Changer has assumed and respect it.

"Tell Arthur, my terms or none. Get me a plane ticket to Brazil, fastest route. Duppy Jonah will be in those waters."

"A private plane might be better," Anson says. "There is an airfield here that might rent one."

The Changer scratches. "I cannot fly one, and I cannot promise patience with a pilot."

Anson grins. "I can pilot."

"And a copilot?" Eddie asks.

"Work out those details without me," the Changer says, getting out of the van, "and be here by nine o'clock. I will try to be here by then."

Without another word, he shifts shape, becoming something with broader wings than a raven's. When his form is blocked out against the starlit sky, Eddie sighs.

"Anomaly. Again."

Anson starts the engine. "At least he is working with us. He could have refused. This is none of his problem."

"No"—Eddie's expression is thoughtful—"but he has not given up his vengeance on those who killed his mate and Shahrazad's brothers and sisters. Even though he has the papers he needs to pass in human society, he knows he may still need us. He wants us to owe him a few favors."

"The favors *that* one would need," Anson says with a shudder, "I do not like to think about."

"Neither do I," Eddie replies. "Neither do I."

19

*There are bad people who would be less
dangerous if they were quite devoid of
goodness.*

—LA ROCHEFOUCAULD

RESOLVE IS ONE THING, EFFECTING THAT RESOLVE IS AN-
other. Therefore, it is a new dawn before Amphitrite and
Vera can depart from where they were marooned.

The craft that Amphitrite has designed cannot really be
dignified with the word "boat," but it is quite a fine raft.
Using their machetes, the two athanor had chopped logs and
lashed them together with vines.

A prow has been trimmed to make steering easier. They
could have managed a mast, but without a sail, it would have
been a useless gesture. Even Vera cannot weave tight fabric
from vines.

Amphitrite's hands are swollen from unaccustomed fric-
tion—calluses are not survival needs under water. Vera has
done better. Her fondness for martial arts and domestic crafts
has toughened her hands, but she favors a slightly sprained
wrist.

Both are scratched, sweaty, and filthy when they launch
the craft. They have had their share of insect bites—although
neither has experienced a severe allergic reaction. Despite
their aches and pains, they are triumphant when the raft
proves serviceable.

"What shall we call her?" Amphitrite asks.

"The *Vengeance*," Vera suggests.

Amphitrite purses her lips. "Too violent for such a little craft. How about the *Pororoca*? It means 'the Big Roar'— that's the local term for a specific type of tidal wave that occurs in the Amazon's mouth."

"The Big Roar," Vera says. "I like it. A big roar is exactly what I plan to make when we get out of here."

Amphitrite scoops out a handful of river water and sprinkles it over the bow. "Be named, then, *Pororoca*. Know yourself whole and essential."

Vera raises her head, which she had bowed during the makeshift christening. "Shall we load our earthly goods?"

"That won't take long." Amphitrite grins.

To the supplies that Isidro and Oswaldo had left, Vera has added four spears with fire-hardened tips. Coils of vines supplement their meager supply of rope, and a basket made from river reeds gives them a place to stow mangoes and other fruit.

"It isn't much," Vera says, "and I would give a lot to know how far we are from the mouth of the river, but it is a start."

"Climb aboard, then." Amphitrite picks up one of the steering poles, wincing at the pressure on her sore hands.

"Do you want me to steer first?" Vera asks. "You can navigate and rest your hands."

"Let me get a feel for how the *Pororoca* handles," Amphitrite says. "Then I will do just that."

As they push off into the river, monkeys scream mocking commentary. An anaconda raises its head, vaguely disappointed that what it had perceived as dinner is leaving. A caiman alligator slides off the bank, not so much hunting as hoping to be on hand if either of them falls in.

"She handles well," Amphitrite says, "for a raft."

"That's all we can ask," Vera replies calmly. "She is a raft—she must do a raft's work. Where Isidro has made his mistake is in believing that we are like this raft—a tool to be turned to his purpose."

She hefts her spear, her grey eyes studying the riverbank, her body adjusting to the motion of the raft on the water.

"But we are more than tools," she continues.

Amphitrite, still fashion-doll pretty beneath the grime, laughs, a sound holding the relentless murmur of the sea. "Oh, yes, my friend. We are far more than that."

¤◙¤

The Changer and Shahrazad are waiting at the turnaround when Anson arrives in the van. Some indication of how fast they must have journeyed can be guessed from the pup's evident exhaustion. She does not rise from where she is flopped beneath a shrub but waits for the Changer to lift her.

He has shifted human-form once again and is clad in the same clothes in which he had departed Arthur's hacienda three days before. His feet are bare.

Inspecting the other's wrinkled attire, Anson chuckles. "I brought clothing for you, old one."

"I cached these when we left," the Changer answers. "They will do for now."

They spare each other idle chatter on the drive back. Only once does the Changer speak. "Did Eddie find me a way to Brazil?"

"He has chartered a jet," Anson says. "I will fly it. We can make do without a copilot if you want to leave quickly."

"I do."

"Then we will."

At the hacienda, the Changer carries Shahrazad into the courtyard, where she takes refuge under her lilac bush. Then, without knocking, the ancient walks into Arthur's office.

If the King had been inclined to protest this lack of courtesy, he is stopped by the cool expression in the Changer's yellow eyes. Instead, Arthur rises and offers his hand.

"Thank you for coming so quickly."

"You need me to negotiate with Duppy Jonah."

"Yes." Arthur gestures toward a seat and takes his own chair. He has not slept in close to twenty-four hours, and his blue eyes are unnaturally bright. "There has been a hurricane off the coast of Florida, flooding in the Netherlands, and all manner of smaller marine disasters. The meteorologists are coming up with excuses as wild as sunspot flares and a sudden acceleration in global warming."

"Duppy Jonah is showing restraint."

"I know. His full fury would leave no coastal area untouched. Still, I would prefer that he hold his temper until we know that Amphitrite is lost."

The Changer nods. "We are both family men, my brother and I. I will speak to him. What are your limits?"

"I cannot promise him anyone else's life. Otherwise, I am willing to grant him anything within my power."

"What about your throne?"

"Would he want it?" Arthur's expression is wry. "If he does, he is welcome to it, remembering, as always, that kingship is subject to the Accord rule of the athanor."

"Of course. Do you have any threats to offer?"

Arthur frowns. "You mean punitive measures I would take?"

"Yes."

"No. He has been wronged. I am not asking him to accept injustice without striking back. I am asking him to reserve his wrath for those who deserve it."

"I see. Do you want me to try to find Vera and Amphitrite and take them from their captors?"

Arthur's mouth drops open. "Are you serious? Yes!"

"Would I have offered otherwise?"

"I suppose not." Arthur regains some of his composure. "From what Lovern recalls, they were stranded somewhere in the rain forest near the river. He has tried to divine more precisely, but whatever they did to him is still restricting both his powers and those of his familiar creature."

"The Amazon River has many branches," the Changer says. "That isn't much to go on."

"His impression was that it was a main branch of the Amazon. They flew from Belém for several hours before landing the plane at a wide spot in the river."

"That's still not much."

"I understand that you might not be willing to attempt the journey on so little information," Arthur begins, sincerely trying to save face for the ancient.

"I didn't say I was not going to find them," the Changer says. "I said that was not much to go on. I understand that Anson is going to be my pilot."

"Yes, he has volunteered."

"Good. I will ask him to go ahead to Belém and see what he can learn."

"Anson?"

"You still underestimate the Spider after all this time, Arthur. He is a wise, dangerous, old soul."

"Perhaps. He has been helpful since Eddie was hurt—helpful and patient."

"We understand each other somewhat, the Spider and I. I believe that we can find our two lost ones."

"And when they are no longer hostage . . ."

"Then you may decide how next to act, but I should warn you that Duppy Jonah will probably want the South Americans dead."

"Yes," Arthur looks sad. "I know. I even understand."

The Changer rises. "I will do what I can. Mind my daughter for me. I place her in your keeping."

"Mine?" Arthur asks, then nods sharply. "I accept."

"I am no kinder than my brother when my dear ones are endangered," the Changer says, opening the office door. "And I doubt that he would negotiate with me for you."

"I understand."

The Changer strips and shifts shape into coyote form. He wishes with all his heart he could use words more complex to tell the pup where he is going. All he can do is try to promise her that he will return, that she is not being forsaken.

Shahrazad seems willing to accept his leaving. His last sight of her shows her standing at the door of the courtyard, her brush held low but striving valiantly to wag.

¤◻¤

The jet that Anson proudly takes possession of a few hours later is a speedy fuel hog. It lacks the elaborate interior appointments of the plane on which Vera and Amphitrite left Albuquerque, but is comfortable enough.

"We will be our own flight attendants," Anson says, "and I will teach you enough to let you copilot in an emergency."

"I am overjoyed," the Changer says.

"I have raided the kitchen," Anson continues tranquilly,

"and we have supplies enough to sustain us."

"Good. More than just sweets, Spider?"

"An entire ham," Anson says, flipping switches and checking clearances, "three pounds of different cheeses, some pasta salad, a few apples, a loaf of fresh Italian bread, butter . . ."

The Changer glances over at him. "You did more than raid the refrigerator."

"Oh, maybe I went to a grocery with Arthur's credit card, eh? He can afford it. There is a herring, too, smoked. A chocolate cake and a box of those little strudels. Some milk, apple juice, and a gallon of lemonade, in case we get thirsty."

And, during the hours of flight, they consume a great deal of the supplies that Anson has laid in. Like most natural shapeshifters, their metabolisms are high, making great demands for rejecting the usual demands of mass and structure.

When they arrive in the vicinity of Belém, Anson lands the plane at a small airstrip whose owners have been paid well to overlook the unauthorized craft.

"A flourishing drug trade," Anson comments, "has its uses. We are within an hour of the ocean. A car—actually, something jeepy with four-wheel drive—awaits. What is your request?"

"Drive me to the shore, I will go from there on my own. Can you find where the South American contingent reside?"

"Easily. Isidro invited me to visit and discuss revolutionary politics."

Anson's expression turns solemn. Once they are in the jeep and bouncing down rutted roads, he comments, "They are not evil, Changer. Isidro Robelo is a passionate advocate of his cause. Cleonice has known almost all her life about the heritage her father gave her. She believes it is wrong that we do so little to affect our world. Oswaldo is a dreamer and a shaman. They are not cruel."

The Changer shrugs. "I will not present them as such to Duppy Jonah. He values Amphitrite more than he does his own life. In attempting to use her, they were attempting to use him. Water is not evil, either, but people get drowned."

"Still . . . I am a sentimentalist. I hate to see dreamers die."

"Perhaps. But I don't think that idealism is an excuse for stupidity. I saw a tee shirt on the kiosk at the airport in Florida. It read, 'EVOLUTION IN ACTION.' I suspect that evolution is about to act once again."

"Humor?"

"No, seriousness. I have seen entire species die out because they could not adapt. If our people cease to accept the cost of killing our own, then we will have lost one of the few checks on our actions."

"You really believe this?"

"I flew over the battlefield at Ragnarokk."

Anson drums his long fingers on the steering wheel. "I wonder if Arthur knows how brutal a negotiator he has sent?"

"I'm the only one who has a chance," the Changer says.

"The road doesn't go much closer to the water," Anson says. "We could find a village, perhaps."

"No. Pull over and let me out here." The Changer unbuttons his shirt. "I'll leave my clothes with you."

"As you wish. Can you shape a local bird?"

The Changer glances at him and continues disrobing.

"Of course you can. Seek me in Belém at Isidro's house."

"Is that wise?"

"I don't expect for him to see me," Anson says cheerfully. "You are not the only shapeshifter among us—merely the finest."

"Flattery."

"Honesty. I will see what I can learn and then, when we are together, work my wiles."

"Very good." The Changer gets out of the car. "Be safe, Spider."

"And you, Changer."

The water is warm as a puppy's kiss. Wading into the shallows off a tangled shore, the Changer dives. Any watcher would have waited forever to see him surface again.

Shifting into a sea serpent with scales of iridescent copper, the memory of which is recorded with more or less accuracy in both Polynesian and Viking carvings, the Changer plunges into water that tastes of mud and decaying vegetable matter as well as of salt.

Each creature he passes flees, darting from memories of primeval predation. From the pattern of their departure he reads the sign of the one he seeks. Arthur had promised to call ahead, but even so the Brazilian coastline is long.

But the Sea King is also seeking him, so they meet more quickly than might have been imagined. Duppy Jonah wears the form of a ponderous elephant seal, but when he sees the Changer he shifts into a form akin to that which the Changer wears, though his scales are of burnished gold.

"Brother," he says in the language of the sea dragons, "I have the honor of your company twice in as many moons. I do not know whether to be honored or suspicious. Have you become Arthur's lackey?"

"Think rather," the Changer hisses, "that I seek to make him mine. Doing him this favor is little enough to me. I may ask more of him."

"Your family, yet?"

"Until I win retribution from their slayer, forever."

"That I understand. What have you come to ask?"

"On what terms will you subdue the storms and tempest that ripple outward from the force of your just anger."

"That is all?"

"All. Arthur sympathizes with you as the one wronged. Yet he is concerned that your unhappiness may harm too many unconcerned with our quarrels."

"Always the advocate of humanity." Duppy Jonah lashes his forked tongue around a fat fish foolish enough to wander within range. "I wonder if they would speak so thoughtfully for him?"

"That is not our issue now. What will you accept to calm your storms?"

The golden sea serpent twines through a thicket of sea plants. The copper follows, knowing that his brother must be given time to think.

"I want the deaths of those who have wronged me and mine."

"Immediately? If we kill them too swiftly, we lose any clues as to where Vera and Amphitrite were left."

"True." More undulating progress, then, "I want the wizard Lovern as my hostage against Arthur returning my wife to me and then against his promising to execute the three who have transgressed against me.''

The Changer coils about himself like a design in Celtic knotwork. ''I was not given permission to treat with others' lives, but I will phone to offer Arthur your terms.''

''There is a line we can tap into within a few miles of here,'' Duppy Jonah says. ''I dread the day that humans forsake cables solely for satellite relays.''

''Humans are lazy,'' the Changer says. ''They will not pull the cables, and we can continue to turn them to our use.''

Shifting into a triton, the Changer places his call. Arthur answers immediately.

''Pendragon Productions.''

''Arthur, this is the Changer.''

''Do you have an answer?''

''The Sea King wants Lovern as a hostage. He will return him when Amphitrite is returned to him and Isidro, Cleonice, and Oswaldo are dead.''

Arthur paused. ''That is all he will accept?''

''Yes. And I think he is being generous given the situation. Lovern did swear to keep her safe.''

''He did. Hold on. I'll go tell him what he must do.''

There is a pause of several minutes, then Arthur returns.

''Lovern has agreed to surrender himself. He wants to know if you consider it likely that Duppy Jonah will kill him.''

''Only if Amphitrite dies. According to his own vow, Lovern's life is forfeit in that case.''

''Yes. So you said. And Isidro, Cleonice, and Oswaldo must die? Duppy Jonah will accept no other penalty?''

The Changer lowers the receiver, and asks, ''Arthur wants to know if you will accept any other penalty for the South American contingent members.''

''Other than their deaths?'' The Sea King snorts. ''No.''

The Changer addresses the phone receiver. ''He says no.''

''They are certain to offer service or goods in ransom.''

The Changer repeats this to Duppy Jonah. The Sea King flares out his fins and crest.

''I want them executed, both as penalty and example.''

The Changer says to the phone, "He will take nothing but their deaths."

"And only then do I get my wizard returned to me." Arthur sighs. "Perhaps I should not care so much how many humans or others uninvolved in our quarrels die."

"Arthur, they have broken the Accord," the Changer says sternly. "You cannot let live those who use athanor as pawns."

"True. I am being softer than I should, or perhaps I am selfishly thinking of the cost to Harmony. Tell Duppy Jonah he will have what he requests. Where should I send Lovern?"

"To your home in Florida. Someone will collect him there. Call when you have his estimated time of arrival."

"Very well. And thank you, Changer. I will not forget."

"I know," the Changer says, and it is perhaps good for Arthur's peace of mind that he cannot see the expression on the triton's face. "I go to rejoin Anson now."

"Good luck."

"Thanks."

The Changer sets the phone aside. "Lovern will meet you or your emissary in Florida at Arthur's private beach. Someone will call to tell you what time."

"Good. I wonder how one keeps a wizard imprisoned?"

"I wouldn't know. Perhaps you should consult Oswaldo. He seems to have managed quite neatly."

"You jest!"

"Of course. If I may take my leave, I need to rejoin Anson A. Kridd. We have further tasks to perform."

"You may go."

With a rapid uncoiling of his tail, the Changer sets off toward the shore. Two to find, three to kill. The order of the day is neat and clear in his mind. He wonders if Arthur will be too angry when he learns that due process has been bypassed, but he doesn't trust the King's idealism any more than he trusts that of Isidro, Cleonice, and Oswaldo.

✡✡✡

After dropping the Changer at the roadside, Anson A. Kridd continues on into Belém. Despite his great age, he has never lost the capacity simply to enjoy a moment and so as he drives along, he savors the light shifting through the green canopy overhead, the red of a delicate anthurium on its slender stalk, the different red of a macaw's feathers, the white of a broken tree limb dead and dry amidst its verdant surroundings.

In Belém, he drops the jeep with a hotel concierge and saunters out into the bustling streets. Here, too, brilliant color and humid heat dominate. Strolling through a marketplace, he realizes how tired he is. The Changer had remained awake throughout their long flight, but the piloting had been left to him alone.

Humans often believe that immortality means having time and enough for any task, but Anson has learned that immortality can make one aware of all the things one should do with any given hour of the day. Today there is less time than usual, for they have no idea what dangers Amphitrite and Vera face.

Stopping at a stall, he pays American money for a stick of sugarcane and a sack of dried mango. The market woman who helps him is dumpy, but she has silky hair the color of jet twisted in a tight braid and eyes of a clear, almost translucent hazel green.

Her skin is brown and her gestures assured—a city woman, then, one who possibly knows less of the rain forest surrounding her than an average American schoolchild for whom it is a place of wonder. To her the surrounding jungle is a haven of ants, disease, and unprofitable acreage.

Then again, perhaps he is being unfair. Taking out a city map Eddie had procured for him, Anson finds the location of the South American contingent's domicile.

After asking directions several times, Anson locates the imposing building, almost hidden inside its lush tropical gardens.

In an alley, he removes his clothes, folding them neatly and placing them, along with the map and sugarcane, inside a string bag that already contains the Changer's attire. Then, with a minimum of effort, he shifts into a small wiry capuchin monkey. He has picked this type because they are frequently kept as pets, so his presence in a civilized area will be overlooked much as a domestic cat would be in most American cities.

Looping the string bag about his skinny shoulders, he swarms up a tree and over the wall into the gardens. Secreting the bag in a crotch of a tree, where it is invisible from the ground, he scouts the grounds.

He sees two anteaters, like long-nosed, hook-clawed bears, prowling the grounds. An ornamental pond conceals a sizable anaconda, lazily soaking its huge, rounded length. He scents a jaguar and sees the marks of its claws on the trees, but the spore is old.

A shaded veranda, with a canopy of gaily striped fabric and walls of woven wickerwork, juts out into the back garden. It is equipped with very modern screens.

Here, forsaking the air-conditioned comfort of the house's interior, Cleonice is stretched out on a rattan divan, listening to Oswaldo read from a handwritten volume, presumably of his own work:

> *Ageless children of Mother Earth,*
> Huldre *folk suppressing voice,*
> *Forsaking Adam's charge by choice,*
> *Indolent wasters of our own births,*
> *We . . .*

"I don't like it," Cleonice interrupts. The composition is in English, and she responds in the same language, her accent flavored with the Spanish of her birthland.

"I have my problems with it, too," Oswaldo responds. "Tell me what you don't like."

"It overgeneralizes. All of us aren't indolent. My father wasn't. Frank MacDonald isn't. Even Arthur, much as I disapprove of some of his policies, isn't."

"Oh, I thought you meant the rhyme scheme." Oswaldo frowns at his piece of paper. "I thought it was forced."

"It's that, too."

"You aren't pulling any punches, are you?"

"You did ask for my opinion."

"And you're testy."

"I can't be. I'm a woman. I don't have the *cojones*."

"Bitchy, then."

"You say the nicest things."

"You didn't like my poem!"

"You asked for my opinion. I gave it to you."

Oswaldo draws a wide, dramatic swath through the page with a felt-tipped pen from his breast pocket.

"I have destroyed it, now. Satisfied?"

"With that, but I am growing worried."

"Why?"

"We left Vera and Amphitrite in the rain forest three days ago. Isidro promised that Arthur would accept our terms immediately. Still, despite phone call after phone call, nothing has been achieved."

Oswaldo drums at the armrest of his chair with his pen. "I know, and I have tried to divine what Arthur is doing. Unhappily, his doings are blocked from me."

"Actively?"

"No, he has long had charms in place. Why else should he keep his pet wizard?"

Cleonice, who knows professional jealousy when she hears it, says, "I wonder if we were foolish to return Lovern?"

"We could not hold him long. I do not know the secret that Louhi wormed from him ages past and she wouldn't share it."

"You asked?"

"I did."

"Ah."

Oswaldo continues, "Nor could we strand him with the others lest they draw upon his magical skills. We could only return him and make necessity look like good politics."

"Yes. I still wonder if we were right. Perhaps we should have killed him and sent his body back as a warning that we were not to be trifled with."

"Hotheaded blood-drinker," Oswaldo says almost fondly, "you spend too much time as a jaguar. Killing hostages only convinces the enemy camp that you will not treat fairly."

"I don't necessarily agree."

"I know, but I also know that you were overruled on this point. Besides, he is ancient. His death would greatly diminish Harmony."

In a perfect universe, at this point Cleonice would say, "I

still think we shouldn't have left them at such and such point on the river." Oswaldo would answer, "But they are near to such and such landmark. We can find them easily." Anson, possessed of the location of the two missing athanor would swing off, locate the Changer, and they would head to the rescue.

Sadly, the universe is not such a tidy place. Instead of worriedly confiding in Oswaldo, Cleonice turns on him, her patrician features distorted with anger.

"You're nothing but Isidro's puppet, did you know that?"

Oswaldo starts up from his seat, no longer the indolent, almost foolish scribbler, but every rounded inch a man of power.

"So! Do you wish to bear my shaman's curse?"

"I apologize," Cleonice says sulkily.

"Good."

Oswaldo does not seat himself again, but, picking up his notebook, turns toward the interior of the house.

"I am going to check with Isidro on the developing situation."

"It won't have developed," Cleonice predicts.

"Nonetheless."

Anson A. Kridd listens and is pleased. He knows what tack he will take when the Changer returns. All that is left is to make certain that he knows if Isidro or his allies depart.

Swinging gracefully to the top of a palm tree, he sets his subconscious to listen for any sign of departure. Then, curling into a small, furry ball, he gets some much-needed sleep.

He is awakened by a red-and-blue macaw landing in the palm fronds beside him and croaking rudely. Uncurling, Anson scratches vigorously, then leads the way downward. He detours to retrieve his string bag and thence to the alley outside. Happily, the shadowy area is deserted.

The only difficulty with animal forms is that, beyond generalized warnings which even humans can learn to understand, there is no *ur*-beast language. Although capuchins (like coyotes and ravens and macaws) are remarkably verbal, their speech does not contain the sounds for the concepts he wishes to communicate.

He shifts back into human form and stands in nonchalant

nudity, waiting for the Changer to follow suit. The other does so immediately.

"We make quite a pair, eh?" Anson says wryly, "brown man and black standing naked in an alleyway. What might the police say?"

"Nothing," the Changer comments, "for we would run and as soon as we rounded a corner there would be only a monkey and a macaw. Now, enough foolishness. I have gained a reprieve from storm. What have you?"

"A plan," Anson says. "I must return human for it. If luck and paranoia are with me, it should gain us the information we lack. Cleonice and Oswaldo both are unhappy and afraid because of Arthur's unwillingness to treat with them."

"I should imagine that Isidro is no happier. Do you need me for your plan?"

"Not for this stage," Anson says. "First I will flush our game, but I would be happiest if you were along on the hunt."

"I shall be. Where would you have me wait?"

"In the garden. There is a patio. I shall get them to take me there, so you can overhear what passes between us."

"And if you do not come out?"

"I shall be. They will not wish to hold me."

"Very well. Dress and be about your business." With a small shrug, the Changer becomes macaw once more and flies to the top of the alley, keeping watch as Anson dresses and tidies himself.

"Your clothing," Anson says softly as he passes beneath the macaw, "is in the string bag. You should be able to lift it."

"Good luck," the macaw croaks, in the strange, almost human voice that parrots possess.

"See you."

Anson tidies his attire, then inspects his face with the help of a small pocket mirror. Certain that he looks as natty as possible in this humid climate, he strolls up to the gate.

A stocky man with Indian features comes to the gate. "What do you want? No solicitors," he says in accented Portuguese.

"I am here to see Isidro Robelo," Anson replies calmly. "You may take my card in to him."

He hands one of his business cards, to which he has added the handwritten line *On Arthur's bidding*, to the guard. Then he waits outside the gate, whistling softly to himself and glancing about as if this is his first glimpse of the place.

The gatekeeper returns three minutes later. "He will see you. Follow the path to the house."

"I thought he might," Anson says, smiling warmly. "Thank you for the directions, my good man."

The gatekeeper locks the wrought-iron gate behind him and takes a post where he can watch the road. Evidently, Isidro expects trouble. He will be disappointed.

Isidro himself meets Anson at the door. Oswaldo stands a few steps back. Cleonice is nowhere in evidence.

"Come in, Anson," Isidro says heartily. "We are rather surprised to see you here."

Anson allows himself to look just a little bit arrogant. "You certainly didn't expect Arthur to come himself, did you?"

A flicker of Isidro's gaze tells him that the revolutionary had hoped for precisely that. Pretending not to notice, Anson continues, "Eddie is still not agile enough for travel, and Lovern was somewhat reluctant to renew his acquaintance with your hospitality. With Vera missing, that left me."

Isidro nods as if he had expected this all along. "Please, make yourself comfortable. We can sit in the parlor or perhaps you would prefer an office?"

Anson pretends to shiver. "Actually, I was wondering if you had somewhere not air-conditioned where we could sit? I have been in the heat all day and the change is not healthy, especially for a tropical creature like myself."

"There is the veranda," Oswaldo says, looking up from the book he holds. This time, Anson is certain, he has been listening, not reading.

"If that would not be too inconvenient . . ." Anson says.

"Of course not," Isidro agrees heartily. "We cannot have you uncomfortable."

He commands a servant woman waiting discreetly in the background to bring drinks. Then he leads the way.

"Cleonice, I regret to say, is not home at this time. I hope you can speak your business with the two of us."

"One would be enough," Anson says, hoping to feed the

dissension he had overheard earlier, "if it was the right one."

Privately, he suspects that Cleonice is prowling in jaguar form in the gardens, alert for any possible attack. He hopes that the Changer is wise enough to stay out of her reach and away from her nose.

They take their seats on the rattan furniture beneath the veranda's striped canopy.

"I am here to inquire for Arthur as to precisely what you expect from him," Anson says, sipping casually.

"I told him over the telephone," Isidro says a bit testily. "We provided a detailed platform at the Review. We wish it to be put into action."

"You really expect Arthur to grant all of that?" Anson chortles. "Come now, it is beyond his power. He is not an absolute dictator, able to command resources of magic and money at a wave of his hand. At best he is a coordinator of other people's talents. True, yes, he has money, but so do many of us. The things you really want—the magic, the skills of our ancient warriors, those are not his to command."

Isidro frowns, drawing his brows down. "He can command Lovern, who is the greatest of our mages. Lovern can teach Oswaldo, who has talent. He could offer favors to bring others into our service."

"You," Anson says brightly, "have wealth enough to offer payment. You must have learned that such is not enough. Certainly some of the hottest heads among us would be happy to act as mercenaries, but that is not what you want, eh? You want the gentle souls like Frank MacDonald or the Smith or even Vera."

Anson nods in agreement with his own sagacity. He wonders if Isidro is foolish enough to believe that Vera is gentle. Celibate she may be, but she is a woman of real passions.

"We want what we said in our manifesto!" Isidro insists.

"So you say, but who is to say that the King will grant your wishes?" Anson becomes menacing, a poisonous spider. "You have taken a member of his household and a fellow monarch hostage. You have shown no respect for rank or kinship. You have put yourselves outside the law that governs us all—you are outside of the Accord. Take care that you don't find yourself declared out of Harmony as well."

Isidro's jaw drops. Oswaldo is making no pretense of reading his book. Outside in the garden, a jaguar screams impotent rage. Anson continues, "Perhaps if you throw yourself upon the King's mercy, you may keep your lives, but even that I will not promise."

He sees the awakening of panic and then hope in the others' manners. Poor fools. Like children who seek to test the limits of their parents, they had not realized until this very moment what a monumental transgression they have committed.

"Arthur may take mercy on you," he says, knowing full well that Arthur cannot, "but I will not promise even that. Your best hope is if Vera and Amphitrite live and are returned by you. Even then, I cannot promise."

Oswaldo starts to protest, then sinks back, his book slipping from nerveless fingers. Isidro has lost his eloquence.

Anson rises, allows himself to be shown to the door by the two men. Isidro mumbles a polite farewell.

"You may leave a message for me at the Hibiscus Suites," Anson continues, still on his dignity. "Good evening to you."

"Thank you for coming by," Oswaldo manages. "You have been most informative."

"I think we now understand each other," Anson says. "Good luck to you."

He saunters out, nodding to the gatekeeper as he goes. Sadly, he imagines them summoning Cleonice, telling her what they have realized, frantically planning how best to throw themselves on Arthur's mercy.

But they have angered the sea, and the sea knows no pity, not for the sailor who loves her, nor the child drowning in its grasp.

The brother of the sea, sea-born son of that element, now perches in the treetops marking their comings and goings, their plans and conferences. He will follow them on red-and-blue-feathered wings, wherever they may go. The Changer does know pity, but like any wild thing, he has none to spare for the foolish.

*Keep your course. Wax fat. Dishonor
justice. You have power—now.*

—AESCHYLUS

SVEN TROUT WALKS IN THE MAIN DOOR OF LOS CUATES
restaurant. Outside, the snap and bang of the occasional fire-
cracker reminds everyone in earshot that today is July 4. He
likes Independence Day: fireworks, loud parties, drunks, bar-
becues, hot weather, and a sense of undeserved holiday.

After all, none of these fools had done anything to earn
"American" independence. In 1776, New Mexico was a
Spanish possession that wouldn't become a state for years
and, even today, its people cling with great pride to that history which predates adoption into the Union.

Yes, he likes Independence Day. That is why he has arranged to meet Monk and his two *tengu* buddies for an early
lunch. After lunch they'll head off for Dukes' Stadium to
watch some minor-league baseball. Later, there will be
fireworks.

Sven has a way with fire, and he plans that this show will
contain no duds, that every cherry bomb will be an ear-blaster
and that every multicolored rocket will burst with exceptional
brilliance. Yes, he is looking forward to this evening.

He's even mailed Arthur a few complimentary tickets, rep-
resenting them as a freebie from the King's bank.

Looking around, he locates the three *tengu* sitting in a row

319

on the wooden bench along one wall of the entry foyer. They look rather like slightly wild Japanese teenagers, all clad in white tee shirts and blue jeans. Monk even has a pack of cigarettes rolled in his shirtsleeve.

"Have you put us on the list to get a table?" he asks.

"Sure have," Monk says. His tee shirt is one of those you only see in Japan; English words are boldly printed in red and black. They look cool, but they don't make much sense.

Sven reads aloud: " 'Apple. Pizza. Love. Gotta Have It!' Interesting."

The *tengu* casts a critical glance over Sven's own sartorial splendor and evidently finds the dark purple cotton trousers and lavender button-down sport shirt lacking *panache*.

"Hey, it beats most of what I've seen here. If I see another shirt printed with a soulful 'Native American' cuddling up to a couple of wolves, I think I'll flip."

Sven nods and politely turns his attention to the other *tengus*' attire. Laughing Enemy (he uses the name "Roy" in conversation) wears a shirt emblazoned with a wide-eyed girl done in classic *anime* style. She wears nothing but a yellow-striped bikini and tiny horns poke out of her mass of green hair.

Joyful Wrath (or "Hiero") apparently doesn't share Monk's dislike for Southwestern style. His shirt is airbrushed with one of Catlin's depressed Indians, a pink-and-orange sun symbolically setting behind him.

The waitress calling out "Monk" saves Sven from the need to comment. Instead, he motions his guests in front of him, feeling vaguely as if he is meeting with a *yakuza* sponsored JV gang.

When they are seated in a booth, Sven orders frozen margueritas all around, along with an appetizer of guacamole. The *tengu* study the menu with solemnity. Food is always an important issue. If the waiter is surprised at the magnitude of their order, he is too harried to remind them that Los Cuates believes in generous portions.

The background hubbub is loud enough that Sven feels quite safe discussing business. "So, are you having fun with Arthur?"

"We were having plenty," Hiero says. "Then he stopped answering the phone."

Monk clarifies. "We were serenading him at all hours with a humbling composition of our own making. Without Lovern around, we could even spy on him from the balcony and check his reaction. Apparently, he forgot to reset the wards' exclusivity programming after the Review."

Sven loads a chip with red-chili salsa. "Why did you stop once Arthur didn't answer the phone? If you could sneak into the hacienda . . ."

Laughing Enemy titters. "We did, a little, but he didn't even notice us. Something big was going down."

"Huh?"

Monk clarifies. "A couple of days ago, the hacienda started resembling a war room. I snooped and gathered that something had happened to Vera and Amphitrite."

"Not really!" Sven exclaims, surprised to learn of mischief not of his making.

"Really," Monk continues. "Lovern came back from Brazil alone. Later, Eddie and Anson went out past midnight."

"Did you follow them?"

"No," Monk grins, "but we know where they went, anyhow."

"Where?"

"They came back alone in the morning, but went out again midmorning to fetch the Changer and his pup."

Sven's eyebrows vanish in his hairline. "But you told me that they'd left for the hills!"

"They did. Apparently Arthur needs the ancient's help."

Thinking of blood, Sven asks, "Is he still there?"

"Didn't see," Hiero replies. "We stopped bugging them."

Sven is aghast. "You did what!"

"We stopped," Roy repeats. "It's one thing to harass a bureaucrat so he doesn't get too full of himself, but Arthur was concentrating on helping a couple of our people."

Seeing that Sven is still surprised, Monk cuts in. "We tease to keep people humble, but if our teasing is going to hurt Vera and Amphitrite by distracting Arthur from his work . . . Don't you get it?"

Sven, who has much less wholesome reasons for his tricks, manages to nod and smile. "Of course. You did just fine."

Sven's mind is whirling, and he feels an almost physical

pain that he doesn't know enough about the situation to exploit it. Still, he cannot suddenly depart without making his too-clever tools suspicious.

With mock heartiness, he applies the edge of his fork to the fiery *carne adovada* burrito the waitress sets before him.

"Dig in, boys!" he says. "Then I'll take you out to the ball game. You've done a good job for me."

Better, he adds silently to himself, *than you may ever know.*

¤◙¤

"I," Vera states happily, poling the raft along, "am one solid mass of mosquito bites."

Amphitrite stares at her from where she is kneeling at the bow of the raft, spear in hand. "Remind me to invite you to visit. I've some Portuguese man-o'-wars you'd just love."

"I'm just feeling lucky," Vera says. "I was feeling miserable, then I remembered that I am immune to malaria and a host of other diseases that a mosquito bite can transmit. What could be a death sentence for even a native of this region is nothing but a source of discomfort for me."

"I'm beginning," Amphitrite says, choking out the words between bouts of laughter, "to understand how you got your reputation for wisdom."

Vera shakes back her tangled hair. Unlike Amphitrite's, it hadn't been long enough to braid, but she's tied it under a strip of cloth torn from the hem of her shirt.

"Don't get me wrong. I'm no Pollyanna, but there's something about being on edge that makes me appreciative."

"I keep going by imagining what I'll do to those three when I get my hands on them," Amphitrite says with soft menace.

"That's it?"

"Well, sometimes I imagine how they'd feel if Duppy Jonah gets to them first. When I want variety, I imagine the looks on their smug faces if they go back to that grove where they stranded us and find us gone."

Vera nods and wipes her forehead with a grubby arm.

"I've thought of that, too. The great thing about the forest canopy is that if we stay near the riverbanks, we're invisible from above."

"That does make it easier for the ants," Amphitrite says, scratching one thigh vigorously.

"True. How's the fishing going?"

"I scared a *pirarucú* off when I started laughing."

"Want me to be quiet?"

"Probably be best. Still, that one was a bit big for just the two of us."

"I don't know. I'm as hungry as a shapeshifter."

"I'd guess it was at least a hundred and fifty pounds."

"That is a bit big. Do you have the spear line anchored?"

"Yep. Wish I could handle a bow like you can."

"Wish I could make something with a bit more pull. It's hard without seasoned wood and sinew."

"Yeah."

"Still, I could try to get us a monkey."

"Not yet. I can't stand the accusing look in their eyes."

"Nothing likes to die."

"Fish don't look the same," Amphitrite says, "or maybe I'm just used to killing them."

"I don't mind eating fish."

They fall into easy silence. During the day and a half that they have guided the *Pororoca* down the Amazon, there have been many of these silences and as many bouts of conversation. Despite their shared heritage, they have been enough separated by environment to be strangers.

Vera finds Amphitrite's *naïveté* regarding life on land fascinating; the Sea Queen is touched by Vera's almost human point of view on many issues. One bound by human shape, the other a shapeshifter currently clinging to a shape alien to her experience, they would enjoy their voyage if the circumstances were not so dire.

This near to the equator, daylight is not the limiting factor on their traveling, but even athanor grow weary, especially two immortals guiding a raft hour after hour.

Coming beneath the protecting shadow of a broad-leafed tropical tree, not listed among those plants that they are to avoid, they haul the *Pororoca* close to the bank.

As they did the night before, they will sleep with the raft roped to the shore, letting it drift from the bank once darkness provides cover. While there is still daylight, they need to forage for fruit, firewood, and take care of other necessities.

"I wonder how far we have come?" Vera says.

"What does it matter when we have no idea far we must go?" Amphitrite asks reasonably. "*O Rio Mar* is four thousand miles long."

"At least we didn't start in the Andes," Vera says. "Certainly we don't have more than a few hundred miles to go."

"If we aren't in a tributary," Amphitrite says. "There are times I wonder if we should even think about progress—only about staying alive."

"And *I'm* the wise one?" Vera smiles fondly. "You're right, of course. For now, we're alive. Let's forage."

They carry their irreplaceable valuables with them. With these they can protect themselves if the need to make another *Pororoca* arises.

Later, richer by various pieces of fruit, some dubious nuts, and, best of all, some reasonably dry wood, they trudge back to the *Pororoca*. Ever distrustful of ants, they kindle the fire aboard, insulating the deck with a thick pad of wet mud and leaves. Amphitrite has speared a smaller *pirarucú* that they cut into chunks and cook impaled on green sticks.

"Hey! It's Fourth of July." Vera laughs self-consciously. "All over the United States, campers are roasting hot dogs over campfires. I wonder what they'd think of our repast?"

"Exotic tropical fish and fruit?" Amphitrite says. "They'd envy us, of course."

"Of course."

"At least the smoke keeps the mosquitos away."

"Yeah."

"I wonder if anyone is looking for us?"

"Sure they are."

The fish sizzles over the fire. In the jungle, a monkey shrieks an unintelligible protest. Something large slips into the river, drawn by the smell of cooking, frustrated by the unfamiliar raft. Ants troop mechanically down the tie rope, knowing only that something edible is in that direction.

✿◙✿

Duppy Jonah emerges from the waters near the isolated *tupa* wherein Louhi dwells. Huge and vaguely human in form, he has taken the shape by which Finns in ancient times had known him, the Great Durag, the monstrous, often capricious King of the Sea.

He has sent his calling card before him, a rumbling herd of the white-maned horses of the sea, waves that froth against the pebbled shore and make sounds like the rattling of dead men's bones on All Hallows' Night.

And Louhi is strolling the shore, her pale hair and white skin seeming as if the fog that crowds the shore has decided to grow flesh and blood.

"Greetings, Great Durag," she says, her voice tinkling with laughter, a brittle sound like crackling icicles. "Welcome to these empty shores."

"You have knowledge I desire," he says gruffly.

"*Ka*! Why am I not surprised?" she answers. "Perhaps because we do not call upon each other with any frequency? Perhaps it is because your Amphitrite is missing?"

"How do you know?"

"What type of sorceress would I be," she says in tones light and mocking, "if I could not learn of such momentous events?"

Actually, her source is the Head. Although it had been affected by Oswaldo's weakening of Lovern, it has not been as severely debilitated as it had claimed.

"Don't you agree that I am powerful?" she purrs. "Now, what do you wish of me?"

"I have claimed Lovern as hostage until my queen is returned," Duppy Jonah replies. "You alone of all our people have held him prisoner. Tell me what I must do to keep him."

"You do not think he will honor his duty to his King?" Louhi says coolly. "*Ka*! Perhaps he will not. His honor is a flexible thing. What payment do you offer me for my knowledge?"

"Pearls, gold, diamonds, jewels of all sorts are mine to give," Duppy Jonah answers, casting a chaplet of pink pearls and gold wire at her feet. "I also can retrieve many things that the sea has claimed. Would you have statuary from Thera? Incan gold from Atahualpa's ransom? Temple archways carved of porphyry and jet retrieved from island kingdoms lost to the memories of humankind?"

"I live a simple life," Louhi says, gesturing back at the *tupa*. "Where would I put a grand statue? How in this modern world would I explain a sudden fortune? My situation for this identity is a simple one."

"There are ways to do this thing," Duppy Jonah says impatiently. "If you do not covet a fortune now, let it be put by for a future life where you may not choose to live so simply."

Louhi picks the chaplet from the sand and caresses its delicate weaving, spinning the pearls between her fingertips.

"A pretty thing, this," she says. "I am not foolish enough to tempt the wrath of the Great Durag, especially when his *kultani* has been taken from him. First, let me tell you that the spell by which I once held Merlin prisoner will do you no good in this circumstance."

She raises a slim hand when the waves begins to stir angrily. "The spell takes time to cast, more time to gather the elements needed for the weaving. You need something that will work quickly."

"I have servants all over the seas and some free to travel the land," Duppy Jonah protests, his tone a low roar. "Anything I desire can be collected within hours."

"Yes, but some must be gathered only under certain circumstances," Louhi says. "Dew from the cup of a saffron crocus on a morning when the moon is waning. A feather from the tail of a blue jay that has just sung its first spring carol. Water melted from snow gathered in Stonehenge on midwinter's night. Do you understand?"

"Yes."

"Still, there are other, less complicated ways to incapacitate a wizard. If I teach you some of these, I will demand a great price, for I am teaching you things that might be used against me in turn."

"Ah . . ." The sound is the groan of waves pulling back

from the shore when the tide is ebbing. "I may know of these ways," Duppy Jonah says guardedly. "I am as old as the seas."

"Then we are at an impasse. I will not offer my knowledge without a promise of a price paid, and you do not wish to promise to pay without knowing what the wares will be."

"Precisely."

They study each other. Somehow, the slim figure standing on the shore is the stronger, for Duppy Jonah concedes first.

"I will give no blanket promise of service," he says. "I am no fool. Nor will I promise any of my get or of my wife's getting for your taking."

"Would you promise inaction?" Louhi asks. "Promise that one time of my choosing you will not interfere, even if called on by Arthur himself?"

Duppy Jonah frowns, beetling brows of dank seaweed. "I might, but not if my Amphitrite was in danger nor if you were trespassing in the rights that are mine as Sea King. I would not provide you the key to my kingdom."

"No." She laughs her icicle laugh. "I did not think that you would."

"Nor would I promise inaction indefinitely."

"A year?"

"No. That is too great a time, even for athanor."

"Half that?"

"I know various ways to imprison a wizard, Louhi, and I do not believe you can breathe water indefinitely. As you commented earlier, my patience has been sorely tried."

"*Ka*! Perhaps a day?"

"A day—define it as twenty-four hours in sequence and I will make this pact."

Louhi pauses to think. "If you add that you would not take revenge for acts done during those twenty-four hours, I agree."

The waves rumble: "As long as those deeds do not violate the other provisions I have stated, yes, I can agree. I am not such a fool as to think that you would need my inaction if you believed that I would approve of what you might do."

"You are too clever, Great Durag."

"Then we have a deal."

"One where you have gotten the better of me," she agrees.

Louhi looks hurt, so hurt that Duppy Jonah casts a small, locked box onto the shore near her feet. "It holds a pretty brooch of emeralds and golden topaz. Call it my gift, sorceress. Now, tell me what I wish to know."

Sitting gracefully on a boulder that has been rounded by the caress of sea and sand, Louhi begins.

"Of course you know that cold iron impedes the use of magic, but what many do not know is that the ingesting of mineral supplements containing nutritional iron can have a similar effect. Essentially, the wizard finds his own blood becomes his enemy. Incidentally, this is why wise sorceresses know (despite male-propagated lore to the contrary) that they are most powerful at the time when their menstrual blood is ebbing . . ."

She continues speaking, and Duppy Jonah listens, nodding, frowning, smiling, and, at last sinking beneath the waves, satisfied that he will know best how to hold Lovern and how to weaken him so that, if his death becomes necessary, the wizard will not be able to prevent it.

Louhi bends to pick up the bracelet of moonstone and jade that washes onto the shore as Duppy Jonah vanishes. It is a lovely thing, scooped from the bottom of the China Sea. Slipping it onto her wrist, she smiles and bows to the salt spray.

"Thank you, Your Majesty," she says.

She waits until she is safely within her *tupa* to release the triumphant laughter she has caged beneath her breast.

¤◼¤

Just shy of dawn's first light on the fifth of July, while Arthur still sleeps the uneasy sleep of a king who hears the rumbles of war and Sven Trout sleeps the uneasy sleep of one who has eaten far too many ballpark hot dogs, three figures depart the palatial house in Belém.

They drive directly to the small airfield where they keep the airplane *Caiman*, unaware that clinging to the roof of their all-terrain vehicle is a sturdy capuchin monkey, or that a resplendent red-and-blue-feathered macaw soars over them, pacing their vehicle with preternatural ease.

Cleonice assumes the pilot's seat, running the small aquaplane through preflight checks. Isidro unlocks the hangar's bay doors, pushing them back on tracks that cry metallic protest.

Oswaldo stands some distance from all this massed metal; red vegetable dye is brushed on his face in ornate patterns, and a short staff topped with feathers and shells is in his right hand. His feet are bare and he stamps the damp ground at the verges of a runoff channel, muttering strange phrases and frowning at the omens he reads in the jungle sounds.

"We're going to run into trouble," he says to Isidro, rinsing off his feet before donning his sandals. "Lots of trouble. I do not see either Vera or Amphitrite; moreover, something dark hovers over the entire picture. I see Death reaching out her long-fingered hands."

"For whom?" Isidro asks, trying to sound casual and failing.

Seduced by the success of terrorist politics in the human world, Isidro had forgotten that the athanor governed themselves by different rules. Anansi's hints that they were in danger of being declared outside of Harmony had shaken him so badly that he had neither slept nor eaten since. Now his eyes burn with something far more dangerous than fanaticism—raw terror.

"I can't tell," Oswaldo says, "but Death rides with us."

"Death," Cleonice says, padding out to them as silently as if she were already in jaguar form, "has always ridden with us. I think the proximity of all this metal has thrown your magic askew, Oswaldo. Or are you like Isidro, too terrified to act?"

"You are insane," Oswaldo comments calmly.

"Arthur says that we are outside of the Accord and in danger of being declared out of Harmony," she answers. "What is insanity to that? Come, the *Caiman* is ready. We will have more concrete answers within a few hours."

They board the plane, unaware that the vehicle already holds two stowaways. Not wishing to be vulnerable, the Changer has taken the shape of a jaguar.

His hope is that Cleonice will think any trace of the scent is a remnant of her own. Normally, this would be a ridiculous risk, but with the odors of gasoline, oil, metal, and human sweat to cover his own, he permits himself hope.

Anson has remained a monkey. Together they crouch in the small cargo area behind the last few seats, one fighting an impulse to kill, the other fighting an impulse to flee.

It is not a particularly comfortable ride, and it lasts longer than the stowaways had believed it would. Clearly, the South American contingent had not settled for depositing their prisoners a few miles from Belém but had taken them far inland.

When at last the *Caiman* splashes to a landing in a broad section of the river, Cleonice motors parallel to the shore.

"I don't like this," she says. "No sign of them. We're going to have to go ashore. Get the raft, Oswaldo."

Suddenly, the Changer and Anson realize what they have been crouching behind. Anson scrambles under a seat. The Changer shifts into a slender snake, not worrying that it is a type once found only in Asia and now extinct for several thousand years.

"Coming ashore, Cleonice?" Isidro asks.

"Yes."

"Very well, come along."

"I don't," Cleonice says with a hard-eyed glare, "need your permission."

Oswaldo raises his hand in a gesture both weary and tense. "Let's wait to tear each other up until later."

He hasn't washed the red dye from his face, and his expression is unfathomably grim. The other two cease their bickering and the raft is readied with experienced efficiency.

When the three rebel athanor are on the water, the Changer slithers to the open door. Slipping into the water, he shifts into a sizable caiman alligator. Then he drifts, waiting for Anson to take his hint and hitch a ride to shore. The monkey does so, chattering nervously. The Changer might be said to be smiling if the long-jawed alligator mouth did not always smile.

Once ashore, Anson takes to the branches. The Changer considers. Given the many shapeshifts he has performed that morning, he is growing quite hungry, but the caiman is not swift on land. Two of his three potential opponents are not shapeshifters; Cleonice, as far as he knows, is restricted to the jaguar form.

Still considering, he creeps forward where he can better hear the rebels' conversation. They have stopped in a clearing bearing the marks of human habitation, although the rain forest is already effacing those marks beneath vines and new growth.

"Gone!" Isidro is saying, inspecting a space where hammocks once hung. "I never imagined they would be so courageous."

"They went by water," Oswaldo states, indicating a tree stump. "Enough trees have been cut to make a decent raft."

"They could have bound it with vines," Cleonice adds, "or with strips cut from those canvas packs. I told you that the machetes were an overgenerous gesture on your part."

Isidro is shaking, reeking of a mixture of rage and terror. "Cleonice, we needed to be able to state beneath a truthstone that we had given our prisoners what they needed to survive. No one but an Indian can survive here without a machete."

"And even they prefer to have one," Oswaldo adds. "Stop passing on the blame, Cleonice. You're being catty."

She sneers down her long nose, looking very catlike indeed. "Vera and Amphitrite will have gone with the current toward the sea. I could track by land. You two could take the plane."

"If they are clever enough to make a raft," Isidro says, "I doubt they will expose themselves to surveillance from above. We had better track them from the boat."

"Ashore," Cleonice insists, "I can catch their sign more easily. They are clever enough to hide it from casual view."

"True." Isidro chews his lip. "There are only three of us and three means of travel. Although we are several hours ahead of New Mexico, we cannot spare the time to fetch reinforcements."

"We could radio from the plane," Oswaldo reminds him.

"No!" Isidro says. "This is athanor business. All our subjects are humans. We must kill them if they learn anything."

Oswaldo frowns. "I could magically alter their memories."

"Are you certain you could?" Isidro asks.

"No."

"Then we have no choice. In any case, even if our subjects left Belém immediately, we would lose several hours waiting for them to arrive." Isidro shakes his head decisively. "We must make do with what we have—at least until we learn more.''

"I can't fly solo," Oswaldo reminds him.

"I know. How about if we . . ."

Whatever alternative he might have suggested is lost when the Changer emerges from the brush. Some vague sense of fair play has made him take the jaguar's form once more, but fair play or not, the shapeshifter has heard enough. More refinement of a plan that will never be put into action is hardly necessary.

Uncertain whether the threat is natural or not, Isidro unholsters the handgun he wears at his waist, but he backs away from the jaguar before firing. Like bears, great cats have a stubborn tendency to fight on after what should be a fatal wound, and the big jaguar is very close indeed.

Cleonice rips open her shirt, obviously preparing to shapeshift, while Oswaldo hefts his pistol in one hand, his feathered wand in the other. A voice from the treetops stops all three in mid-action.

"Didn't know we were with you, eh?" Anson A. Kridd calls merrily. Wisely, he has remained shrouded by the leaves, but even in human form he can climb easily.

"You? Anson?" Isidro's voice has lost its tremor now that he has a physical enemy to confront.

"That's right, and the Changer with me, clad in the lovely spots. Think again before putting your bullet into him, eh? The Sea King would never forgive you if you harmed both his wife and his brother."

Although Cleonice has locked eyes with the big jaguar, she has begun inching back toward the edge of the clearing.

"What does it matter?" she answers. "We are doomed no matter what. Arthur cannot afford to forgive us. There is only one chance—to *make* him do so!"

With her final words, her intent becomes clear. She dives into the concealing brush. When the Changer leaps after her, Isidro fires, his poorly aimed shot grazing the jaguar's flank.

Screaming feline fury, the Changer stumbles. Regaining his balance, he lets Cleonice go, jumping instead for the branches of the nearest tree, his claws raking great furls out of the bark, his blood spattering down to pattern the leaves.

Seeking to avoid the jaguar now above him, Oswaldo

rushes blindly into the center of the cleared area, but his attempted escape only brings him up short against the sinewy form of Anson A. Kridd. The Spider is naked, his brown body scratched from his rapid descent from the treetops.

"Flight or fight, eh?" Anson says, plucking the pistol from Oswaldo's grasp. "Old impulses, even for us."

Oswaldo brandishes his wand. "Back, Spider, or I will curse you!"

"Bold," Anson says, flinching somewhat as screams both human and jaguar make conversation difficult, "but you are not Lovern, to make stones walk."

He levels the pistol at Oswaldo's temple. "And I am not the Changer, to fill my mouth with an enemy's blood."

Oswaldo's eyes widen, twins to his gaping mouth. "You wouldn't!"

"I would," Anson says. "You have overstepped what is permitted, kinsman. Every athanor's hand is raised against you."

He pulls the trigger then, once and then twice. The reports come so close together that they make one long shout. In the distance, a howler monkey hoots defiance.

Lowering the pistol, Anson wipes a stray fleck of blood from his face and turns toward the Changer. The jaguar still bleeds from his flank, but the redness on his jaws and throat belongs to another source. Isidro lies twisted and dead on the sodden ground, his handsome face frozen in terror.

"Messy but efficient," Anson comments. "Are you unharmed but for the one shot?"

The Changer wheels so that Anson can see another bullet graze, this one along his right foreleg.

"You are fortunate he was so terrified he could not aim or plan," Anson says. "Can you find sign of Cleonice?"

The Changer sniffs both ground and air, then, mimicking a bird dog, points downstream.

"When her fury and fear leave her," Anson says, "she may remember the usefulness of airplanes. You check for the keys among her clothes. I'll strip the weapons from these two."

Neither feel any particular pity or sorrow for the two who have just died. Old as they are, they have seen many of their own die. Unlike the younger ones, neither Changer nor Spider believes that any upon the Earth have any particular right to continued life.

The Changer finds the keys to the *Caiman*, then licks his wounds until they stop bleeding. Anson collects guns, ammunition, and the ubiquitous machetes.

"The others were right," he says, "we may never find our quarry from high above. Cleonice has the advantage of us on land. Can you shift again?"

The Changer licks his muzzle in the universal feline sign for "I'm starving."

"Then you must eat and we must travel. Come. The plane is too bulky, but we will lock it and hope it will await our return. Then I shall take to the river in the rubber boat and, when you have eaten, you can take wing and try to outdistance Cleonice."

The Changer's response is to nod once and vanish into the brush. Without a look back at the two corpses, Anson follows more slowly, burdened with equipment they may not need but they dare not leave behind.

Let the ants and the scavengers tend to the funeral.

✵✵✵

As far down the river as several days of determined rafting can take them, Vera and Amphitrite greet the same morning that saw Isidro and Oswaldo die with something like routine.

While Amphitrite handles casting off and the first round of poling, Vera refreshes the fire, the coals from the previous night having been kept smoldering in order to burn various noxiously scented leaves that keep the even more noxious mosquitoes somewhat at bay.

Over this fire, Vera boils water in an aluminum canteen from which the decorative nylon casing has been removed. When the water is boiling, she brews tea from leaves that Isidro's handy little book has assured them are not poisonous. This is served with peeled mangoes, some Brazil nuts, and the remainder of the fish from the night before. They have learned to keep a portion of this from rotting by wrapping it in leaves while still raw and burying it in the wet mud over which their fire is built. There it bakes and is sealed from the air.

Once breakfast is eaten, Vera takes over poling so that Amphitrite can tend to her ablutions. Then Amphitrite returns to her post, and Vera does the same. Once fed and vaguely clean they are ready to face another long day of heat, humidity, mosquitoes, and uncertainty.

"Did you ever read *Huck Finn*?" Vera asks idly. She's been busy sharpening shafts for her makeshift bow.

"I've heard the story," Amphitrite answers, "but I don't know it well. Reading is one of those things that doesn't work too well underwater."

Vera frowns and sucks at a place where she has nicked her finger. "It seems to me that you and Duppy Jonah have done without a great deal. You don't have books, computers, fax machines, rapid transportation. In many ways, the modern improvements have passed you by."

"We do have the telephone," Amphitrite says, "a useful thing, now that Arthur has chosen to reside in a desert. It was easier getting messages to him when he lived in Great Britain."

"I hadn't really thought about how living underwater handicaps you and your people. If athanor are going to rely more on modern technology, we should find a way to hook you folks in."

Pausing between strokes, Amphitrite examines her pole. "We need to cut another one of these. This one has been chewed on by something. I wouldn't trust it if I needed to do something more strenuous than guide us with the current."

"Take mine," Vera suggests. "Or let me take over and you can scan the banks for the right kind of tree."

"I'll keep poling," Amphitrite offers, making the switch. "All land plants look rather alike to me."

"Fine, just don't wear yourself out. We've a long day in front of us." Vera sighs. "Again."

Amphitrite smiles at her. "Don't get discouraged. Let us talk instead about the interesting point you just raised. Life beneath the sea has its own advantages. We have much property and, as humans have yet to learn how to live beneath the water, we are not in any great danger of discovery.

"When we're not administering our kingdom, Duppy Jonah and I have a great deal of fun. Some of the sea dwellers are quite old. There are athanor turtles and whales with fascinating tales to tell. Sometimes we go to Loch Ness and stir up the tourists."

Vera giggles. "I always wondered if that was you, but I never had the courage to ask."

"It was Duppy Jonah's idea. He was a plesiosaurus long ago. I think he misses the age of dinosaurs. That's the only time he lived on land."

"I didn't know that he ever had," Vera says surprised.

"He tried it then, along with the Changer. The Changer took to land and never really returned to the oceans. Duppy Jonah made the opposite choice. One became a monarch, the other the ultimate vagabond."

"Would you really call the Changer a vagabond?"

"What else is he?" Amphitrite barely manages to keep a teasing note from her voice, for, at the mention of the Changer, Vera has cheered up. "He not only has no fixed home or responsibilities—he has no fixed form!"

"Still, he's very loyal to Shahrazad."

"He is that."

"And he wants vengeance on whoever killed his mate."

"Perhaps he wants vengeance because the attempt may have been on him."

"Perhaps." Vera sets her pile of shafts aside. "Pole over to the right bank. I see a stand of bamboo."

She rises to use the chewed pole to help steer them out of the current's pull. When they close, she leans across to the bank and hacks away at a nice, sturdy cane.

"Hard to believe," she says when she is stripping off the leaves, "that this is a grass."

"Really?"

"Really. There, will this pole do?"

Amphitrite flourishes the bamboo cane. "Can you take about a foot off the top? I feel like I'm wielding a ship's mast."

"Why don't you trim it yourself? It's my turn to pole."

"Fine."

Amphitrite sits and begins trimming. Several moments

later, she utters a shrill shriek and leaps to her feet. The bamboo pole rolls into the water unnoticed.

"What is it!" Vera exclaims, spinning to look.

Amphitrite is beating at her leg where several bright red forms are moving. They are so tiny that Vera can hardly believe that they are the source of such evident agony.

With another shrill cry, Amphitrite jumps into the river.

"Watch out for the piranhas!" Vera yells, hurrying to pull her friend aboard.

"Piranhas be damned!" Amphitrite exclaims, treading water a safe distance from the raft. "Watch out for the fire ants!"

Vera shudders and begins brushing at her extremities.

"I'm going to splash the deck," Amphitrite says in a tone that brooks no argument.

"Splash me, too," Vera says. "Can't you do that from here? I'm worried about the piranhas getting you."

Amphitrite grins sheepishly. "We've got something new to worry about. You see, when I hit the water, the only thing I wanted was to be rid of my legs, they hurt so."

"You didn't!"

"I'm afraid so. I've broken Lovern's spell. We'd better hope that the piranhas don't think that mermaid smells appetizing, because I'm not sure I can haul myself onto the raft without sinking it. All my other forms are water creatures."

"Oh, my," Vera says softly. "Oh, my!"

✿▣✿

On the private beach in Florida, Lovern is met by a stocky fellow of freckled complexion, with a very Irish pug nose and mop of red hair. He wears nothing but a pair of brilliant orange hibiscus-print shorts.

"Himself sent me to take you to Him," the man says. "I'm by way of being a selkie. I've brought you my granther's pelt. 'Tis just a loan, mind you."

"I understand," Lovern says humbly. He has been watching the news channels, and the destruction caused by Duppy Jonah's temperamental weather reminds him of Calcutta.

The selkie motions for Lovern to come down to the shore.

Two sealskins have been tucked in a tide pool. The waters move them so that they seem to swim of their own accord.

Lovern kneels to help the selkie pull them out. The wet pelt is heavier than he had expected, but he manages to pull it out without letting it drag on the sand.

"Contrary to what the old mothers would have you believe," the selkie says, "the pelts last better kept in water. 'Tis a bit chill when first you're being about putting them on, but it warms fast enough."

"Interesting," Lovern says. Then, fearing that he sounds haughty, he adds quickly, "What's your name, sir?"

The selkie cocks a bushy eyebrow at him. "I'm no 'sir,' but the courtesy is welcome as offered. This life they're calling me Connel O'Conaill. Once I was the self-same Conaill."

"I'm Ian Lovern," Lovern says. He does not mention other names he has been called. With men and women drowned and desperate because of his folly, anything that might smack of a boast is beyond him.

"Ready, then, Ian?" Connel asks. "Then just set granther's pelt on that rock while I prepare you."

Lovern does so. "Is your grandfather still alive?"

"That's right enough. The pelts lose their virtue soon after the owner goes on."

"Are you selkies born as seals or human?"

"Now that would be telling, wouldn't it?" The selkie's dark eyes twinkle. "First, Himself spoke that you should strip off everything about you down to the least bit of jewelry."

The selkie's brown eyes are large and kind. His expression is sweet and a touch mournful, but Lovern has had enough doings with various branches of Celts over the centuries to know how quickly that mild mood can turn to storm.

He strips, feeling self-conscious, for Connel's gaze never leaves him. When he has finished stacking his clothes and placing his rings, earring, belt buckle, and bracelet atop them, Lovern takes a deep breath. He has not been so bereft of supplements to his natural power since he was a small fey boy.

"Now," Connel says, "will you swear to me that you are indeed without any power but that which you were born to?"

"Yes."

"Again tell me. I'll warn you that Himself will have you

flayed and given in gobbets to the sharks if you lie."

"I have nothing but the natural power that I was born to," Lovern says firmly. "I am not lying."

"You're a wise one—a wizard. I'll be thinking that you know the binding power of an oath." The selkie picks up his own pelt. "Let's be about this. You start by draping the skin over your shoulders—make sure it falls smooth or you'll pinch a fin. Then lift it over your head. When it touches your head, be ready to fall forward. Let the waves catch you."

Lovern takes the wet hide, some small part of him wondering if he is being toyed with, for the procedure seems so simple compared with his own elaborate enchantments. The selkie stands with his own pelt over his arm.

"Excuse me," Lovern says, "but can I store my clothing and tools somewhere?"

The selkie strikes himself on the forehead. "I'm almost forgetting. Himself said the Land King has a safe in the house, and I'm to stow your gear there. Why don't you put on the skin and practice some swimming while I run up to the house?"

Lovern complies, quashing his nervousness with reminders of cottages turned to nothing but storm wrack, and land creatures bloating and drowned where the waters had risen.

Almost as soon as he puts the head skin over his own, he feels the tingle of transformation. His upper body becomes far too heavy for his legs . . . No! Flippers. He falls forward and the waves rise to catch him.

"There, you're looking much more fine." Connel sets his own pelt back into the tide pool. "Practice in the shallows and don't be going too far out. Himself might just have sent some sharks out to welcome you if you're after coming out without me."

Lovern splashes agreement. What else is he going to do? He isn't likely to flee into Duppy Jonah's own kingdom. In any case, he doesn't even know how to take this thing off!

The selkie returns after about ten minutes, already naked.

"Seemed a crime to waste such a fine pair of short pants," he explains, lifting his pelt and shaking out the kinks. "So I left it in the mud room. Even so this pink-skinned ass burns from just a few moments looking back at the sun."

He slides into his pelt and into the water with the grace of long practice and natural affinity. When Connel the Seal barks, Lovern understands that he is being told to follow.

Their journey is not a short one. Each time they surface to breathe, Lovern tries to judge their location by the position of the sun, but, except for being certain that they are swimming east and south, he feels no certainty. Day becomes night, and that night eventually becomes day again.

Connel feeds him with fish caught along the way, but otherwise does not pause. The original owner of Lovern's pelt must be a hale fellow, for all his being a grandfather, for Lovern doesn't grow particularly weary.

At last they come to a fortresslike cluster of coral and rock. The sun has been clear above the horizon the last several times they have risen to breathe, but the day is still young.

Wearing the form of a massive triton with dark green hair and brows, from beneath which ink black eyes fix Lovern with a hard gaze, Duppy Jonah greets him. "I am prepared for you, wizard. Over yonder you will glimpse a domed cage with bars of iron. Within those limits, you will be able to breathe and be comfortably warm. Should you stray, the only question is whether the pressure will crush you before you drown."

Lovern blinks, hoping that his eyes are as soulful and innocent as those of most seals.

"Go into the cage," Duppy Jonah says. "If Amphitrite returns to me and requests that I forgive you, then you may again claim your life above the waves. If not, the cost to Harmony will be as nothing to me. You will die."

Lovern goes. Once inside the cage, he follows the Sea King's instructions and removes the selkie's pelt. Passing it outside of the bars (taking great care not to touch the iron bars), he bows.

"Thank your grandfather for me, Connel."

His guide wrinkles his whiskers in agreement or maybe even a smile. The wizard is miffed that Duppy Jonah has not softened at his cooperativeness. He's been everything a hostage should, but damned if he'll beg for clothing! With a surge of his great tail, Duppy Jonah swims away. Connel follows and only an octopus remains.

"I don't suppose you play chess," Lovern asks it. "No, I suppose not."

He sinks to the sandy bottom of his cage, deciding that Duppy Jonah's prison is less horrid than Louhi's. He takes odd comfort in remembering what he has survived, but it is not enough to banish the fear that this imprisonment will be brief—and terminal.

21

He who has a thousand friends has not
a friend to spare,
And he who has one enemy shall meet
him everywhere.

—RALPH WALDO EMERSON

"THE PHONE'S BEEN RINGING RIGHT OUT OF THE CRADLE,"
Eddie says, coming into the doorway of Arthur's office.

"That's an archaic phrase," Arthur says mildly. "Phones
don't ring anymore. They bleep and beep and chime. And
receivers are so slim that they don't really need cradles."

"True," Eddie says, "but I stand by what I've said. The
damn thing is shaking down the wall. Listen!"

Arthur winks. "I'll do better." He lifts the receiver. "Pendragon Productions."

He listens. "Yes, yes, I am aware of the odd weather. No,
no, I don't think Duppy Jonah is aware that you own property
in the Netherlands. Yes, I am certain that flooding does the
tulip crop no good. I assure you, measures have been taken."

Hanging up the phone, Arthur smiles weakly. "Have all
your calls been like that?"

"Pretty much. The humans are treating the odd weather
patterns as a mystery. They have plenty of theories. The most
popular is that El Niño has shifted. The next is that there is
suboceanic volcanic activity. Jonathan has been up on the
Internet flagging the really interesting theories."

"The one about volcanic activity is about right," Arthur says. "Duppy Jonah's temper *is* volcanic. The problem with these bloody phone calls is that I don't dare ignore any call on any line. It could be Vera or Anson."

"That's true."

The phone begins to ring again.

"Damn!" Arthur grabs for the receiver. His tone is calm when he speaks. "Pendragon Productions. No, I haven't had an opportunity to check my e-mail. I haven't had my second cup of coffee. The phone hasn't stopped ringing all morning."

He waves a resigned dismissal to Eddie and Eddie departs, going to his office where another phone awaits his attention.

"We never should have had multiple lines installed," he mutters, and goes about the business of running a government.

¤◙¤

In the courtyard of Arthur's hacienda, the coyote pup called Shahrazad is digging. Already she has made a great deal of progress. Her tunnel loops under a root of the ornamental juniper and is widening. Dirt showers out behind her, scattering over the patio in a fanlike pattern.

She digs faster, imagining that she is nearing a mouse nest or, better yet, that of a ground squirrel. There is dirt in her ears and eyes, but she feels none of it, busy envisioning a successful hunt. Mice are just a warm, wet crunch, but a ground squirrel is big enough to tear and shake.

Growling, she digs faster. Yet, as distracted as she is, she hears a faint sound and feels a thump as something drops onto the patio behind her.

Her tunnel is not yet big enough to hide her, nor will she leave her tail facing an unknown threat. Demonstrating the speed and agility that her father fears has been tamed from her, Shahrazad backs out of the tunnel and turns, protecting her back against the juniper.

Lips curled back from puppy teeth white and strong in a long muzzle, she growls, whimpers in confusion, and growls again.

A man stands on the patio. He looks as her father does when he takes human shape: lean, muscular, with long, black hair and eyes of coyote yellow. His scent is wrong, though, and it is that wrongness that turns her whimper back into a growl.

"Easy, kid," the man says and his voice is the deep rasping voice her father uses.

Rather than comforting her, the sound deepens her fear. Shahrazad feels her fur standing out all over her body and she stiffens. In an adult coyote, the display is quite frightening. Even on her gawky young form, it is impressive.

The man who is not her father takes an involuntary step back and glances toward the upper reaches of the courtyard's balcony. A woman with pale hair, clad in something loose that flaps in the gusting summer wind, stands outside one of the doorways.

"Louhi, I don't think the pup's fooled."

"Deal with her," the woman replies. "Didn't you once claim the Fenris Wolf as get?"

"Yeah," he says. Then he mutters softly, "Frigid twit."

He hunkers down and takes a delicious-smelling chunk of raw liver from a plastic bag. This he tosses in front of Shahrazad.

Impulses war within the coyote pup. Her growing body clamors that this is food and that neither the dark, furry man nor the golden one has fed her for many hours. Her wary mind holds memories of the Big One growling at her when she stole carrion. She flattens her ears, recalling his punishing bites.

Her tail creeps between her legs and she piddles, wetting both belly and tail. Now that she has decided to be afraid rather than confused, her mind is free to sort this man's scent from all the scents in her memory. With remarkable speed she places it as the scent of the man who had slept in the room beside her father and hers during the Time of Crowds.

The Big Male had not liked that one, had been guarded when he came near and had not let him touch Shahrazad. Fear deepens and becomes defensive ferocity. When the man tosses another piece of meat near her, Shahrazad is not even tempted, but takes the opportunity to spring forth and slash at his hand.

Her aim is good and she slices open a deep furrow. The man curses and strikes out. Too late she sees that his arm has grown burly and that muscles bulge from it. His blow catches her solidly, and Sven hisses at her from a mouth suddenly misshapen.

"You've made me ruin my suit, bitch."

From where she lies on her side, Shahrazad has no idea that the bulky monstrosity that Sven has shifted into is what a younger age of the world would have called a troll. All she knows is that it stinks of death and rot. His mouth has more teeth than her father's. Some are curved like a snake's fangs and others twist like trees growing from windswept crevices.

If she was afraid before, she is terrified now. Her coyote programming tells her to submit and hope that the foul thing will not hurt her further. Something slightly wiser, but less strong warns her that some creatures do not honor surrender.

She drops and rolls, tail flat against her belly, throat fur exposed. Craven and defeated, she trembles and hopes the thing will not kill her.

There is a terrible moment when the troll looms over her, slavering with rage, the blood from its wounded hand steaming on the patio stones. Its claws curve, and a hand raises to strike. Then the woman's voice says sharply, "Kill her and I will turn you into garden statuary. Have you forgotten the power of the sun on troll-kind? It would be little enough trouble to sweep away the foliage that shades you."

The Sven-troll stops. There is a blur of motion and Sven stands over the pup, again slim and fiery-haired, clad in a ripped suit too large for him.

"I wouldn't have killed her."

"You'd better not. At least not yet." Louhi gestures imperiously. "Put her in the carrier and get up here. Who knows how long it will be until Arthur remembers his charge."

"Long enough," Sven answers, stuffing Shahrazad in a dog carrier too small for comfort. "He's a workaholic."

"Come!"

Shahrazad feels herself carried up the stairs and lifted onto the roof. The woman does not help Sven, for she, too, is encumbered with a box. When they reach the rooftop, they cross to a wing unused except when guests stay on the estate.

From there, they climb down a ladder, cross the grounds, and hasten to a side road where a van waits.

Shahrazad is put in the back and the luggage door is slammed shut. Once alone, she begins to howl mournfully but fearfully, sobbing out her sorrow and knowing that there is no one near enough to care.

¤◙¤

Anson A. Kridd watches as the Changer thumps a gaudy yellow-and-orange curved beak against a cypress branch and spreads his wings, flaunting his new toucan shape before taking flight.

The most recent shapeshift has not completely healed the grazes from Isidro's gun, but, as neither has done significant damage to muscle, the wounds will not impede him much. For now, they present a certain soreness and a marring of his plumage.

Anson believes that Cleonice will attempt to take a hostage—or to kill both women in revenge for the deaths of her allies. There is still the chance that she will seek more immediate vengeance on himself or the Changer.

When the Changer flies ahead, Anson will need to watch out for himself, but the wiry African ancient is an old hand at avoiding ambush. His various monkey and insect forms have more agility than either the jaguar or the human. Waving farewell to the Changer, he paddles the rubber boat down the center of the river, knowing that he will make better speed than a raft.

Still, he is not hopeful. Even without a crazed athanor tracking them, the rain forest offers dangers and to spare— poisonous snakes and insects, anacondas, piranhas, jaguars . . . To survive with so little, the two *must* stay on the water.

Trying to believe that the Changer will find more than a few broken and rotting remnants of what had been two fine women, Anson A. Kridd paddles strongly, keeping where the current will carry him most swiftly.

¤◙¤

Above the winding path of the river, the Changer travels on toucan wings. Before relinquishing the jaguar form, he had dined on a sloth. The meat had been rank, but his strength is renewed. As a toucan he can replenish himself on the plentiful fruit and nuts without ever coming within striking range of predators. All he needs to do is keep a weather eye out for the hawks and eagles which might find the rapidly traveling toucan tempting prey.

His first several miles offer no sign of the fugitives, and he considers shifting shape into a water bird so that he will be better equipped to scan the shoreline. He dismisses this option. Speed first. Meticulous search later. What he seeks is fairly large and, unlike an airplane, he can fly below the tree line. Until evening comes, he will fly ahead. Then he will return to Anson and report.

As he flies, he sees occasional signs that make him hope: a deadfall that has been chopped at by a machete, a low branch overgrown with vines that appear to have been pruned, a few crude arrows caught in a snag of driftwood.

These might not be sign of those he seeks, but he permits himself to believe that they are. Unfortunately, the omnipresent river washes away scent, so even when he drops and shifts into an anomalous coyote to seek confirmation he cannot be certain that his quarry made the marks. He can only store the information away against despair and fly on.

Yet, even as alertly as he is watching, he nearly misses the raft. The equatorial sun is at its height and, despite the myriad discouragements offered by ants, snakes, beetles, and the like, Vera and Amphitrite are rafting close to the shore in order to benefit from the shade it offers. The Changer swallows an urge to break into song and comes around for another look.

They—or, as the Changer sees when he swoops lower—she. Only Vera stands on the deck of the raft, poling along in a fashion that makes quite clear that she has been about this labor for hours and expects to be about it for hours to come.

The impulse to song vanishes as swiftly as it had arisen. If Amphitrite is lost or dead, Duppy Jonah's wrath will be limitless. In the days of old, his temper gave rise to floods that still crop up in the myths of dozens of cultures. His hurricanes and tsunami make men fear and distrust the vast stretches of water. That Amphitrite's birth coincided with the development of seamanship more ambitious than a tentative paddle around the shoreline was no coincidence. Happiness had tempered the Sea God and his tempests alike.

Disconsolate, the Changer lands on a tree limb some distance in front of the raft, intending to shift into a macaw and hail Vera from there. His respect for her warlike spirit has only been intensified by the determination she is demonstrating in her solitary voyage to the sea.

Then the Changer sees something that puzzles him. A rope made of thick vines braided together by skilled fingers is tied firmly to the front of the raft. From his initial vantage, he had thought it was a painter for mooring the raft at night. Now he can see that it drops under the surface at an angle far too sharp to be caused merely by the pull of the current.

It is almost as if something is pulling the raft.

He hops and flaps to another limb so that he can continue to study the situation before revealing himself.

Does Vera have the magic or skill to have trained a river porpoise to pull her vessel? Could she have chanced upon one of the athanor water dwellers? Or could . . . ?

His unformed, hopeful supposition is confirmed as a head crowned with seaweed green hair emerges from beneath the waters. Pearlescent skin untroubled by the sun, shoulders bare but for a harness of vines that has cut ruddy lines in their purity, Amphitrite rises from beneath the river waters.

"Time for a break, Vera," she calls. "I'm not used to this kind of work, and I haven't had any luck convincing the river dwellers to do my bidding."

"At least," Vera says, setting down her bamboo pole and wiping her forehead with a grubby arm, "the piranhas have decided that you are not edible."

"At least that," Amphitrite agrees.

Squawking, the Changer swoops down onto the raft. Forgetting decorum and his customary restraint, he shifts into human form. Vera's greeting is not at all what he had expected, but what, in a less emotionally charged moment, he should have known it would be.

She drops her bamboo pole and, with a single practiced movement, brings into play a spear that she has anchored point down in the deck of the raft. The Changer looks down to where the blackened but undeniably sharp point rests on the hollow of his breastbone.

"And hello to you, too, Vera," he says in admiration.

She doesn't let the point of the spear drop—a smart thing, given that many athanor are shapeshifters—but the expression on her grimy face becomes a smile.

"Changer?"

"In the flesh," he answers.

"Prove it."

He shifts into coyote form, then into raven, toucan, macaw, jaguar, raccoon, and back into human, the entire process a blur of color and motion devoid of the gestures a mage would need to trigger the spells and with variety enough to identify himself.

"If I did larger shapes," he says, "I might upset the raft."

Vera lowers the spear but keeps it near to hand. "Did Arthur send you after us?"

"I volunteered, more or less. Duppy Jonah is causing a great deal of harm. Locating Amphitrite seemed a wise thing, else the world would be destroyed by water."

The Sea Queen has slipped the vine harness from her shoulders and swum close to the raft.

"Hello, brother," she says, her expression both rueful and wistful. "How is my husband?"

"Furious," the Changer answers honestly. "He has taken Lovern as a hostage. I am not certain that even when you are returned, he will release his prisoner."

"I wish I could phone him."

"No such luck." The Changer gestures over his naked form. "I had to travel light."

"You've been wounded," Vera comments, looking candidly at the fresh pink scars against his naked skin.

"By Isidro Robelo," he answers, "the late. He is dead, as is Oswaldo Barjak."

"You killed them both?" Vera asks.

"No. The Spider accounted for Oswaldo. Anson is trailing me in a rubber boat. His shapes do not include any that fly."

"And Cleonice?"

"We don't know for certain," the Changer says honestly, "but our best guess is that she is tracking you by land with the intent of taking one or both of you hostage."

"Let her try." Amphitrite's voice is low and full of frustrated anger. "I have had enough of being a pawn."

The Changer nods. "Anyone with wisdom would have known that Lovern would make a better hostage. He has a less refined sense of self-preservation and a firm belief in his own importance."

He sits on the deck, crossing his legs. "We stowed away in the light plane *Caiman*. If you ladies do not mind, we would probably do better to return to it and fly out."

Vera nods. "It will be faster, and Amphitrite can use the radio to get a call relayed to Duppy Jonah."

"Moving the raft against the current won't be easy," Amphitrite says.

"But Anson is on the water," the Changer says, "and Cleonice on the shore. Moreover, you are limited to the water, so even if Vera and I went by land, we would need to stay near the river."

Amphitrite shakes back her hair, spraying the air with droplets that create a rainbow halo in the afternoon sun filtering through the green canopy above.

"If you shift into something aquatic," she says, "we could tow the raft."

"We can also move out of the mainstream," the Changer says, "and reduce the pull of the current."

Vera frowns. "I hate the idea of you two towing me."

Amphitrite reaches to pat her hand. "Don't worry. I would say you could ride on one of our backs, but I do not trust the piranha to ignore such a toothsome morsel."

"And they will ignore the Changer?"

"My husband says that most creatures who value their lives avoid the Changer. He claims that the ancient have a scent about them that warns away all but the most foolhardy."

The Changer does not comment on this, but looks about. "I will need to eat before I can change and then swim for hours, but my hunting will not take too long if Amphitrite hasn't frightened off all the game fish."

"There are both *pirarucú* and *piraiba* near," the Sea Queen answers. "The *piraiba* have nothing much to fear and so have done little but move slightly at our passage. Try downstream.''

"I shall.''

The Changer rises, shifts into a many-toothed, vaguely alligator-like creature, the like of which vanished from the Earth before humans ceased to be monkeys. He slips into the water and is gone.

Vera cocks an eyebrow. "I could pity the *piraiba* if I knew what they were.''

"Catfish,'' Amphitrite says, lifting her vine harness, "large enough to swallow monkeys or children. I haven't caught any for us because their flesh can taste muddy.''

"Shall we start the raft upstream?''

"May as well, but keep your spear at hand.'' Amphitrite glances up where far too many branches arc out over the water. "We don't know when Cleonice will find us.''

Neither of them even think "if.'' They know the power of fear can drive even an athanor to insane measures.

✡◻✡

Night is falling when the jaguar catches the sought-for scent. Ears flare at the sound of rhythmic splashing. A rumble somewhere between a purr and a growl muddles in her throat.

Cleonice has allowed the jaguar's instincts to rise to the fore during her hours of travel and tracking. The athanor within her has simply served to force the jaguar to persist long after a natural animal would have given up.

Now she lets the athanor mind take full command. Her quarry is near, and she must plan. Amphitrite would be the best hostage, but Vera will do, especially if she can use her to command Amphitrite. The two seemed to have become friends. Amphitrite might surrender herself to save her friend, especially if Cleonice demonstrated a willingness to mutilate her captive.

Although long-lived, athanor heal at different rates. Some, like the Smith, bear old wounds for life. Others, especially the shapeshifters, can regenerate. However, although Vera's father was a shapeshifter, there is no evidence that Vera is herself. Mutilation should be a serious threat and has the advantage over death that it can be repeated.

Having resolved this issue, Cleonice begins to creep close enough visually to assess the situation. A few things puzzle her already. For one, the raft seems to be traveling upriver. For another, it seems to be moving at a fair clip. Clearly, this is not a time to attack as her jaguar instincts are urging.

The sight that meets her astonished gaze is a raft a few logs wide being towed upstream by a pair of bull sharks. Vera sits aboard, watchfully scanning the banks and the trees overhead. She holds a spear in one hand and at least four others rest on the abbreviated deck, along with a makeshift bow.

That Vera does not spare attention for guiding her particular steeds confirms what Cleonice has already guessed. Isidro and Oswaldo had failed to stop their rivals and they, in turn, have beaten Cleonice to her quarry. Nor is she terribly surprised to see that Amphitrite has returned to a form adapted to the water.

Spotted tail lashing, Cleonice assesses the odds of success. They had been poor before. They are worse now. She is not likely to take a hostage. Amphitrite is outside her reach, and Vera is alert to the possibility of attack. With others to assist them . . .

No. She would be a fool to continue on this course of action. Isidro would have leapt into the fray out of idealistic desire to avenge his comrades, but Cleonice's father was a soldier, and she has learned the value of retreat.

Why shouldn't she vanish into the rain forest? As a jaguar she could live quite easily until her crimes are less immediate. If she could locate a native enclave, she could live as a human—perhaps a queen—and do some good against the encroaching civilization that threatened their ancient ways.

The idea is tempting. Arthur is a bleeding heart for the oppressed. If she reappears in a century or so with a history of fighting for the underdog, she might find herself readmitted to the Accord.

She will wear iron about her and keep on the move. Eventually, her enemies will grow weary of searching for her. If they leave her in Harmony, what is a few centuries of fear compared to immortality?

As silently as she had come, Cleonice Damita melts into the surrounding jungle and runs on velvet paws toward life.

¤◙¤

"Face it, Arthur," Eddie says, coming out from behind the lilac bush. "Shahrazad is gone."

"Gone!" Arthur exclaims. "She can't be! Where would she go? How could she get out? I locked all the doors into the courtyard myself before we started work."

Eddie glances around. What Arthur has said is true, but that does not change the fact that the three-month-old coyote pup is no longer in the courtyard. Jonathan Wong, emerging from behind a small stand of juniper, adds, "It may be impossible for her to be gone, Arthur, but that does not change the fact that she is not here."

"Could she have gone out over the roof?" Arthur trots up the courtyard stair to the balcony level. "I seem to recall that coyotes can climb."

"Maybe," Eddie says doubtfully. He's kneeling beside some of the dirt Shahrazad had kicked out over the patio. "Arthur, Jon, take a look at this."

"Just a second," Arthur calls, frowning at a mark on the stuccoed wall before coming down.

"Look." Eddie indicates a partial footprint in the dirt. "That isn't any of ours."

"No," Arthur agrees. "A rubber-soled shoe. I've got moccasins on."

"It's a right print," Eddie says. "I'm still wearing a scuff over that foot."

"I," Wong says, extending a neatly shod foot, "am wearing dress shoes with hard, smooth soles."

"Why?" Eddie says.

"Why not?" Wong answers, his expression a parody of Chinese imperturbability. "Actually, I was planning to go to the courthouse and do some research for a case I am pursuing."

"Oh."

"So someone came in here and stole Shahrazad," Arthur continues, ignoring the digression. "A man, judging from the size of the print."

Eddie scouts about and now comes up with several small scraps of fabric. "I think that Shahrazad accounted well for herself. Apparently, her kidnapper had his clothes rather badly torn. There's blood, too, hastily covered with fresh dirt."

Arthur nods, remembering the mark on the wall and understanding its significance. "I'm going up onto the roof. Since none of the doors were unlocked, her captors must have gone out over the roof. Maybe we can find which way they took her."

Arthur's investigation finds another partial footprint, another scrap of cloth, and, when he goes out and inspects the grounds outside of the hacienda, the place where a ladder had been leaned against the house.

Glumly, he reports his finds to Eddie and Jonathan.

"I checked the grounds, but I'm no tracker. My guess is that the kidnapper had a vehicle parked along the road—maybe along a side road where it wouldn't be noticed. I found what could be the outline of a dog carrier in the gravel. The ladder was dropped behind some shrubs."

Eddie rubs his temples and pours them each two fingers of good Irish whiskey. "I know it's early in the day, but we need bucking up."

"Thanks."

"*Gracias.*"

"I guess we forgot to make certain that Lovern reset the wards before he left for South America," Arthur says.

"I just assumed he would do so," Eddie adds.

"Assumptions are not strong means for running a secure establishment," Jonathan Wong comments.

"I know . . . I'm kicking myself," Arthur says, "I assure you."

"We have a big problem here," Eddie cuts in.

"We know," Arthur says.

"If the Changer returns and finds Shahrazad gone . . ."

"I know." The King swirls the amber whiskey in his glass. "He entrusted her to me specifically. How can I tell him I didn't want his daughter peeing on my carpets so I left her locked in the courtyard?''

Eddie takes a deep swallow of his own drink. "You won't need to if we find her before he gets back."

"Whoever took her was athanor."

"Probably the same person who killed the rest of the Changer's family," Jonathan adds helpfully.

"Yes. That doesn't bode well for her."

"Poor pup," Eddie says softly.

"Poor us!" Arthur protests. "Have you forgotten that the Changer is the brother of the Sea King? What if he shares Duppy Jonah's affinity for controlling the ocean?"

"We've seen no evidence of this," Eddie answers, "but with the Changer that means little. He keeps much close."

"I took responsibility for Shahrazad," Arthur repeats, "therefore, I must find and ransom her before her father returns. That's the only acceptable answer."

Eddie nods. "I never thought I would say this, but I hope Anson and the Changer take their time in South America."

"Heaven forgive me," Arthur says, "but I share that sentiment."

⚙◼⚙

Although the three slogging up the Amazon expect Cleonice every hour, she does not come. Once they rendezvous with Anson, they discard the *Pororoca* for the rubber boat and reach the *Caiman* before the next morning. There, Amphitrite radios the Smith, who links her to Duppy Jonah, and thus the Sea King's anxiety is somewhat relieved. Even so, a rumble of anger in his voice bodes ill for Lovern.

After Duppy Jonah has been contacted, Vera has the Smith relay news of their success to Arthur. Although the Smith is clearly curious as to what secret mission they have been performing, he promises to pass on the information without question.

When dawn breaks, Anson takes the *Caiman* into the sky and, before morning is many hours old, they are back in Belém. While Anson readies the rented jet for its transatlantic flight, the Changer takes on Isidro's shape and goes to the estate in Belém. Arthur eventually may need to delegate someone to deal with the "disappearance" of the owners, but for now it is enough that the servants be told that Isidro, Oswaldo, and Cleonice will be traveling for a time. Following Vera's counsel, the Changer arranges for severance pay and the like.

Doubtless, he overpays.

While Anson and the Changer are dealing with these mundane arrangements, Vera drives a panel van to an isolated stretch of beach. There, she backs close to the water. Then she wades out to open the doors and set a ramp in place.

Amphitrite slides off the ramp like an otter going down a mud slide. When she is in water deep enough to cover her fishy lower half, she looks back at Vera.

"Thanks." The Sea Queen is feeling a conflicting mixture of emotions: eagerness to be away, relief at coming home at last, and a sharp realization that she will miss Vera. "You will come visit, won't you?"

"I'll need to learn how to breathe water," Vera says, wiping what might be sweat, but might be tears, from her cheek with the back of her hand. "But as soon as I have that under control, I certainly will. We can still talk on the phone, right?"

"Right!"

"And I'll try to do something about getting you folks onto the Internet."

"Great. Talk with you soon."

"Have a safe trip."

"I will."

And, waving once more, Amphitrite dives beneath the waves, heading to one who would have destroyed the world in grief over losing her. Vera watches the empty water for a time, wondering at such passion, then she packs the ramp, closes up the van, and heads to the airfield.

Noontime finds Vera, Anson, and the Changer on their way to New Mexico. They chase the day across the oceans, unaware that the rest they each believe awaits them is as much an illusion as the movement of the sun about the world.

To be excellent when engaged in administration is to be like the North Star. As it remains in its position, all the other stars surround it.

—CONFUCIUS

Monk>> Hi! Sorry, I've been out of touch for a while. Me and some buds decided to do the tourist bit in Albuquerque.

Rebecca>> Tourist! Lucky! Tell!!

Monk>> Well, we went to a ball game on July 4. Doubleheader. Home team won one, lost one. Ate way too much.

Demetrios>> King Arthur go? He's a baseball fan.

Monk>> Didn't see him. Think there was some admin trouble he was busy with. Wouldn't have been with him anyhow. We went with Sven Trout. He and Arthur aren't exactly buds.

Rebecca>> Sven Trout. Loki? Brrr . . . What's he like?

Demetrios>> Sven Trout? Never felt comfortable with those fire-types. Doesn't blend with earth and water.

Loverboy>> Lucky stiff!! Sven knows how to party hearty! He knows about a hot time on the old town tonight!!

Monk>> Sven's okay. He likes to shake things up, that's all. Loverboy, you would have gotten into this party. We ate and drank until we were sick. And babes!!!! Albuquerque goes for pretty fine bimbos. Fuck-me pumps. Skirts up to . . . and necklines down to . . . :)!!!!

Rebecca>> Ah-hem! :(This is a family site!

Monk>> Sorry. Just playing to the crowd. I can't help it. There's lots of genteel action, too. The ballpark has a place where families can picnic with their kids during the game.

Demetrios>> Do you think we could have brought in the non-shifters at this time of year?

Monk>> You might have managed if you were willing to wear a cap, baggy pants, and boots, but the heavy-wear that the sasquatches and yetis will need would have really been uncomfortable, not to mention noticeable. We've been looking to see what styles might fit them best. There're some far-out religious groups in New Mexico. There's a colony of Sikhs who all wear turbans and white clothes, but they don't cover their faces. Men often are bearded, but ladies don't wear veils.

Rebecca>> I guess I should be the one to say it, but lady sasquatches don't look much like lady humans, even when bundled and veiled. Maybe we should dress as Sikhs. The turbans would hide our more pointed head shape.

Demetrios>> Nothing will hide the height.

Rebecca>> So we brazen it out. Aren't the Sikhs warlike?

Demetrios>> Don't know. Time to research.

Monk>> And I'll see what I can do to learn about the local Sikh communities. You'd need to know enough but not too much.

Loverboy>> Tell us more about the babes and the beer!! :(This stuff bores me!

Monk>> Sorry. Don't want to get tossed off the site by the Moderator. Use your imagination.

Loverboy>> !!! That good!! Oh, baby!!

Arthur greets with mixed emotions the news that Amphitrite and Vera are found, and that his emissaries are returning.

"We might have time to find Shahrazad while they tie up loose ends there and fly back," he says to Eddie.

Eddie nods. "I've called all the Humane Society and Animal Control locations. No one has taken in a puppy that matches Shahrazad's description. I didn't precisely say 'coyote,' but I think at least Animal Control twigged."

"And they still didn't have her?"

"No."

Eddie continues, "I checked with the neighbors. No one has seen anything peculiar."

Picking up a pencil, Arthur begins to drum the eraser end

on his desk. After a moment he stops, pencil poised in mid-thump.

"Now that he has Amphitrite back, Duppy Jonah will return Lovern to freedom. We can ask him to scry or dowse or something and find her! If we hurry . . ."

He picks up the phone and punches in Duppy Jonah's phone number. Patiently waiting while it rings several dozen times, the King is rewarded by Duppy Jonah himself answering the call.

"Yes?"

"Duppy Jonah, this is Arthur Pendragon. I'm calling to make certain that Amphitrite returned home safely."

"We met off the coast of Brazil a few hours ago," Duppy Jonah says, his severe tone softening. "She is well enough except for welts on her shoulders."

"Welts?" Arthur envisions the lovely woman being beaten by her captors and frowns. "Was she tortured?"

"If you do not count being stranded in fresh water, surrounded by poisonous beasts and insects, and hunted by homicidal maniacs as being tortured, no, she was not tortured. She obtained the welts towing Vera, who could not swim with impunity in the Amazon, to safety."

"What courage!"

"Yes. Now, what do you want?"

Arthur draws in a deep breath and chews on his mustache with his bottom teeth. "Now that you have Amphitrite back, you will be releasing Lovern. I'd like to make arrangements for his return. If you'd tell me when I can expect him in Florida . . ."

Duppy Jonah cuts him off. "I have not released Lovern, nor do I have any immediate plans to do so."

"But!"

"He gave himself as guarantor of Amphitrite's safety. As I have made amply clear, I do not think she was kept safe. That she is alive at all is no thanks to him."

On his side of the conversation, Arthur refrains from stating that Lovern could do very little to help Amphitrite while kept hostage himself. Instead, he lets Duppy Jonah rant.

"I am considering keeping Lovern hostage for a time, long enough to give him ample opportunity to meditate upon his incautious behavior—perhaps a decade for every day that Amphitrite was lost, perhaps a century.''

Arthur quickly ticks off days on his fingers. Five days or six, depending on how one counts, and he suspects that Duppy Jonah will be liberal in his counting. Far too long, even if Duppy Jonah settles for decades rather than centuries.

Keeping his tone level but commanding, Arthur says, ''Lovern is important to me and to my administration. I would prefer that you found another way to make your displeasure known to him.''

Duppy Jonah bellows like a bull seal.

''You prefer? *I* reign in my kingdom, Arthur. These past centuries, I have worked with you, but I will not subject my justice to your whims. Lovern gave his oath willingly in order to retrieve the toy he had hidden within my ocean . . .''

Ah, that old crime still rankles, Arthur thinks despondently.

''. . . Now he must live with the consequences of his actions. For too long has he lorded his connection with you over his betters, even when he would have been wiser to have not.''

Arthur swallows a sigh. ''I quite understand. I shall not trouble you further on this issue. If you reconsider . . .''

''Then *I* choose.'' Duppy Jonah's tone leaves no doubt that he considers the interview over.

''As you say, Your Majesty. Do tell Amphitrite how delighted I am that she is safe. Her captors will be duly punished.''

Duppy Jonah guffaws. ''That has been taken out of your hands, Arthur. Isidro Robelo and Oswaldo Barjak are already dead. Cleonice Damita has fled. I wish you the pleasure of finding her. Perhaps I would trade her head for Lovern's freedom. Then again, perhaps I would not. Good day!''

''Good day.''

With a limp hand, Arthur hangs up the phone.

''I gathered some of that,'' Eddie says. ''Duppy Jonah will not release Lovern?''

''No. Isidro and Oswaldo are slain. I assume by Anson or the Changer. Had Amphitrite or Vera managed it, I believe Duppy Jonah would have boasted.''

''Cleonice?''

"Fled into the rain forest."

Eddie rubs a hand over his five-o'clock shadow. "Well, they would almost certainly have been executed in any case. This saves us some trouble."

"But raises all sorts of other problems. I can't have my subjects believing that I would send assassins out against those who would question my decisions."

"You didn't."

"The events could be so distorted. I had better speak with Jonathan Wong and get his counsel on this matter. Is he here?"

"He has gone to see if he can trace the ladder. It's a slim hope, but he was growing restless."

"It is difficult to imagine Confucius becoming restless," Arthur comments. "I thought he would contemplate universal truths or something."

Eddie smiles. "You confuse the legend with the man. It's easy to do, isn't it?"

Arthur, who often wishes he possessed all the virtues his legends attribute to him, nods. "Too easy and too easy for the legend to fail."

¤🞖¤

In a rented house in Bernallio, a few miles north of Albuquerque, a strange household is gathered. Elsewhere it might draw comments, but Bernallio hosts many illegal immigrants. Neighbors have learned to mind their own business.

Moreover, the house is set on several acres of land and is bordered on all sides by pasture. Except for the few people who have rights to use the dirt road, there is no one likely to comment on the young coyote crying in the adobe-walled yard. No one at all is in a position to see the grotesque Head suspended by its own grey hair over a coffee table in the living room.

"Nice place," Louhi says, setting her luggage on the kitchen's brick floor. "A bit far from the airport, but I can see why you wouldn't want to be in the heart of the city."

"Not with the bitch whining," Sven agrees. "I thought about knocking her out, but I don't know what her tolerances might be."

"Don't do it," Louhi says. "I want to take a blood sample. Perhaps she has enough of the Changer's traits to serve us."

"Right." Sven's grin is sly. "Besides, you can have a nice chat—sister to sister."

Louhi raises one slim, pale hand. "Would you like to be a pig? Or perhaps the fish you name yourself?"

"You forget yourself," he says sternly. "I, too, am a shapeshifter."

"Want to test me? I might find it amusing to discover how long a fish would take to gasp its gills to dryness in this air."

They stand for a long minute, its seconds marked by the miserable sobs of the coyote pup. Neither will step back.

A gruff voice, rasping and hoarse, breaks the impasse. "Ill it becomes the fiery one to forget, when fire meets ice one melts, one is quenched. Destruction and damnation ensue."

Deliberately, Sven turns away from Louhi, forcing his mouth to quirk in something like a wry grin. He walks down the short brick staircase into the living room.

"You're quite right, of course," Sven says, his cheerfulness brittle. "We would be fools to spat so close to victory."

"Wiser to wait, brighter to bide," the Head agrees, "until the race is won."

"Yes," Louhi says, and her agreement is hissed. "Sven and I can play the old wizard's game another time."

Sven holds a straw to the Head's parched lips, ignoring the other slobbering over his hand. When the Head has finished, Sven carries the glass up to the kitchen to refill it.

"This house," he says to Louhi, as if their quarrel had never occurred, "has three bedrooms. Two on the ground floor and a rather grand master suite on the upper floor. I will give you first choice."

"I'll take the master bedroom," Louhi says promptly, "and thank you for your courtesy."

"Not at all," Sven sweeps a bow. "May I carry your bags?"

"Thank you. I'll take the small one. It's warded."

"A good precaution."

As they cross the living room, Louhi glances out the floor-to-ceiling windows to where Shahrazad, chained to two different cottonwood trees, voices her misery.

"No rope spun of the sound a cat makes when it walks,

the breath of fish, the spittle of birds, the hairs of a woman's beard, and all the rest, is needed to hold her,'' Louhi says scornfully. ''Has she stopped crying at all?''

''Hardly,'' Sven says. ''She is persistent.''

''When do we call the Changer?''

''I have an informant at the airport who will call as soon as their plane touches down. I want him to learn that Arthur has failed to protect the pup. Then I will call.''

''Very good.''

When Louhi comes down, she is dressed in sturdy denim trousers and a heavy cotton work shirt over a white tee shirt. With her hair swept back in a ponytail, she might be a horse-crazy young woman but for the coolness of her gaze.

She stops alongside the Head.

''How are you?''

''Butterfly wings beat against ribs I lack. I long for length.''

''Soon,'' Louhi assures him. She opens a jar of ointment she has brought. ''This will preserve your skin against the dryness.''

''Your fingers feel sweeter than a mist in the highland.''

She arches an eyebrow at the monstrosity. ''Did you study your maker's pickup lines?''

The Head coughs and refrains from further comment.

When Louhi walks out into the yard, Shahrazad stops whining. Her tail, already held low, tucks tightly between her legs. She backs as far as the limits of her dual chains will permit.

''You know that tears won't work with me, don't you?'' Louhi comments in a menacing purr. ''I don't have an ounce of pity in my soul—at least not for such as you.''

Shahrazad strains back, her paws making furrows in the gravel mulch. Her ears fold against her skull; her lips peel back from small white fangs.

''Bite me and you'll regret it,'' Louhi says, ''even if you are blood of my father's blood.''

Darting out one hand, she grabs Shahrazad firmly by the scruff of the neck. Fixing the panicked animal's yellow eyes with her own pale blue, Louhi mutters a few words. Instantly, Shahrazad stops crying, seems even to stop breathing. A careful observer would see that she does breathe, but slowly.

Keeping the pup mesmerized, Louhi draws a syringe of dark blood. When it is safely sealed in a test tube, the witch pauses, puzzled. Holding one hand just barely away from the coyote puppy's fur, she makes a stroking motion. After studying the palm of her hand, she lifts each of the pup's feet and studies the pads.

"Oh, my!" she mutters softly. "There's more to you than meets the eye. Does the Changer know what he has begot? Is that why he watches you so carefully, little sister?"

Anger flushes her pale cheeks and she surges to her feet, breaking the spell that has kept the pup mesmerized. Then she stalks away, furious that she must let her rival live.

As Louhi departs, Shahrazad trembles so that she can no longer whimper. Her weeping has become the silent cry of one who knows that no one is listening.

¤◙¤

Arthur, to his credit, does not delay telling the Changer the bad news. That afternoon, as soon as the returning three have entered the hacienda, Arthur requests that the Changer come to his office. Eddie and Jonathan Wong take the others off to tell them what they must know and recommend that they stay clear.

Once in his office, Arthur forsakes the security of his fortresslike desk to stand before the Changer like a boy before a schoolmaster.

"I regret to tell you, sir, that Shahrazad has been taken."

The controlled fury of the ancient's reaction chills Arthur's blood far more than any outburst could. Yellow eyes with nothing human in them look out of a face that, despite its sculpting, also seems other than human.

"My daughter is taken?"

"Yes."

"By whom?"

"I don't know. He left tracks, but none of those here with the exception of Eddie have the skill to learn much from them, and Eddie cannot move freely enough to track. We did not wish to call in the police . . ."

"No."

"And Duppy Jonah will not release Lovern to me. I did

not wish to consult another sorcerer without your permission.''

"No."

"We have left them untouched. Perhaps you . . ."

"Yes."

The Changer turns without any courtesy and departs. Watching him stride forth, Arthur knows that he is seeing something other than human which has taken human form and is finding that form inconvenient. The revelation makes his skin crawl.

The Changer has always taken care to conceal that essential *otherness*, becoming a perfect mimic of whatever shape he wears. It is a measure of the ancient's anger that what he shapes now is fury that happens to have a human outline.

Coming into the courtyard, the Changer inspects the footprints with his human head held low. Arthur wonders that he does not shape something better equipped for such sensing, then the Changer raises his head.

Framed within the straight black hair is a coyote's face, long muzzled, yellow-eyed. The sharp-toothed jaws move and a voice that is part canine whine, part deep-chested rumble comes forth.

"I know this scent. It is Loki."

Arthur nods. He would not be the King if he could not make the gesture casual and controlled, yet it takes an effort.

The Changer touches the sandy earth where it is marked by his daughter's struggles, a soft pat that offers comfort to the absent one. Then he rises and lopes up the courtyard's wooden staircase, dipping his head as if tracing scent.

"Another was here—Circe, I believe. Here, where they mounted the wall to the roof, she set something down." The coyote whine shrills into a laugh as the Changer trots smoothly down to the French doors to Lovern's suite. "I believe your sorcerer will find some of his belongings are missing."

Eschewing the staircase, the Changer swings over the railing, human arms becoming raven wings that tear through the light cotton of his sport shirt. He flutters to the ground, shifting wings into arms again so smoothly that Arthur could believe he imagined the initial transition if the torn fabric did not bear witness.

"You have searched for her, Arthur?"

"We have."

"And have not found her, despite."

"No."

The Changer tosses back his hair, and when it settles his features are human again, but Arthur knows he will never lose the feeling that they are merely a mask.

"You must tell me what you have learned. Then . . ."

Eddie opens the courtyard door. "Arthur! There is a phone call for the Changer from Sven Trout."

"Get a tracer on it," Arthur says, even as the Changer pushes past Eddie and seizes the kitchen receiver.

"Speak, Loki."

"Changer!" Sven is using his perky, door-to-door salesman voice. "Good talking with you!"

The Changer waits, patient as death—and as silent. If Sven is disappointed, his tone doesn't give anything away.

"I've got something you want."

Silence.

"You'll only get her back—intact and alive—if you give us what we want."

"You and Circe."

"We thought you'd figure us out. Yes. Me and Circe."

"What do you want?"

"Deliver yourself to us. Circe needs you to make a blood-and-organ donation for a project she's working on."

"I will not die, even for a daughter."

Sven laughs, cheery as if they are discussing floor wax or boxed chocolate creams. "Of course not! She wants an eye and about a quart of blood. Surely you can survive that."

"I can."

"Then you'll do as we wish?"

"Will I be released after?"

"Of course."

"And you expect me not to take revenge?"

"Circe has made a charm that will instantly kill Shahrazad if she chooses. We consider that our insurance."

"Ah."

The Changer doesn't need to be told that Circe hopes to make some similar charm against him. Blood and body parts are particularly efficacious for such things.

"And if I refuse?" the Changer asks.

"If you did, we would have no further use for Shahrazad."

"Except as insurance that I will not attack. I will not forget this affront."

"Louhi is quite the mistress of magic," Sven says, cheer untouched. "She has some interesting plans for a child who is of our kin and who might, judging from the Harmony Dance, have inherited certain affinities from her father."

"Ah."

"So, will you take our invitation?"

"Shahrazad must be released on my arrival along with any and all charms made to affect her."

"That is possible."

"And you and Louhi both must swear over a truthstone that this has been done."

"You don't trust us?"

"I am not a fool."

"I can agree to that."

"And I plan to take measures to assure that I am released alive once you have obtained your pint of blood and eye."

"Quart."

"Yes, quart."

"We had expected that you would."

The Changer considers. He could let Shahrazad be slain or corrupted, but that would be unwise—almost as unwise as letting these two continue to live, something he suspects he will be forced to do.

Were it not for what had happened at the Harmony Dance . . .

No. He decides to be honest, at least with himself. Shahrazad has claimed his affections, his love. She looks like her mother, whom he also loved. To refuse to sacrifice himself for her would darken every sunrise, distort every birdsong.

"Tell me, Sven. Were you the one who had my family slain?"

"You have sworn a terrible vengeance on that one." Sven chuckles. "I would be an idiot to admit to anything."

"Still, I had to ask."

The Changer steels himself. For the first time, he is aware that Eddie and Arthur stand one to either side of him, that Vera, Jonathan, and Anson listen from the edge of the kitchen. He knows from this that the call was either untraceable or the information so gained useless. No matter.

"What is your answer, Changer?"

"I will come to you. How many may come with me to bring Shahrazad away?"

"Two. And if they act against our agreement, then we shall consider your safety forfeit."

"I understand. Tell me where to come."

Sven gives directions, ending, "Can't wait! See ya!"

The Changer hangs up. He surveys the watching group.

"Did you listen in?"

Arthur shakes his head. "That would be intrusive."

Anson A. Kridd grins broad and white. "But I did tape the call in case you wanted to review it. Do we erase or keep?"

"Keep." The Changer gives his old friend a wry smile. "You would in any case."

"*Moi*?"

The Changer does not respond to the banter. "Sven Trout and Louhi Maki have Shahrazad. They have agreed to release her to me in return for my surrendering myself so that they may extract an eye and a quart of blood."

No one gasps or pales. All are well seasoned in the horrors intelligent beings can inflict upon their own. Still, Arthur stiffens—he would rather be the one to suffer.

"The details of our agreement are on the tape," the Changer continues. "Jonathan, can I hire you to write a contract?"

"Inside an hour?" Jonathan nods. "Of course."

"If you would, I wish you to come with me as one of my witnesses. Anson, would you be the other?"

"Certainly."

"King Arthur"—the Changer almost sounds pitying—"you failed to protect Shahrazad. Therefore, from you I extract this promise. If I die, you will avenge me to the deaths of the two who call themselves now Sven Trout and Louhi Maki."

"I will."

"You will find my daughter fosterage—perhaps with Frank MacDonald—and serve as her guardian. If she proves to be naught but coyote, guard her first year and then find her a safe, isolated place and set her free. If she is athanor, guide her for her first century.''

"I will."

The Changer nods. "You are honest, but I will have Jonathan draw this up as a contract as well.''

"Of course." The King manages a smile. "It will protect me as much as you—though vendetta killing may cost me my crown."

"Then wish me life," the Changer says, "so that I may spare you the responsibility.''

When the clock marks thirty-five minutes to the rendezvous, Jonathan Wong enters with two contracts. "Sign this one, Arthur. It's the vengeance and custody agreement.''

Arthur does not even read the fine print but signs, adding his thumbprint beside his signature.

"Done."

"Are you ready, Changer?"

"I am." He rises, turns to the King. "Keep my room."

✿❂✿

Sven Trout wishes that his interior calm matched the poised exterior he sees reflected in the windshield of his car. He permits himself a quick moistening of his dry lips, even while admitting to himself that he gets into these damned escapades mostly for the adrenaline rush.

Why else would he get caught up in things just about certain to get him killed? He's put himself on the line again, closer than ever before. In some ways, he's his own biggest victim.

Self-pity quiets his roiling guts just as a van he recognizes pulls into the space next to his car. Anson A. Kridd is at the wheel, his dark features unbrightened by his usually omnipresent smile. The Changer sits beside him and, when he gets out, pauses to open the sliding back door for Jonathan Wong.

Wong rises, bows formally, and presents Sven with several sheets of paper. "These are contracts my client requires you to sign over a truthstone, pursuant to your telephone agreement."

Sven glances over the pages, then folds them and stuffs

them into his pocket. "Louhi and I will need to review them."

"Of course. Do you wish us to wait here?"

"No, come along. You can wait outside our place."

He has his reasons. Louhi has warded the area immediate to the house against eavesdropping and intrusion. The enchantments won't hold up against a concerted attack, but they're better than nothing. The rented house is about a mile from the gas station. Sven tells the Changer and his escorts to wait outside and hurries in.

"They're here," he tells Louhi and the Head, suddenly breathless with excitement. "The Changer had Jonathan draw up our agreements."

Louhi snaps a sheet of paper from his hand, scans it while he does the same with the other sheet; then they trade.

"It seems a fair transcription of the phone conversation," Louhi says when she is finished. "Let's sign it. I want the Changer locked down for midnight tonight. I'm not certain how long certain protections I've set up will last."

"Right." Sven nods toward the door. "Come along and we'll get the swearing and exchange over with."

Jonathan Wong supplies a truthstone as well as a tidy little item that permits him to assure that it is not being jammed.

"I had it made back during the Opium Wars," he comments. "Very useful."

The contracts are read, witnessed, and signed, Jonathan retaining the Changer's copies. Then the Changer turns to Louhi.

"My daughter?"

For a moment, her expression becomes hopeful, as if she believes he has done other than ask for Shahrazad. Then it grows neutral, even stormy. Removing a garage-door opener from her pocket, she presses a button. One of the two garage doors opens and a streak of brown and gold races to the Changer's side.

He kneels beside her, muttering soothing noises and running his hands along her flanks and head, checking for injuries. He finds the bruising caused by the collar, but little else.

"Shahrazad," he says sternly, taking her puppy head in his hands and turning it so that she must look into his eyes.

She licks his nose.

"Shahrazad, go with Anson and Jonathan. I will come to you . . ." He glances at Louhi. "How long with this take?"

"You should be free by tomorrow at this time."

"Tomorrow," he tells the puppy. Then he picks her up and sets her in the back of the van. She droops, but makes no effort to jump out.

"There are certain items . . ." the Changer prompts.

Sven removes an embroidered suede bag from his breast pocket. "Here are all the items we promised you," he says, and the truthstone does not gainsay him.

"Then the first part of our business is concluded," the Changer says. "May my escort return for me? I do not fancy I will feel at all well when you are done."

Sven is completely the gracious host. "Of course, of course. We'll even have tea and cookies."

"I think we can skip that," Jonathan says mildly, "but we will return at this hour tomorrow evening."

"Until then," the Changer says, shaking each man by the hand and patting Shahrazad.

"Until then, you know it!" Anson promises.

Jonathan bows and then closes up the van.

Sven lets the Changer watch them drive safely out of sight. Then he smiles and gestures toward the house.

"Shall we go in?"

The Changer nods. Louhi opens a wooden gate and motions for him to precede her. He does so, sparing her no acknowledgment, knowing that any acknowledgment, false or true, would come far too late.

23

Non est, crede mihi, sapientis dicere "vivam."
Sera nimis vita est crastina; viva hodie.
*(It is not, believe me, the mark of a wise man
to say "I shall live." Living tomorrow is too
late; live today.)*

—MARTIAL

WATCHING FROM BEHIND HIS CURTAINED OFFICE WINDOW,
Arthur observes the return of the van. A few minutes later,
Eddie taps on his door.

"They got her back," he says, coming in and closing the
door behind him, "and she seems fine."

"And the Changer?"

"Stayed with them, just as he promised. Anson says they
can get him back tomorrow at about the same time."

"Yes. I expected he would stay." The King turns to face
his liege man. "And yet I hoped . . . that he would be less
honorable."

Eddie nods sadly. "Yes. We have no reason to trust the
word of Sven Trout."

"Did the Changer mention the promise he extracted from
me?"

"Not that I know. You'd need to ask Anson or Jonathan."

"It doesn't matter. I plan to keep it."

"I know."

372

There is a long silence during which Arthur paces back and forth across a handmade rug of Navajo design and Vera's weaving. Eddie limps to a chair and takes the weight off his leg.

"Eddie," Arthur says at last, "troubles are upon us, troubles akin to those that brought about the fall of Camelot."

Eddie does not say yea nor nay, but listens. Arthur begins ticking points off on his fingers.

"This matter with the Changer is but one. Even if he lives, we must decide whether what Sven and Louhi have done violates Harmony. The acts of the South Americans most definitely did, but their hostage-taking was done in an effort to manipulate all athanor. I'm less certain about this last."

"Nor I. Louhi has her long resentments against . . ."

"Lovern?"

"Yes, but I was going to say 'the Changer.' She believes herself his daughter and resents his lack of acknowledgment."

"I had forgotten," Arthur admits. "It is not as if there is a great estate to be contested."

"No."

"Another challenge we must face is how to present the deaths of Isidro Robelo and Oswaldo Barjak. Delicate and ticklish. Even those who are our supporters will frown at what could be seen as political assassination."

"Anson would swear otherwise."

"Who would believe the Spider," Arthur says, "even with a truthstone in his hand? Even now I wonder at the firmness of his support. What does he want?"

Eddie, long accustomed to Arthur's distrust of Anson, does not bother to defend his friend, but his shrug is eloquent. *Take the Spider as he is*, it says.

"Don't be angry with me, Eddie," Arthur pleads. "I can only speak honestly to you. I am made furious by my inability to act. The Changer deserves better from me than to act in my service and then be consigned to a sorceress's shambles."

"I know."

"Perhaps if I called Duppy Jonah . . ." Arthur muses. "He might act for his brother."

"Does his brother need acting for?"

"A strong force camped within sight of neutral ground has oft swayed the course of negotiations in the past."

"True. Make your call, then."

Arthur punches buttons and after several rings a human-seeming voice with an Irish accent answers. "Who would you be wishing to have speech with?"

"Duppy Jonah."

"And who may I say is calling?"

"Arthur Pendragon."

"One moment, sire."

Arthur cups his hand over the lower end of the receiver. "I'm on hold. Nice music. Waves on the beach. Whale song. We might want to try something similar here."

Eddie frowns. "Certain parties might chose to misinterpret it as a sop to powerful allies."

"Hm. True."

The music stops and Arthur raises a finger to Eddie.

"This is Duppy Jonah."

"Arthur Pendragon."

"We seem to speak more frequently these days, Arthur," the Sea King says gruffly. "What do you want of me?"

"To tell you that the Changer is in difficulty."

There is a rough sound, like a strangled exclamation. Then, "Does this trouble involve Louhi, perchance?"

"It does," Arthur admits, amazed.

"Then tell me no more. I . . . I have taken oath not to interfere in her business at this time."

"You have . . . Oh. Very well. I thought . . ."

"Although I consider informing me just and courteous, King Arthur, I should not know what I have been asked to overlook."

Arthur is familiar with the business of trading favors and the like not to guess something of what has restricted Duppy Jonah's actions. He tugs at his beard, trying to think of a way to enlist the Sea King's aid if the need arises.

"I appreciate your position, sir. If there is anything you would care to know . . ."

"No. I will call if I need information."

"Then if there is nothing I can add, let me at least ask after the well-being of my wizard."

"Lovern?" Duppy Jonah's tone becomes distrustful. "Is

this all some ploy to get me to release that scrawny-shanked troublemaker into your keeping? I swear to you . . .''

"No, Your Majesty, no, nothing of the kind," Arthur says swiftly, though he realizes that something of the sort *had* been lurking beneath his conscious mind.

"The wizard lives and breathes and is taking lessons in the wisdom of manipulating those who may one day be in the position of remembering and acting on those recollections.''

Arthur smiles grimly. "A lesson we all should recall, don't you think, Duppy Jonah? The Wheel of Fortune turns steadily and those on the top are the ones who have the farthest to fall.''

"An apt metaphor, King Arthur, one for all of us to remember," Duppy Jonah replies, undaunted. "Lovern has fallen to the depths of the sea. From here, he can only hope to rise.''

"Give him my greetings, if you would, good King.''

"I shall. And my thanks for the courtesy of your call.''

"My pleasure and my duty, sir.''

The connection ends, and Arthur shrugs, his sigh eloquent. "I expect that you followed all of that, Eddie.''

"Easily enough. I wonder what keeps Duppy Jonah from interfering against Louhi?''

"Some promise given, who knows how long ago or for what trifling service. He regrets it some now, will more so if the Changer comes to lasting harm.''

"I expect so. There is nothing we can do but wait.''

"I know. I'd better visit Shahrazad. I should grow more familiar with her. Carpets be damned! She'll sleep in my room.''

Eddie chuckles. "You might be wiser to sleep in the courtyard. She is but indifferently housebroken, and coyote urine reeks!''

"No matter," Arthur says. "The courtyard lacks a roof. I would have at least that between Shahrazad and having to answer again to the Changer for not keeping her safe.''

"Wise.''

Together they depart, flipping off lights as they go, both wondering about one whom they imagine to be in darkness.

¤◻¤

After watching the van drive away, the Changer follows his captors into the house.

"Since you're here of your own free choice," Sven says, his voice as cordial as if he is discussing the menu for dinner, "I don't see any reason for you to be imprisoned. Do you, Louhi?"

Louhi shakes her head stiffly. She has yet to look squarely at the Changer.

"We have another colleague with us," Sven continues. "I doubt that you have actually met. He's lived a life of rather enforced isolation."

The Changer refrains from guessing who this other is, although he has strong suspicions. Still, to voice them would be to play Sven's game, and that is something he wishes to avoid. Obediently, he follows Sven down the stairs into the living room and faces the Head hanging there by its lank grey hair.

"Hardly a comfortable seat," the Changer comments.

Before speaking, the Head sips from a straw that has been rigged so that it can drink without help. Despite its care, water trails down its chin, emphasizing the dryness of the skin.

"Wizard-wrought wight, basely born but baseless," Mimir's Head replies, " 'til remedies woven by witch and woe will bring forth a body to bear me."

"I understand," the Changer says, "and does Lovern know that you are gone?"

"Lovern," Louhi snaps, "is still captive to Duppy Jonah. Even if he knows—which I sincerely doubt—he is in no position to act."

Without asking permission, the Changer crosses to a beige sectional sofa and slouches among the cushions as if at his ease. He isn't, but nothing is gained by letting his captors know.

"A bit of luck for you, then," he says, "that the South Americans did what they did, or did you have a hand in that, too?"

"Regretfully," Sven says, taking a seat at the other end of the sofa, "I did not, except for encouraging them in their sense of righteous indignation. They were helpful, but we had contingencies planned to keep Lovern from interfering."

The Changer nods. Louhi still stands at the top of the stairs, looking down from the kitchen. He can almost hear the argument she is aching to begin.

How can you love a dog more than me? Why didn't you care for me as you did for her? Aren't I a daughter of whom to be proud?

His answers—that he does not believe she is his daughter, that even if she is, she is clearly capable of caring for herself, and that he does not find her particularly admirable—would not help matters, so he lets the argument rage: unspoken, unresolved, unresolvable. He only regrets that he will suffer from her unrequited desire for acknowledgment.

Since Louhi will not speak, and he does not care to, conversation cannot thrive. Sven's attempts at banter fail, as do the Changer's attempts to gather some knowledge of what their plans are beyond his impending mutilation. At last, Sven reaches for a remote control and they watch television reruns.

Half an hour before midnight, Louhi descends from her room. She wears a black-silk robe embroidered with arcane devices in silver thread. It caresses her slender body as she walks, hinting that the robe and her suede slippers are all she wears. In one hand, she holds a slim velvet band, also embroidered in silver, a hammered-silver crescent moon stitched onto its center.

"Sven," she says, her voice soft yet carrying, "I'm having trouble getting this on straight. Would you please tie it on?"

With notable alacrity, Sven springs to his feet and fastens the headband about Louhi's brow. Watching the redhead trying to slip his hand inside the sorceress's silk robe, the Changer decides that the two are not lovers. He also notes the expression of lust and envy that ripples across the Head's features and files that knowledge away for the future.

"Changer," Louhi says peremptorily, "come with me."

He follows her up a short flight of stairs, twin to those leading down from the kitchen but across the living room, and into what proves to be a palatial bathroom. The fixtures are dove grey and the tile vaguely art deco. The dominant feature is a large, deep bathtub, freestanding on its own pedestal against a backdrop of windows curtained from prying eyes by climbing roses.

Louhi has modified the room for her own purposes. Set at a right angle to the tub is a high platform, which he recognizes as a hospital gurney. It is oriented so that one end protrudes over the bathtub. A bracket, just the right shape to hold a human head, has been attached at this end. A basin has been placed within the tub beneath.

With a barely concealed shiver, the Changer realizes these tools' purpose. He swallows hard and waits to be told what to do, fighting back contradictory impulses to flee and to meekly place himself where he knows he will end up.

Louhi studies the arrangement. Then she places a few glass vials etched with arcane symbols on a broad part of the tub meant, doubtless, to hold such things as bath oil and soap. Finally, she shakes out over the gurney a cotton cloth beautifully embroidered with yet more symbols.

"Undress," she commands, "then lie down there with your head over the tub."

"Why does he need to strip?" Sven asks from where he lounges against the doorframe, trying unsuccessfully to hide his discomfort at the situation. Perhaps it reminds him overmuch of a time when he resided in like confinement. "Can't you get what you need just from his upper body?"

"I can and I cannot," Louhi says, and refuses to say more.

The Changer knows that arguing would be undignified and, ultimately, useless. Moreover, he does not share the frequent human psychological reaction that equates nudity with vulnerability.

He obeys Louhi's command and, once he is in place, begins the physical restructuring he has delayed until now lest some small action of his give it away.

Reaching inside himself, he numbs in both eyes and the nerves that carry sensation in their vicinity. Next, he stimulates his bone marrow to build replacement blood. This is more tricky, since the body normally does so only after a crisis, rather than in anticipation of one. He knows, vaguely, that some human athletes "blood dope" themselves before an event, but without knowledge of the details, he had not wished to attempt any such with so little time to prepare.

Louhi sets out various pieces of vaguely surgical equipment on a wooden TV table that has been covered with red velvet. She makes no move to sterilize them or to create a sterile environment. Doubtless, she trusts the Changer's own resilience to keep him from infection—or she simply may view the risk as his own to take.

With the portion of his attention he can spare from keeping his heart from racing, the Changer notices that Sven has retreated, closing the bathroom door behind him. Louhi also notices this, and her lip curls in scorn.

Glancing at a portable alarm clock set on the washbasin counter, she tightly straps down his arms and legs. Obscurely, the Changer feels grateful. He cannot disgrace himself by struggling overmuch.

Then she assumes a parade-rest pose and glances down at her victim. "You may wonder," she says philosophically, "why I don't knock you out either magically or chemically."

The Changer does not trust his voice to remain steady, so he keeps quiet and hopes she takes silence for stoicism.

Louhi smiles. "I could do so, if you must know, but my tests show that either type of anesthesia seems to retard the processes that I am working toward. It is as if the magic knows that sensation has been deadened and perpetuates that lack of sensation in the new host."

Dread emanates from the Changer's heart as he realizes in what direction this speech is heading.

"We are but a few minutes before midnight, at which time I would like to begin my work. The time, however, is only a matter of esthetics. I can work at a later hour. What that means to you, however, is a prolongation of suspense and pain."

She raises a hand in which she holds a pinch of something white. "This is fine-ground salt. To it, I have added some citric acid. I am going to sprinkle it in one of your eyes . . ."

The Changer winces despite himself.

"You understand my purpose." Louhi's tone is gently lilting, like a little girl explaining to a doll why it must be spanked, reveling in having power over someone. "If there is no reaction, I must convince you to alter your physical composition until the nerves react as they should. My methods of persuasion will not be verbal."

She raises her other hand, showing a scalpel. "And will make clear to Sven why your nudity was preferable."

Even as she speaks, the Changer has been shifting his nerves back to full sensitivity, never once doubting that the sorceress will do as she has indicated. A threat is not a threat when there is every intention of turning it into action.

When Louhi sets down the scalpel and holds open the lids of his right eye with her free hand, he has finished the reversal. The powder burns like a sandstorm on the shores on the Dead Sea. His tear ducts well to clear away the intrusion.

Louhi squirts saline solution to rinse the tormented orb. "Very good . . . or very wise. Do not alter the situation. I have little patience with those who toy with me."

The Changer would nod, but his head is held fast. "No doubt," he says gruffly. "Now, get on with it."

"The hour is just midnight," she says. "I believe I shall."

Singing in Finnish, her words a parody of an ancient love song, she raises a tool rather like a *demitasse* spoon, though the bowl is a bit less deep and the edges are sharpened.

The Changer does his best not to pay attention, yet he cannot help but flinch as it comes toward his right eye. Louhi impatiently pries his eyelids apart.

Trying desperately to disassociate himself from what is happening, the Changer is aware of pressure against the bone beneath his eye. The pressure intensifies; then he feels pain and heat as blood pours along his cheek.

He screams.

Louhi continues to sing.

Afterward, he hears Louhi talking to Sven. "I took all the blood from the catch basin and needed to drain about a half pint more to reach my quota. Neat work, eh?"

"Neat indeed," Sven replies in strangled tones.

The Changer, free now from Louhi's constraints, deadens the nerves around his right eye. He wonders if Sven's ardor for the sorceress is at all dampened and marvels at the resilience of his own odd sense of humor.

"Keep the Changer strapped down," Louhi orders, "and wheel him into one of the other rooms. Then bring me the Head. I wish to place the eye within the hour."

"Aye-aye, ma'am," Sven says.

He is still chuckling over his pun as he wheels the Changer from the bathroom.

Although the Changer longs for nothing so much as sleep to speed the healing that he has already set in motion, he forces himself to remain awake so that he can eavesdrop.

"Does the Eye-father live?" the Head asks Sven as the other brings him to Louhi. "Thunder loud, tempest terrible were his pained plaints."

"He's alive," Sven answers, "and I suspect you'll be screaming pretty loudly yourself in a couple of minutes."

"The babe, newborn, bellows at birth," the Head says, complacently, "so bellow I at body's birth."

"I'm glad you feel that way about it," Sven says. "I wouldn't. I've had enough of pain."

The Head's reply is muffled by the closing of the bathroom door. Several minutes later, the Changer hears Louhi begin to croon another spell song. Then the screaming begins. It sounds less like the squalling of an indignant newborn than the shrieking of a soul in torment.

¤◙¤

Tommy Thunderburst lounges loose-limbed in the midst of his drum kit, the sticks balanced rather than held in his long-fingered hands. His eyes are closed, his head lolling slightly so that his golden brown hair brushes to the middle of his bare back. To one who does not know him, he might seem asleep or utterly stoned, but he is far from either.

Touching the snare, he warms into a swirling, almost military tattoo, a sound that can make even a pacifist straighten with unconscious pride. That sound holds part of what he wants, but there must be more than pride. Pride alone is empty.

Leaning behind him, Tommy picks up a syrinx from the windowsill. He likes its haunting notes, its simple, limited scale. Almost every culture has its drums and flutes. The syrinx is a simple flute in a way—its sounds akin to the music every child learns to make by blowing across the neck of a bottle. There are more tones, of course, but the similarity is there.

Drums and flutes. Many types of each, not just the skirl of the snare, but the heartbeat thump of the tom-tom, the raindrop patter of fingers on a tight skin, the thunder of a timpani.

He'll avoid the shrillness of the fife, but the silvery notes of the *flute d'amour* would be nice, and perhaps the simple hooting of the ocarina.

What about strings or woodwinds?

He considers. Yes. There must be some of each. Violin played as a fiddle for joy and an oboe for secret sorrow. No keyboards, though. They wouldn't be quite right.

Each instrument will carry the melody at some point—even the percussion will do its part.

The theme of the composition will be the different elements of the self: emotions, life stages, loss, and gain. If he does it right, he should be able to touch every athanor, whether someone millennia-old like Arthur or alive merely a couple of lifetimes.

Joseph Campbell was onto something when he talked about the hero's journey in every person's life, but for the athanor that journey is made more difficult by its very extension. There is no quiet fading off into age, no basking in glory. No wonder so many of their most ambitious have chosen suicide, however disguised as heroic risk or self-sacrifice.

"Lil?"

Lil Prima, who has been lounging on the sofa, reading *Variety*, rolls to face him. In honor of the summer day, she wears a very short skirt in a multicolored cotton print and a coordinated sleeveless blouse.

"Yes?"

"I think I'm about ready to start recording the different instrumental tracks for this new piece."

"I'm glad. It's been taking a lot of your attention this past week."

"Oh," he says innocently, unaware that she means this as a criticism. "It's going to be taking a lot more. What I have in mind is orchestral in scope."

"Can't we just hire musicians to perform it?"

"No way! I've got to play all the parts. What I want you to do is sit in on the sessions and try that trick you've been working out for the new video."

"Why?"

"I want to make certain that more than just the music gets recorded. I want something of my own . . ." He stumbles under her critical gaze.

"Charisma?" she supplies, her tone acid.

"Yeah. That. This is an important piece. I don't want to just trust to the sound alone."

Lilith swings her long legs to the floor and studies him. "Your 'charisma' came across pretty well via audio recordings during our last venture."

"I know, but, please, Lil. For me?"

"This is the piece you're composing for Sven Trout, isn't it?"

"Well, yeah. He gave me the idea. What of it?"

"What's in it for me? Why should I use my powers for Sven, of all people?"

"You're not using it for him. You're using it for me. Darling."

He smiles a slow, sleepy, sexy smile and despite herself Lilith is stirred. Still, she is not instantly won over.

"I don't understand why this composition is so important. What I've heard is nice, but it's not precisely marketable."

Tommy looks affronted. "I've given you marketable stuff. I've made us both rich time and time again. Now I'm writing a song that I want to write."

"Don't tell me you're going John Lennon on me!"

"Lil, I'm never going to become a hermit and give up the crowd. I love them, too, babe. I just want to do this one piece. It's important."

"Important."

"Yeah." He pouts, his expression akin to a little boy threatening to hold his breath until he turns blue. "And until I get it recorded just right, I won't be able to do anything else . . . like that new album you've promised the record company."

"That's blackmail!"

"Turnabout, sugar, darling mine, love. Turnabout is the best type of fair play."

Lil gets up from the sofa, saunters across the room, threads her way through the drums, and drapes her arms about his neck. Looking deep into his eyes, her Cupid's bow lips only inches from his own, she nuzzles him.

"You drive a hard bargain."

"That's not the only thing that's hard . . ."

"And I've been wanting a chance to practice that ritual anyhow. I'm not certain I can do it fast enough . . ."

"Fast isn't what I have in mind . . ."

"To pull it off in a recording studio."

"So you'll do it?"

She glances down. Tommy has set aside the drumsticks, and is unbuttoning her blouse.

"What are you asking about?"

"Uh . . . the ritual."

"I'll do the ritual for you, Tommy."

"Later," he suggests, his breath coming fast. She can feel his heartbeat against her breast. "There's something I need first. Inspiration."

Lil lets him stand, then wraps her legs around his hips, her arms around his shoulders. "Those jeans are in the way of inspiration," she comments.

"That can be taken care of," he promises. "As soon as I get out of all these drums."

Amused, Lil lets him carry her, lay her against the carpet, consider the open curtains and damn them. In the midst of the frantic activities that follow, they seal her promise to help him record his composition. Somehow, though, they both forget Sven Trout's role in instigating the whole thing.

¤◙¤

Anson A. Kridd tries to hide his nervousness as he awaits the time when he can reasonably leave to collect the Changer. Still, by the time he paces into the kitchen for his third glass of iced tea in an hour, Vera must smile.

"Come and sit with me in the courtyard," she offers. "I'm taking a turn minding Shahrazad. Arthur has decided that she cannot be left alone."

Anson nods. "I took her for a run around the grounds this morning. Though I can have more legs than two, I was much pressed to keep up. She has energy and to spare, that one."

"I like her," Vera says in the tone of one who is still surprised to discover this. "I even like her father."

"The Changer," Anson says, walking with her into the courtyard, "is a difficult person to understand, but there is much to like about him."

The courtyard is warm and sunny. Shahrazad is happily basking in a sunbeam, her sides round from a recent heavy lunch. On the table, Vera has set up a small bead loom and arrayed a dozen shallow bowls, each holding a different-color bead.

"You've known him for a long time?" she asks, picking up a line of beads and working them into their places between the warp threads before fastening them with a stroke of her needle.

"Truer to say, I've known of him for a long time," Anson begins, then stops and corrects himself, "but I forget, you are of the younger ones."

"Hardly!"

"Sweet lady, I meant no offense." His tone is melodious, just barely teasing. "I thought a lady didn't like being reminded of her age."

Vera accepts the teasing with a smile and continues her weaving. "But I am not precisely young. I remember when the Greek city-states were being formed, and I saw Athens rise to glory and fall again."

"Long enough," Anson admits. "You knew the Changer when he was called Proteus, then?"

"Like you said, I knew of him. The myths capture well how he was one of the old ones even to those of us who called ourselves the Olympians."

"Yes. Not one to seek out athanor company, even then."

Vera nods, tilts her head, and examines her pattern. Not liking something, she rips out a line or two and sorts the beads back into their appropriate holders.

"What are you making?" Anson asks.

"I'm trying to evoke the Amazon river," she says, tilting the loom so that he can see the twisting blue bordered by green, splashed with brilliant colors. "It's more abstract than representational, and I'm not completely happy with it."

"Ah."

They sit in silence for a time, Vera weaving, Anson watching. When the Spider drains his glass and begins swirling the ice cubes about the bottom of the glass, Vera asks: "Are you worried about the Changer?"

"Impatient to know what has happened, maybe, and, yeah, maybe worried, too."

"Jonathan doesn't seem worried."

"I know. I tried to talk with him this morning before I took the pup for a run, and he smiled inscrutably, quoted himself, and walked off to his room with a law book."

Vera smiles. "Jonathan told me once that he didn't say half of the things attributed to Confucius, but, since everyone thought that he did, he memorized all the sayings."

"No!"

"Truth." She runs a line of blue and green, the latter interrupted with splotches of orange, then looks at Anson, her grey eyes serious. "I think that Jonathan's worried, too, but I'm not certain he's worried about the Changer."

"No? Maybe not. And what are you worried about, Vera?"

"Does it show so clearly?"

"You've been tearing out almost as much as you weave, dear lady, not exactly what I've learned to expect from you."

"Ah." She considers, rips out a line, puts it back in again after replacing some of the light blue with a darker shade. "I am worried. I'm worried about the Changer—I'm more worried that Sven Trout has chosen to make war on him."

"Sven. Yes."

"Sven is not one to forget that fire burns," Vera says. "Any hold he has over the Changer is flimsy at best. What does he believe will stand between him and the Changer's vengeance?"

Anson crunches a bit of ice. "An ally in Louhi."

"Not enough. There are other sorcerers, even with Lovern imprisoned, who could neutralize her. There must be more."

"When we rescued Shahrazad," Anson offers, "we were given a token made from her blood, spittle, and hair that would have enabled Louhi to slay her even at a great distance and to control her from a lesser one. They are taking the Changer's blood. Perhaps they believe they can bind him in some similar way."

"That's a thought," Vera admits, "but I doubt we have the full picture."

She stares at her beadwork as if tempted to tear out more, then stops and adds another couple of rows. "I feel a desperate need to know more."

"Perhaps the Changer will tell us," Anson says.

"But will he share what he knows with us?" Vera says. "I admire him greatly. I'll even admit to finding him almost painfully attractive, but I don't trust him to realize that his needs and the needs of the larger group are the same."

"And do you think they are?"

"I don't know," Vera admits. "Arthur has been badly shaken by the South American contingent's rebellion. He hates when he must declare someone outside the Accord, and he nearly had to ask for them to be declared outside of Harmony as well."

"True."

Vera beads. Anson rattles his ice. Shahrazad whimpers, her toes twitching as she chases something in her dreams.

Or perhaps it is she who is chased.

✡▣✡

The Changer awakens as the sun is westering. He lies on the bed in the house in Bernallio. Listening, he knows that he is alone in the house.

Painfully, he sits upright. His entire head aches; his lips are parched. The area where his right eyelid hangs limp over an empty socket throbs to the beating of his heart.

Taking inventory of his resources, he realizes that he is too weak for even a minor shapeshift. Louhi may have taken only her quart of blood, but he has lost more over the night. It soaks the bandage wrapped loosely around the side of his face, crusts along his temple and mats his hair.

His attempt to replenish the anticipated loss may have made matters worse by raising his blood production beyond the level his system could sustain with an open wound. Absently, he wonders if Louhi was careless or if the injury was deliberate. Given his capacity to heal, he is willing to believe the latter.

Standing, he totters to the bathroom and re-dresses his eye socket with a folded washcloth tied on with strips torn from a towel he curses for its fluffy bulk.

His suspicion that he was meant to bleed, if not to death, at least to incapacity, is confirmed when he finds the refrigerator stripped of every last item of food. Even the bottles of condiments are gone. The freezer is also bare, but in the back of an otherwise empty cabinet he finds a partial box of stale dog biscuits. These he softens in water and devours. He has eaten far worse.

Unable to hunt, unable to shift into anything that could metabolize grass and weeds, he must wait until Anson and Jonathan return for him. The hours pass with glacial slowness. The phone is disconnected, so he cannot call for help. The drone of the television only makes his head hurt more.

At last, he curls into a ball on the sofa, his head on the remnants of the shredded towel. He realizes the extent of his weakness only when he is awakened by the front door opening. Had it been an enemy, he would have been dead.

But it not an enemy. It is Anson, followed by Jonathan Wong. Etiquette forbids comment on his state, but he can tell they are shocked to find him so pale, bloody, and weak.

Reasonably, they should expect his condition, but reason does not govern emotions, and he is one of the ancients, the great shapeshifter who normally mends his wounds with a casual shrug. Even athanor are subject to their private legends.

"Can you walk, Changer?" Anson asks.

"After a fashion," he says in a rough, dry voice that testifies to his dehydration, "but I would prefer to lean."

"Then lean on me," Anson says, handing him a glass of water.

"First, do you have anything to eat?"

Anson pats his pockets and produces a candy bar, a partial roll of hard candies, and a stick of gum. The Changer all but grabs them and wolfs them down.

"Didn't anyone ever tell you not to swallow your chewing gum, Changer?" Jonathan Wong comments with a hint of a smile. "Let Anson get you to the van. I'm going to make certain no trace of you is left behind. From what I can tell,

you bled pretty freely. We don't want the homeowners calling the police when they get back.''

''Thanks.''

As the Changer hauls himself up on Anson's bony shoulder, he sees Jonathan pulling on a pair of disposable surgical
gloves.

''First piece of evidence,'' the lawyer says, plucking the
torn and blood-splotched towel from the sofa. ''I wonder if
there are trash bags in the kitchen.''

''There are,'' the Changer says. ''I couldn't eat them.''

''Still a sense of humor, old one? Good,'' Anson says.
''Now put your weight on me, and we'll go out slowly. I
have a box of donuts in the van and maybe a thermos of
coffee.''

The Changer considers asking him to fetch them to him,
but an animal nervousness advises him to flee this place of
pain—a place to which his enemies could too easily return.

When Jonathan finishes, the Changer is sprawled in the
back of the van, finishing off the doughnuts with a voracious-
ness that Anson watches in admiration.

The portly Asian tosses a full trash bag into the back of
the van before getting into the front passenger seat. ''I had
to take the bed linens. They were ruined. The mattress should
be salvageable. Mostly, he bled into a pillow—which I also
removed.''

The Changer swallows coffee. ''Thank you.''

''A pleasure. It is easier to prevent an investigation than
to derail one once it begins.''

''Confucius say,'' Anson chuckles.

''Not in so many words, but yes,'' Jonathan agrees. ''I'm
going to advise Arthur that someone should come back and
treat the sofa cushions and mattress to remove the stains.''

The Changer studies him. ''I will owe you.''

Jonathan bows slightly. ''I do not insist.''

They depart then, and, after a short stop at a fast-food place
where Anson places an order that astonishes even the bored
teenage clerk, they drive back to Arthur's hacienda. The
Changer cannot possibly devour everything Anson has provided, but he makes enough progress that he can patch the
bleeding wound.

''It was made with an enchanted tool,'' he comments as

he feels his body resisting the prompt to shift and close. "I cannot heal it completely—at least not quickly."

"Dr. Kocchui . . ." Jonathan suggests.

"No. I don't wish anyone else to know how weak I am. Louhi will wonder whether her enchantment had power over me. She may even have spies watching our best healers. Leave her wondering."

Anson nods somberly. "He has a point."

When they arrive at the hacienda, Arthur, Eddie, and Vera come to meet them. Shahrazad wriggles from Eddie's hold and leaps into her father's lap as soon as the back of the van is opened, her tongue trying to bathe his wound in puppy kisses.

"Easy," the Changer says, but his tone is fond, not angry.

He holds her with what firmness he can manage, and she, sensing his weakness, obeys, content to flop on his lap and be fed cold french fries.

"You look terrible," Eddie says bluntly.

"I don't feel very well," the Changer agrees, "but let me sleep and eat, then I will tell you what I have learned."

Arthur nods. Anson briefed him via the car phone, so he already knows that Sven and Louhi have vanished once more.

"There will be time enough," he says.

"I sincerely hope so," the Changer responds. "I most sincerely hope so."

His smile is not a pleasant thing.

24

Dime con quien andas, decirte he quien
eres.
(Tell me who your friends are and I'll
tell you what you are.)

—CERVANTES

THE CHANGER SLEEPS THE CLOCK ROUND AND INTO THE
next day, waking only to eat with animal concentration and
then to sleep again. No one, not even Arthur, dares to question him during his infrequent waking spells. There is something cold, and, if they had the courage to admit it, something
desperate, in his single yellow eye.

Shahrazad keeps vigil over her father, leaving only for
twice-daily runs—the morning one with Anson, the afternoon
with Arthur. Thus, she is the first to note when he awakens
more in possession of himself. She does not think to notify
anyone, so the Changer has time to stretch, compose himself,
and inventory his injuries.

He is not pleased with what he confirms. Normally, as long
as he has the energy, he is able to shift his shape into one
that is uninjured. Whatever Louhi has done to his eye socket
is preventing this. He can shift shape, but the shape always
lacks an eye. If he is not cautious, the socket begins to bleed.

Growling, he devours the food left out for him and goes
to sleep, this time as a coyote, delighting Shahrazad to no
end. She curls next to him, half-guarding, half-cuddling.

Vera, making a routine check, finds them thus, nods politely to Shahrazad, and does not disturb the Changer further. She suspects that he has heard her entry, but as he chooses not to acknowledge her, she does not press her company.

Two hours later, he emerges from his room, human-form, freshly showered, and clad in jeans and a tee shirt. Shahrazad prances at his side, pleased and protective. They walk together into the kitchen and he systematically raids the refrigerator. While he is building a sandwich that seems to defy the capacities of a human mouth, Vera comes in.

"I thought I heard you moving. How do you feel?"

He angles his head to look at her from his one eye as if that is answer enough. Then he recalls that she has been kind to him: "Weak. Impaired. Angry."

"Reasonable," Vera says, studying the sandwich with a clinical gaze. "Want me to get Shahrazad some of her kibbles?"

"If you would. She'd prefer my sandwich, but I want her eating as well as she can."

"Oh?" Vera considers what this might mean as she fills a dish for Shahrazad.

The coyote pup falls to as if this is a duty rather than a pleasure, but doesn't refuse the food. The Changer eats with something of frustration in his steady chewing.

"Will you sleep again when you finish?" Vera asks.

"I don't think so. Is Arthur available?"

"He has asked to be interrupted whenever you would see him."

"Then tell him that I will be in the courtyard."

"Only Arthur?"

"No. Whoever is here. I may as well tell my story only once."

Vera nods, her hand straying as if to pat him reassuringly. Remembering who he is, she aborts the motion and pats Shahrazad instead. Leaving the room without another look at the Changer, she misses seeing the small smile that lights his face.

They gather quickly: Eddie with his computer to take notes, Jonathan Wong looking sleepy and fooling no one, Anson making himself popular with Shahrazad by dropping her pieces of his doughnut, Arthur leaning forward in his chair, elbows on his knees, and Vera, thoughtful and alert.

Her gaze strays to a bird perched on the courtyard roof. Disconcerted, it decides to move on. Chewing on the edge of her thumbnail, Vera resolves to get Lovern's wards reactivated.

"I want," the Changer says, his voice deep and gravelly, "to thank each of you for your assistance these past days. I am not accustomed to depending on the mercy of others. It was pleasant to discover it exists—even for me."

"You are in Harmony," Arthur says. "That counts for something."

"So I have seen." The Changer rubs beneath his empty eye socket. "You have waited patiently for my story. I have little enough to tell, but what I must tell has implications enough."

Eddie's fingers stop racing over the keys of his computer. "Before you go on, Changer, tell me how you feel."

"I hurt," the ancient answers bluntly, "more than I can recall since the days when we stopped warring on each other. Louhi was meticulous in taking only what she bartered for . . ."

Jonathan Wong smiles ironically. "No chance of using Portia's gambit from *The Merchant of Venice* against her?"

"I'm afraid not," the Changer says. "She took her quart of blood and the eye only, but she enchanted her surgical tool to leave a wound that will not heal—even with my considerable skill at such things. I cannot easily regrow the eye and, if I do not take care, I begin to bleed again."

Anson hisses angrily between his teeth. "You may not, old one, but I call that a violation of the trust."

"I forgot to forbid such," the Changer says ruefully, "for it did not occur to me."

"A jury of your peers would be hung on this one," Jonathan says.

"The Changer has few peers," Anson answers curtly, "even among us."

"Let's not quibble," Arthur says steadily. "The issue may never come to court if I read the Changer correctly."

"Your Majesty"—the Changer bows without rising—"you may try them if you wish. I plan to treat those who did this to me in a fashion that will remind all why me and mine are not toys.''

"But did you discover why Louhi wanted your eye?" Vera prompts.

"I did," the Changer says. "When I went inside the house, I discovered that they had another with them."

"What?" Arthur says. "Athanor?"

"In a sense," the Changer answers. "In a sense. Jonathan, you and Vera are too young to recall the time we name Ragnarokk, but these others remember."

"Remember and were there," Arthur says. "It was in the early days of human civilization."

"I fought at Ragnarokk," Anson comments, "but my sympathies were torn, shapeshifter that I am. Still, in the end, I believed that humanity should not be slaves."

The Changer nods. "I, too, was torn, but like you I sided with those who would tolerate rising humanity as equals, not dominate them as vassals. In those days, Lovern was among us, too, though he called himself Mimir."

"Yes," Arthur adds. "Already he was counselor to monarchs and recognized as a wizard."

Vera clears her throat as a means of getting attention. "One thing I've always wondered. Why do our people speak of that battle using the names given in Norse legends? Other cultures, even my natal Greek, tell tales of the battles of the gods."

"There was an athanor skald," Arthur explains, "who told the tale among the Norse. It fit their dark and desperate view of the universe. He used our own names—altering them slightly to fit the language in which he composed. Since his version was closest to what had happened, we borrowed his nomenclature."

"Ah," Vera says. "That explains it."

The Changer continues. "The king—though he would have called himself a god—that Mimir served in those days is remembered by the name of Odin. He was mostly just, but eager for knowledge and for power."

"He traded an eye," Vera recalls aloud, "for wisdom."

"He traded an eye," the Changer says, his voice becoming more gravelly than usual, "but not for wisdom. He traded it for Mimir's service. From it Mimir crafted a magical tool that he promised would give them great power, power that would assure that Odin's battle would be won.

"Mimir kept his promise," the Changer continues after a sip of fruit juice, "though ultimately the loss of that eye cost Odin his life. Using Odin's eye and, I suspect, his own blood, Mimir grew himself a second head."

Eddie stirs. "I recall that his cowl was deformed, but I could not tell why. Nor was I bold enough to ask what was the reason. There were rumors thereafter . . ."

"I heard," Anson says, "that he later removed the head and used it as some wizards use a crystal ball."

"That is so," the Changer confirms.

As the Changer has revealed these old secrets, secrets that do not cast a kind light on his wizard, Arthur has grown somber.

"Changer, you know that Lovern still has that Head. It was the prize he regained from Duppy Jonah's realm."

"Lovern *had* it," the Changer sighs. "Lovern—Merlin—Mimir has kept the Head through many lives, many roles. Until we brought it forth, he visited it only astrally. However, when he grew afraid for his life he feared to make the astral journey. Unwilling to do without his valued tool, he brought it from the sea and stored it in his chambers here. The Head is here no more."

"This Head," Anson guesses, "is the other you mentioned."

"Yes. I believe that my blood and my eye are to be used to enhance the Head. From its cryptic words, I believe they will make it a body."

Vera clears her throat. "Maybe Louhi means to make herself a match for Lovern's tool. Their rivalry is millennia-old."

"I do not think she would," the Changer says. "Even if she knows the means, she knows now what Lovern has willfully ignored. The Head is not a tool—it is a person in its own right, a talented, powerful person. I believe that it hates its master and has willingly misled him for who knows how many centuries."

"Lovern must have known what it was!" Arthur protests. "How could he not?"

"If the Head did not give him sign," the Changer says,

"or if Lovern chose to ignore those signs, then such ignorance would be simple to cultivate. Many athanor have nursed the one who would betray them. We are no different than humanity in this."

Jonathan Wong clears his throat. "Do you have any idea how much power the Head might possess?"

"I do not," the Changer says. "Does any here know what Lovern most used it for?"

Arthur frowns. "Predicting possible futures, designing spells and enchantments, and storing bits of lore."

"In that case," Vera says somberly, "it could be as powerful as Lovern himself."

"Potentially so," Jonathan agrees, "though it may not know how to employ its vast knowledge. Magic is more than knowledge. It is the skill to perform the rotes that manipulate the power."

"But Louhi will know how to perform those rotes," Eddie says. "Lovern has long admitted that she is nearly as powerful as he is and, in some ways, more skillful."

The Changer nods. "Lovern has had the Head as a crutch—or at least an assistant. It may have made him lazy. Louhi has had nothing of the kind."

Arthur rises and begins pacing. "So we are faced with Sven Trout—as great a mischief maker as has ever lived—Louhi Maki—a potent sorceress and one with no great love for this House—and this Head. Changer, did you get any indication of what they desire?"

"No."

"Will you hazard a guess?"

"Rather, let me offer a question in return." The Changer's tone makes quite clear that he is not merely playing games. "What might they want—what might they believe that they could gain—that would make the enmity of both myself and Lovern a fit price? What could they hope to achieve that would be worth the cost of being declared out of Harmony? The South American contingent did not really believe they would be so declared. Isidro Robelo was an idealist. These three are not."

Arthur shakes his head. "I know not. They are endangered already—if not by your actions, by Lovern's. Even if they faced the lesser penalty of being declared out of Accord, they could not call upon our protection. Many of our more warlike people will welcome the challenge of hunting them down.''

"I don't know either," Jonathan admits, "but I have suspicions."

"What?"

"Let me brood a while," Jonathan says. "This is not a time to jump to conclusions."

Arthur looks as if he, too, has suspicions, but that he would prefer not to dwell on them. The others wait in silence for the Changer to go on.

"I have nothing more to add," he admits. "Suspicions of intent do not interest me. My goals are to heal, then to neutralize this threat to me and my child. That is all."

"You will not consult a physician?" Eddie pleads.

"Not at least for now," the Changer says stubbornly. "Were I my enemy, I would have spies reporting on Aesculapius and the best of the others. The lesser ones cannot help in a matter that is medical and magical at once. As I said before, I do not wish to confirm that I am sorely hurt."

No one gainsays him, and he continues. "Shahrazad and I will return to the wilds. There, I can keep her safe, and in solitude I can concentrate on healing. Wild things often go to earth and rise from injuries that would kill a human."

"Then?" Arthur says.

"Then I will contact you and trade information."

"You will not be in contact for the nonce?"

"No. They drew me out once before by your summons. I will not permit that to happen again."

"Ah." Arthur muses silently that the Changer's egocentric view of events is annoying but predictable. "Then you have made your plans."

"I have."

"When will you leave?"

"If your hospitality extends for another three days, I will leave on the fourth."

"It does, and it will continue to do so even if you change your mind."

"I will not."

"I have not forgotten what you did for Vera and Amphitrite."

"I did what I did for my reasons, Arthur."

"Still, I am grateful."

"If that gratitude will keep me sheltered and fed for three more days, then I, too, am grateful."

Arthur shakes his head. Perhaps if one has no set form, arrogance can be a form of its own. He wonders if it is one he would choose, wonders with unusual honesty, if it is not one he has already chosen.

❁❖❁

The Changer makes arguing with him over the course of his recuperation impossible by the simple expedient of staying a coyote. He is a singularly polite coyote, to be sure, refraining from peeing in inappropriate places or tearing up the furniture, but beyond thumping his tail in agreement when offered food and barking when he needs to be let out, he does not communicate.

Resigning himself to the fact that the ancient cannot be swayed, Arthur ignores the shapeshifter with equal courtesy. He and Eddie begin searching for Louhi, Sven, and the Head, though they don't feel a great deal of hope. Locating even a human who does not wish to be found is difficult. Finding a sorceress and a shapeshifting trickster who do not wish to be found is pretty much impossible.

Still, they must try. Jonathan Wong departs on the second day to tend to his neglected law practice, promising to continue the search from the East Coast. Anson agrees to stay a bit longer, but, he notes, he has been in Albuquerque over a month and eventually even his casual business dealings need his personal attention.

On the fourth day, the Changer walks up to Arthur and barks sharply. To all appearances, his is fully recovered from his injury. His fur is glossy and his flanks have lost their slatsided look. Only the thin black line where his eye should be testifies to what was done.

When the King looks down, the Changer barks again, pointing with his sharp nose in the general direction of the garage.

"I believe," Eddie says, amused, "that he is reminding us that he is leaving today and requesting a ride."

The Changer barks again, wagging his brush just enough to acknowledge that Eddie's interpretation is correct.

"Well, we can't have him and Shahrazad running through the city in broad daylight—or even after dark." Arthur sighs. "I'll drive them out myself."

The Changer takes his leave with a wag of his tail, angling his head to favor his remaining eye as he looks at each one. Shahrazad does not seem aware of any greater significance to the parting than that she is going for a ride in the van— something she has come to regard as a great treat.

Vera and Anson come to the hacienda's main foyer to see them off. The Changer seems to smile, but then coyotes often seem to smile—something that has led to their bad reputations.

Once on the highway, Arthur soliloquizes, "Changer, I've been wondering what you think of me. You've never sworn yourself to me as a member of my court, yet you have been supportive. You have more power and—in a way—more influence than many others, but you have shown no desire to use it. And I've been thinking about the question you asked.

"Loki—to be impolite and use a name with some bad associations—has chosen to use some dangerous tools in this most recent gambit. Yet, he has nullified you, if we accept as given that he prompted Louhi to damage you and is behind Duppy Jonah's refusal to free Lovern.

"Perhaps I give him too much credit. Perhaps Louhi is the dangerous one. I don't know. I wish that I did. Maybe the Head is the one to fear. I wish I could ask Lovern about it. I almost dread asking him, too. I'd never realized that the thing might have a mind of its own—no pun intended. Working with it as closely as he did, could Lovern have failed to know?"

If the King expects an answer, some burst of ancient wisdom, he is disappointed. However, perhaps he does not. Arthur, too, is ancient. Perhaps he is just thinking aloud.

When they reach the same general vicinity in the Sandias as once before, the Changer barks. Arthur finds a wide shoulder and pulls off the road. Then he slides open the van's back door.

The two coyotes, one young enough still to be a puppy— though a growing puppy—one a grizzled male with a blind eye, jump out. The young one doesn't pause, but vanishes into the brush. The elder gives Arthur an eloquent glance from his single yellow eye and follows his daughter into the darkness.

✿◉✿

To the east of those very mountains in which the Changer takes refuge with his daughter, the Head grows a body. Each day small but perceptible changes occur. Tendrils of flesh grow from the base of his neck and, as these grow longer, the internal network of bone, vein, artery, nerve, and other such things takes shape. Even as these form, more skin grows to cloak shoulders, chest, abdomen, and such.

His skin loses the unwholesome translucence of a thing that has never seen the sun. When, after over a week, his heart begins to form, he takes on something like healthy coloring. His skin is not so prone to chapping, which is a great comfort.

Long accustomed to isolation and immobility, the Head observes these changes, remaining stoic even when new-grown bone aches or when a partially formed organ belches into function. It has no one but Louhi and sometimes Sven to talk with, but in this place, at least it can watch cable television, a pleasure that it had not experienced in his dark prison beneath the ocean.

Still, Louhi might be uncomfortable if she knew how often a gaze that she believes is occupied with watching a movie or news program is actually devoted to watching her. Proximity to the woman has only increased the Head's lust. At first the feeling had been intellectual, but as his body grows, it takes on a distinctly physical component.

Hormones needed for growth and the triggering of dormant programming contained in the DNA of his cells surge through his nascent circulatory system. As he develops glands, organs, bones, and tissue, he becomes more appreciative of the way Louhi wears her own flesh.

Desire enflames him. For the first time in his cold existence, it affects his ability to plan, to calculate. He wonders if Louhi will desire him. He believes his new body will bear a strong resemblance to Lovern, who had been her lover and teacher. Does she hate Lovern enough to despise his likeness?

The thought panics him for several days. Then he calms. He will never be the shapeshifter the Changer is—most of the potential contained in the blood Louhi injects into the artery at the base of his throat is used to stimulate his cells to shape the new body. Still, some small virtue may remain. If none does, he will learn shapeshifting magics like those Lovern works. It will take time, but what matters time to an athanor?

He grins a broad, cruel grin that Louhi takes to be a response to the television program. She might fear if she could see his fantasies, if she knew what channels he watches when she is not in the house. She should fear, for his desire holds nothing of mature love, but only the wild possessiveness of a small child. This child will have the body of a grown man, and power to threaten the greatest wizard among them.

But Louhi doesn't know to fear. She goes on mixing her potions, singing her spell songs.

And the Head grows a body.

❁▣❁

Two days after the Changer and Shahrazad have departed into the wilds, Vera taps on the door to Arthur's office.

"Come." He rises when she enters. "Vera. Any news?"

"None." She pauses, her grey eyes tranquil. "Nor do I believe there will be. Arthur, Sven has much skill in hiding. Louhi is a recluse by temperament. Ours is a futile quest."

"Like the one for the Holy Grail, eh?"

Vera shakes her head. "Don't tease, Arthur. I have an invitation to visit Amphitrite."

"And?"

"And I have a mind to take it. Duppy Jonah has commanded Lovern to create a spell to enable me to live beneath the waves."

Arthur looks hurt. "That should be easy enough for him. Such magics have been worked before."

"Arthur," Vera crosses to him, astonishes him by enfolding one of his hands in her own. "I am not abandoning you—not at this time of all times. But I am too old to hope idly."

"I am older," Arthur reminds her ruefully. "Are you saying I am a fool?"

"No. A warrior who doesn't know when he is beaten, perhaps, but never a fool." She sits, and, after a moment, Arthur follows suit. "If I go beneath the sea, I may be able to convince Duppy Jonah to release Lovern."

"Do you think you can?"

"I don't know, but I do know that we will never convince the Sea King over the phone. He can hang up too easily. The Changer is not here to assist us . . ."

"I wish he was."

"If wishes were horses, my liege . . . Let me go to the Sea King's home as Amphitrite's friend. I will listen, learn, plot, and plan. She may even help me if she can do so without taking a public stance against her beloved's policy."

Arthur's face brightens. "Yes, that's true. She can't disagree with something he is doing to avenge her—at least not publicly. But if you confided in her . . ."

Vera nods. "I shall. I shall tell her about the stolen Head, about its implications. She will be furious about the injury done to the Changer. Not only is he her husband's brother, but he did us a kindness out there in the rain forest."

"Yes!" Arthur says, now as eager for Vera to depart as he had been reluctant moments before. "Go and see what good you can work, lady. When can you leave?"

"I have a reservation on a flight this evening," she says, catching a glimpse of irritation in the King's face that she had not waited for his permission to make plans. "I can be with Amphitrite tomorrow."

Arthur nobly banishes his pique, acknowledging that it is unjust. "I'll drive you to the airport. Do call regularly!"

"Daily," she promises. "If not more frequently."

"Very well, then." Arthur shakes his head. "The hacienda is going to be quiet. Everyone except Eddie is leaving."

Vera grins. "And just a few weeks ago you were griping about how the Review was interrupting your privacy."

Arthur laughs. "Go pack. And godspeed, Vera."

"Thanks."

Unbelievably, after the pressures of the previous month or so, the next weeks pass fairly peacefully. July melts into early August, August into later August. Yet Arthur feels little peace. Nothing has been heard from the Changer. No one has located Sven Trout or Louhi Maki.

Vera has not succeeded in convincing Duppy Jonah to release Lovern. She reports that she is hopeful. Arthur, hearing a certain relaxation in her voice, noting that her phone reports are becoming less frequent and less detailed, wonders if she is enjoying her vacation too much.

He worries, spends excess energy working out with Eddie (who is taking physical therapy quite seriously) until his torso regains some of its former firmness. They are discussing the possibility of taking up fencing again when the telephone in Arthur's office rings.

"Arthur," says a deep voice, "this is Bronson Trapper."

"Bronson! Good to hear from you. Everything going well with the new equipment you ordered last year?"

"Well enough. No problems we can't deal with here." Bronson pauses. Arthur has the impression the sasquatch is searching for words. "Arthur . . ."

There is another pause.

"Yes?" Arthur prompts gently.

"Are you planning on being in Albuquerque in September?"

"I have no plans to be elsewhere. Do you need me to visit?"

Bronson clears his throat, a sound rather like a bear coughing. "Actually, we're planning on coming to visit you."

"Me? Here?" Arthur's eyebrows rise. "In Albuquerque?"

Reaching down, he switches his phone to intercom so that Eddie can listen in on the call.

"That's right. I thought you knew we were coming, then something Rebecca said made me realize that you still didn't. I had made her promise that someone would tell you to expect us."

Arthur has the feeling that Bronson assumes that his

speech has clarified matters instead of muddling them further. "Bronson, should I have the impression that when you say 'we' you are speaking of a group larger than yourself and Rebecca?"

"Why, that's right."

"Uh, how many are in this group?"

"I don't know exactly," Bronson admits. He sounds embarrassed. "The Moderator is handling the arrangements. Rebecca talks with a small group via a private chatroom—not everyone is on the Internet, you know . . ."

"Yes, I do."

"But from what she has gathered, I think there will be several dozen."

"Several dozen sasquatches?" Arthur manages not to sound horrified by dint of great effort.

"Well, no . . ."

Arthur relaxes slightly until Bronson continues:

"There are going to be some fauns and satyrs as well. My cousin Snowbird is bringing his family from Alaska. I think some *kappa* are coming in, along with a group of *tengu*. The *tengu* may be there already. I'm not quite clear on that point."

"Oh."

"And there may be a *pooka* or two," Bronson hastens to add. "I'm not certain about the details. I do know that the trolls couldn't be convinced. They were worried about the intensity of the sunlight out there."

"Oh." Arthur swallows hard. "Is that all?"

"I'm really not certain. Apparently the Moderator has had the most luck recruiting from first-world countries where there is a developed computer network."

"I can understand that. Even I have trouble reaching those athanor who reside elsewhere without magic." Arthur is pleased with his matter-of-fact tone. He decides to essay a more awkward issue. "May I ask why you are coming?"

Bronson says, "Well, Rebecca really wanted to go. When I realized that she'd be brokenhearted if I forbad her—never a good idea in any case if you want a healthy marriage—I decided to accompany her."

"No, no . . . I mean, that's very interesting and very responsible of you, Bronson. What I was wondering is why is this convocation coming to call on me?"

"Oh," Bronson can be heard swallowing hard. "Well, most of them aren't very happy with how you've been administering the theriomorphs, most particularly those of us who aren't of animal nature. Isolation works fine for a rabbit or bird . . ."

Arthur recalls the Changer, raven-form croaking, "Nevermore."

"Yes."

"But many of the others feel as Rebecca does, that we must make ourselves known to the world at large."

"Oh, bloody hell," Arthur moans softly. "That again!"

"That again," Bronson says apologetically. "I'm happy with the current situation, but the younger ones are more ambitious."

"So, when can I expect you?"

Bronson sounds relieved to leave the philosophical issues alone. "The Moderator is sending in a small plane to pick us up. I believe one of the *tengu* is piloting. We're arriving at an airstrip in Albuquerque."

"Not Albuquerque International!"

"No, I have the impression it's a smaller place, maybe a private landing field."

Arthur exchanges worried glances with Eddie. Even at a small strip there will be humans who may see more than is wise.

"And will you be availing yourself of the facilities of my hacienda?" he says hopefully. "Your dues do go toward its upkeep against such need."

"I think the Moderator has arranged for all of us to stay at a hotel," Bronson says, the note of apology back in his voice. "That's part of the issue, you see. Being permitted out in public."

"Oh, quite right. If you change your mind . . ."

"I'll mention it to Rebecca, but I think she has her heart set on visiting with some of her Net friends in the flesh."

"She could do that here," Arthur reminds him.

"Only if all of them were convinced to stay at your hacienda," Bronson explains.

"Right." Arthur swallows another sigh. "I say, Bronson, who is this Moderator you've mentioned?"

"I don't really know," Bronson admits. "Rebecca just calls him the Moderator. He set up the chatroom and now has arranged for this trip. My guess is that he is a shape-shifter, since he doesn't seem worried about his mixing with the humans. Maybe he's a *tengu*. They seem pretty active in this."

"But you have no idea who he is?"

"None at all. I don't even know if it's a male. I've just gathered that. I can't say I haven't wondered, but, honestly, I don't think Rebecca's fervor for the issues would change if she learned it was Satan himself."

Satan, Arthur thinks, *doesn't exist, but I know someone as mischievous who does. I wonder if this is how Sven's been spending his spare time since his meeting with the Changer?*

Eddie holds up a note that reads: " 'Get the website address for this chatroom.' "

"Do you have the address for the chatroom?" Arthur asks casually. "I might as well send along an invitation myself for folks to stay here."

"Sorry, that's Rebecca's bailiwick. I don't care for computers myself. My hands don't keyboard comfortably."

"Ah. Could you ask her?"

Bronson sounds uncomfortable. "I'll try. She's out now."

"How sweet," Arthur says dryly. "Well, if you get an opportunity . . ."

"Yes. I'll send it on."

"I hear Rebecca coming in," Bronson says, his voice suddenly soft. "She only went out to the henhouses. I'd better go."

"Thanks for calling, then," Arthur says.

"And I'll get that order to you directly," Bronson says, his tone firm and businesslike. "Thank you for calling."

"Good-bye," Arthur says, fully aware of the implication of his own words. "I'll be seeing you."

25

Das Ewig-Weibliche/ zieht uns hinan.
(The eternal feminine/ draws us up and on.)

—GOETHE

BY THE FIRST WEEK OF SEPTEMBER, TOMMY THUNDER-burst has completed his composition for Sven Trout. It is beautiful and, despite the primitive simplicity of the instruments, curiously compact. Rich and vibrant, owing something to classical orchestral composition, something to the "wall of sound" approach, and something to a cappella harmonies, it is none and all of these things.

Lil Prima, draped elegantly in a heap of pillows on the floor of Tommy's studio, listens to the final work and shakes her head in amazement.

"I take it all back, Tommy. That's one of the best things you've ever done. I don't know whether it makes me want to laugh or cry." Her lips frown, but the bliss doesn't leave her eyes. "Or dance. Or none of that. What contract did you give Sven?"

Tommy blinks. "I don't know. One of the release things."

Lil's blissful expression becomes calculating. "Good. I'll make certain we review the terms before Sven gets his CD. I think this would make a great radio release."

"Cool." Tommy imagines concert arenas filled with gently grooving souls, all those eyes turned up to him like he's a priest of some lost mystery. "Really cool."

"Do you have a number where you can reach Sven?"

"Nah. He said he'd be in touch."

"We give him no more than a month, then we tell him that his piece is something else and take this one," Lil says decisively. "He won't know the difference, and I'll want a month to build momentum for this release anyhow."

"Cool," Tommy says, somewhat saddened that he might need to wait a month to see the effect of his composition on the multitudes. "What if Sven doesn't want it released?"

"If you gave him the standard contract," Lil assures him, "he can't stop us. Underneath all the double talk, it doesn't sell him anything but the right to pay us for first use. Can you put something together for us to toss him in case he shows up after we have this one in production?"

Tommy nods. His mind is still buzzing with all the music he didn't use for this opus. "Sure. I can do something. It won't be *this*, but it will be good."

Lil unfolds herself from the pillows, eager to get to work on the promotional aspects. For a moment, she considers not letting Sven have this composition at all. Then she shrugs. If he wants to pay them for something that will ultimately resound to Tommy's glory—and indirectly to her own—then let him.

"Tommy, can I have a copy to listen to while I work?"

"Want to work on the release copy?"

"Well"—she reaches out and touches the side of his face—"that, and I just want to listen to it. It makes me feel good."

He grins, almost blushes. Hard-edged Lil doesn't usually admit such an emotional attraction to a piece.

Music to soothe even the savage breast.

¤▧¤

Feet that have never before touched a floor prove to be difficult things to manage. So learns the Head—now possessed of a body—the first day he tries to walk.

"Put the entire foot down," Sven urges impatiently, "flat against the floor. Don't walk on your toes!"

"That's how babies walk at first," Louhi says more patiently. "They test their balance while leaning forward. It takes them longer to shift balance onto the entire foot."

Sven sighs gustily. "But we don't want a baby!"

The Head disciplines himself to put all of his left foot flat against the carpeted floor. Although he is angered by Sven's impatience, he knows that he only has himself to blame. Louhi had suggested that he begin by crawling. He had been the one to refuse such an undignified method of locomotion.

"Now the other one," Sven says, steadying the wheeled walker he had brought the afternoon before.

The Head holds the metal rail, hoping they cannot see how tightly he clutches with his new hands. These he trusts somewhat more than he does his feet, for they had formed earlier. During all his waking hours he has striven to strengthen them, first with a rubber ball, then by pulling against a series of weights.

The body that Louhi has grown for him outwardly appears that of a hale man in his mid-thirties. He is moderately tall, neither lean nor heavy, built to suggest strength without advertising his potential. The Head has surreptitiously compared his new appearance with those of the men he sees on the television and has decided that he is attractive without being overtly handsome. Except for his silvery grey hair (something he plans to remedy by means of dye or magic when present needs are past), he does not bear any marked resemblance to Lovern—something he alternately regards with pleasure and concern.

His new body does not possess an invalid's flaccid muscles—indeed, superficially, he is in fine shape. His calves are cabled with muscle, his torso and arms suggest regular exercise—nothing as distorting as weight training, rather something like swimming several times a week.

However, just as owning a racehorse does not make one a jockey, possession of this body does not make the Head confident in its use. He has only had soles to his feet for a day— these being the last things to form—but the time for the long-anticipated confrontation with Arthur is growing close. Thus, he cannot dawdle in learning how to use his new equipment.

Taking a deep breath, the Head sets both feet flat on the floor. Motioning Sven to one side, he lifts his right foot and moves it forward about six inches. Then he does the same with the left. The walker against which he leans rolls forward.

"I'm holding it so that it won't roll too far, too fast," Sven assures him.

The Head wonders if to trust him, decides that he must. Sven has little to gain by damaging his new ally and, surely, he must realize the vengeance the Head would wreak.

Louhi crosses so that she is standing about six feet in front of him. "Come, *kultani*," she says sweetly. "Come to me. Walk as you have dreamed."

He shuffles forth, fired by dreams of other than walking. When he reaches her, Louhi strokes his cheek before stepping out of range again.

Obediently, the Head shuffles forward, an idea forming, one he cannot undertake until Sven is gone and Sven will not leave until he is assured that the Head is practicing.

A step at a time, the Head walks toward his goal, noticing the shine in Louhi's eyes and wondering if it is pride alone, or if perhaps it just might be love. At that moment, to his dreams of possessing her body, he adds that of possessing her heart.

Might she love him? She has reason, for he is made largely of the two men with whom she has been the most deeply obsessed. He is shaped, however, by her hand and craft, rather than by their own capricious whims.

Never mind. Soon Louhi will look at him with love . . . whether she chooses to or not. Her own words have reminded him of the way.

✿ ▣ ✿

"I have him for you!" Vera crows over the phone. "Duppy Jonah has finally relented."

Arthur is stunned to silence. He has grown accustomed over the past two months to the idea that he must deal with his present difficulties without his wizard to counsel him. The situation has taken on the light of a particularly bad omen. After all, didn't the legends agree that part of the reason for

Camelot's fall was that the king was without his mystic guide?

"You did! How? When?" he sputters, unable to word his requests more clearly.

"I did. How?" Vera chuckles. "I suggested that Lovern get to work on some magical means to permit electronic equipment to work underwater. He complained at first . . ."

Arthur can imagine this easily.

"Then he got to work on the project. Duppy Jonah was pretty generous with him—gave him Odd and Pod for assistants—and had the selkies fetch him whatever gear he requested. I think Lovern's fidelity to his captivity was what finally decided Duppy Jonah. Lovern could have requested the means for weapons or escape, but he kept faith."

"I'm proud of him," Arthur says. "I didn't know he possessed such humility."

"Lovern isn't humble," Vera qualifies, "but he isn't a fool. I'd like to believe that he has learned something."

"Have you told him about the theft?" Arthur says delicately. He had requested that she not, being uncertain how Lovern would react and not wishing to torment the wizard when he was effectively helpless.

"I have acceded to your request and not done so," Vera says formally, "but I did tell Amphitrite, and if she told Duppy Jonah . . . Well, Arthur, the Sea King is no fool either."

"No," Arthur agrees. "He is not. Are you returning, too?"

"I am. I promised you that I would be there for this new visitation." Vera sighs. "Have you learned anything further about what we may expect?"

"Sasquatches, yeti, satyrs, fauns, *kappa*, *tengu*, a few *pooka*. That seems to be it."

"Quite an 'it,' " Vera comments.

"True. Frank MacDonald will almost certainly be there with his jackalopes, ancient ravens, the Cats of Egypt, eagles, and such. I'm not certain whose side he's on. He's accepted hospitality here, but that may be because he isn't certain that the animals would be comfortable at a hotel."

"And the Changer?"

"No word."

"And Sven and his crew?"

"Nothing."

"How's Eddie's leg?"

"Doing better. Anson is coming back, too. Jonathan Wong has promised his help if I need him."

"Have him come," Vera prompts. "Everyone respects him, and he may be vital if some sort of amendment to the Accord needs to be drawn up."

"I'll call, then." Arthur is happy enough now to chuckle. "Eddie has been after me to do much the same. Are you certain that you two aren't coordinating behind my back?"

"Positive."

"How long until you are home?"

"Tomorrow afternoon. We're catching an early flight." She pauses, but Arthur can tell by some nuance in her breathing that she is not finished speaking. "And we won't be alone."

"No?" Arthur has already guessed but he must ask. "And who will be coming with you?"

"Amphitrite, Duppy Jonah, and at least one of their selkie courtiers. They have decided that if changes are being discussed about such important matters, they wish to be present."

Arthur takes a deep breath, whooshes it out. In all his memory the Sea King has never come inland. Sometimes he has come onto a beach as a great seal, but never has he taken human form.

"Tell Their Majesties that I am awed and honored. Will they do us the honor of staying with us?"

"Yes," Vera says. "I suggest that you give them my suite. I never moved back after Anson's visit."

"Thank you for the offer."

"One of the reasons we're coming back a few days before the meeting starts is so that Duppy Jonah will have an opportunity to adjust to the new surroundings," Vera says, her tone balanced between pleasure at having brought Arthur the good news about Lovern and concern about how the King is reacting to the rest.

"That seems wise." Arthur projects approval into his tone.

"Well, then," Vera says, sounding relieved, "I'd better

go and finish coordinating everything on this end.''

"Go then, Lady Grey Eyes," Arthur answers. "I can see that we will have much to do as well.''

"See you tomorrow.''

Arthur Pendragon, once King of all the Britains, sets down the telephone receiver. He cannot decide whether to laugh or cry. The Lustrum Review which he had so worried about had been a rumble of thunder before the real storm.

He sighs and shrugs. He'd better go find Eddie and make certain that the roof doesn't leak.

❁◙❁

In the higher reaches of the Sandias, the nights are now most definitely chilly. Shahrazad is growing into her ears and limbs. These days, no one could mistake her for either a puppy or a somewhat canine fawn. She is definitely a coyote.

You look so much like your mother my heart weeps tears as bitter as pine tar, the Changer thinks, looking at her. *I wonder what she would think of you. Nothing, probably, except that vague, warm joy that another young one has lived to see the moon's face turn. And I, too, feel that joy, even as I look at my lover's image growing out of puppyhood.*

The Changer has had much time for introspection during this last long unwrapping of days. Unlike many of his animal incarnations, he has not permitted himself to lapse into the animal life. No matter how much he longs for that simple, animal oblivion, he does not dare. One-eyed, with potential enemies unpunished, he cannot simply be coyote.

One-eyed.

That angers as much as it inconveniences. Despite his most skillful reworking of his body—reworking that has descended into the level of the cells and even deeper—he has not been able to rid himself of the magical taint. His entire identity is wrapped up in being the Changer. To be saddled with an infirmity he cannot change not only pains him—it makes him doubt his essential identity.

Moreover, it makes him ravenous.

Time and again, he has considered going to Arthur and requesting help. Time and again he has rejected the idea. Nor does he have any illusions why he has refused to ask for help. He knows that he is proud. He likes giving aid or requesting what is his due. But creeping down, crippled, begging for the same aid he had refused weeks before.

No!

The Changer rises from where he had denned beneath a spreading evergreen and shakes the needles from his fur. Shahrazad comes romping over, eager to join him in whatever venture he plans. Evening is coming on, a good time for hunting, and she is always hungry. Vaguely she remembers a place that was always warm and where her belly was never empty. She views its loss with philosophical regret.

Most things change: day into night, wet into dry, hunger into fullness, warmth into cold. Perhaps this will change as well. For now the Big Male is up and walking about. There will be mice to eat, perhaps even a rabbit.

The Changer knows the immediacy of her viewpoint. With quiet sincerity he envies her as he never envied all the rulers of the earth.

¤▣¤

Whistling happily, Rebecca Trapper unfolds lengths of dark green cloth from the wide, flat, shipping box that had arrived that morning. When she holds it up and shakes it, the cloth resolves into a forest green robe, long enough to conceal her feet. There is a matching sash trimmed with gold and a turban.

Donning the ensemble, she discovers that the sleeves can be buttoned away from her hands or draped forward to conceal them. The fabric is lightweight, but the color is dark enough that even a strong lamp doesn't turn it embarrassingly translucent.

"Bronson! Bronson!" she calls. "Come see what came in today's mail!"

Bronson Trapper stomps in from where he has been cleaning the mink pens. Seeing his wife clad all in flowing green, a turban on her head, her large eyes shining happily, he hoots softly.

"You look like a man," he says.

"Thank you!" She hugs him. "Do you really think I'll pass? Try on yours!"

Bronson wonders if any of them will pass, but he must admit that Rebecca looks like a tall, rather hirsute man. She resembles a Neanderthal (Poor sods. His grandfather had said they just couldn't compete.) rather than an Arab. Still, a veil would attract more attention than it would dissuade.

"Try combing your facial hair into a shape closer to the way human males wear it," he suggests, trying on his own robe. "It's a pity we don't grow mustaches."

"We could get some false ones," Rebecca suggests, combing her side whiskers so that they more closely resemble a silky black beard.

"No," Bronson grunts. "That's asking for trouble."

As if all of this isn't, he thinks morosely.

The green robes fit with tailored perfection—not surprisingly, since Rebecca had measured both of them with persnickety care. Looking at himself in the mirror, he has to admit the color goes well with his reddish brown fur—far better than the Sikh's pure white would have. The discussion group in the computer chatroom had decided to avoid white lest they insult any real Sikhs. The stylistic similarity had been viewed as far safer.

"Bronson," Rebecca says admiringly, "you look wonderful!"

She comes over to him and rubs her nose against his. He feels a groin-warming thrill and hugs her tightly. "Maybe I should wear a robe all the time if this is how you feel about it," he teases.

"Oh, no!" she protests. "I always like how you look. It's just that you look so . . . formal and mysterious. Like a high priest of ancient Persia."

Bronson's rambles had stayed within North and South America, but he has seen pictures of the men to whom Rebecca is alluding and is complimented.

"Are all the theriomorphs dressing like this?" he asks, thinking that a mob of them would make quite an impression.

"No, just the sasquatch and yeti. The fauns and satyrs can get by with baggy pants and tailored boots. *Tengu* shapeshift, as do *pooka*. I really don't know what the *kappa* are planning."

Bronson, recalling some of the disgusting practices rumor attributes to the yellowish green, monkeylike *kappa*, swallows a rather rude comment.

"I'm certain that the Moderator has something in mind for them," Rebecca finishes happily. "I only wish we could include more of the dispossessed. Monk told me that some unicorns were actually considering attending, but Frank MacDonald convinced them that their safety couldn't be even as assured as ours is."

"As safe as that will be," Bronson mutters.

If Rebecca hears, she chooses not to comment.

¤⊠¤

Now is the moment to make his attempt. For the last four hours the Head has been siphoning small amounts of magical energy into his personal store, has analyzed the wards around Louhi, has reviewed the spell that Lovern had stored within his memory.

It is a simple spell, only a few lines long, but in order to work it the caster needs to establish a bond between himself and the spell's recipient. There must be a moment of vulnerability and contact. He thinks that he knows how to achieve this.

Hauling himself to his new feet by means of the ropes that Louhi had anchored in the ceiling studs a few days earlier, the Head pulls himself erect. His walker is within reach, and he edges into it, releases the brake, and rolls toward where Louhi is reading a paperback copy of *The Compleat Enchanter*.

She lowers her book to watch his progress, her expression both analytical and approving.

He continues to exercise, coming closer to her with every pass. Sweat forms along his hairline and trickles down his back. It still seems odd to him that his skin can involuntarily leak water. Louhi continues to watch.

Carefully, the Head reviews the spell one more time. Softly, keeping the sound trapped within his throat, he taps the reservoir of power he has been storing in tiny increments all afternoon. When magical energy wells so full and potent that he feels as if he will choke, he deliberately slips.

Jumping to her feet with such speed that her book thuds to the floor, Louhi takes him into arms strengthened by hours of gathering driftwood and sea-polished stones on the Finnish beaches.

Perhaps she thinks it peculiar that what issues from his lips is neither startled cry nor frightened scream, but instead a thin, pure note of song, a sound so clear and beautiful that it catches the hearing and holds it prisoner.

Perhaps she does not.

Whichever is the case, by the time she notices, the chance to do something other than listen in rapt attention is past.

Her voluntary touch has brought him within her wards. She had not thought to proof herself specifically against him. Her perception of him is still as of a passive thing that needs her care and guidance, not as a wizard-spawned creature of power.

The Head sings a brief lyric in Finnish, the same lyric that a Durag is said to have sung to enchant his captive bride. Neither the words nor the melody alone spin the spell; they must be fused by the magic that he weaves into them. A less-gifted person could sing the same lyrics to no effect; a more greatly gifted (though nonesuch may exist) might not need to be within Louhi's wards to assure success.

Louhi listens, her pale eyes growing first more pale, then returning to their usual cool blue. As the color returns, they hold a greater warmth; for the first time since the Head has looked upon the sorceress, her eyes are framed with a smile that is neither sarcastic nor ironic but warm and loving.

She knows that she has been ensorcelled, but part of the power of this spell is that it convinces the recipient that the spell is not the cause of the emotions welling up within a heart and soul too long cold and vengeful, but merely the excuse for releasing what she has always known.

"I love you," she whispers softly, and pulls his head against her small, round breasts.

"You do?" he asks, his tone equally soft.

"As I have never loved another," she says honestly.

Except with some shrilly screaming part of herself, she is unaware of the irony of this statement. Truly, never before, even when she loved Merlin, has she loved like this, for never before has she been ensorcelled to love.

"And I love you," he says. His reply is somewhat less honest, for he does not so much love her as desire her, but love and lust are as muddled within his mind and body as within that of any teenage boy.

"*Kultani*," she says, caressing him. "My darling."

He turns her face to his, kissing her cheekbones, the corners of her eyes, and finally her coveted mouth. She returns his kisses with enthusiasm, then, as he wishes it, with heat.

"Sven will not be here tonight, will he?" the Head asks, as she helps him to his feet.

"No. He is preparing for the last stages of our grand challenge to Arthur. You and I are alone tonight."

"And that is how you wish it?"

"Of course!" She is not so far from herself as to fail to sound indignant that he would question her, but she smiles immediately. "I wish to ravage your virgin body, to make you feel what you have only fantasized."

He licks his lips. "I'm capable of quite a lot of fantasy."

"And I am capable of quite a lot of satisfying," she purrs.

Leaning on her, the Head has a momentary qualm that perhaps he should have waited to cast this spell until he was stronger. He had no idea what a tigress lurked beneath Louhi's cool, silvery exterior.

"We won't tell Sven about us, now, will we?" he asks, seeking to reestablish control.

"No, that wouldn't be wise," Louhi agrees. "He's been lusting after me since we started this gambit—and long before that. It wouldn't do to make him jealous. At least not while we still need him."

Her hand drops from his shoulder to slip inside his loose sweatpants. "My, you're shaping up nicely. Come along now."

And he does, quite content to let her appear to lead since he knows with the certainty of the song that still echoes within his mind that he is the true master.

Judicial reform is no sport for the short-winded.

—ARTHUR VANDERBILT

EARLY IN THE SECOND WEEK IN SEPTEMBER, MONK DECIDES he isn't really pleased with the way things are turning out. It was one thing to help Sven with a few tricks and turns. Not only had it given him and his buddies something to do (Nippon is wonderful, but realistically it is a small archipelago. The combination of highly developed electronic security systems and a few stodgy resident athanor make it tough for a *tengu* to have any fun.), but they sympathize with theriomorphs who, like the trickster *tengu*, are becoming imprisoned by the advancement of human technology.

But this . . . Hiero out flying shuttle service. Roy meeting fauns and satyrs at the airport. And Monk himself shapeshifted into a respectable Japanese businessman so that he can meet with hotel managers and caterers. Where the hell is Sven as the great mess he has orchestrated gets ready to begin? Monk doesn't have the slightest idea.

Oh, the Fiery One checks in by telephone or e-mail several times a day, but a few interesting things have become clear. Monk can't decide whether he's more pissed off that Sven won't be arriving until a couple of days *after* the meetings with Arthur begin or that he insists that the *tengu* keep the secret of the Moderator's identity just those few days longer.

"It's a matter of life and death, Monk," Sven had said seriously during a recent telephone conversation during which Monk had complained. "My life and death, I admit, but I feel no less strongly about it for that. I've stirred some hornets' nests in setting up this meeting. I've made some enemies. Let me make my appearance in my own time. Please!"

Monk agrees reluctantly. "The first two days of the meeting, Sven-san. Two days only. Then the cat is out of the bag. I'm not taking the fall for you."

"Great, great. Two days should be plenty."

Huffing to himself as he remembers this, Monk reaches for the listing of foods he's ordered for the guests who will be arriving today. He notices that he's forgotten to order cucumbers. With *kappa* coming that wouldn't do. Their alternate food choices can get very vulgar.

Cucumbers.

Sighing, he reaches for the telephone, shifting his throat to produce the voice of his Japanese businessman persona.

Cucumbers.

¤◼¤

Leaving the courtyard where Vera is visiting with Duppy Jonah, Amphitrite, and Anson, Arthur snags Eddie and takes him to his office.

"How are we going to entertain all these people?" Arthur says, unaware how closely his concern mirrors Monk's own.

"Vera has said that she'll be able to handle the Ocean Monarchs." Eddie leans forward. "I'm more concerned about the other lot."

"You mean the Trappers and their friends?"

"Right. They're coming into Albuquerque for a vacation—not just for this meeting. In a way, I expect that this meeting is an excuse for the vacation."

"I think you're right. They aren't going to be content staying in their hotel or roaming around this estate."

"No, not if their entire platform is based on unhappiness at being kept undercover," Eddie agrees. "I suppose we could arrange a tour to some of the museums."

Arthur shakes his head. "I'm not certain about that. There are security cameras. One slip . . ."

"Yeah."

"If Lovern were here to work some hoodoo on the cameras, I might risk it," Arthur says. "Museums are amusing—and educational about human understanding of the Earth."

Lovern, however, has made his apologies and is busy searching for the Head. Lovern's dismay at its disappearance had been equaled only by his fear when he learned who had taken it and what they were planning to do. When he hasn't been driving about the area with divining tools, he has been in his room performing strange rites that leave the air smelling of burned spices.

"A public event then," Eddie offers. "Fiesta in Santa Fe wouldn't be a bad idea. There are lots of galleries and the burning of Zozobra. I can check the dates for this year."

"Wait!" Arthur says. "I have a better idea. How about the State Fair? It's close to home, crowded, and has lots of different activities. There are rides and games as well as art exhibits, farm animals, and music acts."

"You're right!" Eddie agrees excitedly. "Do we offer or wait for them to ask?"

"Let's offer. That way we can avoid the charge that we were forced into taking them out."

"Needless to say, that opens us to the charge that we are trying to steer where they do and don't go."

"So we lose either way." Arthur shrugs. "I'd rather err on the side of generosity."

"They should be arriving today," Eddie says. "I'll call over to the hotel and make our offer to their liaison."

"Good." Arthur frowns. "Who *is* their liaison? Is it this Moderator?"

"No." Eddie shakes his head decisively. "I asked him when we talked, and he flatly denied it. He wouldn't identify himself. I have the impression he's not completely happy about his job."

"Interesting." Arthur makes a note. "We may be able to play on this during the meetings."

"How formal do we want the meetings to be?" Eddie asks.

"I want to model them on the Lustrum Review," Arthur

says promptly. "There must be no protest raised that we are treating the theriomorphs any differently than we do other athanor."

"Well, that will make things easier," Eddie says, "or maybe more difficult. We won't need to worry about a change of format, but to realistically parallel the Review, we should have sent out invitations to all the rest of the Harmony."

"We can't do that," Arthur says, "not on such short notice, nor do I think it would serve any of our needs. However, let's make certain we have video cameras set up and make regular postings to those members of the Harmony who are on-line."

Eddie nods, his mind racing as he considers all the different things he will need to prepare. Vera won't be available to help—not with acting as liaison for visiting royalty. Anson might help and Jonathan . . .

"I think we can pull it off," he says, hesitantly, "but if you want full coverage, we're going to need help."

"Let's not worry about full coverage," Arthur decides easily. "We'll be able to brief folks later. It isn't like this is a proper Review."

"Okay," Eddie says, relieved.

Neither Arthur nor Eddie realizes that they have just made a tactical error.

✿◼✿

Getting off the small plane at an airfield on the northern edge of Albuquerque, Rebecca Trapper sniffs air so dry that her nose aches. She grabs Bronson's hand tightly.

"Look how bright the stars are!" she says rapturously. "And how broad the sky is!"

Hiero, their *tengu* pilot, chuckles. He still resembles a Japanese street punk, but he has donned a black bomber jacket over his tee shirt. A white bandanna printed with a red sunburst is tied about his brow.

"It's a good sky," he says, "but there are lots of them around the world. Come along. Monk should have a van waiting."

Monk, back to looking like a punk himself, is waiting at the edge of the airfield in a silver-grey van. He welcomes them warmly, admiring how well they wear their green robes.

"You're the last of the crew," he says. "The yeti handled most of their own transportation. We just shuttled them in the last leg. The fauns and satyrs took the public airlines. Demi saved the day when Loverboy pinched a flight attendant on the . . ."

He catches Bronson's warning glower, ". . . tail."

"How many are there in all?" Bronson asks.

"Snowbird and Swansdown brought their daughter Dawn, their infant son, and someone they call Great Uncle Winter. There's another Alaskan yeti family that I haven't met yet."

Bronson interrupts. "That must be Joelle Buxkemper's group."

"That sounds right," Hiero says. "Then there is the Olsen clan from up your way."

"And the Moderator?" Rebecca says hesitantly. "Is he here?"

"He isn't yet. We're to start the meetings without him." Something in Monk's voice keeps them from asking more.

Monk has taken an entire floor at the hotel, selecting one with several conference rooms. It is in one of these that Rebecca finally has the opportunity to meet the people who have become her closest friends.

Loverboy proves to be a hulking, olive-complected fellow with wild hair and beard. He wears baggy black pants belted low on his hips, a loose pink shirt, and cowboy boots.

He greets Rebecca with a bellow of delight and an appreciative leer. When he sees Bronson, he becomes somewhat less openly enthusiastic.

"Baby, baby, baby!" he shouts, loping over to her, a glass of beer in one hand, the other hitching up his pants.

"Loverboy?"

"You know me, sweet fuzzy lady!" he answers. "But here you call me Georgios, okay? Let me introduce you to my *compadres*."

Rebecca hangs back. Even though she is several inches taller than Georgios, he is an intimidating figure.

"Maybe in a moment," she hedges. "I was hoping to meet Demetrios."

"And I have wished to meet you," a courtly voice says, coming from around Bronson's towering bulk.

Demetrios is a natty fellow with neatly combed, reddish brown hair cut stylishly long to the nape of his neck and a matching goatee. Clad in tweed trousers held up by tan suspenders and a white shirt, he might have been a particularly short college professor were it not for the curling goat's horns jutting back from his forehead and the tidy goat's hooves peeping from under his trouser cuffs.

He puts out his hand for Rebecca's and, although she could have easily engulfed his hand in her own, he raises her hand to his lips and kisses the air just above it as if she is the finest lady in the land. Then he bows to Bronson.

"I am delighted to make your acquaintance, sir," he says. "You wife speaks of you frequently and with great fondness."

Bronson, who had been prepared to dislike this confidant of his wife, bows as well. "I am pleased to meet you as well, Demetrios. How was your trip?"

"Exhausting," Demetrios admits. "I was traveling with three of my more rural brethren. Additionally, we were escorting five satyrs. Those horse-tailed fools could have gotten themselves in serious trouble."

"Oh?"

Demetrios sighs. "I'll spare you the details. I'm simply pleased we arrived here without one or more of the satyrs getting arrested. Would you like a glass of wine? There's a fine red on the table by the window."

"That sounds wonderful," Rebecca says, tucking her hand into Bronson's. "I want to look out over the city lights. I've never seen so many. And where are the yeti?"

"They've gone to bed," Demetrios says. "They had a longer trip than many of us, came by small plane in jumps with stops for refueling. Your Aunt Swansdown asked me to give both of you their love and to say that they'll see you in the morning."

Rebecca nods. "I'm tired myself, but I'm too excited to settle down."

Demetrios continues, "Not all of your relatives have retired. The Olsens are here."

Bronson nods, a smile lighting his broad face. "I see Netherton and Arel over talking to the *kappa*."

Pouring them all wine, Bronson listens as Demetrios and Rebecca chat. She sounds so very happy. He decides that they have done the right thing coming here after all.

As if she can read his mind, Rebecca reaches out and squeezes his hand. Despite his hands being even bigger than hers, their fingers fit together quite neatly.

The next morning, the first session of the meeting begins with the roll call of those who have died before. Perhaps it is due to the group gathered in the conference room, but Arthur is acutely aware of how many of those who are dead were theriomorphs—all of the dragons, the minotaurs, the largest of the giants. Only those who could hide or shift shape or blend into the changing world seem to have survived. Some of this must be the natural course of evolution, but he feels obscurely guilty.

Then he calls for introductions all around. This is a slight departure from the usual Lustrum Review procedure, but so many of those gathered here have known few but their own isolated communities. In any case, the members of his staff have not met many of these people for centuries. A reminder may save an awkward *faux pas*.

Vera surprises him by asking Demetrios the faun with unfeigned cordiality after a number of women of whom Arthur has never heard. When he inquires, she tells him that they are dryads, naiads, and oreads, the female counterparts—in some sense—of the fauns and satyrs.

"They have long withdrawn from contact with most members of the Harmony, as have the naturals in many regions," Vera says calmly, "but they take part in Harmony nonetheless."

Arthur, who still views these creatures as myths, does not contradict her, but reminds himself to chide her privately for adding yet another element to the morass confronting them.

The meeting then progresses to a formal statement by Rebecca Trapper and Demetrios Stangos of the business that they have brought before him.

"Simply, Your Majesty," Demetrios says, hands on his hips, "we would like Harmony to consider a change in policy regarding the theriomorphs. We are weary of being hidden away, unable to participate in the world around us."

"And what a world it is!" Rebecca adds, enthusiasm making her dark eyes shine. "For the first time, it is possible for anyone to fly, to go beneath the seas, to visit all the places of the Earth. And," she continues darkly, and a touch too theatrically, "to destroy them."

Arthur swallows a groan. Not another eco-nut! He listens patiently, however, and is rewarded by the pair keeping their introduction brief. That, at least, is a pleasant change from Isidro Robelo and his partners.

When they take their seats, he rises and clears his throat. "Thank you both for that *concise* introduction."

He smiles warmly and is rewarded with a some chuckles— and the soft whistles that are the same for the yeti and sasquatch. Organizing his next statement, he realizes how long it has been since he looked out over an audience where the participants did not appear human. The nonverbal cues are harder to read on faces that are broader, furred, more heavily ridged with bone.

Yes, he has visited them in small groups within their own communities—gone ice fishing with the yeti, danced with the fauns, pretended to haunt ancient ruins with a laughing-eyed *pooka* who then transformed into a wild steed and carried him along the beach. Yet in each case, he was the honored guest and they were trying hard to make him welcome. This time the situation is different. He is on the spot. He must make them welcome, make them accept his policies.

Oh, my. Omah. He puts on his most fatherly expression and begins. "I think the first question we need to raise in considering this issue is that for many centuries the theriomorphs who are not shapeshifters have *wanted* to be hidden. In effect, the Harmony's policy regarding the theriomorphs grew out of a desire to accede to your own wishes."

He and Eddie had designed this approach during the many brainstorming sessions that followed Bronson Trapper's call. Effectively, it puts the responsibility back on their heads.

Demetrios raises his hand. "Your Majesty is absolutely correct. In fact, many of us still desire a certain amount of privacy."

Georgios the satyr interjects, "Not us! We want to bring joy to the babes. We're ready to go out and plant the seed!"

His pals start guffawing and making lewd gestures in the direction of their groins. Demetrios sighs. Bronson Trapper silences them with a dark glower.

Arthur nods. "So am I to understand that you are not united as to exactly what level of exposure you desire?"

Rebecca Trapper frowns at Georgios and sighs. "I suppose that is so, Your Majesty."

The King says softly, but firmly, "And have you considered that we may not be able to grant you these varying desires? I am a king—in this age little more than an administrator—not a god. I cannot grant wishes. I can only advise policy."

Bronson Trapper's deep voice dominates the murmured responses. "I, at least, understand this all too well. I hope that everyone here realizes that this meeting should not be expected to change policy overnight. These issues are ones that will affect all the Harmony."

"But," Rebecca says angrily, waving a massive fistful of computer printouts, "the world is ready for a return of the creatures of myth and legend! Many first-world nations have lost the underpinnings of faith that gave them a cultural unity."

She takes a ragged breath and continues. "And with them they have lost the uniformity of prejudice. We would find ourselves welcomed as proof that the Earth holds more than what their science has discovered."

"Welcomed?" Eddie asks. "Or viewed as a threat? Some of those within Harmony have lived since the dawn of life."

Duppy Jonah bows his head in acknowledgment. His human form lacks his typical blue-green coloring and fishy lower body, but otherwise bears strong resemblance to his long-haired, flowing bearded triton-form.

"How," Eddie says, "will humanity feel when forced to admit to its relative youth? We have enough rivalries of that type among the athanor. How will humans feel when they know that some who have been thought gods and goddesses still walk the Earth?''

Vera, who has been called both goddess and saint within her own comparatively short span of years, adds, ''And will they welcome us or view us as subjects for study? I, for one, do not care to end in a laboratory, yet the risk to me is far less than to a yeti or sasquatch, faun or satyr. Some of you may be termed animals, not people, and until your sentience is acknowledged what horrors will you meet?''

Rebecca Trapper, who for this meeting has put aside her green robes and sits clad in her fur and a few pieces of jewelry, shouts out, ''What do you mean that they would think us animals? Fur does not make a person less sentient! We can talk and craft and manipulate our environment!''

''So could the African natives imported to this continent as slaves,'' interjects Anson A. Kridd in a strong, level voice. ''Yet their basic humanity is *still* in doubt in some circles. Equally, look at the Africentric rewriting of history that seeks to make everyone from Nefertiti to Aristotle black. Humanity has not come to terms with the fact that under the skin they are one race. Why do you expect them to come to terms with us?''

''Perhaps,'' says a *kappa*, its voice thin and shrill, like that of an infant just finished weeping, ''they will see our differentness and realize their own similarities. Perhaps our reality will inaugurate an ending to racial strife.''

''And perhaps,'' says Jonathan Wong, looking at the little yellowish green, vaguely simian creature, ''it will instigate more strife as elements in each area seek to learn the secrets of our long life. I, for one, join Vera in my fervent desire not to end up in a laboratory or as a stud.''

''Hey, don't worry, Jonny-boy,'' Georgios says. ''Me and my brothers will do stud service whenever and wherever necessary. I'm so tired of mares that I could f . . .''

Whatever he is planning to say is cut short by Bronson Trapper placing a firm hand on his shoulder. ''Kindly remember that there are ladies present, satyr.''

''I can't forget,'' Georgios says with a forlorn glance at his trousers, ''and it hurts.''

Somewhat hastily, Eddie adds, ''There is no reason to believe that human unity would be to our benefit. We will be the aliens among them—never mind that many of us were born to human parents and have no greater gifts than an extended life span. If one looks at the evidence of film and fiction, humans do not often welcome the stranger.''

''I disagree,'' says Swansdown, her voice deep but melodious, rather like the lower pitches of a skillfully played cello. ''There are many legends—both ancient and modern—that indicate humanity's desire for gods and teachers among them.''

The discussion continues in this vein throughout the morning and, after the lunch break, well into the afternoon. Arthur's fingers grow cramped from taking notes, and he knows that he will be working well into the evening trying to organize the various threads of the discussion into a coherent form.

He realizes that the issue is not some vague, self-important desire for change and recognition. The complaints are carefully considered, the needs complex.

Why shouldn't the sasquatch have some say on government policies that affect the woods on which they depend for both their living and their protection? Shouldn't the fauns be able to protect the naturals that they claim depend on their care? Arthur thinks guiltily of the time and resources he has spent on lobbying for water management in New Mexico. The theriomorphs can do something similar only from a distance.

To make matters more complex, not all of the theriomorphs want the same thing, and very few have considered the vast public attention they will all receive—at least for the first fifty or so years until enough humans who have knowingly lived in a world with immortals and monsters mature.

Calling a recess for the evening, Arthur invites everyone to stay for discussion and picnicking on the hacienda's grounds. To his guilty relief, he learns that Monk has activities planned back at the hotel. Most of the theriomorphs are getting over a certain shyness regarding mingling with humans. A venture into the hotel restaurant or cocktail lounge seems daring.

Although Monk invites Arthur's household to join them, Arthur explains that he and Eddie, at least, must remain home to prepare today's minutes for tomorrow. Vera plans to venture out with Amphitrite and Duppy Jonah. Both women are giggling about dancing in the hotel's club. Even Rebecca Trapper seems tempted.

After seeing his guests to the door, Arthur wonders somewhat wistfully where Lovern is and if he is having any luck tracking down his missing Head and those who have taken it away.

✿▣✿

Flicking off the headlights, Lovern parks his four-wheel-drive cruiser on the shoulder of the road. For the last several days, ever since Arthur informed him that the Head had been stolen, he has been searching for his missing . . .

Once he would have automatically thought of it as a tool or perhaps a homunculus. Now he doesn't know how to term it. Certainly a tool does not make its own alliances and arrange for favors. "Servant" might have been a better way to view it, but now is too late to confer even that relative dignity.

"Enemy" is the only term that really fits what the Head has become. It has permitted itself to be removed from Lovern's keeping, apparently has lied to him and misdirected him, possibly for years. Now the Head strives for autonomy, and only Lovern fully realizes how dangerous this could be, for only Lovern knows what vast resources he has given over to the Head's keeping.

Getting out of the cruiser, the wizard inspects his wards and amulets. All are active; all are fully charged. He feels a small fear. Most of these were crafted with the Head's assistance. Could it have designed them in such a fashion that it can disable them? For how long has it resented Lovern?

Lovern tries to shrug away the apprehension but cannot. Assuming that the amulets have been tampered with is only logical, but doing without them completely would be foolish. What if he is wrong and the Head has dealt with him honestly? Then he would be denying himself protection for no reason.

Contrary to popular belief, held even by many athanor, wizards cannot work magic at random. Even the most simple spells take preparation. Amulets permit preparation beforehand, make wonders on demand sometimes possible. Without them, he is little better than a skinny man who has not kept himself in decent physical condition.

Now on another's turf, he reaches out tentatively around himself, seeking warning of the magical equivalent of barbed wire. Perhaps because this place is not meant as a permanent stronghold, he finds nothing more elaborate than a light alarm.

This is neither foolishness nor carelessness on the part of the residents. Creating wards keyed to three and only those three could be time-consuming (as well he knows from his work for Arthur). Even more difficult is creating wards that admit the harmless while refusing the harmful.

After thoughtful consideration, Lovern trips the alarm. He is not coming here to steal or kidnap; he is coming here to confront. He may as well be mannerly about it. And perhaps his good manners will keep them off guard.

One can hope.

He raises his right hand and raps lightly on the door. The house, he notices as he stands waiting in the small circle illuminated by a single, unshielded yellow lightbulb, is a very simple place, probably no larger than a few rooms. Quite different from the rambling modern abode in which the Changer had undergone his unwilling surgery. The reason for this change in residence becomes quite evident soon after the door is opened.

Louhi stands before him clad in eggshell white linen trousers and a loose but low-cut blouse of pale blue silk. She wears sandals with slim straps and a few slender silver chains about her throat and wrists.

She smiles at him. "Lovern, do come in. We thought that our visitor might well be you."

"Thank you, Louhi."

He steps past her, looking about attentively, and sees the Head coming toward him. "Head" is hardly an appropriate name for his creation, for he has a body now, a strong, muscular body, much better developed than Lovern's own. The wizard feels vaguely envious, but why, if Louhi took the trouble to craft an entire body, should she make one that was weak and effete?

The Head leans on a walker, which he rolls with a fair

amount of command across the wooden floor. This, then, is why Louhi selected this particular house when the need to relocate arose. The floor plan is open, all on one story. Only a few doors, presumably to bedrooms and bath, are closed. The rest of the house is divided by broad archways and different shades of paint.

"Hello, Lovern," the Head says.

"Hello." Lovern nods a bit stiffly. "I'm not certain what name to call you."

" 'Head' will do for now," the Head says. Interestingly, he is no longer using his characteristic alliterative speech pattern. "I'm still considering what I wish to be called."

"Would you like a cup of tea or coffee?" Louhi calls from the kitchen area. "I was just putting on the kettle."

"Tea would be fine," Lovern replies.

"Please take a seat, Lovern," the Head says. "I will not hide that I need to rest."

Lovern sits in a low-slung, Bauhaus-inspired chair, while Louhi helps the Head onto a sturdy Spanish colonial–style bench.

He is puzzled by her attitude. She seems somehow younger, yet it is not a matter of her appearance, which has always been as fluid as any shapeshifter's. It is a matter of mannerisms; she seems gentler, less guarded. His puzzlement increases when she sits next to the Head, resting her hand near his, not precisely holding it, but not remaining aloof.

"So, Lovern, why are you here?" the Head asks.

Lovern has considered this himself. How can he state his reasons tactfully?

"I was wondering why you left." He realizes that he sounds like the ineffectual husband in a romance novel.

The Head laughs, not unkindly, but not kindly either. "I'm certain that's not what you really want to know, but I'm going to tell you anyhow.

"You created me and then stuck me in a dark pit in the bottom of the ocean. For millennia, I lived without light, without friends, and with only your infrequent companionship. Then I was left in isolation during your captivity."

The Head stops to spare Louhi a fond smile. "I decided that I had tolerated enough. When I was given the opportunity to leave, I did."

"When I was a captive." Lovern's expression is pure astonishment. "Head, that was centuries ago! Why didn't you talk to me?"

"What are a few centuries after two or three millennia?" the Head says caustically. "I had practice waiting, and I didn't care to plead with you. I wanted freedom on my own terms. Now I have it—and I owe you no favors."

The teakettle begins whistling. Louhi rises, drifts off to the kitchen.

"What are you going to do with your newfound freedom?" Lovern asks.

"That's the question you really wanted to ask, isn't it? One of them, anyhow," the Head says. "You'll know soon enough. I'm not giving away anything in advance."

"I don't suppose you'd be interested in coming with me, becoming my apprentice," Lovern offers awkwardly. "I didn't realize what a terrible wrong I had committed. That doesn't mean I'm not willing to correct it."

"Sorry." The Head looks to where Louhi is rejoining them carrying a tea tray. "You have nothing to offer me. Don't you wish you could say as much, Wise Wizard?"

There. Lovern stiffens, knowing that last was a shot meant to hurt, unable to conceal that it does indeed hurt.

"I trusted you!" he says.

"No more than an office worker trusts his computer or a banker her safe," the Head taunts. "What you gave to me, you simply stored away, as if with all my vast potential I was little more than a filing system. Now you've learned that I am not."

"But what you are contemplating is theft!" Lovern says.

"I consider my actions more comparable to a bonus for many years of faithful service. I might even make a deal with you if you wish to have copies of what I hold."

Lovern, thinking of the spells, the research, the rituals, the personal conjectures that he has stored within the Head since its creation, swallows a wail of despair. Of course he has copies of much of this, but since the Head made access so easy, cross correlation so painless, basic spell design so tidy, he has never really codified his notes. They were written mostly so that he could dictate to the Head.

And now the Head has it all. Why had he never invested

in a computer when Arthur and Eddie had pressed him? Had the Head subtly dissuaded him?

"Yes," the Head says, not answering his question although for a terrifying moment Lovern thinks that it has read his mind. "Yes, I might be willing to let you purchase the knowledge of which I am custodian. I fear, however, that I would not assist you for as little as I did before."

"I see," Lovern says, proud of how calm he sounds, for his fury is raging within him like one of Duppy Jonah's storms.

He glances at Louhi, wondering what he will see in those cool eyes: Contempt? Malicious humor? Boredom? Calculation?

Yet, there is none of this. She hardly seems to notice him; her gaze rests with calm fascination on the Head.

Is she so proud then of her creation? Her obsessed expression reminds Lovern of a mother with a firstborn child. Louhi, like so many of their kind, is unable to bear a child. Perhaps this man grown from her art fulfills her as none of her shapeshifted pets ever did.

"Louhi," Lovern says, desperate enough to appeal to this old lover, old rival. He thought that she might have welcomed his tentative attentions during the Lustrum Review. "Louhi, do you agree with what the Head is doing?"

"I do," she says. "He has been most cruelly used by you—as you use most of those you teach. I think that even if all the Harmony were asked to judge, they would agree with the Head."

This answer is enough to break through Lovern's careful self-control.

"You think so, do you? The Accord rules against theft from each other!"

Louhi shakes her head pityingly. "Theft is a minor crime compared to slavery. Long ago, the Accord ruled against keeping athanor slaves, yet what else was the Head?"

"I made him!" Lovern protests.

"A parent," Louhi says with ice in her voice, for she has no love for parents, "gives a child life, protection, and eventually autonomy. You could argue that you gave the Head the first two, but never that you gave him the latter."

"You have always resented that the Changer did not claim

you as his get," Lovern protests. "Now you are speaking out of the other side of your mouth."

"One act is pure neglect, the other pure possession," Louhi spits back. "Neither is correct behavior. I cannot deal with my own father—or at least not more than I have already—but I can help the Head free himself from one who should have been a father but proved only to be a slave master."

Lovern rises, sets down his tea untasted. "I see that we cannot agree on these matters. I beg to take my leave."

"*We* will not hold *you* against your will," the Head jeers. "Louhi will show you to the door."

Lovern departs hastily lest they change their minds. As he drives back to Arthur's hacienda his mind races, balancing accounts and realizing that this time he is coming up very short.

❁❁❁

There had been no practical way for Chris and Bill to gain reentry into Pendragon Estates after their encounter with the two drug dealers. Chris had done some light surveillance and had confirmed that quite a large group had gathered for about a week. The names Dakar Agadez and Katsuhiro Oba had proven to belong to two businessmen, one Nigerian, one Japanese, visiting the U.S. on perfectly legal passports. He hadn't been able to find out anything remotely interesting about either of them.

That had been all he had been able to manage. Bill had been taken by his parents to visit relatives in Jamaica for the summer. Chris's workload at the *Journal* had increased as he covered for vacationing reporters. Then he had his own summer break, a satisfying interlude featuring a lady in Maine.

Despite such distractions, he can't get the Arthur Pendragon story out of his mind. Bill Irish returns to register for classes and for the first few weeks of September is too busy to do more than periodically hassle Chris to take up where they had left off. In the second week of September, he phones.

"Guess what? Pendragon Estates has put in another order

for folding chairs and card tables. What do you want to bet that our favorite drug lords are planning another meeting?"

Chris swallows, remembering the preternatural terror he had felt when he had seen Dakar's eyes. "You don't want to sneak in again, do you?" he says, pleased to find his voice so steady.

"I don't think the rental company's owner would let us," Bill says sadly. "I think he got asked questions last time. Do you want to stake out the place? Maybe we could get some pictures to match against the FBI's most-wanted list."

"That's an idea," Chris says, "but we'll be rather obvious. It's a single-lane road in front of Pendragon Estates."

"It's worth a shot," Bill says. "I'll do it if you can't. I can bring my laptop and do homework from my car."

"Just be careful," Chris urges. "The police get nosy in a nice neighborhood like that."

"My Yugo doesn't have a window on the driver's side, has spiderweb cracks on the windows that *are* there, and is mustard-colored. Any cop who sees it is going to think it's abandoned."

It must be nice to be young and confident like Bill, Chris thinks as he hangs up the phone. Or maybe he hadn't seen quite as clearly the look in Dakar Agadez's eyes.

"Some of Pendragon's cronies are staying," Bill says, before Chris can say more than "hello" into the receiver, "at the Crown Plaza Pyramid Hotel. Meet me there."

He hangs up, giving Chris little choice but to meet him or to abandon his young friend. Sighing, he heads out. Bill meets him in the parking lot.

"C'mon! They should be here any moment!"

Chris and Bill have hardly settled in the central atrium when a very strange group enters the lobby and heads for the nearby bank of elevators.

First come a dozen or so bearded men, the smallest of whom is at least six feet tall. These are dressed in forest green floor-length robes. Following them are several tweedily dressed men, all wearing fedoras and pushing baby carriages. Bringing up the rear are three Japanese street punks, a gorgeous blond woman, a man with the flowing hair and beard of a biblical patriarch, and Arthur's assistant Vera Tso.

"My feet hurt," complains one of the men behind a baby carriage as they come to a halt by the elevators. "It's these boots. I don't know if I can dance in them."

"When in Rome, Demetrios . . ." a green-robed man says.

"I never worried about boots in Rome." Demetrios sighs. "Of course, I haven't been there for years."

Vera Tso smiles at Demetrios. "I'll help you pad your boots, Demi. We wouldn't want you to miss coming to the Pyramid Club with us tonight."

"Thanks, Vera," the little man says. "Save a dance for me?"

"I promise."

When the elevator carries the rest of the group off to the eighth floor, Bill and Chris exchange triumphant grins.

"We've got 'em now!" Bill crows. "No more barred gates and no more thugs."

"No," Chris says more cautiously, "just giants in green robes and one of the drug lord's most intimate cronies. It's a little too early to celebrate."

The reporters dine in the hotel restaurant that night, choosing a table that lets them keep an eye on both the elevators and the corridor to the hotel's Pyramid Club. They are lingering over colas—Chris's straight, Bill's laced with rum—when the first of the odd group begins descending from the eighth floor; Bill and Chris hurry ahead to get a table in the club.

"I'd been hoping we'd overhear something," Chris says after about fifteen minutes, "but the music is too loud."

"I wonder if we should ask someone to dance," Bill says thoughtfully. He has noticed that, like men everywhere, the group across the room seems more interested in talking and drinking than in asking the ladies to dance. Characteristically turning thought into action, Bill rises and asks the fashion-model blond to dance.

"I'd love to dance," she says with a friendly smile and a deep sigh, "but my husband is the jealous type."

The fellow with the patriarch's beard nods solemn agreement, but he takes the hint and ushers his wife onto the dance floor.

"How about you, miss?" Bill asks Vera Tso, desperately

hoping she won't remember his stint as a deliveryman.

Vera hesitates but accepts. As if this was a signal, several of the green-robed types venture onto the dance floor.

Watching from his table, Chris notes that despite their size, the green-robes are quite graceful, moving with a gliding, shuffling step that billows their gowns out around them. Men dance in pairs, demonstrating none of the self-consciousness often seen when homosexual couples dance in public.

Chris considers his own next move. He knows there are cultures where dancing with someone of the same gender is just good, healthy exercise. In those same cultures, couples of the opposite sex dancing would be scandalous.

He decides to put American prejudice aside and take the plunge. When a new song is beginning, he walks over to one of the smaller green robes. This fellow's whiskers are silky black but fairly sparse and oddly proportioned across his face—almost as if the man is simply hairy, rather than bearded. Combined with the shape of his nose and set of his eyes, he looks unfortunately simian.

"Hi," Chris says, swallowing hard, hoping that Bill won't notice and start laughing, "want to dance?"

"Uh, sure," the hairy guy says, glancing as if for reassurance at the much bigger, much hairier guy with whom he had been dancing. "Sure."

As they move to the dance floor, Chris shouts over the music, "Where you from?"

"Oregon," his partner says, shuffling vigorously.

Chris realizes that they're both nervous and that gives him courage. "I'm local. What brings you to the Duke City?"

"Duke City?"

"Albuquerque, it's named for some Spanish duke, except he spelled his name with an extra 'r.' "

"Oh. Albuquerque is hard enough to spell without that!" Amazingly, for all his height and bulk, the hairy man giggles.

Chris conceals his surprise. "Purists keep agitating to change the spelling. I don't think it'll ever happen."

"Good! When we were making our travel plans, I kept spelling it wrong."

"Happens all the time. You here on vacation or business?"

"A little of both. We have some meetings to attend, then

e're going to sightsee. I've never been in a desert before."

"Wear shoes or boots with good soles," Chris advises. "There are lots of stickers and thorns. And allow for the higher altitude if you go up to the Crest or plan to exert yourself. People pass out all the time."

"Thanks." The guy—Chris is sure now that he's young— seems genuinely grateful. "Can I buy you a drink?"

Chris swallows a hallelujah. "Sure. Sounds good. I'm Chris Kristofer."

"I'm Reb . . ." The young man coughs. "Rob Trapper."

"Rob Trapper," Chris repeats. "Pleased to meet you."

He steers Rob over to his table, suspecting that the other green-robes or Vera Tso might attempt to interfere with any further conversation. From the alacrity with which Rob follows, he suspects that Rob thinks the same thing.

Perhaps Rob's a prisoner of a cult! That would be a banner headline: "Albuquerque Investigative Reporter Busts Cult!" "Religious Group Used As Cover By Drug Gang!" Then he mentally kicks himself. What kind of cult recruits only six-foot (or taller) hairy men?

"So, what business are you in?" Chris asks. Bill has stayed out on the dance floor where he is creating quite a stir by demonstrating a classic waltz. *Good guy*, Chris thinks. *Keep them distracted.*

"It's international," Rob says evasively. "We're meeting to discuss internal regulatory matters."

"You a religious group?" Chris asks.

"Uh." Rob giggles again. "Sure! You could call us a representational theocracy." He smiles at his own joke. "Seriously, we're no more religious than most people."

"But the robes, the turbans, all the guys wearing hats and boots and beards . . ." Chris presses.

"Private symbolism," Rob says. "It's a family thing, from the old country."

Chris doesn't miss the nervous glance Rob casts in the direction of the others. Maybe his theory was closer than he had thought. Given American devotion to freedom of religion, a religious group *would* be a great cover for drug smugglers.

"So, what do you plan to see in Albuquerque?" Chris asks, changing the subject.

"Our host suggested that we go to the State Fair," Rob answers, relieved. "Do you think that's a good idea?"

"A great one," Chris agrees. "I go every year. It has something for everyone: art, animals, rides, lots of food, a whole building devoted to cool junk."

And, Chris adds silently to himself, *if you go there, we'll have no trouble locating a crew of six- and seven-foot-tall green-robed men. And maybe, just maybe, your host will be with you and we can finally uncover the secret of Arthur Pendragon.*

All that is necessary for the forces of evil to win in the world is for enough good men to do nothing.

—EDMUND BURKE

LESS THAN AN HOUR AFTER EDDIE AND ARTHUR FINISH posting the day's events, the phones start ringing. Anson and Frank, who had planned to join the group at the Pyramid after dinner, conscript themselves to help and never make it out the door.

The questions, despite the various accents and inflections, are all variations on the same theme. "What is going on?" "How can you expect to decide such a crucial issue without a full quorum?" "Whose idea was this meeting anyhow?"

The answers satisfy some, enflame others. Several callers announce that they will be coming to join the meeting, among them Lil Prima, Tommy Thunderburst, the Smith, Garrett Kocchui, and Patti Lyn Asinbeau.

Finally, Arthur orders the answering machines put on with a new message that says: "This is Arthur Pendragon. Thank you for your concern about recent developments. Answers to the most frequently asked questions have been posted on our website. We will open for business at the regular time tomorrow."

Then he calls over to the Pyramid to ask that the meeting start a few hours later the next day. Monk quickly agrees.

"Almost everyone is down in the bar," he says, "dancing and drinking. It made me so nervous that I came back up here to visit with the *kappa*. Hiero and Roy are down there, though. They've shifted to look female so that there would be enough dance partners. A couple of the *pooka* did the same thing. The sasquatch and the yeti are dancing with each other. I can tell you that *that's* raising some eyebrows."

"Oh," is all Arthur can think to say.

"How do you manage it, Arthur?" Monk asks. "I've been in charge for just a couple of days, and I want to fly out the window and never come back."

"You won't though," Arthur says.

"Naw, these folks would be lost without some help."

"And that's what keeps me going," Arthur answers. He forces a laugh. "Besides there are great benefits like a fancy house and lots of angry phone calls."

"See you in the morning, Arthur," Monk replies with a chuckle. "And thanks."

Arthur heads to the kitchen, where his team is sharing a plate of cookies.

"Want a drink?" Eddie asks, gesturing with his beer bottle.

"Earl Grey tea, I think," Arthur says, "decaffeinated. I don't dare be kept up all night. Any word from Lovern?"

"He called in on the line I've been covering," Frank says. He holds one jackalope on his lap, another sits on the counter in front of him. Both hands hold carrots. "He said to tell you that he found what he was looking for, and he's on his way back."

"Ah." Arthur absently strokes one of the Cats of Egypt— the same one who had been his advisor during the reign of Akhenaton.

The kettle whistles. Motioning for Eddie to keep his seat, Arthur moves to brew himself a cup of tea.

"Did Lovern say when he'd be getting in?"

"Just late."

Arthur glances at the clock. It's almost midnight. He decides he'll finish his tea, then go to bed. Lovern will wake him if his report is important. When the grandfather clock in the front hall chimes midnight, Arthur puts his cup and saucer into the dishwasher.

"Please excuse me," he says, "but I believe I will be off to bed. I expect that I will need to rise early."

All but Anson, who is taking the first night shift, agree that they, too, should be getting some rest.

Anson waves to them as they troop up the stairs. "I'll tell Vera all about our expected guests when she comes back," he promises. "All of you rest easy. Tomorrow will be another day and a hell of a day at that."

✿▣✿

The meeting the next day begins late and ends later, extending through the dinner hour and necessitating canceling the planned outing to the State Fair.

No one minds; indeed, problems are being hashed out. The theriomorphs realize for the first time that what they want differs within their own group. Even those like Rebecca Trapper, who had advocated a full, public introduction into society, are forced to confront the truth that the world might not be ready for them.

But she and her cohorts are unwilling to abandon their dreams. The memory of the night before, when they had blended so successfully with the normal humans in the Pyramid Club, is as intoxicating as strong drink, teasing and enticing them.

"Would you be willing," Arthur offers, late in the night, "to develop a compromise? Up to this point we have helped the theriomorphs obtain legal identities within the human societies of their various countries of residence. Would you be willing to take this a step further and begin your entry into human society clad in an illusion that makes you appear to be human?"

Rebecca, who has found herself the speaker for her contingent in the absence of the Moderator, rises. "I cannot speak for the rest, Your Majesty, not without further discussion, but your offer has its positive points. Can you explain how the illusions would be created and how we would maintain them?"

"And how much they would cost," says one of the *pooka*, who recalls the days when athanor paid high sums for magical communication or similar services that technology now performs.

"An illusion," protests Snowbird the yeti, "would only serve part of our needs—the need to blend in without being seen, but it would merely be a stopgap. It might even cause more troubles than it solves. We live in relative secrecy now, but what would happen if humans thought of us as like themselves?"

His wife, Swansdown, adds, "I don't want to deal with authorities trying to take Dawn or the other young ones off to school. If we were recognized as yeti, our place on the fringes of their society would be understood."

Lil Prima interjects, "But you are saying, are you not, that you wish to be part of the human society for those things that would benefit you? Why shouldn't they regulate how your children are educated?"

"We live centuries longer than humans," Demetrios protests. "Our educational needs are not their needs!"

Like a judge gaveling for silence, Rebecca pounds on the seat of her chair with one massive fist. She gives Arthur, who has been watching the argument with a bemused expression, a smile that is partially apologetic, partially embarrassed.

"Shall we," she says, once silence is restored, "let Arthur explain to us how these illusions would be achieved . . ."

"And how they would be paid for?" repeats Padraig O'Faolain, the *pooka*.

"And how they would be paid for," Rebecca agrees, "before we accept or reject them out of hand?"

There is no further protest, and Rebecca turns wearily to Arthur. "Your Majesty?"

The King smiles thanks. "Actually, I wish to let Lovern, who is known to many of you, explain how the procedure would be handled magically. Then Eddie has some comments about how the illusion would be correlated with your current identities."

Padraig shuffles irritably in his chair. His shape keeps migrating between that of a wild-eyed, scruffy-maned black pony and an impish boy. Arthur glances at him and smiles soothingly. "And then, as Padraig O'Faolain has requested, we will deal with the question of expense. Let me say at this time that any figures would be broad estimates. We had not seen the need to develop this program until yesterday's meeting.''

The theriomorphs settle into their chairs, ready to take notes, prepared to frame protests, certain, at least, that they will get their say.

None of them realize the secret fears harbored by the wizard who so nonchalantly brushes his hand through his silvery beard, the apprehensions that keep the King and his intimates glancing toward the windows and jumping to answer any phone call.

Even as they work toward a modification of their working Accord, those who would shatter that Accord and perhaps even the Harmony on which it stands are preparing for their own entrance into the meeting.

¤▣¤

The next morning, Monk is particularly edgy as he and Hiero gather their associates into the vans that will take them to Pendragon Estates.

"Brighten up, *tengu*!" Swansdown says kindly as she settles her children into their seat belts. "Arthur has promised that tonight's meeting will not go as late."

"We're going to the Fair," Dawn says happily. "I'm going to see a baby lamb."

Monk manages a smile and a quip that makes the young yetis giggle, but his inner tension does not fade. Today, if he keeps his promise, Sven Trout will join them. If he does not, tomorrow Monk must decide whether to reveal who the Moderator is (and risk undermining everything) or keep his silence.

The latter option is only superficially agreeable. If Sven comes to believe that Monk will remain biddable, then he may continue to play his games from a distance. The extension of his uncomfortably responsible role doesn't please Monk at all; nor does the realization that he and his fellow *tengu* would be alone in their brooding concern about what the Fiery One intends next.

No, if Sven does not appear today, then at the first stroke of midnight, Monk will call Arthur and tell him what he knows. He can handle the King's certain displeasure; maybe he can even imply that Sven forced the *tengu* into doing his bidding.

Yes . . . he could turn that little incident with the prank phone calls to their advantage if he works it just right.

Looking around, a more relaxed smile on his face, Monk sees that everyone is aboard except for Rebecca and Bronson Trapper.

The two sasquatches are standing at the main entry to the hotel. Rebecca is in animated conversation with two human males. He thinks, from Hiero's description, that they may be the same two she had been talking with in the bar the night before last.

"Hey," he calls. "We're ready to go."

"Sorry!" Rebecca calls back.

She makes another quick comment to the young men, then, when Bronson takes her arm, hurries to the van.

"See you tonight, Rob!" the darker-skinned of the men calls after. "Have a great day!"

"Bye!" Rebecca answers, waving before she bundles into the van. She looks around and realizes everyone is looking at her. "They wanted to know if we'd seen the Fair yet. Chris is a local. He said he'd be glad to show us around. I told him we hoped to get there about six."

Monk swallows a protest. This is what they had all wanted, a chance to mingle with the natives on their own terms. He can hardly deny them. He'd only be opening himself up to accusations that because he can shapeshift, he doesn't really sympathize.

He wonders if he *does* sympathize. Then he guns the engine and leads the caravan over to yet another day of argument. And maybe a little more.

☼◙☼

By the third day of the meeting, the group has grown so large that Eddie and the Smith take down the semipermanent wall dividing the two largest conference rooms in order to accommodate the numbers. The theriomorphs are still commuting from their hotel, but the guest rooms at the hacienda are rapidly filling.

The hum of conversation is constant, except during the meetings themselves. Unlike the Lustrum Review, there is no routine business. Everything focuses on the linked issues of the theriomorphs' desire to move from the fringes of human society and what this might mean for the athanor as a whole.

Still, when the athanor break for lunch, the overall mood is optimistic. Now only the most wildly idealistic of the theriomorphs believe that a sudden revelation is a good idea. The plan that is slowly gaining favor blends the use of illusion and a gradual education-and-awareness program to prepare the humans for a revelation some fifty or so years hence.

As the afternoon meeting is opening and Eddie has finished reading a summary of the morning's business, the double doors at the back of the room dramatically blow open.

"And why," says Sven Trout, projecting his voice so that it fills the entire room, "should anyone wait fifty years? I say we should tell them now!"

He strides down the center aisle clad in a green robe similar to those worn by the sasquatch and yeti. Behind him, also clad in robes, though these are almost painfully blue-white, are Louhi Maki and a man no one but Lovern has ever seen before.

The Head walks with a hitch to his step, but his gait is confident nonetheless. He looks deeply into the faces of those seated at the curved table in the front of the room, and Arthur and his allies must fight down a deep, visceral fear.

Human legends hold the memory of when black sorcerers walked the Earth. The athanor had slain them long ago, leaving only those who practiced in shades of grey like Louhi, Lil, and Lovern.

The roomful of people had fallen silent at Sven's grand entrance, but now murmurs of shock, surprise, and indignation rise. Sven shouts his next words loudly enough to dominate all the other voices so that the silence seems to have fallen again.

"Why should we let humans dictate our actions? We are their seniors. We could be their masters—their guardians— their guides. Now they flounder, lost and lonely in a universe their science has stripped of magic and wonder. They search for God and know that, if he is not dead, he is no longer the thundering Jehovah they once worshiped, trusted, adored, and feared.

"I say that Arthur has led us wrongly. The time for caution is gone. The time for action is now! Why should we blindly follow a hidebound administrator—a man without imagination or depth, a man whose closest advisors are a sycophant and a corrupt slaver who abuses the very system he claims to uphold?"

Eddie's face darkens with anger, knowing well enough who is being called "sycophant." He rises, balling his fists. In his arms and shoulders muscles strengthened by his reliance on his crutches threaten to rip the sleeves of his short-sleeved sport shirt.

"Sven! What grounds do you have for coming here and making such inflammatory statements?"

"The same as those whose robes I sent to them." Sven turns and looks out over the gathering, smiles at a horrified Rebecca Trapper, who is just now realizing who he must be. "I am the one who has summoned them. I am here to make certain that they do not forget their purpose beneath your lulling words."

"You are the Moderator?" Rebecca asks, her normally bell-like voice cracking.

"I am the Moderator," Sven says, "and lest my old rivals frighten you, let me remind you that I am here as an advocate of moderation. What else am I calling for if not a moderation of the policies that have dominated the Harmony for too long?"

The Smith rises. "How about rebellion? Chaos? Destruction?"

Sven faces him. "I thought you would understand me, Smith. You work with fire. Without fire, metal must be sifted from dirt. The finest crafting comes only when the metal is softened by fire. I am here to soften the ore of the Harmony so that it may be reworked into a new shape."

"I admire your metaphor," the Smith says, "but I cannot say I trust you any more than I trust the coals in my forge not to burn my smithy to the ground."

"There is so much I must say," Sven says, his expression

open, appealing, warm. "So many things I must tell you all, but I know that I am on shaky ground here. Therefore, first I must ask for the protection of this gathering."

He is so busy appealing to the group that he does not notice Duppy Jonah departing from his seat at the back of the room. The Head notices, but knowing that Duppy Jonah has himself grown restive at Arthur's rule, he does not comment. Whatever Louhi thinks is muted beneath the cushion of love that binds her will.

Arthur stands. When he speaks, his words are chosen with a respect only partially feigned. Sven remains a master of manipulation. The Fiery One has supplied himself with allies and with an admirable cause that cannot be easily dismissed. Yet Arthur permits himself to hope that, as in the past, Sven has somewhere laid the grounds for his own defeat.

"I am amused," the King says, "that you should appeal for protection to those very hidebound forces that you claim need 'softening.' Yet, I am willing to grant you the protection of this gathering. You may speak within the house. You may even claim rooms here for yourself and your allies. For now . . ."

He pauses so that those listening will perceive the implied threat, "For now, you are still within Harmony and protected by our common Accord."

"Thank you, Your Majesty," Sven replies promptly, "though let me remind the younger ones that, for all you imply that they are of your making, rather than of your use, neither Harmony, nor Accord originated in you or your administration."

"No," Arthur agrees, "we have merely upheld them. Do you plan to do the same?"

"Of course not!" Sven says cheerfully, allowing horrified murmuring to fill the hall. "How can I advocate change and promise to uphold the Accord in one breath? I'm no politician . . ."

A wave of nervous laughter interrupts him, disconcerting him temporarily. He quickly adapts his speech: "I am no politician to make impossible promises. My goal is change but not, for all the good Smith has said, the change of Chaos. My change is that of amendment, not destruction."

"Fire," comes the rich, laughing voice of Anson A. Kridd,

"usually destroys as it changes. We will remember that, eh?"

"Do," Sven answers, "as long as you remember that fire in a forest may destroy disease, weak undergrowth, and saplings that could not have lived in any case. Fire in a hearth destroys old wood in exchange for heat and light. Fire's destruction often clears the way for things we might prefer."

Jonathan Wong raises his hand and, when he is acknowledged, bows first to Arthur, then to Sven.

"I would like to request that this meeting continue without such a wealth of metaphors. When you entered, you made several accusations that need answering. I am certain that Eddie would be willing to overlook as mere literary license your calling him a sycophant . . ."

Eddie growls something inarticulate, but nods stiffly.

"However, you have stated that one among us is a"—he glances at his notes to confirm the wording—" 'a corrupt slaver who abuses the very system he claims to uphold.' "

None of Sven's aplomb deserts him, although he had wished to lead up to this issue in his own time. Lovern, seated on the dais in the front of the room, keeps his expression neutral, but his gaze is fixed on the Head.

Sven gestures theatrically. "Very well, Jonathan. You wish me to be blunt, blunt I shall be, though it is against my very nature."

"Don't we know that," grumbles Katsuhiro Oba, who had hurried to New Mexico in hope of a fight and has found himself immured in the type of debate he despises.

Sven steels his gaze and fixes it on Lovern. The wizard refuses to quail, even smiles a touch ruefully.

"The slave keeper sits before us, at the King's left hand. And his slave stands behind me, freed at last from the bondage in which he has been kept since the days of Ragnarokk!"

The Head walks unsteadily forward until he stands directly in front of Lovern. Then he turns and stares proudly out over the assembled throng.

"Born of sorcerous spell," he says, "and Odin's eye, I grew into life upon Mimir's shoulder. When war was near won, he slashed me free and set me in solitude in the seal's bath, beneath the whale's road. In darkness and despair resided I there, but though my master deemed me a wise worker in spellcraft and safe store for legend lore, never did he acknowledge that I was as his son and as much a member of Harmony as any here.''

Louhi has cut the Head's hair and trimmed his beard in a style similar to Lovern's own. The facial features, no longer gaunt and pale, no longer distorted by the ichor in which they had been stored, hint at the kinship. Moreover, those who remember Odin see that likeness as well, especially in the brown eye set beside one of coyote yellow.

''Cast what spells you wish,'' Sven says cheerfully. ''Seek to unmask illusion or trickery. Use a truthstone to test the Head's words if you desire. You will find that there is no deception here. What the Head tells you is the truth.''

''Or,'' says Jonathan Wong, ''what he believes to be true. You and Louhi could have created him yourself and given him a false history he believes. I would hear Lovern testify to the truth or falsehood of this case.''

Only Arthur's belief that Jonathan Wong is acting as an impartial judge, as a free member of the Harmony, keeps him from feeling that this trusted counselor has betrayed him. Lovern must feel the same, for he rises without hesitation.

''I will answer you, Jonathan. I did create the Head, in much the fashion that he has told. I did store it, much as he has said, although for his safety rather than out of malice or fear.''

Murmurs rise from the assembled group.

''What he does not say, I will,'' Lovern continues. ''Until a few days ago, it never occurred to me that the Head was in any way a person, nor did he attempt to inform me of such. Therefore, I thought him only a creation of my magic with no more volition than is held by a truthstone or ward. That, Jonathan, is my answer to these charges. I hold I was not a slaver, for I never knew I kept a slave.''

Lovern sinks back into his chair. Jonathan's polite ''Thank you'' is drowned out by the rising tumult. Arthur makes no attempt to still the rising argument. He turns to Eddie, smiles a smile both wry and rueful.

''Well, this is what we have been awaiting and dreading these long months. The end is come at last.''

¤◙¤

Duppy Jonah, ruler of all the oceans of the Earth, stands in the corridor outside of the meeting rooms talking to Connel the selkie in low, urgent tones.

"What do you mean that you are not certain you can find him? You have seen the Changer. Vera has told us that he is within an hour's drive of this house."

Connel rubs the side of his freckled pug nose. "Lord, the rules of the Land are not those of the Sea. If the Changer has taken himself away, I certainly cannot find him."

"You can find me one whale in all the pods within all the oceans if I so bid you, but you cannot find me a creature as unique as the Changer in a span that cannot be more than a hundred miles—less! We know he has gone into the mountains."

"Lord, the creatures of the sea know you and do your bidding," Connel says patiently. "I do not so much find that whale as he is found for me—for you. Perhaps Arthur commands such obedience from the land dwellers."

The selkie permits himself a grin, secure in the knowledge that he is among those favored by his tempestuous lord. "Although I do not think that this is the case if the arguing and debate we have heard these past days is any indication."

"Then how will we find the Changer?" Duppy Jonah muses. "He must be told that Sven is here. After what was done to him at this one's instigation . . . yes, most certainly, even sore wounded, the Changer will wish to know where Sven is to be found."

The door from the meeting room opens and Anson exits. His bow to Duppy Jonah is such a fluid thing that it seems more the first step in an elaborate dance than an obeisance.

"So you mean to seek the Changer, eh?" he asks, his smile only widening when Duppy Jonah frowns angrily.

"Have you been eavesdropping, Spider?"

"No. Even if I wanted to, I wouldn't find it easy. Those doors are soundproofed."

"Then?"

"I saw you leave soon after Sven made his entrance. Nei-

ther Amphitrite nor Vera made any move to stop you.
Therefore, you were either going out for some routine business or for something serious. When you didn't return
quickly, I decided the reason was not routine and hurried to
place myself at your service."

"And why would you wish to do that?"

"Because the old Changer and I are friends. Because I
think he should know what is happening here. Because I
think that he's more likely to listen to you than to me. Because if he's going to help himself, I'd like it to be at a time
when that helping would help Arthur, too."

"Oh." Duppy Jonah considers. "Can you find him?"

"I have a good idea where to start looking. Not only that,
I know where the keys to the van are kept. May I accompany
you?"

"When should we go?"

"Sven has claimed the protection of this house," Anson
says, "so the sooner the better. If he knows the Changer is
coming, he will stay inside until his damage is done. Tonight,
however . . ."

"A trip is planned to the State Fair."

"Yes. I slipped a note to Rebecca Trapper—who is having
some mighty powerful mixed feelings now that she knows
who has been pulling her strings—suggesting that she invite
Sven to join them during their outing so they can get better
acquainted."

"And why should she listen to you?"

Anson winks. "I signed the note from her friend Demetrios. She won't know otherwise until it's too late."

"Then I see only one problem," Duppy Jonah says. "I
agree that my brother will be more likely to heed me—moreover, I may be able to find him by virtue of our shared
blood . . ."

"Neat trick, that."

"But I will most certainly be missed in the assembly. If
we do not want Sven warned, how can I go?"

Anson strokes his chin, then he turns to Connel.

"Are you a shapeshifter, lad?"

"After a fashion. I can shape from man to seal and back
again, if I have the proper skin."

Without asking leave, Anson reaches up and with a knife

he produces (apparently from nowhere) he slices off a piece of Duppy Jonah's hair. This he places on Connel's head.

"Pretend this is your 'proper skin,'" Anson tells the astonished selkie, "and shift into your master's shape."

Connel glances at Duppy Jonah for permission. The Sea King nods. Closing his eyes, the selkie begins to concentrate so hard that his skin pales and sweat dots his forehead.

"Not like that," Anson chides, pressing down on the selkie's head. "Easy, just like man into seal."

Connel sighs, then motions as if pulling a pelt over his shoulders. As his hands drop to his side, he shakes the heavy purple-black hair of the Sea King from his eyes.

"I . . ." he says, and his voice is Duppy Jonah's as well.

"There. Go and take your lord's place in the meeting," Anson orders. "Write a swift note to Amphitrite so that she will help you with the deception."

"Go!" Duppy Jonah adds when Connel hesitates. "We will return soon."

"And we'll call first so there will be no trouble over folks seeing two Duppy Jonahs," Anson assures the selkie.

When Connel has returned to the meeting, Duppy Jonah grabs Anson by the shoulder. "I didn't know you could work magic."

"Small things," Anson replies glibly, "learned when I stole magic from the Spirit in the Sky. The ability to shape-shift something else is particularly useful if you get into trouble as often as I do, but I couldn't have done it so quickly without the selkie's own abilities to support me."

"And my hair?"

"Theater." Anson grins. "I can never pass up a chance for a grand effect."

During the drive, Duppy Jonah questions Anson about the Spider's relationship with the Changer and assures himself that the ancient trickster is truly his brother's friend.

"When I saw the condition that Louhi left the Changer in," Anson explains, "I knew then that even though I am a signatory to the Accord, I would do anything I could to help the Changer."

"The Changer is not a signatory to the Accord, is he?" Duppy Jonah asks.

"No. He's in Harmony, but otherwise he protects himself and expects no protection from anyone else."

"Then he is not bound by Arthur's offer of the protection of his house."

"True, but I don't think the Changer would relish having all the Accord forced to protect Sven against him. I wouldn't enjoy that much either, come to think of it. Such a conflict could break the Accord and Arthur's administration as easily as whatever game Sven is playing."

"Yes. I can see that, but will the Changer?"

Anson fumbles with a bag of cookies with one hand as he drives. The Sea King rips it open for him.

"I think," Anson says around an oatmeal-raisin cookie, "that the Changer will realize that Sven could use the conflict between them to weaken the Accord. He may not be a member of the Accord, but he will not wish to break it. Surely he realizes that the Accord is Shahrazad's best protection."

"True," Duppy Jonah says thoughtfully. "Even if it were not, the Changer would not wish to be Sven's tool."

"So the Changer will moderate his actions to preserve Arthur. May I beg leave to ask you a question, Sea King?"

Duppy Jonah responds to the sudden formality of Anson's words with formality of his own. "You may ask, Spider."

"I was curious," Anson says, "if you planned to ask the Accord to move against Cleonice Damita."

Duppy Jonah fidgets as if the question makes him physically uncomfortable. Anson does not press for an answer, but drives on, munching cookies. At last, the Sea King replies: "I am a creature much like my beloved oceans. My anger can be a tempest, but then I can calm into the most placid doldrums that ever stole the wind from a ship's sails."

Anson makes a noncommittal but encouraging sound.

"When Amphitrite was taken from me, I was furious and would have done anything to regain her. I cared for nothing but my loss and for the punishment of those who had wronged me.

"But when Amphitrite was returned to me and I learned that two of those who had done her this wrong were dead, I exhausted my rage keeping Lovern captive. As long as Cleonice is formally severed from the Accord and I am made part of any committee that considers her reinstatement, then I am content.''

Anson nods. ''Magnanimous in victory.''

''Perhaps,'' Duppy Jonah says, ''I was also influenced by Vera's belief that the South American contingent did not plan to kill them. I find . . . to my embarrassment . . . that the fury of my reaction was expected. My anger was used to manipulate Arthur. I dislike this immensely.''

''I understand,'' Anson says. ''So Cleonice may live?''

''I will not seek her death,'' Duppy Jonah says, ''but I would not attempt to prevent it if another sought it.''

''And could someone gain your favor with her death?''

Duppy Jonah rumbles laughter. ''No. I will not pay for the head of John the Baptist—nor request to be rid of a troublesome priest. Cleonice was a fool. Leave it there.''

When they arrive in the appropriate section of the Sandias, Duppy Jonah gets out of the van. He breathes deeply, shaking his head in disapproval.

''The air is so thin, so dry, so empty.''

''There are places that are worse,'' Anson says philosophically. ''Any ideas as to how we find your brother?''

''A few. I have been recalling old practices during our drive, but it has been long since I used them.''

Anson, who knows that Duppy Jonah speaks of millennia, not centuries, nods and opens a box of doughnuts. He has eaten three when the Sea King shakes himself from his revery.

''There was a call we used long ago when both of us ventured onto land,'' he says, ''a carrying thing. That would surely reach him, especially in this clear air.''

''So?'' Anson asks, for Duppy Jonah is not calling.

''I cannot make it from this human throat, nor am I at all certain that I can shapeshift this far from water or without unspelling the spell that Lovern has used to make me seem human.''

''That last is a risk we can't predict,'' Anson says practically, ''but I can guide you to shifting just like I did your selkie.''

'' 'Tis a good thing then,'' Duppy Jonah says with a belly laugh, ''that your use of my hair was just theater.''

''True enough,'' Anson says. ''Let me place my hand

upon your head. When I give the word, concentrate on the shape you wish to take. Don't worry about channeling energy. That's my part.''

The Sea King complies and, perhaps because he is more powerful than Connel, or perhaps because he has more confidence in Anson's abilities, within about a minute he stands on the roadside in the form of a massive bull elephant seal.

"That's quite a trick," says the Spider, wiping his forehead and eating two more doughnuts. "Now, you make your great cry."

The seal shuffles to face the seemingly empty forest. Then a weird and eerie sound rings out, seemingly too high-pitched to come from the baggy throat. There is volume behind the call, volume and strength, and it carries through the evergreen-forested slopes, echoes off the rocks, and finally fades away.

The Sea King calls thrice, each time pausing five minutes between calls to listen. After the third repetition, there is an answer. It is fainter, as if the chest behind the cry is smaller, but the notes are unmistakable.

Snuffling his bulbous, trunklike nose, the Sea King nods solemnly to Anson. Then he flops over, and Anson puts his hand lightly on the seal's head. When Duppy Jonah has been returned to human form, both he and Anson are trembling.

"I don't think we should try that again," Duppy Jonah says. "I drew upon the pattern of Lovern's spell for the human shape, which, since I did not undo it with the command word, remained."

"And the Changer?" Anson asks.

"He comes," the Sea King says from a throat made rough and weary. "He comes."

✿▣✿

When he arrives hours later, the Changer needs very little explanation. He listens to their report in silence, his single yellow eye almost unblinking, his hand (for he had shifted human-form) resting on Shahrazad's head.

"We go, then," he says, when Anson finished his speech, "and I thank you both."

He tilts his head to one side so that his gaze can rest on

Shahrazad. "You are nearly old enough to be left alone now, little girl. Yet . . ."

Again the tilting of the head, the inspection by the yellow eye, this time of the Sea King and the Spider.

"But I am reluctant to do so. Twice she has been used against me: once when my enemy would have killed my family to set me on Lilith, once when they kidnapped her." He makes a dry sound that passes for an ironic chuckle. "I have a weakness, and she is a few pounds of baby coyote. Shall I leave her where she may be safe but I shall wonder, or shall I take her with me?"

Anson tosses the pup a chunk of doughnut. "She danced the Harmony Dance, Changer. How much longer must you fool yourself that she is a pup to be sent on her own way when she reaches six months or a year? She is one of us."

Duppy Jonah nods and, to emphasize his point, gets on his knees so that he can stroke the coyote pup. "This is my niece, Changer. You have had young before, but most take after their mothers. This one has found her heritage young. Let us bring her with us, have her declared in Harmony. She will be guaranteed a juvenile's protection within the Accord. It is more than you alone can do for her."

The Changer smiles one of his rare, open smiles. "Good. You've convinced me to do what I wanted to do. Now I am certain that Shahrazad will be safe even when I must leave her."

As they spiral down the mountain roads toward the outspread gleam of the city lights, the Changer asks question after question, formulating his plans.

"Drop me off near the fairgrounds," he says. Then he glances at his nudity, which to this point had not been an issue between them. "No, I will need clothing."

"And we will need to put Shahrazad somewhere safe." Anson chuckles. "We cannot bring a coyote to a place filled with livestock. It would not be fair to her."

The three men frown. Shahrazad whines sadly.

"Can we put her in a room at the hacienda?" Duppy Jonah asks. "Or will she howl?"

"She may howl, but she knows the place, so she may not." Anson drums his fingers along the steering wheel. "This is the answer. I will call ahead. We will drive around, maybe get something to eat, until we are told that Sven and his crew have left. Then we go to the hacienda, get some clothes for the Changer, and put Shahrazad in the care of some stay-at-home. Then we head to the Fair.''

The Changer nods. "Make your call.''

¤◙¤

For Rebecca Trapper, the wonders of the State Fair, revealed in the light of early evening, are almost enough to make her forget her uneasiness regarding Sven Trout. She had grown to maturity hearing from her Aunt Swansdown and the Olsens the legends of the athanor. In these Sven Trout, by his various names, had often had an unsavory role.

Yet, watching him stroll along, dressed now in jeans and a garish Western shirt, cotton candy in one hand, an inflatable rubber hammer in the other, she cannot find him a figure of fear.

The Head is easier to fear. Like most of the theriomorphs, this is his first outing of this sort, but even the satyrs' open lust as they stare at the pretty girls in their short skirts or tight pants, as they whistle admiringly at the cleavage revealed by low-cut blouses, is warming and natural compared to the grasping avarice and weird complacency with which the Head gazes around from his mismatched eyes.

"It's as if he has seen the world,'' Rebecca whispers to Bronson, resisting an urge to cling to his hand, "and not only has he decided that it is good—he's decided to have it gift-wrapped and sent to him at his hotel.''

Bronson grunts agreement. "I won't let him harm you, dear. Now, what do you want to see next?''

"Swansdown and the Olsens want to take the children on the rides. The *kappa* want to go, too, but I'd rather see the Indian Arts Building.''

"We can split into smaller groups.'' Bronson reaches into his sleeve pocket. "I have a watch.''

"Let's do that then.''

They have just finished making arrangements with the other yeti and sasquatches when two voices call out.

"Rob! Rob!''

Looking over they see Chris Kristofer and Bill Irish hurrying up. The two men seem genuinely pleased to see "Rob."

Bronson quietly notes that they did not have any trouble picking one green-robed figure out of the group. Maybe they hadn't blended in quite as well as Rebecca had thought.

Rebecca shakes Chris's hand, noticing again how big her own is in contrast, and dips a bow to Bill. He bobs back.

"Having fun?" Bill says.

"Yes." Rebecca gestures to Bronson. "This is my . . . best friend, Bronson."

"I think we saw you this morning," Chris says, looking up into the hairy face. "Pleased to meet you."

"And I you." Bronson offers his huge hand briefly.

With instinctive caution, Swansdown and Snowbird have moved the rest of their group along, so more introductions are not needed. Demetrios lingers on the fringes, but seeing Georgios licking his lips and leering after a pretty Hispanic girl, he hurries to defuse the situation.

Bill asks, "Where you headed next?"

"We were going to see the Indian Arts Building," Rebecca says shyly. "We've just finished looking at the Spanish art."

"Want a local guide?" Chris asks. "I'd say 'native,' but that has other meanings around here. I'm no expert, but I do know an inlay from an overlay."

Rebecca notices that Bill's gaze has wandered after a couple of pretty high-school girls.

"Do you know Indian art, too, Bill? I mean, I wouldn't want you to be bored. And we'd be stealing your friend."

Bill shrugs resignedly. "I'll come along. It's not as if I'll have any luck with the babes. I'm cursed."

"You should talk to our friend Georgios." Rebecca giggles.

"No!" Bronson says firmly, taking her elbow and steering her toward the Indian Arts Building.

"Did someone call for Georgios?" says a voice filled with lusty enthusiasm. The satyr comes up, Demetrios trailing behind.

Chris quickly offers his hand. "I think we met last night

n the Pyramid Club. Rob was saying that you could teach
ny poor young friend something about getting girls.''

"Nobody does it better," Georgios says smugly.

Over both Bronson and Demetrios's protests, Bill is escorted off, linked arm and arm with Georgios. Rebecca no-
ices that Chris looks as pleased as Bronson does worried.
She wonders about it for a moment, then decides to relax.
They're all blending in wonderfully. There's no need to be
concerned.

¤◙¤

At the main gates into the fairgrounds, the Changer stands
with Eddie, Anson, and Duppy Jonah. Arthur is already
somewhere on the grounds escorting one group of theriomorphs. Vera is with another, Jonathan with a third. Sven
had insisted on guiding a fourth and no one had been able
to come up with a polite reason why he should not. The rest
of the athanor are either loosely attached to one of the groups
or about their own business.

The Changer looks about the milling grounds, a dissatis-
fied expression on his face. "It will take hours to find Sven
in this crowd if I stay a human. I may even miss him entirely."

"He's certain to be with some of the sasquatch and yeti,"
Eddie offers. "The group we assigned him had the Trappers
and the Snowbirds. That should make finding him easier."

"Still," the Changer grumbles, "it will be easy to miss
him. I had no idea the Fair would be so crowded. I may do
better to wait until he leaves."

"We sent over vans," Eddie says. "He won't ever be
alone."

"And you're in a worse situation if you confront him in
a place where there are members of the Accord," Duppy
Jonah reminds his brother. "He can appeal to them for protection against you and even if they don't like it, he will be
within his rights."

"I still think," the Changer repeats, "that finding him will
be nearly impossible."

"Then what do you want to do, eh, ancient?" Anson asks. He's already wandered over to a cart and purchased a large bag of buttered popcorn.

"Let me shift into a raven. I can scout the grounds and narrow our search."

"And your clothes?"

"I'll give them to you."

Duppy Jonah sighs. "Do it. You have a point. And if you see Amphitrite, would you tell me where she is?"

"Gladly."

The Changer and Anson step into an empty rest room and the change is effected. A large black raven soars out the front door and into the twilight.

"He says," Anson comments as he rejoins the others, "that he will shift to an owl when the full darkness comes, but he prefers to be a raven while he can. They're common here."

"And what do we do?" Duppy Jonah asks.

"I suppose we enjoy the Fair," Eddie says dubiously.

Anson finishes his popcorn and licks the last of the butter from his long fingers. "Of course we do!" he says enthusiastically. "I've had enough of this health food. I smell barbecue, sausages, pies, and carmel apples. Let's go!"

A grin of pure amazement glints within the rich darkness of Duppy Jonah's beard. "Yes, Spider, let's go."

¤◙¤

Over the fairgrounds the Changer soars, catching the warm thermals from the food stands, the rides, the clustered people.

He perches on a tented bandstand beneath which a boy plays a country fiddle before a small but supportive audience. There are several green-robed yeti in the crowd and a faun pushing a *kappa* carefully propped up in a baby carriage. The *kappa's* wizened features and indented skull are covered by a frilled infant's bonnet. The Changer examines the group carefully but finds no flame-haired Sven.

Pushing off into the air again, he soars over a long avenue lined with booths selling souvenirs and food. He sees Jonathan Wong helping a selkie select a tee shirt, notes Vera seated on a bench instructing her charges how to eat cotton candy.

He soars on. Near the barns where prize farm animals are waiting to be judged, he sees a pair of *pooka* giggling in a corner. He is not at all surprised when on his second pass two more ponies wait for the judges' inspection.

In the horse arena, Arthur Pendragon sits in the stands with a contingent that includes a few green-robed figures, the Smith, Frank MacDonald, and a brace of *kappa* sitting in their laps.

Passing back over the avenue, the Changer sees Anson purchasing hats from a vendor. They resemble those worn by the Cat in the Hat in the book of that name. The ancient shapeshifter pauses long enough to watch the great and revered King of the Sea don his unlikely crown. Then he quorks laughter and flaps toward the midway.

Full darkness is now falling, and the lights of the various rides glow and sparkle. The Changer sweeps down to the lip of a wire trash barrel to scavenge some french fries soaked in cheese. Thus fortified, he flies to a rooftop and turns into a small owl.

Continuing his search, he lands between the cars on a towering Ferris wheel. He sees several green robes in line and soars down to check their company.

He is in time to see a satyr get his face resoundingly slapped by a pretty red-haired woman, but, although he watches and listens, he does not think that this woman is Sven.

Again over the grounds. Bronson and Rebecca Trapper, in the company of two humans that the Changer does not know, are walking from the Indian Arts Building. Bronson carries a package under one arm.

Remembering that Sven was supposed to be escorting this group, the Changer examines the humans carefully, lest one of them be Sven in another form. Looking at the open, laughing faces, he finds no trace of mockery. Sven is not here, either. The Changer must fly on.

In the animal barns, one of the *pooka* has been awarded a blue ribbon. The other has shifted human once more and is proudly parading his fellow out of the ring. There will be certain confusion when the authorities realize that these did not have proper entry forms.

And the Changer soars on. He is not despairing—he is far too old for this small delay to bring him to despair, but he is growing tired. Little birds need a great deal of food, and the owl cannot scavenge as a raven can. He compromises by shifting into a slightly anomalous raven and eating his fill and more from a trash can behind a line of food-vendor stalls.

An old Navajo woman touches her bag of gall medicine when she sees him. He answers her gesture by cawing loudly, then launching into the dark skies. Let her believe she has chased the witch away. She will be comforted.

He shifts back into an owl and flies over to the Indian Village. In a central space, six Pueblo men in elaborate beaded and befeathered costumes dance the formal, ritualized steps of some dance accompanied by music played on drums and flute. In the shadows, two fauns who have discarded their boots join hands and dance in company.

None of those who wander about the perimeter of the dance area, eating fry bread smeared with honey or browsing the displays of jewelry and pottery, notice the fauns except to smile at their joyful romp.

Next the Changer soars into the Mexican Village, and there he finds his prey. Sven Trout sits in a folding chair before a bandstand watching, with evident interest, a performance by a mariachi band. Over to one side of the bandstand, the Head and Louhi are inspecting a display of garish Mexican sombreros and sequined shawls.

None of them look as if they are planning to depart anytime soon. In any case, the avenues away from this section of the fairgrounds are limited. The Changer marks the place, then flies off to find Anson and the others.

He finds them at the intersection of the fairgrounds' two main avenues with Bronson, Rebecca, and their two humans. Duppy Jonah is no longer with them. Presumably, he has found Amphitrite and joined her party.

By the simple expedient of dropping a small rock on his head, the Changer gets Anson to look up. The he lures the Spider to a place where he can shift and they can talk.

"Sven's in the Mexican Village," the Changer says, as soon as he has shifted.

"Put on your pants!" Anson says, handing them to him. "Now, have you thought about how you will catch him?"

"I thought I would simply walk up to him and say I wished to have a word with him."

"It might work." Anson hands the Changer his shirt. "I have a more complicated plan in mind."

"Why bother?"

"What if he wishes to flee?"

"I will hold him."

"And if he calls for help?"

"Will he?"

"Can you say he will not?"

"No."

"I believe if he thought that he could use the Accord against you, then he would not involve ordinary humans."

"I see . . ."

"Rebecca Trapper has friends who can help us. What I have in mind is . . ."

Sven Trout sincerely likes mariachi music and Mexican food, but both are better for their location away from the midway.

In Sven's restless state of mind, long waits in line for a minute or so of artificially created terror hold no appeal. Realizing that Snowbird and his family will be engaged by the rides for some time and that Demetrios is fully capable of keeping track of the satyrs, Sven had used the excuse of checking up on Bronson and Rebecca to make his escape.

No one seemed terribly sorry to see him go. He is certain that everyone was relieved when the Head and Louhi left with him.

"Hello, Sven," says a voice at his right shoulder.

He finds Anson A. Kridd and Eddie sliding into seats behind him. They wear matching red-satin jackets emblazoned with the logo of the Albuquerque Dukes and floppy, striped hats. Anson's is red and orange, Eddie's blue and purple.

"Having fun?" Anson asks, popping an éclair into his mouth.

"I am," Sven says. "I love mariachi music."

Eddie grins. "I won the jackets in one of the basketball-shooting arcades. You should have seen the look on the proprietor's face. I'm sure the hoops are rigged, but after just one shot I got a feel for the spin."

He mimes shooting baskets.

"Did you win the hats, too?" Sven asks, sincerely interested. Something for nothing has always interested him.

"Nope." Eddie gently punches his buddy on the shoulder. "Anson got them for us."

"Where're the lady and the Head?" Anson asks, digging through his pockets and discovering only an empty bag where he clearly had hoped to find another snack.

"I think they're in one of the stalls."

"We should go pay our respects," Anson says, "and I want another éclair. That one was too small."

Eddie chuckles. "I wish I had your metabolism, Spider. I bet that Arthur would like it even more."

"Sorry, I'm not giving it up."

Sven waves casually as they wander off. The band is starting a new piece. He leans comfortably back in his chair. About halfway through the song, he hears a deep, gravelly voice at his right shoulder.

"Hello, Sven."

Sven feels his bowels tighten. He fights down the urge to flee wildly.

"Hello, Changer."

"I heard you were in town and thought that it was time for us to chat."

Sven turns slightly in his seat. The Changer is directly behind him but he can see that the ancient studies him out of only one eye.

"Why?"

"I don't approve of what you did to me, and now that you're outside of Arthur's protection . . ." The Changer lets his words trail off.

"We made a deal!"

"I didn't deal. You offered terms I had no choice but to accept if I wanted my daughter to live."

The gravelly voice speaking directly into Sven's ear seems louder than the mariachi music, but that music is making their conversation quite private. The people nearest to Sven have moved away, perhaps made nervous by his one-eyed visitor.

Sven looks around anxiously. Neither Louhi nor the Head is in sight—he doesn't dare guess in which direction they have gone. Then, at the fringes of the Mexican Village, nearly hidden by the darkness, he sees two red jackets, two silly hats, a tall black man and a shorter white man.

They're sharing a huge cotton candy between them.

Hadn't Eddie and Anson said they were going to look for Louhi and the Head? And even if his cronies aren't nearby, he can always claim the protection of the Accord . . .

"We can't talk here," he says. "Let's walk."

The Changer grunts agreement. Sven ambles as if picking a direction randomly, but really walking toward Eddie and Anson.

"Now, Changer," he says bossily (must keep him from noticing where they are headed), "what do you want from me?"

"Restitution," the Changer says, "and your binding word that you will not act against me or Shahrazad again."

"And why do you think you can get away with this?"

They have almost reached Eddie and Anson.

"I am who I am," the Changer says simply.

"And if I don't agree?" Sven says cockily.

"Then reluctantly," the Changer says, raising his hand and grabbing Sven by the throat, "I will break your neck."

They are in the shadows now, away from the shops, away from the loud mariachi music. Sven knows that the Changer can do as he threatens, but still he is filled with surging triumph.

"I call," he says loudly, "on the protection of the Accord!"

Eddie and Anson turn slowly and face him full on for the first time. Sven feels a prickling of adrenaline, for now he is close enough to get a clear look at the two men.

They wear the hats, the jackets. The white man even has a brushing of something dark across his jawline to simulate Eddie's five-o'clock shadow, but neither is Eddie nor Anson.

They nod politely to the Changer and start walking away.

"Wait!" Sven shrills. "Help me! He's going to kill me!"

"I don't think so," the white man says.

"And even if he was," the black man adds, looking pointedly at the Changer's missing eye, "he might have a really good reason for doing so."

They walk away and Sven realizes that he is alone with a creature out of nightmare. The grip on his neck is firm, and he knows that even if he shapeshifts, the other will keep his hold.

"So," the Changer says almost conversationally, "do you agree by our blood to foreswear the protection of Arthur's house and of the Accord in the matters associated with your kidnapping Shahrazad and the price you extracted for her return or . . ."

He gives Sven a shake that pops the vertebrae in his neck. "Or do I break your neck here and now?"

"You're going to break it eventually," Sven sulks.

"Perhaps. Perhaps not. Think for yourself, Fiery One. Would I stop to talk if all I wanted was you dead? I want restitution and an opportunity to remind you what happens when you use your elders as toys in your games."

"That's all?"

"When I am finished with you, it will be enough."

"Then I guess I can do what you want."

The Changer does not release his hold, and their proximity is such that Sven feels his dry chuckle as much as hears it.

"Sven, I must have you swear. So that none will misunderstand my desire to bring you harm, I want my complaint against you to be a public one."

"Public?"

"I think that, if you swear as I have asked, we can use the athanor forum that is already gathered beneath Arthur's roof. However"—the dry chuckle again—"I am not such a fool as to let you go there without your promise to foreswear—in this instance—the protection you have already claimed."

"I never thought you were a fool, Changer."

"But you have misjudged me, Sven. You would never have drawn me here if you believed I would move against you."

Sven sighs. "You're right, but I wasn't certain if you would attend the Review this time. Louhi had made promises."

"Your explanations will not sway me, Sven. Now, are you

going to swear, or am I going to break your neck?''

"I swear by our shared blood," Sven says stiffly, "that in matters related to the kidnapping of Shahrazad and the ransom extracted from you for her safety, I do not and shall not, claim the protection of Arthur's house."

"Very prettily said," the Changer says, "and our blood stands witness."

Sven cranes his neck in an effort to face the Changer. "Let me remind you that this is an oath under duress."

"That seems only right," the Changer says, moving his hold to Sven's arm, "for what you have taken from me was taken under very similar circumstances. Come along. Eddie and Anson are waiting for us, and our night at the Fair is coming to a close."

¤▣¤

Chris and Bill walk quickly away from where the one-eyed man holds the red-haired one prisoner.

"Do you think we did the right thing?" Bill asks worriedly.

"I do," Chris answers firmly. "Those guys reacted just like Rob Trapper told us they would. I don't think the guy with the one eye is going to hurt the other one."

"No." Bill ponders. "Chris, I'm beginning to wonder if these people are dealing drugs after all."

"I'm not so certain anymore, either" Chris admits, "although this last bit could have been some sort of gangland rivalry. Listen, Rob Trapper promised that he'd be calling. He hinted that he had something important to tell me. That's one of the reasons I agreed to go along with this whole thing."

"Even if we never learn the truth," Bill says, cheering up, "we got these cool jackets and hats for our night's work. And that Georgios taught me some amazing things."

Chris stares disbelievingly at him, then laughs. "So he initiated you into the deep secrets of romance. Is that it?"

"You never know," Bill says mysteriously.

He grins flirtatiously at the next pretty girl who passes. To his amazement, she smiles back and winks.

"You never know," Bill repeats wonderingly.

Chris slugs him lightly on the arm. "Come on, Romeo. You can try your luck some other time. I want to beat the traffic and get some rest. Who knows what Rob has up his sleeve?"

"But I wanted an ice cream cone!"

"After all that cotton candy?"

"Sure" Bill grins. "It's the only way to finish a day at the Fair."

The reasonable man adapts himself to the world: the unreasonable one persists in trying to adapt the world to himself. Therefore, all progress depends on the unreasonable man.

—GEORGE BERNARD SHAW

CHRIS KRISTOFER'S PHONE RINGS ABOUT AN HOUR AFTER e gets home from the Fair.

"Chris, this is Rob Trapper."

"Hi, Rob."

"Chris, I need to see you. Bill, too, if you can get him."

"You're in luck," Chris says easily, his mind racing with cenarios varying from Rob giving him a full confession to ob setting him up to be assassinated by Dakar and Katsu-iro. "Bill crashed here—he didn't want to miss your call."

"Can you come by our hotel?"

"Sure," Chris hears himself saying. His mouth is a lot nore confident than his imagination. "Is a half hour okay?"

"Come to Room 805. We'll be waiting."

"Right." *We*, Chris thinks as he hangs up the phone. *I ope to hell that "we" doesn't include Dakar and Katsuhiro.*

Rob opens the door to Room 805 and hurriedly ushers hem in.

"You remember Bronson," he says nervously. "This is my Aunt Swansdown and my friend Demetrios."

"*Aunt*"? Chris thinks, looking at the white-bearded fellow sitting stiffly upright on the sofa. He glances at Bill, who shrugs ever so slightly.

"Pleased to meet you," Chris says, accepting the seat Rob offers. Bill echoes him.

"We . . . well, *I*," Rob begins. Demetrios interrupts.

" 'We' is okay, Rebecca. Otherwise, we wouldn't be here. We're all taking a considerable risk."

Chris raises one hand. "I think we need to start at basics. Who are you folks? Is Rob's name really Rebecca?"

Rob nods. "Yes. I'm Rebecca Trapper. Bronson's my husband. We're . . . We're sasquatches."

Chris finds himself gaping.

Bill sputters, "Like Bigfoot? All of you?"

Demetrios gives a thin-lipped smile. "Not all of us. I'm a faun. Swansdown is a yeti."

"An Abominable Snowman," she says. "Or Snow-woman."

Explanations take quite a while, but by the end the two humans have a fair grasp of what the athanor are and what risks the four theriomorphs are taking by talking with them.

"So if you could get thrown out of this Accord for talking to us," Chris asks, "why are you doing it?"

"Arthur and the others need to see that all humans aren't like what he fears," Rebecca says eagerly. "You helped us last night, trusted us. We want to trust you now. It might be the first step toward something a whole lot bigger."

"You mean," Bill says, "you want us to be ambassadors for the whole human race?"

"What's to keep Arthur from killing us?" Chris says in almost the same breath. "We're dangerous to his secret."

"Rebecca thinks," says Swansdown, "that the secret can't be kept for much more than a century. I'm coming to agree with her. The amendments to the Accord that we've been negotiating include an information campaign. You two could help."

"And you trust us not to blow the whole thing wide open?" Chris says, visions of headlines running through his head.

"I think," says Bronson, and something of his bearing reminds Chris of Dakar Agadez, "that you realize there are certain risks involved."

"So we're in whether we like it or not," Bill says.

"Pretty much," Swansdown says. "There are ways to make it impossible for you to speak about any of this, but I prefer not to use them. They can be painful and noticeable."

The two humans trade glances.

"Actually, we'd like to help," Chris says. Bill nods, suddenly solemn as he realizes this is a lot more exciting than a career in computer engineering.

"First of all, we need to sneak you into the meeting," Rebecca says. "Aunt Swansdown has worked out an illusion . . ."

✿◙✿

The next morning, Chris and Bill take seats in a crowded room buzzing with conjecture and rumor. Thanks to Swansdown's art, they are disguised as two fauns who have agreed to hide back at the hotel. Demetrios assures them that no one but the fauns and satyrs, who are in on the secret, should notice the switch. In any case, they have no desire to draw attention to themselves for both Katsuhiro and Dakar—as well as other menacing figures—are among those in the meeting room.

King Arthur sits at a curved table at the front and slightly to the side of the room. The central position is commanded by a speaker's podium.

Near the front of the room, off to the left, is the one-eyed Changer from the night before, a puppy leaning against his leg. Someone Rebecca has identified as Frank MacDonald sits near him. Amazingly, he has a falcon on his shoulder and what has to be a jackalope in his lap. Something like a half dozen cats occupy other chairs.

Bill excitedly points out Tommy Thunderburst, the rising musical sensation, sitting toward the back, his manager Lil Prima beside him. As Chris makes a mental note to see if he can get an interview, he is shaken to realize that Tommy's presence means that he both he and Lil are immortal. Somehow, the concept had been easier to apply to sasquatches and legendary kings than to people one reads about in gossip magazines.

Arthur rises and taps the bell, requesting a silence that comes before the last clear note has faded away.

"Our business," he says, with a rueful smile, "keeps getting increasingly complex. We began with an appeal by the Harmony's theriomorphic members (supported by some others) that our Accord reform its policy regarding secrecy.

"Then, yesterday, Sven Trout, speaking as a supporter of these reforms, directly challenged my administration, proposing a complete overhaul.

"Finally, last night, the Changer came to me requesting a hearing before the Accord regarding a complaint he has against Sven Trout. I would like to ask this assembly if we might begin this day by hearing the Changer's appeal. Yes, Jonathan?"

Jonathan Wong rises. "Your Majesty, why should we hear the Changer's case? He is not a member of the Accord, nor has Sven Trout requested the Accord's protection."

"A good question," Arthur answers. "The Changer asked that we hear this case because Sven *is* a member of the Accord. Moreover, as we will hear when the case has been presented, the Changer is bringing his case in part on the behalf of one of his children, a daughter whom he wishes recognized as in Harmony and, thereby, protected by the juvenile's clause in the Accord."

This last statement brings many murmurs, some of surprise, some of approval. All eyes turn to where Shahrazad leans against her father's leg. (*"The puppy's his child?"* Bill whispers. Rebecca nods matter-of-factly and hushes him.)

"Thank you, Your Majesty," Jonathan says formally. "I withdraw any implied objection."

Lil raises one elegantly manicured hand. "Your Majesty, why should the Changer's business take precedence over existing business? Can't it wait until we have settled the other issues?"

Arthur gestures for the Changer to speak.

"Lil, I want everyone to hear just what Sven will stoop to in order to get what he wants. I think they should know this before they consider replacing Arthur's government with his."

Lil laughs. "Don't we know too well what Sven is willing to do? But perhaps some of our younger kin need a reminder. Very well, I do not make any formal objection. Let the Changer's business be handled first."

"Does anyone else have a question about this new issue?" Arthur asks. "No? Then we will vote. A show of hands will do and, please, hold them high so that Eddie and Vera can see them. All in favor of hearing the Changer's case as our first item of business, raise your hands."

Eddie and Vera make a quick count.

"All against?"

One hand rises. Katsuhiro Oba shrugs.

"I'm so tired of all this talk," he says, thrusting out his prickly beard defiantly.

A varitoned chuckle fills the room, then Arthur motions for the Changer to come to the speaker's podium. He does so, Shahrazad hugging close to his legs.

"Thank you all," he says, his gravelly voice carrying easily through the packed room.

In a brief, concise speech, the Changer tells of Shahrazad's kidnapping, of the evidence that she had been taken by Louhi and Sven, of Sven's phone call and the demands he had made.

The Changer's missing eye is testimony enough that he has paid the ransom and at a cost higher than what had been asked. He then tells of what he had overheard regarding the use to which his blood and eye would be put. Several in the audience look ill, and many glance uneasily at where the Head sits impassively beside an equally impassive Louhi.

When he has finished, various hands fly up. Arthur recognizes one at random. "Smith?"

"Changer, why did you bring your charges against Sven alone? Louhi seems to have done her share, and this Head, if he is as intelligent as he claimed yesterday, knew what was going on."

"I know from the scent that Sven carried my daughter from Arthur's hacienda. He made the phone call. I would like the others to be punished for their roles, but I have no proof that they were not merely his tools. He has a special talent for using others."

Louhi colors, but she is smart enough not to protest and thus condemn herself. The Head also keeps his peace.

Arthur recognizes Bronson.

"Changer, could you clarify Shahrazad's position regarding the Harmony? We were not at the Lustrum Review."

"Shahrazad is my daughter by a coyote who was murdered this last May." Mutters of surprise and consternation rise, but the Changer is permitted to continue uninterrupted. "I brought her with me to the Review. During the Harmony Dance, she surprised me by joining the Dance."

Bronson asks, "But you did not have her recognized then?"

"No," the Changer says. "She is a young thing. I thought that there would be time enough when she had avoided the things that kill little wild creatures."

Frank MacDonald is recognized. "Changer, if you didn't know she was in Harmony, why did you bring her with you?"

"I am her father," the Changer says simply. "A coyote parent raises a pup for the first six months of its life. My business in Albuquerque did not discharge my responsibility."

The Head raises his hand. "Do you believe, Changer, that Sven Trout knew that Shahrazad was in Harmony?"

"He was at the Dance," the Changer says simply. "All who were there saw her join in."

Chris can tell that the crowd is becoming angry. He looks questioningly at their guide.

Rebecca whispers, "Many athanor are sterile. Most athanor children do not inherit our gifts. A new athanor, no matter what shape or type, is a blessing to the Harmony as a whole."

When there are no further questions for the Changer, Arthur calls Sven to the podium.

"What do you have to say that might mitigate the right the Changer has to claim restitution from you?"

Instead of speaking in his defense, Sven Trout begins to laugh. It is a loud laugh, a belly laugh, and he laughs until the tears run down his face.

"You have me, don't you, Arthur Pendragon? I came here to challenge you, and now, through this little courtroom drama, you have turned me from a serious contender to a cringing criminal begging for the mercy of the court.''

Arthur begins to speak, but Sven waves him down with the hand that isn't wiping his streaming eyes.

"Don't deny it, Arthur, my dear. It's all over you. Why else bring this matter up in front of the whole assembly?''

The Changer says from his seat, ''I asked for restitution and for my complaint to be heard first. I thought that those who had followed you should know about your deals.''

Sven looks at him, laughter fading as he sees the ancient shapeshifter's single yellow eye upon him. ''Well, Changer, you're getting your restitution. You've ruined my reputation.''

Anson calls out, ''That's not much, eh, Changer?''

The Changer says dryly, ''This is not all that I want, Sven.''

"I don't doubt it,'' Sven persists, ''but while I have the podium, I am left with a few questions.''

He looks to where Louhi rests her hand lightly on the Head's thigh. She smiles a sweet, sleepy smile.

"One question is just how far I should rat on my associates. I'm not good at taking a fall on my own, and I'm ruined anyhow. But before I get to that, what I want to know is, why is Arthur always left on top?''

Sven spreads his arms in a broad, appealing gesture. ''How many of those of us who have mingled in human society have left so many enduring legends behind us? Arthur is Gilgamesh, Akhenaten, Rama, Frey, and, of course, Arthur Pendragon. Isn't it strange that the athanor who has most actively advocated our hiding ourselves away from the humans is the one who lives over and over again in their memories?''

Arthur answers gruffly, ''Over and over again, I have failed, Sven. My immortality is a legend of lost causes. In those societies where physical memorials could not be escaped, such as in Egypt, I distorted my physical resemblance. Did you think I liked being portrayed as an emaciated, long-jawed hunchback?''

"I bet that your daughters and Nefertiti liked the art even less,'' Sven says caustically, ''but I forget, they weren't really *your* daughters, not like the Changer's little coyote bitch.''

He smiles sweetly. "That is the proper term, isn't it? And as to that art, Arthur, didn't it guarantee your being remembered? Everyone who knows anything about Egyptology remembers the unusual representational art of Tel el Amarna. Everyone remembers their heroic king who tried to substitute a kind monotheism for the dictatorship of the priest-kings.''

"Would I immortalize a failure?" Arthur protests.

"Some people prefer tragedy to comedy," Sven says. "Perhaps you enjoy being the tragic hero remembered through the ages—valiant, unlucky in love, struggling against the odds to establish kingdoms of virtue and . . .''

"Enough!" Eddie bellows. "You are on trial for your crimes against the Changer. Stop campaigning!''

"Why?" Sven retorts blithely. "I need all the votes I can get.''

Eddie paces from behind the table toward the podium. "Votes may be what you need, Sven, but I can ask a few awkward questions, if you wish. Can you swear under a truthstone that you did not come to my hospital room and try to kill me? Can you swear that you did not create the circumstances for the accident that put me in the hospital in the first place?''

Sven smiles charmingly. "I don't think I'd better answer those questions. And maybe you don't want to ask them.''

From where she sits, Vera says softly, "That sounds rather like a threat to me.''

Sven's smile becomes vaguely snide.

"Your Majesty! Your Majesty!''

Chris and Bill watch in silence as the assembled athanor wave their hands in the air, one after another raising various complaints they hold against the red-haired trickster. Much refers to events they've never heard of, but it's clear that Sven doesn't have many friends among his peers—and equally clear that he doesn't particularly deserve them.

At last, the attorney Jonathan Wong raises his hand and is recognized. "Your Majesty, I have been privately asked by a number of those gathered here to present a motion that Sven be ruled both out of Accord and out of Harmony.''

Even the humans realize the import of this request.

"Both?" Arthur says sternly, cocking an eyebrow. Ruling a member out of Accord—often for a limited period of time, the sentence to be reviewed thereafter—is considered a strict but standard penalty. Ruling someone out of Harmony is a much more serious punishment and is often irrevocable—for once separated from the sustaining force of the Harmony, the criminal dies.

"Yes, Your Majesty. Both."

"I cannot deal with two such penalties in tandem," Arthur says. "They must be dealt with separately."

"Very well. That is acceptable."

Jonathan's motion is seconded and passed.

Anson A. Kridd, who has himself been ruled out of Accord several times, raises his hand. "I'd also like to suggest that the same penalties be considered for Louhi and the Head."

"Again, I must insist that the penalties be dealt with separately," Arthur says.

"I can adapt my motion to that," Anson agrees.

This motion, too, is seconded and passed.

✡ ✶ ✡

The next day, Rebecca Trapper walks out into the Pendragon Estate grounds with Chris, Bill, and Demetrios.

"Rebecca, you don't look very happy," Demetrios says. "Are you annoyed that this business has interrupted our agenda?"

"No!" She looks shocked. "These are serious matters. I'm still adjusting to the fact that our Moderator is Sven Trout—and the things he did, the deals he made, to advance our cause."

"His cause."

"Yes. I suppose so. What he did doesn't change the fact that much of what he said was right. I don't want to go back to hiding in the woods."

"I know," Demetrios says, putting a reassuring hand on her arm. "And Arthur will listen to us."

Bill laughs nervously. "I sure hope so. I don't want to be on trial next."

"You won't be," Demetrios says.

"Good." Bill relaxes, only to stiffen at Demi's next words.

"You aren't an athanor. Humans don't get trials."

"I'm surprised," Chris says bravely. "You seem like a very judicial group."

"Taking someone out of Harmony is a serious matter," Demetrios explains. "It affects each athanor."

Rebecca frowns. "Bronson said the same thing, but I don't understand. Not really."

"Rebecca, Harmony is what makes us immortal; it is what rejuvenates us. Harmony grows more powerful according to our numbers. That is why we rejoice when a child is born."

"But, Demi, no one is censuring the Changer and Anson for killing Isidro and Oswaldo," Rebecca says, referring to events that had been debated at great length earlier. "Didn't their deaths reduce Harmony?"

"They did, but the Changer and Anson had no choice. They acted in self-defense and have sworn so under a truth stone."

"Yes, I saw." Rebecca sounds almost sulky. "I still think they could have knocked them out or something."

"Maybe so, Becky, but we weren't there. In any case, the loss of Isidro and Oswaldo is minor to what we would suffer if we were to lose Sven or one of his allies."

"What?" The sasquatch looks surprised and startled.

"You have yet to live through a time when we lose many of those in Harmony," Demetrios says, "or you would better understand. The closest you came was in World War II during the bombings. Even then, we lost comparatively few athanor. Most of our people fled."

"We do that a lot, don't we?"

"Rebecca . . ."

"I'm sorry."

"Now all of you listen to this old faun. Not only is Harmony diminished by the loss of any of our number, the loss of an old one costs us more than the loss of a younger one."

"Really?"

"Yes. Your Bronson is probably worth both you and me. The Changer . . . Some say he is the oldest of us all. Why do you think we give so much deference to those we term ancient?"

Rebecca shrugs. "I thought it was just good manners, like with the Chinese. The older ones *do* know more."

Demetrios pats her, a gesture that could be ludicrous given the differences in their sizes, but is not.

"Now can you understand why taking these three members out of Harmony is such a serious matter? Truly we are diminished by the loss of anyone, but three such . . . Sven was present for Ragnarokk. If the Head has been in Harmony since its creation, which I think is likely, he is almost as old. Louhi is the youngest, but even she is millennia-old. Our late, lamented South Americans could not claim even Louhi's years between them."

"I don't like what I'm learning," Rebecca admits. "What do you think will happen?"

"I think that all three will be ruled out of Accord. I think that Sven will also be ruled out of Harmony."

Rebecca nods stiffly, clearly frightened by his bluntness as she had not been by the detached parliamentary procedure.

Demetrios continues, "The Head is making a good claim for relative ignorance—the only one who says otherwise is Sven, and he's not exactly trusted."

Rebecca takes up the thread. "Louhi . . . She's so cold. What she did to the Changer was terribly cruel, but with Garrett testifying that he can reverse the effects of her spell, even if she will not, and her testimony that she acted for the Head's own good . . . They won't kill her for that, will they?"

"*We* won't," Demetrios says quietly, firmly. "Remember, in these matters the Harmony is a true democracy. One reason these proceedings are taking so long is that an effort is being made to contact everyone from the unicorns in their secret valleys to the least bunyip in the Antipodes."

"And when that voting is done, Sven will die." Rebecca wrings her hands. "I don't even like him, and I'm afraid for him. Why doesn't he flee?"

"It won't matter," Demetrios answers. "When he is severed from Harmony, wherever he is, the effects will reach him."

"I'd be terrified!"

"So, I expect, is he."

✡◻✡

And when, two days after the Changer had made his initial complaint, the vote is taken, the result is much as Demetrios had predicted. Louhi and the Head are severed from the protection of the Accord; Sven is also so severed.

Then, his face suddenly old, Arthur looks up from the notes on the speaker's podium. He does not meet the gaze of any in the meeting room, but stares at the back wall.

"The vote for taking Sven Trout out of the Harmony passed two-thirds for to one-third against. Since this exceeds the simple majority I have no choice but to ask each one present to accept that Sven Trout is . . ."

"Wait!"

The voice that speaks is Sven's, but it is neither shrill with fear nor crippled with anger. Instead it is deep and raw with confidence. "Wait a moment before you speak those words, King Arthur."

Sven leaps up from where he had been sitting onto the raised dais. "Do you think that I am so foolish as to take on *you* and not make any contingency plans? I knew you would use your power to slay me, whether by the hand of your lackeys as Isidro and Oswaldo were slain or by some trick of law."

He thrusts his face into Arthur's and hisses, "I knew you would not get your own precious hands dirty."

Arthur pushes him back. "I will not rise to these petty insults, Sven. Tell us what you have done. Have you bartered the sun and moon once more?"

"Better," Sven says, "for that was only legend. What I have done is real and will work."

Deliberately, he turns his back on Arthur and struts down the platform: "You all thought you could sever me from the Harmony, did you? Oh, I know that some of you voted for me, but I doubt it was from any great love. I suspect you feared to lose my considerable force within Harmony.

"Well, when you were so smugly judging and choosing, ruling and voting, did you ever consider that *I* might have the power to do the same to you? I have come up with a way to sever the bonds of Harmony for all but myself and a few chosen allies.''

He looks at the Head and Louhi. "I wonder if you voted for me or against? I don't think I want to know.''

Jonathan Wong calls out, "What is this madness, Sven? How can you sever Harmony?''

"We reinforce Harmony by means of a dance," Sven says, pulling from his pocket a tape player, "and I will break it with a song—a song composed by our own Tommy Thunderburst . . .''

"No!''

The wail of protest rises from where Tommy sits, but Sven airily waves him down.

"The song has a few additions put in by my good Louhi, a few additions that I doubt Tommy would have written even in his darkest moments. Louhi is different. She's far more dangerous than any of you believe. I tried to warn you about her . . .

"If you declare me out of Harmony, I shall press a button and the song will play, not from this little recorder, but from recorders I have hidden throughout the hacienda while enjoying Arthur's hospitality. You'll never find them all in time.

"However, even if you do, I have arranged that on the same signal a message will be sent out via e-mail to radio stations all over the world, radio stations that have been playing Tommy's newest hit. They will be informed that there is a new song by the rising new superstar . . . Digital transfer is wonderful. They'll be able to download it right off the web.''

He laughs. "None of you have ever been my match in trickery! Do you dare see if I am bluffing?''

Arthur ignores him. "Tommy, is what he says possible?''

"I'm afraid so, man.'' Tommy's expression is wild and pleading. He faces the assembled athanor. "Look, I didn't know what he wanted. He said he wanted a song to make Harmony with the self. It *could* be perverted to sever Harmony with others!''

Lil Prima cuts in. "No one blames you, *mon petit*, Tommy. We all know too well where the blame should rest. Arthur?''

"Yes, Lil?''

"Sven could do it. Tommy's performances have a magical

component that we've long since fixed in his recordings. I did the magical work on this piece, both the audio and video recordings. If Sven wanted magic that could be broadcast, he's got it.''

Sven grins. ''I told you I was smarter than all of you combined. I've even arranged a feedback loop, so that what you lose should help sustain the three of us through the transition.''

''Set down the box, Sven,'' Arthur says calmly. ''I see we have more to discuss.''

''Sorry, Your Majesty,'' Sven replies, ''but I'm not letting it out of my hot little hand.''

The fear building in the room is contagious. Even Chris and Bill must fight back an urge to join those imploring Arthur to take a new vote, that they will renounce the sentence.

''Fools!'' mutters Bronson. ''Don't they realize that merely getting Sven to surrender that black box won't be enough? If he isn't completely neutralized, either he or his allies could use the Disharmony spell in the future.''

Katsuhiro Oba also reaches this conclusion. Leaping from his seat, he screams, ''You can't do this to us, you bastard!''

The one time god of storm and iron sprints down the aisle between the chairs, preparing to rip the box from Sven's hands and beat his secrets from him. Not nearly as quickly, but with an implacable steadiness, Eddie moves from his chair and interposes himself between Katsuhiro and Sven.

''Out of my way!'' Katsuhiro shouts.

''No!'' Eddie says. ''We don't do . . .

Katsuhiro doesn't listen further. As he tries to shove Eddie aside, Sven panics and his finger closes for a moment on the black box. The sound of bright flutes accompanied by drums surges from the hidden speakers for a few devastating chords.

Eddie's scream as his leg is rebroken is nearly lost in the keen of pain that emits from almost every throat. Only the two humans, Sven, Louhi, and the Head do not reel. The ancients are the first to recover.

Shifting into a raven, the Changer knocks the black box from Sven's hands. In the audience, Duppy Jonah seizes the Head. Amphitrite pins Louhi's hands, whispering, ''Not a word, not a gesture. I'd love to hurt you for what you did to the Changer.''

Anson A. Kridd pushes Garrett Kocchui through the crowd to tend to Eddie. The physician, still a bit staggered himself, gains strength when he realizes he has a patient.

"Now," Arthur says through gritted teeth, "we are in a better position to discuss this matter."

"Physical violence!" Sven says in the tones of one appalled. "Arthur, you only support my thesis that you will do anything to preserve your power structure."

"Stow it," suggests Bronson Trapper, stepping up onto the platform and picking up Sven as easily as a child might a doll. "Arthur, why don't you retrieve that box? I suspect it cut off before his electronic signal was sent, but we should check."

"I think I can find out," the Smith says. "Arthur, I'll use your computer."

Swansdown rises with her infant son cradled in her arms. The yeti child is unconscious, his pink face contorted with pain. To one side, Snowbird is chafing Dawn's wrists, trying to bring the little one around.

"Do that again, Sven Trout," Swansdown says, "and before my last breath passes I shall curse you with such pain in every joint and tendon that though you are immortal you shall pray every day for death. Look what you have done to my babies!"

"And mine," says the Changer, lifting Shahrazad's limp and barely breathing form. "The children are not strong enough to survive for long the pain of separation from Harmony."

All around the room, the younger athanor have collapsed, but Sven's luck has held, for none has died.

Arthur paces up and down the platform while Eddie and the children are carried out to a makeshift infirmary. Then he restores order with a single, commanding gesture.

"Well, my friends. You see how our judgment has been perverted. I have no doubt that, even with Swansdown's curse hanging over them, Sven or his allies will carry out their threat if we remove them from Harmony. Shall we change our sentence?"

The Changer says into the silence, "Perhaps we should."

Arthur looks at him in astonishment. "You are the last one I thought would say that!"

"What other incentive can we offer Sven?" the Changer answers reasonably. "In any case, I never said I wanted Sven's death, only retribution for what he has done to me and my daughter and an opportunity to remind him what happens when he uses his elders as tools."

"What about those of us who are not so ancient?" Rebecca Trapper protests. "That is, what about his using us?"

The Changer turns his head to study her from his one remaining eye. The sasquatch bravely holds her ground, and he nods slowly.

"Rebecca, you have learned an important lesson about blind trust over these last few days, but does that mean the cause that brought you here is without merit?"

Rebecca frowns. "No. I still don't want to hide in the woods for the rest of my life."

"Very well. Then, for all the ill he has done, Sven has done some good as well."

Vera calls out. "Changer, he's dangerous!"

"So is stagnation," says the Changer. "Look at human history—a history many of you have helped to make. Stability and stagnation often go together. Egypt, Rome, various Chinese dynasties, the great empires of South and Central America, more recently this mid–twentieth-century United States: all of these have suffered from the lack of competition and challenge."

The Changer smiles at the amazed King, then turns back to the gathered membership. "Perhaps Sven Trout—Loki, Firebrand—is what Arthur *needs*."

This is not what the athanor want to hear. They want punishment and security against this threat and any like it.

"Maybe you're tired of living, ancient," shouts Netherton Olsen, "but we are not. Why should we leave this rat free?"

"His manipulation is the reason you are here," the Changer says stubbornly. "If Sven's Disharmony Dance can be disabled, his threat to Harmony is removed. Exiled from the Accord, any of you will be free to attack him."

"Yeah!" Sven says, with manic cheer. "I'm in a shitload of trouble! Save me! I'm open to suggestion!"

"Can we disable his Disharmony Dance?" asks Duppy Jonah.

Lovern rises. "Your Majesty, a charm could be crafted to

reate an aversion that would develop into physical illness if
Sven or his allies even think about using this Disharmony
spell.''

Tommy Thunderburst nods. ''Like tetraethylthiuram di-
sulfide for alcoholics, right?''

Amazed gazes center on the musician. He shrugs and
blushes. ''Hey, I've been on it. Aversion therapy. Nasty stuff,
but it can work.''

''Something like that, Tommy,'' Lovern continues, ''except that the spell would be woven into the same force that
connects them to the Harmony. They could not dispel the
charm without breaking their link to Harmony.''

Swansdown hands Dawn to Snowbird. ''I volunteer to
help. My curses would weave well into this.''

Tommy, who has had his own experiences with pain, asks,
''But, like, how bad would this torment be?''

''Horrible,'' Lovern promises. ''The mildest reaction
would be vomiting and blinding headaches. Persisting against
the aversion could well lead to death.''

''And,'' growls Katsuhiro, ''can we get all copies of the
Disharmony Dance so that we can destroy them?''

Lovern smiles unpleasantly. ''I'm certain you could coerce
Sven and his allies if truthstone questioning suggests they are
holding out.''

Frank MacDonald sighs, his hands nervously stroking the
jackalope hunched nervously in his lap. ''The solution is
cruel, but, then, so is what they intended for us.''

Chris and Bill listen in a mixture of horror and fascination
as debate and discussion further refine the plan. In the end,
a formal resolution is passed permitting Sven Trout to remain
within Harmony as long as the Disharmony Dance is destroyed and suitable precautions are taken against its being
used again.

Vera slides a note across the table to Arthur: *Should we
raise the issue of taking Cleonice Damita out of Harmony
while we have everyone here?*

Arthur scribbles back: *Let someone else raise it. I'm weary
of death sentences.*

Rising, Arthur addresses the group at large, ''If there is no
further business . . .''

Even when he looks pointedly at Duppy Jonah, the one

who had demanded Cleonice's death, no one speaks.

"Then I adjourn this meeting into smaller committees. Jonathan, Lil, and Swansdown, would you assist Lovern with the preliminary design of the aversion spell? I think that the theriomorphs' problems would benefit from smaller group discussion. I'll head one meeting in Meeting Room A. Jonathan will take one in Meeting Room B. Vera, will you head another in C?"

He smiles tiredly. "First, let's break for a half hour. Refreshments are in the kitchen. Help yourself."

Rebecca whispers to Chris and Bill, "Let's talk with Arthur later. He's not in a very good mood."

Arthur watches as the meeting disperses. A small whine and a throat being cleared makes him realize that the meeting room has emptied of all but the Changer and Shahrazad.

"You surprised me, Changer."

"I know."

"You didn't get your restitution."

"Sven has been disarmed; he has been removed from the Accord. I assure you, that is better than martyring him."

Arthur frowns. "But your family . . . Isn't that why you came out of the hills, to gain retribution for them?"

"Yes," the Changer nods, "and to learn who would dare play with me. I was simpleminded not to think of Sven sooner, but he diverted me with Lil, and by the time I had spoken with her, his trail was cold. Even his other attacks were subtly handled."

"That is true." Arthur still looks uncomfortable. "Yet, you have gained very little for yourself—and you have taken more harm than many."

The Changer shrugs. "In some ways, that is so. However, if Sven had not drawn me out, I might never have learned that Shahrazad was athanor. She might have been long dead by this June's Harmony Dance, being litter's runt and all."

He reaches down and scratches the puppy behind her ears. "Moreover, I watched my brother being manipulated by the South Americans. I don't care to be predictable. Lil and I could have killed each other for Loki's gain. Even an ancient can learn."

Arthur nods, thinking of the lessons that *he* has learned.

"And remember, Arthur," the Changer says, "without the protection of the Accord, Sven is fair game to any of those he has made an enemy. I would not want Katsuhiro or Dakar on my trail—not to mention Swansdown. I wonder if he will be slain after all."

"True. But is his pain compensation for your wounds?"

The Changer smiles. "Aesculapius has examined the damage. He will be able to negate Louhi's magic. When he is done, I will be whole once more."

"Good!"

"The process may take several surgeries," the Changer says, "and Garrett has warned me that it will be painful. May Shahrazad and I stay here during the procedure?"

Arthur thinks fleetingly of coyote piss on carpets, of the upheavals the Changer has brought, of the finality of death.

"Of course." He steps from the dais and strokes Shahrazad's ears. "I'd be delighted to have you both."

Injustice is relatively easy to bear; it is justice that hurts.

—H. L. Mencken

"ARTHUR?" REBECCA TRAPPER STANDS AT THE DOOR TO the King's office some days later. "A few of us would like to speak privately with you."

"Come in." He stands to greet the small group of theriomorphs who file in. Anson follows them and closes the door. "Is there something wrong with the amendments? If so, I should call Jonathan in."

"No," Rebecca says, "or maybe yes. You don't need to call Jonathan. We're quite happy with the illusion disguises. We want to suggest members for the research group."

"The one investigating possible human reaction to theriomorphs?" the King says. "Would you like to be a member?"

"Yes," Rebecca says, "I would, but I want you to hire two other members." She gestures sharply, and Swansdown's illusions are broken. "Two human members. Meet Chris Kristofer and Bill Irish. They've attended the last several meetings."

Chris and Bill bow slightly. "Pleased to meet you, Your Majesty," they chorus as they have been coached.

Arthur stares, first at them, then at Rebecca, and finally at Anson, who is trying very hard not to laugh aloud.

490

"You do realize that you are in violation of the Accord," he asks incredulously.

"Yes, Arthur," Rebecca says. "I am, along with at least half of the theriomorphs here. I guess you can put us to trial."

"Oh, Lord, not that!" Arthur moans, pressing his face into his hands. "I don't think . . ." He stops, collects himself, becomes stern. "This is a serious matter."

"We know." Rebecca becomes pleading. "Arthur, I think we need the human point of view. We've been in isolation, guessing what they think, for too long. Chris and Bill can help."

Chris decides it's time for him to speak. "King Arthur, Bill and I don't want to let your secret out—it's Rebecca's secret, too, and Bronson's, and other people we've rapidly come to value as friends. Sure, I started out looking for a news story, but that's before I knew what the news really was."

Bill adds, "Rebecca is right when she says you athanor don't know how humans think. You live among us but not with us. It's like a cat trying to understand a school of goldfish."

"Half the theriomorphs know?" Arthur asks.

"Half of those who are here," Rebecca corrects.

"That's still quite a few." Arthur turns to Anson. "What do you think, Spider?"

"I'm for it, or I wouldn't be here, eh? I convinced Rebecca to bring her friends to you quietly. You will hire these two men into your personal service—there is a provision for that within the Accord. Keep their role secret for a while—perhaps until the next Review, when all of this is due to be raked up again anyhow. If they violate our trust . . ."

He makes a dramatic throat-cutting gesture.

"Some of the athanor will have to know," Arthur says. "My counselors, for example. The word may get out."

"If it does," Anson says, "you can say that you very, very carefully examined the candidates and trust their honesty."

Chris adds, "King Arthur, we'd be happy to swear on one of those truthstones or take any oath you'd like to design. I can't say I liked the sound of that aversion spell, but I'd even let you use one of those.''

Arthur shakes his head violently at the last suggestion. ''No! Either we extend some trust, or this experiment is useless. An oath is a nice idea, though, as is a truthstone examination.''

''Then,'' Rebecca says, ''you agree?''

''It seems to be a time of changes,'' Arthur says. ''Very well, gentlemen, consider yourselves hired. We'll work out salaries and job descriptions and cover stories at our leisure. Your first job is to make certain that the remainder of the Trappers' visit is a safe and pleasant one.''

''That,'' Bill says happily, ''will be no trouble at all.''

¤▣¤

Once the amendments to the Accord are signed, most depart, including Vera, who is going to escort the Sea Monarchs on a brief tour of the United States.

She bids the Changer good-bye. ''Connel has said his wife can loan me her pelt. I plan to try shapeshifting.''

''Good.'' He touches her shoulder lightly. ''I will be taking Shahrazad to the Sandias again. Come and tell us how you liked being a seal.''

The mages remain, working on the aversion spells. Tommy Thunderburst, still shattered by the use to which his most wonderful composition had been turned, smashes the amethyst eagle and flushes down the toilet the last of the blue powder that Sven had given him. These cathartic actions completed, he takes some relief in assisting with the spellweaving. Still, many notice that he has begun drinking heavily.

¤▣¤

Shahrazad is among those who gather to watch the wizards place the aversion spells on Louhi, Sven, and the Head. She crouches between her father's feet, growling as her enemies are led into the room. Daily she has visited the rooms where they are imprisoned, peeing derisively on the door. No one will let her get any closer.

Perhaps only the Big Male recognizes the level of her wrath, but not even he knows of the channel dug in her psyche by the pain of the Disharmony Dance. Through that channel, something courses, building force, waiting only for an outlet.

Shahrazad stares at the three, hating them with all her soul. Soon the Big Male will be taking her back into the wild lands, and her enemies will be out of her grasp. She growls.

The last pinch of scented powder is dropped into the silver censor, the last melodic words are chanted, and the three subjects tremble as if a powerful wind has buffeted their bodies. With a sixth sense, Shahrazad knows that the mages have done their work, that the three are now bound against using that hateful Dance against her.

Is this all that will be done to them? She had understood that the three could be hunted once the mages were done with their workings. Somehow, she had envisioned them changed into prey animals, as her father changes into birds or humans.

Now cold Louhi finishes shaking. Anger darkens her pale, delicate complexion. Spinning on her heel, she raises her hand. Shahrazad bares her teeth, but Louhi's anger is for the Head, whom she slaps soundly across one cheek.

"Come near me again," the witch hisses, "and I will make you so miserable that you will pray to return to your bodiless existence beneath the cold, dank ocean waters."

The Head stares at Louhi, his mismatched eyes full of hurt. For the first time since any has seen him, he looks human.

Sven Trout tosses back his fiery head and laughs. The others join in. Only Shahrazad does not laugh. This is not enough! These three stole her away, tortured her father, made the great pain-song! Her family is a dim memory to her now, but she feels sure that their deaths and the terror she had felt then are these ones' doing as well.

Would that she could hunt them as her father promised! If only they were little like ground squirrels, like mice, like . . .

There is a surging within her as the channel finally overflows and then heals. Her bark of delight fills a room suddenly bereft of laughter. She leaps forward toward the rat that crouches where Sven Trout had stood. The rat dives between Lovern's legs and Shahrazad bounds after, determined to grab and to shake, to twist and break.

She hears the Big Male yelling for her, but ignores him.

¤◙¤

"Grab her!" yells Arthur. "Grab them!"

Chaos ensues as everyone tries to obey. When it is resolved, two small animals—a silvery mouse and a ground squirrel with mismatched eyes—have been trapped in a corner by two of the Cats of Egypt. Frank MacDonald hastens up with a box.

The third animal, a reddish rat, has made his escape. Lovern is wrapping a handkerchief about the wound in his leg where Shahrazad bit him when he fell on her. The coyote puppy hangs growling from her father's hand.

"Did they do that?" asks Lil Prima, glancing at the Changer, "or did someone else?"

The Changer, his lost eye now restored, shrugs and sets his daughter down, swatting her when she makes a lunge for the remaining animals.

"I don't know," he says. "It's beyond my knowledge."

"It could have been a clever ploy to escape," Swansdown offers. "In order to make the aversion spell hold, we had to remove the iron manacles. That means either Louhi or the Head could have worked a spell."

"Is there any way to test?" Arthur asks.

"Too fast," Lovern says. "The signature is gone now."

"Damn."

Frank MacDonald clears his throat. "These two don't seem to want to go anywhere. If no one objects, I'll take them to my ranch. They can stay there until they resume human form."

Arthur looks more cheerful. "We don't *have* to restore them, do we? They're out of the Accord and all that. If you want them, Frank, you can have them."

"And Sven?" says Katsuhiro, for once standing shoulder to shoulder with Dakar. "What about him?"

"He's yours if you can find him," Arthur says. "He's no longer my responsibility."

The warriors hurry out, trailed by the assembled Cats of Egypt. The falcon leaves Frank MacDonald's shoulder and sails out the window. Even the jackalopes depart.

"I wouldn't," says the Changer, "want to be Sven right now."

✿◙✿

While Chris and Bill stand watch, at the small, private airfield to the north of Albuquerque, tearful farewells are said. Rebecca wipes her cheek before bending to enfold Demetrios in an embrace that lifts the faun right out of his boots.

"Promise you'll come visit us," she pleads. "Bronson and I are going to be so lonely out in our forests."

Demetrios sneaks a glance at Bronson, not certain how the big sasquatch is taking his wife's emotional outburst. He is relieved to see that Bronson is smiling and nodding agreement.

"Do come," Bronson rumbles, "you and any of your fellows. You may find that you could be as happy in our misty forests as in the California sunshine."

Demetrios looks doubtful. "But our dryads and naiads . . ."

"They were transplanted once," Bronson says with the composure of one who has seen many impossible things made possible. "They could be again. You don't need to decide overnight. Come and visit first."

"Hey, fuzzy lady," Georgios says, strutting up in new cowboy boots and a garish fringed jacket, "don't I get a smooch, too?"

Smiling now, Rebecca gives him a hug that bends his ribs. "You come and visit, too," she says.

"Any babes in your woods?" he asks, leering.

"You'll just have to settle for visiting me and Bronson."

Georgios grins. "I can do that. With this new illusion magic, I'm going to be able to get out on the town a lot more. The mares are going to get awfully lonely."

"Loverboy!" Demetrios says, despairing.

"That's me," the other replies contently. "That's me."

⌖⌖⌖

As Anson A. Kridd sets his suitcases by the front door, the door to Arthur's office opens and the King himself emerges.

"Are you leaving now, Anson?"

"That's right, back to interrupted business. You'll take care of Eddie, not work him into the ground while his leg heals?"

"I promise."

The King stands silently for a moment. Patting down his pockets until he finds a bar of chocolate, Anson watches Arthur, an expression of open amusement on his broad, dark face.

"Yes, Arthur?"

"I didn't say anything."

"But you want to."

Arthur looks at one of Vera's weavings hanging over the fireplace, at the tiled floor that desperately needs mopping, at anything rather than facing that teasing brown gaze.

"Yes, I guess I do. I want to thank you for everything you've done—helping Eddie, going to South America, managing the Changer . . ."

"Nobody can manage that one unless he wants it," Anson chuckles.

"That may be, but you are one of those who can influence him. I am grateful you were here."

"It was an interesting time, eh?"

"More than." Arthur glances at the Spider. "Anson, I was wondering if you would like to be one of my formal advisors."

"Me? The troublemaker? I thought as you see it, I'm nearly as bad as Sven Trout."

"Not quite." Arthur grins. "I've been thinking about what the Changer said—about stagnation and stasis. Eddie is a good counselor—one of the best—but he knows me and my feelings on certain matters too well. Jonathan Wong delights in order as, in a different way, does Vera. Especially with these new humans on board I need someone who will tell me when I'm . . ."

"Getting stodgy?"

Arthur looks affronted, then relaxes. "In a nutshell, yes."

Anson considers. "Do I need to live here?"

"No. Jonathan doesn't. You could check in every day or so by e-mail. And if you would visit . . ."

"Visit?"

"So you can look at me and grin that irreverent grin and make me realize that I'm being an ass."

"Oh!" Anson rubs his palms together briskly. "I can do that!"

"I'm sure. Will you accept my invitation?"

"What's the pay?"

"We can work out something either in terms of favors accumulated or money."

Anson grins. "I like the idea of favors."

"Somehow, I thought that you would."

"Okay. Here's my first piece of advice. Work more closely with Duppy Jonah."

"I have already planned to do so."

"And second. Get yourself at least one more woman as a counselor."

"A woman? There's already Vera."

Anson wags a finger at him. "Stodgy, Arthur. You need the distaff perspective. Trust me. Women see things differently. They can't help it. Vera has some of that perspective but not enough. You need women—maybe a human-form woman."

"A woman."

"Right."

"Very well. Anything else?"

"Yes." Anson watches Arthur stiffen. "Get at least one of the theriomorphs as a counselor."

Arthur relaxes. "I had thought of that. It will keep them from feeling left out."

"Wrong reason," Anson says. "Like the women, those without human shape see things differently. You need that, too."

"Any suggestions as to who I should pick?"

"Maybe the faun Demetrios. Maybe a yeti or sasquatch. Not a *kappa*. They're too isolated yet. I can think on it and get back to you if you wish."

Arthur takes a deep breath. "Please do."

Anson takes Arthur's hand and shakes it vigorously. "I am honored by your offer, Your Majesty."

Arthur returns the handclasp and adds a slight bow. "And I am honored to have you on my staff."

A horn toots outside. Eddie swings in on his crutches.

"Your ride's here, Spider. Have a good trip."

Anson hugs him. "See you soon, Eddie." He hefts his bags. "See you, Arthur."

Arthur watches him depart, wondering what he has just invited into his life.

✿❂✿

When night falls, a reddish brown rat trembles in the *bosque* down near the Rio Grande. An owl hoots. Cats yowl. Heavy feet trample through the growth.

The rat presses closer to the ground. There is something he should remember. Something he should do. An almost memory beats like panic in his tiny brain. He scurries a few paces across open ground.

An owl hoots. He hears the near inaudible rush of its wings and freezes.

There is something he should remember.

ACKNOWLEDGMENTS

I WOULD LIKE TO THANK THE PEOPLE WHO CONTRIBUTED IN ways great and small to the creation of this book. Jan and Steve (S. M.) Stirling encouraged me by asking pointed, intelligent questions about the work in process. Both Sage Walker and Walter Jon Williams offered tidbits of information that saved me making stupid mistakes. Phyllis White of Flying Coyote Books steered me toward many fine texts on coyotes and shared with me anecdotes about coyotes and coy-dogs. David M. Weber read the manuscript and provided feedback. Jim Moore, my husband, read the manuscript and offered me detailed comments on the developing story. For his thoughtful assistance and for his simply being his wonderful self, I am very grateful.

AVON EOS PRESENTS
MASTERS OF FANTASY AND ADVENTURE

THE SILENT STRENGTH OF STONES
by Nina Kiriki Hoffman   77760-6/$5.99 US/$7.99 CAN

THE WILD HUNT: VENGEANCE MOON
by Jocelin Foxe   79911-1/$3.99 US/$3.99 CAN

GRAIL
by Stephen R. Lawhead   78104-2/$6.99 US/$8.99 CAN

THE SANDS OF KALAVEN: A NOVEL OF SHUNLAR
by Carol Heller   79080-7/$5.99 US/$7.99 CAN

THE PHYSIOGNOMY
by Jeffrey Ford   79332-6/$3.99 US/$3.99 CAN